Good News
From
Outer
Space

Good News From Outer Space

by

John Kessel

A TOM DOHERTY ASSOCIATES BOOK
NEW YORK

GOOD NEWS FROM OUTER SPACE

Copyright © 1989 by John Kessel
All rights reserved, including the right to reproduce this book or portions thereof in any form.

Portions of this novel have appeared, in substantially different form, in *Isaac Asimov's Science Fiction Magazine, The Magazine of Fantasy and Science Fiction,* and *In the Field of Fire.*

A TOR BOOK
Published by Tom Doherty Associates, Inc.
49 West 24 Street
New York, NY 10010

Library of Congress Cataloging-in-Publication Data

Kessel, John.
     Good news from outer space / by John Kessel.
          p.   cm.
     "A Tom Doherty Associates book."
     ISBN 0-312-93178-6
     I. Title.
PS3561.E6675G6   1989   89-5108
813'.54—dc20   CIP

First edition: August 1989
0 9 8 7 6 5 4 3 2 1

For Sue

My heartfelt appreciation goes to the following people for advice, suggestions, information, encouragement and moral support: Bayard Alcorn and Sally Roberson, Richard Butner, Jack and Jeanne Dann, Patrick Delahunt, Gardner Dozois, Ed Ferman, Molly Hays Glander, Betsy Hall, Col. Robert M. Hall, M.D., T.E. LeVere, David Parker, Larry Rudner, Rana Van Name, Allyn Vogel, Sheila Williams, Dorothy Wright, and the participants in the Sycamore Hill Writers' Conferences, Clarion '86, and the North Carolina State Fiction Writing Workshops.

I'm especially indebted to Kim Stanley Robinson, Lucius Shepard, Mark Van Name, Bruce and Nancy Sterling, James Patrick Kelly, my editor Beth Meacham, and, in more ways than I can count, Sue Hall. Thanks, pals.

CONTENTS

April

Heaven and Earth are not humane.
They regard all things as straw dogs.

—*Lao Tzu*

1: THURSDAY, APRIL 15

Carla Hazard entertains a Visitor from Out of Town

Late in the evening, as she rode the Main Street tramway to the central post office of Kansas City, Missouri, Carla Hazard met a stranger.

At first she mistook him for her ex-husband. He was sitting across the aisle, two seats ahead, and the way his long, straw-colored hair fell over the collar of his jacket, blown back by the breeze through his window, made him look just like Stuart. He carried no umbrella, wore no overcoat. No one sat beside him. Like Carla, he was completely alone.

Her first reaction was panic. She wanted to run away, yet wished she had the nerve to get up and slap his face. She wondered why he had not noticed her when she passed by him down the aisle. He looked so calm, so self-assured. That was only one of his lies.

Maybe this was just her fate—to meet him on the street-car that she would never normally have the nerve to ride so late at night. That very morning, when she'd called it up onto her home screen, Dr. Fate of the *Hemisphere Confidential Report* had told her:

Why such a stay-at-home? It's time you got out and had a little fun. Meeting some new people should help dispel the depression that's been keeping you down.

Be open to new possibilities. The Gemini bach-elorette has the chance to find enlightenment tonight. But she must be willing to let her true self show.

Eight blocks of porn shops, pop dens and peepshows lined Main Street from 39th to 31st. When the car stopped opposite Bob's Sport Shoppe three Dadaist punks got on. One displayed his true self as a geisha, the second dressed like a banker, and the third had disguised himself as a space alien, complete with ray gun. As he dropped a five-dollar coin into the fare box, the eyes of the alien flicked over Carla, as cool as if she were a flattened squirrel in the street. The punks sprawled across a bench seat and began to talk about the 1040 Short Form.

Some fun: Stuart and porn nihilists. She distracted her-self by looking around the car. To her right sat a young woman in a Grecian shift and a man wearing a frock coat. In front of them a tiny black woman clutched a large rat-tan purse. Next to her a boy was reading the *Revelations Grapevine*. The headline read, "Saucer Men Run Pen-tagon." Like Carla, the ones lucky enough to have jobs were going to the post office to beat the income tax dead-line.

At the corner of 35th a pale, plucked-looking man got on. He sat down in front of Stuart, turned and leaned over the back of his seat and said, "The fact that He doesn't destroy us all is proof of His Love."

"You don't say," Stuart said, and suddenly Carla realized that it was not Stuart at all. Stuart would have ignored the man.

"It's all predicted," the pale man said. "Things falling apart. The war in Israel. Dead people rising. Diseases. Take my word for it." He poked the top of the seat with his index finger. "It doesn't make a blessed bit of difference whether you file that form. It's the end coming."

The end had already come for Carla and Stuart. She was filing her tax return at the last minute because until now she had never had to do her own income tax. That had been his department. Stuart had never filed anything late in his entire life, including the divorce papers.

In all his habits Stuart was meticulous. Carla had been attracted to that. He was the wine steward for The American Restaurant, and wore his European jackets and silk ties like the son of a coal miner who hopes to rise to a higher station. After awhile, when she realized how much Stuart's punctiliousness grew out of his desire to please others, his stiffness began to wear on her. He gave his control over to the people who set the fashions, surrendered his judgment to a set of rules he could not stand to see broken. When she met Ben at the university she was vulnerable, and had fallen hard. That didn't last long.

"I can't seem to get hold of my emotions," she'd confessed to Stuart. "I didn't mean to hurt you. You know I would never deliberately hurt you."

She should have known that Stuart could not reserve judgment. The minute she told him about the affair, he moved out. She got the call from his lawyer within a week, and the decree was final by Christmas, in time, she supposed, for Stuart to get a date for New Year's without having to lie about being single.

She hadn't even gotten her W-2 form before she heard rumors he had been banging a cocktail waitress during the last year of their marriage. It seemed unlikely, but by then Carla was prepared to believe anything. It explained his giving up so easily. Banging. That was the term Mary Halloran had used when she'd told Carla. Mary made it sound like Stuart was using a gun. Sitting on the streetcar, Carla imagined Stuart standing naked, holding his penis in his hand like Jimmy Cagney holding a pistol in an old movie. *Public Enemy*. "The bastard," she said aloud.

The blond man turned. Carla could see now that the line of his nose was wrong for Stuart, the plane of his cheek too angular.

"I'm sorry," she said, flustered.

"Thinking out loud?" He smiled. He looked so understanding. The pale man kept talking, and the blond man turned back to listen.

Carla tried to get control of herself. She stared out the window. It was a warm night for mid-April: afternoon rain had left the streets damp, and wet pavement reflected the headlights of the few cars left in the city. She was not used to rage. Somehow the anger hadn't hit her until a week ago, as she'd sat down to do her income tax. Calling up the receipts for the previous year had been like reliving it: the house payments, the pitiful remnant inflation had left of the inheritance from her father, the ticket stubs from Stuart's wine buying trip to California. With each receipt the dam that held back her emotions crumbled a little, and by the end of the afternoon she found herself crying uncontrollably. Stuart had deceived her. It must be true about the cocktail waitress.

She drank a third of a bottle of scotch and stayed up half the night watching the HCR call-in show. While a young man from Tucson described the difficulties of finding a job once employers realized he was revived from the dead, Carla's tears transmuted to fury, then to an immense, boozy self-pity, finally descending to cold contempt for Stuart. She hoped he'd turn black. She had been a fool, and blind. But now it was over. No more comfortable illusions. She was going to construct a world of the things she could depend on. She would not be deceived again. The penalties were too great.

"The penalty for the unbelievers is too horrible to imagine," the man in the front of the streetcar was telling the tall blond man. "Why do you think the market crashed? The signs are in the sky."

"Signs in the sky?"

"These UFOs. They aren't spaceships. That's just the modern man's way out. In the Old Testament it would have been angels. You ever seen one?"

"A spaceship?"

"Spaceship, angel—same thing. That's my point. It's just terminology. I've seen them, and they're real. Take my word for it."

"I have no reason to doubt you." The tall man's voice was scratchy, nothing like Stuart's—one of those voices that always sounded hoarse. He had an accent like a German who had learned English from a British tutor.

"Crown Center," the streetcar announced. Carla slid out of her seat and moved to the rear doors. The two men followed. The tall man's expression, it turned out, was also nothing much like Stuart's: mildly amused, very unlike Stuart's sober stare. He seemed content to listen to the madman indefinitely. He caught her watching him and raised an eyebrow as if to say, "He does go on, doesn't he?" She turned away, smiling. The car stopped suddenly and she let herself be thrown against him. "Excuse me," she said.

"Quite all right," he said. They got off.

In the post office lobby, a table of indentured workers in faded army fatigues collected forms and read disks into terminals. A couple of postal clerks supervised.

"Here we are at Grand Central," the UFO expert said to the tall man. He stuck out his hand. "The name's Kyle Igoe. Nice talking to you, Mr.—"

"Stuart," said the tall man. Carla stared at him again.

"Stuart what?"

"Stuart is my surname. My first name is Holman."

"I get you. Well, take it easy." Kyle Igoe turned and began haranguing one of the clerks. Holman Stuart got behind Carla in line. She'd decided that only an Aquarius—straight as an arrow, but eccentric—would act the way he had toward Kyle Igoe. A person lonely enough to listen. She felt an uncommon boldness.

"I'm surprised you put up with that man," she said.

He looked at her. "Tolerance," he said. "It's the best way to get along in a strange place." From the front the man's nose seemed straighter, and his hair, though too long, was neatly trimmed. "My name is Holman Stuart."

"So I heard. It took me by surprise for a second. My husband's name was Stuart. His first name."

The corner of his mouth flicked upward in a fleeting grin. It was very appealing. "Did he change it?"

"What?"

"His name. You say it was Stuart. Did he have it changed?"

Carla searched his face for sarcasm. "No. It's still Stuart, but he's not my husband any more."

"Ah." The man smiled.

The line moved up and Carla gave her disk to the worker who, without looking at her, slid it into the reader and asked for her ID. He keyed the information off to the IRS. "Next," he said. Holman Stuart handed him a small envelope.

"This isn't in disk form," the worker said.

"No." Holman stood there, head cocked slightly forward.

"This table's just for instant filing. Why do you think we set it up out here? You—"

One of the clerks came over. "What's the matter, Bishop?"

The worker went poker faced. "He's in the wrong line."

The super took the envelope. "You could have just put this in the stamped mail slot over there, sir."

"I'm so sorry."

The super studied Holman. The others in line were getting restless.

"It's okay. Only you wasted your time standing in line."

Holman patted his hand delicately on the table, a gesture

of conciliation, amazingly feminine. Carla felt a sudden need to protect him. "I have lots of time," he said.

"Well I don't, pal," said the man behind him in line.

Holman turned from the table and Carla realized that she'd been standing there waiting for him. Flustered, she turned—and ran into a woman. Carla stumbled; Holman Stuart caught her. The woman looked angry.

"Please excuse us," Holman said to her.

The woman huffed away.

Carla could feel her face flush. "Thank you," she said.

"You're welcome."

"I don't know why I'm so clumsy tonight."

"The full moon."

Carla smiled. "You're not from Kansas City."

"It's that obvious?"

"I can tell by your accent."

"I'll work to perfect it."

"I like it fine. Do you mind if I walk with you?"

"Not at all." They walked together toward the streetcar stop. Carla felt excited. Off at the top of the bluff she could see the illuminated phallus of the Pershing Memorial. "How long have you been here?" she asked.

"Two weeks ago yesterday."

"Do you like it?"

"It's a human city."

They caught the next southbound car and sat together. Carla looked at her watch: eleven-thirty. She supposed she ought to go home but she didn't want to. She didn't have to be at the office until ten the next morning.

Holman sat looking out the window. "I meant to say humane," he said. "I have trouble with the language still."

"You speak very well. Where are you from?"

"Brussels, Belgium."

"What brings you to the states?"

"Business. Pleasure." His mouth tightened in that sudden smile. "Tomorrow I leave. Would you have a drink with me tonight?"

Carla considered. "For someone who doesn't know English you handle it pretty well."

"I'm a good mimic."

She decided. "Someplace in Westport?"

"You choose."

They got off at Westport Road and walked along toward the restaurants. There were no clouds now and above the street shone the bright moon, high in the night. The sidewalk was swept clean; the police kept the beggars out of Westport. On a street corner a young man in a white Panama hat played the hammered dulcimer. A movie let out and people flowed into the street. At just that moment a group of Millennialists turned the corner: they rolled their cart plastered with pictures of the coming Paradise on Earth, chanting about the Final Days. Their white jumpsuits had green crosses stenciled on the back. Some people stopped to watch. The dulcimer player stopped playing.

Carla and Holman passed through the onlookers to the patio behind The New Parnassus. The waiters and waitresses were dressed as Greek slaves. While they chatted, waiting for a table, Holman played with the analyzer beside the bar. He inserted his index finger. After a moment the LCD read "clear," and the machine discharged the dated blood test. Carla wondered what he had in mind for the evening. He didn't ask her to take the test.

They moved to a table under the oak at the center of the patio. Carla meant to ask what his business was, and how someone from Belgium had come to have a Scots name. She meant to ask him a lot of questions, but the conversation never seemed to turn that way. Not that he ever avoided questions; he just seemed content to listen to her talk. She found herself speaking about the divorce. She told him what a monster Stuart had proved to be, how she had been deceived. In the middle of this torrent she realized that she might be saying too much.

"Have you ever heard of Spiritual Economics?" Holman asked.

"Spiritual Economics?"

"Yes. The basic notion is that a person's spiritual well-being is dependent on her taking in more love than she expends. In this way she incurs a spiritual profit. The object of Spiritual Economics is to maximize spiritual profits. This leads to a steady growth in well-being and, at the time of death, a surplus that can be passed on to any designated successors."

He looked at her as levelly as if he were describing stamp collecting. Maybe the gin had affected her hearing. "Are you serious?"

He smiled. "Surely."

"You try to get more love than you give? That sounds a little cold blooded."

"To think otherwise is to ignore human nature. No one ever kept a relationship together that way."

"Stuart—my husband—would love it. He would use this system as an excuse. I mean, he could say sleeping around on me was so he could get more love, and his lying was so that he could keep getting my love. The more the merrier."

"This is true. A reckless person could apply Spiritual Economics in this short-sighted way. But that is true of any system of thought. In the long run such strategies don't work. Look at your husband, for instance—assuming he did deceive you—"

Carla was stung. "What do you mean 'assuming'?"

Holman's composure broke. "Did I say something improper? I don't know—please excuse me."

"It's okay. Go on."

"Yes. I mean, assuming your husband mismanaged his spiritual account with you—he no longer has you. We find his relations go poorly with anyone else once his reputation is known. It is like a business—a store that sells shoddy merchandise loses customers. Eventually it goes bankrupt. Why?—because of bad faith."

"It still sounds like you're saying I should take more love than I give out. Isn't that selfish?"

"Do you believe it is possible not to be selfish? All people, even those who claim to be altruists, act according to self-interest. The difference is that some are more honest than others. Or if you insist that some people are sincere in their altruism, the Spiritual Economist would describe such sincerity as a sign of self-delusion. It is better to be honest about it than to hide your motives. Isn't that exactly what bothered you about your husband—that he was not what he seemed, that he put on a false front?"

He was as earnest as a Labrador retriever. "Can't a—a Spiritual Economist—act falsely?"

"Of course. But what we're talking about with kindness or unkindness is merely the manner in which people apply the principles of Spiritual Economics. The laws are the same regardless."

"You're strange," Carla said. "Talk like this doesn't exactly put me at ease."

Holman smiled. "What makes you think I want to put you at ease?"

"Well, I did notice you take that blood test."

He blushed.

Carla poked at the lime in her glass with her finger. It bobbed back to the surface. "Tricky. Still, I'm not sure I'll buy your contract."

"Don't buy anything you can't afford. I wouldn't want you to overextend your finances."

Carla smiled, but she felt sad. Stuart had screwed her over, Ben had screwed her over. She'd been so lonely. It occurred to her that loneliness wasn't being alone—it was being unable to say the things that were important to you. She looked across the table at the foreigner. He did resemble Stuart. Well, screw Stuart.

He watched her, his head tilted so that he was peaking at her up from beneath his eyelids. It gave him a sheepish look.

A flush of sexual attraction swept over her, so strong that her thighs felt like water. She was a Gemini bachelorette. "Where are you staying?" she asked.

"The Hilton Plaza."

"Would you like to come to my house tonight?"

"Are you serious?"

Carla laughed. "I think so."

"Let's go, then." His accent seemed to have diminished to nothing.

Holman left two fifties for the drinks and they went to her home. It was a safe neighborhood. Carla and Stuart had had to stretch to buy it, but crashflation had boosted her salary to where, even without Stuart's income, the mortgage payments were no problem. Holman played with the music box on the end table while Carla poured two glasses of Chivas. They sat on the sofa for a half hour, leaning on one another, sipping the scotch and talking in low voices. She rested her hand on his chest. She could feel the warmth of his body, the faint and steady beat of his heart. How strange to think she had touched him for the first time not three hours before, brushing against him in the streetcar. They went upstairs.

That night Carla felt totally released, comfortable, unembarrassed. Holman seemed to read her mind; he knew what she wanted before she knew herself. She was without thought or emotion other than the simple desire to let her body have what it wanted.

She wasn't sure how much time had passed when she was awakened by a clinking from the bathroom. Moonlight threw the rumpled bedclothes into sharp relief. Holman was not there. She tried to move and discovered that, beneath the bedspread, her hands and ankles were tied together.

Holman came out of the bathroom carrying a small bottle. "I couldn't find any isopropyl alcohol," he said. "We'll have to make do with rubbing alcohol."

"What are you doing?" she asked. The shakiness of her own voice terrified her.

Holman set the bottle on the bedside table. She stared up at him. His face, crossed by bands of moonlight, was now too familiar.

"I want to continue our conversation." He sounded exactly like Stuart. He sat down beside her and reached for the bedside lamp. Her heart thudded in her chest. She wanted to tell him to stop. He switched on the light.

It was Stuart. Not just a resemblance now—it really *was* him.

"Stuart."

"Call me Holman."

She tried to remain calm. How could he have tied her up without waking her? "You bastard! How did you trick me?"

"Here is a lesson in Spiritual Economics. I am not Stuart. Would you have gone to bed with Stuart?"

"I'd die first."

"Such a lack of charity. But you are economically correct. So I must not be Stuart, right? I'm not like Stuart in any important way but appearance, am I? I am kinder than Stuart. I listen more attentively. I care more about your emotions. I'm better in bed. You have clearly profited from this transaction."

"What are you talking about?"

"Could Stuart have been as good for you as I was tonight?"

"I don't know," she said. She felt dizzy. She looked away from him and saw on the table, next to the alcohol, a bag of cotton balls she used to remove makeup, a small bowl from her kitchen, a bottle of india ink from her desk, and a box of pushpins.

"Either I am not Stuart, or else you are guilty of having misjudged him. Here is where the 'Stuart' in this analysis suffered a debit. You were so certain, as you rode on the streetcar, that you knew the truth about him. So self-righteous. If I were really Stuart, I might be angry about your unfairness to me. It's a good thing that I'm not Stuart. It's a good thing I do not get angry."

Carla tried to sit up. He leapt on top of her, inhumanly quick. He straddled her, naked, pinned her arms against her belly. She twisted her head from side to side. He poured alcohol into the bowl, soaked a cotton ball and tried to swab her forehead. She bit his hand.

"It will just feel like some pin pricks," he said calmly. "But you'll need to hold still."

Carla stopped struggling. Her face felt flushed, her legs weak. "I'll scream," she said.

"Poor Carla," he said in Stuart's voice. "You never get a break. You always get used. You're a loser. It's written all over your face."

He grabbed her chin with one hand, and with the other dipped the point of a pushpin in the alcohol. He studied her face like an artist studying a blank canvas. "Or if it isn't, it should be."

2: THURSDAY, APRIL 15

George falls down the Rabbit Hole

The first thing George remembered was falling down a brightly lighted well. He did not know where the well was or how he had happened to fall into it. The light, from a continuous vertical strip on the wall that swept upward by him as he fell, grew brighter until it attained a deadly, depthless whiteness. George could not see well enough to tell how far away it was. When he tried to reach out he found he could not move his arm. It was as if he were falling down Alice's rabbit hole, giddily, swiftly, but instead of shelves and cupboards the wall of this hole had only the single strip of light. He ought to have been afraid. Instead he wondered what would happen when he hit bottom. Would he land lightly, like Alice, a bit of dandelion fluff on the air—or disastrously, like Humpty Dumpty? Suppose he never landed at all?

He heard a sound. A low rumble, not loud but steady, it surrounded him without diminishing or increasing. George thought it might be some distant engine; the rattle that punctuated it reminded him of the pinging of his '64

Plymouth when he tried to take a hill on low-octane gas. That was a long time ago. Like the light, the sound grew more distinct as George fell, and with it came gradual feeling: cool air wafting past his cheek, a slight vibration. He tried to move again and felt his arm respond sluggishly. An oval shape floated into his field of vision. "Don't try to move," a voice said. A woman's voice, perfunctory but not unkind. He was willing to trust her. Perhaps she would break his fall.

George found he could blink his eyes. His eyelids responded immediately to his mental command. He had never understood what a miracle that was, and he enjoyed this feeling of control so much that he blinked his eyes again and again. As he did his vision cleared, and like a revelation it came to him: he was not falling. He was lying on his back. The light that swept past him was a strip of fluorescent ceiling lights. He was on a table being wheeled down a hallway. The rumble was no distant engine, but the sound of the table's wheels on the tile floor. The voice was that of some attendant. The shape that had hovered before him was her face.

George struggled to accept this Copernican revolution. He was not falling and need not worry about crashing; he was being taken someplace and needed to worry about where that was. The new order settled around him. How powerful the workings of his mind; how reasonable, how true! Through them, in seconds, the universe had been remade.

Then George remembered something very important. He was dead.

He felt mildly chagrined, like a man who opened the refrigerator to realize he had forgotten to stop at the supermarket for milk. Of course he was dead! Now that he remembered, many details came back to him. He recalled the slide of his heart into irregularity, silence. The difficulty breathing. The slowing of his thoughts. The vast sleepiness. He remembered floating six feet above himself as his body sat slumped forward in a chair; he remembered realizing that it was dead. Of the time between that moment and now he remembered nothing.

The table slowed and the angle of the fluorescent lights changed until they were passing crossways to his body. The table stopped. He heard a door open, and he was pushed into a room. The woman's face appeared above him again, much clearer this time. Her brown hair fell in curls across a lined brow. "Here we are, Mr. Eberhart," she said. Other faces appeared; hands took him by the shoulders and hips and legs and he was laid on a bed. They connected a number of wires to his chest. A tube bore fluids from a machine on a wheeled stand into his arm. George tried to ask "Where am I?" but it was as if his throat had rusted closed: all that came out was a croak. The nurse gave him a sip of water.

"Thank you," rasped George. He drank some more. "Where am I?"

"In Recovery," she said. "Don't try to talk."

They rolled the table away. They closed the door and left him. George lay there and stared at the ceiling. It was white and full of tiny holes. Was it the ceiling of Heaven or Hell? His eyes felt dry, as if he had not closed them in a hundred years. He wondered how long he'd sat there, dead in his chair, before anyone found him. Perhaps when you died your soul remembered things about your body. That would explain why, despite the fact that he felt quite awake, his eyes were so tired. It was becoming clear to George that he would have many things to ponder before he understood what it meant to die.

For he had died, and now he was in Recovery. He wondered what that meant. He wondered what happened next.

Death was like a hospital. Within a day George understood this. The fact that there were days and nights was difficult for him to accept, but it was only one of the similarities to life that made death so confusing. He had expected that there would be some summing up, and after that a change. Instead he found, as he lay in the bed, and eventually, as he grew stronger and got up to walk about the room and look out of the window, that the surface of things had not changed at all. The sheets were dry and cool where they lay beside him, and dry and warm where they touched his body. When he moved he heard a sweeping rustle and felt the tickle of the fabric against his newly hairless legs. He grew hungry and they gave him food. Meatloaf tasted like meatloaf, boiled potatoes like boiled potatoes, and the sprig of parsley like parsley. Before he had died he had not liked parsley, but now he found its taste quite dizzying. When he got out of bed, he wheeled the machine with the tube beside him like a hall tree on casters. The floor was cold. He rolled himself into the bathroom to use the toilet. There were stainless steel handles beside it by which he could support himself. The face in mirror, that of an unfamiliar bald man, stared as if it were judging him. He did not like that.

The glass of the room's one window was hard and cool. His fingertips left little haloes of moisture on it that evaporated as he watched. Through the window he could see the tops of two budding maples and a parking lot and a booth where a young white girl sat during the day and a young black man sat at night. Beyond was an expressway where, all evening, he watched the tops of semis speed by under mercury-vapor lights. The sun was hidden behind haze during the day and the stars behind glare at night—assuming sun and stars existed in the afterworld.

For a moment during the night, as he lay awake assessing what he had learned, George doubted whether he was dead at all. His surroundings did not give him any proof that he was dead; on the contrary, they offered him overwhelming evidence that he was alive and in an ordinary hospital. He was a logical man, and could not come up with any logical reason not to accept that evidence. Still, evidence was not enough in the face of what he *knew* to be true. There were some forms of knowledge that did not arise from observation or logic.

Granted that this world was not a hospital, still George did not know enough to figure out what it really was. But he

had to be there for a reason. Eventually something would
happen to show him that reason. He had been naive to expect the explanation to come suddenly and overwhelmingly.
It might be that whoever was ordering this experience for
him was watching to see how he would react. The man in
the mirror could be one of their spies. George would show
that he had the faith to accept appearances for the time
being, and the patience to wait for a sign. In the meantime
he would watch carefully, question everything, and keep
what he knew to himself.

Not that George suspected he would come to harm. That
would be paranoid. But it would not do to give himself
away, either.

The next morning one of the nurses told him that someone was there to see him. He felt a moment of panic. Before
he could properly prepare himself a woman and a man came
into his room. The woman sat on the edge of the bed,
leaned toward him, touched his cheek with her fragrant
hand. "Oh, George," she said. "George." She smiled and
blinked back tears.

George recognized her as Lucy, his wife. She was a tall
woman with long black hair; her gray eyes were worried and
intelligent. She wore a conservative suit and a loose-fitting
blouse with a high neck, as if she wished to conceal her sex.
It didn't work.

"I'm so glad you're alive," she said. "You'll never know."

Never know what? "Lucy. It's good to see you."

She pulled back a little. The man who had come in with
her drew a chair close to the bed and sat down. "You look
good," he said.

The man was his friend, Richard Shrike.

"I feel fine," said George. "What is this place?"

"St. Andrew's Medical Center," Richard said. A slender
man, dark hair combed straight back from his forehead. His
coat, with button-down cuffs and embroidered buttonholes,
must have cost six thousand dollars. His hands, strong and
broad, were impeccably manicured. George had a sudden
memory of those hands at the keyboard of a piano.

"How did you get here?" George asked.

Lucy's hand moved on his chest.

"We drove, George," Richard said. "We've been waiting for them to let us see you."

"You've been very ill," said Lucy.

"You had a heart attack," Richard said. "We found you in your study, slumped in front of your computer. I had dropped by because you'd missed four days of work. We had to leave the series about the Suicide Hall of Fame in Debbie's hands and Abramowitz was asking me about you. Lucy didn't want to disturb you, but if we hadn't come in we might have been too late."

"What was on the screen?"

Richard stared at George calmly, then smiled. "Some notes. Ones I would have been embarrassed taking to Abramowitz to justify your absence. Fortunately, we won't have to face that."

"Never mind that now," said Lucy. She embraced George; her cheek was warm against his. Her perfume made him dizzy. "The important thing is you're all right and you'll be coming home soon." She reached across George to pull Richard's handkerchief from his pocket, then dabbed at her eyes. George felt overpowered by her physicality, which threatened to shake his conviction that he had passed beyond the material world. "I don't know what I would have done if you had died," she said.

Richard looked annoyed. She gave him back the ruined handkerchief; he folded the black stains inside and stuffed it back in his pocket. "I don't know what I would have done, either," he said. "I suppose we could have run a three-take story: '*Hemisphere* Staffer Murdered by Brazilian Spies.' But I'd rather have you around to bitch at." He smiled again. "Let's not worry about that."

"What shall we worry about, then?" asked George.

"We could worry about whether you're going to grow your hair back fast enough for us to let you on the air," Richard said. "I imagine it must be pretty boring lying around flat on your back. If you like I could bring along your notes for you to read."

"What notes?"

Richard looked unruffled. "The special report. On the Millennialists? Maybe you're too woozy for that. I don't want you getting all wrought up again before you're back on your feet."

George tried to remember something about this report. "So what's it supposed to be about?"

Richard turned to Lucy. "Brain damage for sure, Lucy. Maybe we can rent him out as a hat stand."

For the first time since he had died, George felt like laughing. This Richard, at least, was the same as the real one. "Very funny, Richard. I'm doing a Special Report, right?"

"Somebody is. Abramowitz has already suggested we give it to Stan Levine. He said Stan could be your collaborator. You know what that means. Stanley will collaborate you off the main menu before you know it. I told him you were the only one who could do this report for him. You have this innate understanding of lunacy. He—"

"Richard," Lucy said, "it was work that put George in here in the first place. You don't need to push it at him before he's even on his feet again."

"You're right. My apologies."

George felt the warmth of Lucy's hip against his leg. "Forget about HCR," she said to him. "You don't ever have to do another report if you don't want to. Just come home."

George didn't say anything. They tried to make small talk but he would not hold up his end of the conversation, and eventually, smiling, reassuring, they walked out, leaving him to his thoughts.

Lucy visited him every day. George watched her beautiful face and wondered what she was thinking, if she was thinking at all and was not just a simulacrum of the woman to whom he had been married. Simulacrum. An intriguing word. George rolled it over his tongue like a sourball. Like a candy it was a tart-sounding word that eventually, worn at by imagination, gave forth a bitter sweetness. A simulacrum was something that appeared to be genuine but was fraudulent, offered in place of the real thing. The world of St. Anthony's Medical Center offered many simulacra. Air conditioning in place of the real breeze you never got because the windows could not be opened. The concern of the nurses which was no more than service delivered for salary. The red-white-and-blue busses that he saw on the highway beyond the fence, cattle cars full of indentureds being shipped from one posting to another—George wondered whether the vehicles existed below the line of his sight. The young woman and young man in the parking lot. There weren't enough cars left to justify parking lot attendants. In the afterlife, would God assign people to makework jobs?

Lucy made him think harder. Here he was up against a mystery he could not solve so easily. They talked. Lucy told him about the latest feuds in the Department of Corrections, punctuating her complaints with rueful jokes.

"A lawyer and his friend go backpacking," she said. "On the trail they run into a mountain lion. They freeze. Then the lawyer takes off his backpack. His friend says, 'What are you doing? You can't outrun a mountain lion.' The lawyer says, 'I don't have to outrun him. I just have to outrun you.'"

George stared at her. "But *you're* a lawyer," he said. He had just remembered.

"Yes. But if you were in trouble, I would never run away."

She laughed. Lucy's laughter was the first thing George had heard that sounded real. He studied her. Their conversations became an almost perfect simulacrum of their relationship.

At times George caught himself wondering how far that resemblance would go. From her first visit he had felt the stirrings of desire. Soon this became a real factor every time she walked into his room. The curve of her hips through the fabric of whatever suit she wore that day became something he could not ignore.

Along with Lucy came more of the outside world. He received shelves of flowers and plants which the nurses fussed at him about. With them came a raft of get-well cards. George would look at the name on each card and the memory of the person would come, but it was a more conscious process than memory ought to be. It felt as much a feat of miraculous control as his earlier discovery that he could blink his eyes.

George decided to test out this memory. He asked for a newspaper and they brought him one. Here was an imitation of the imitation world. He remembered it all, yet its absurdity screamed at him: President to Meet Brazilian Foreign Minister; Secessionists Dominate Dixie Debate; Ex-Hubby Denies Tattooing Wife; Oregon UFO Reports Soar; Leading Indicators Down for 16th Month. He sought the principle that would prove that this world was not simply a duplication of reality. He could find no principle. He felt himself slide toward acceptance that he was indeed in the real world. The prospect filled him with terror.

Still nothing happened. He read the papers, switched through the 140 menus available on the hospital cable circuits. He came across the Hemisphere Confidential Report. With dismay, it all came back to him:

Tragedy Triggers Touching Teen Romance
Judge Puts Dead Back on Streets
—Daughter says "Daddy, how can you defend these zombies?"
Amazing Fiscal Rosary Brings Money to True Believers
Commandante Jesus Jams NBA Broadcast
Pace of Miracle Cures Up as Millennium Nears

George was head of Special Reports at HCR, and Richard was his boss. He had started the Millennium series himself.

There was a whole world out there, a world that included something called revival. That would explain why he knew he had died—he had. He was one of these Revived. Although the explanation did not satisfy him, he felt compelled to accept it. The world was real.

A restless energy that was not strength, but impatience, grew in him. He asked Richard to send over his notes. They were a puzzle. First there was a thick folder of hard copies from all over the country. Many told of sudden death. A fifteen-year-old girl in Spokane who went out into the front yard one evening with a shotgun and blew her brains out. A family of four in Des Moines killed when a drunken college professor set fire to their house. A city councilman in Houston murdered by his wife when she discovered he had Acquired Melanin Production Syndrome and was turning black. HCR made a living sending such stuff out over the computer services. George could make no more sense out of the stories than he could out of the front page of the newspaper.

The other folder was easier to figure out. These notes concerned various religious movements, in particular the Millennialist preachings of the Reverend Jimmy-Don Gilray. The Millennialists believed that, as foretold by the scriptures, the end of the world was coming. The signs were there. The Antichrist was alive, and the movements offered various candidates to fill that role in the drama of the Last Days. The Reverend Jimmy-Don tied the prophecies in with the wave of UFO reports that had swept the world in recent years. His followers called him a prophet. They said he heralded the new order, a thousand years of peace and freedom under the rule of the Lord, after which would come the final judgment. Richard told George that he had been trying to set up an interview when he had the heart attack.

George did not know what he was supposed to do about these notes, but they were the first thing—besides Lucy—that he had found himself interested in since he'd woken up. He spent hours reading through them. Among the clippings George found one that drew him more than others:

UFONAUT THREATENS FINAL JUDGMENT!
. . . But leaves Miracle Cancer Cure as Sign of Good Intentions

Austin—Mar 18—HCR—In a monumental revelation that threatens to change the course of human history, a strange being from another galaxy has delivered the final ultimatum to earth people: change or be exterminated by an Outer Space Hit Team!

The astounding message, along with a miraculous gift from outer space, was delivered to retired plumber Hank Gansvoort in late February in the basement of the historic Driskill Hotel in downtown Austin. The 60-year-old escaped workie was caught there by the saucer alien while in the process of stealing building materials to help finance terrorism by his senior citizen's group.

The space alien appeared to Gansvoort disguised as a human. "At first I thought he was the house dick. I'd told the bell captain I was the building inspector, but I was really lifting some one-inch copper tubing."

"He had his police alarm out," Gansvoort said. "I was going to stick him but he saw it coming and zapped me. He read my mind.

"He made me realize it was wrong to go against God's commands. He made me repent, and he gave me the message."

The Divine Invasion

The star creature said that the Galactic Union has been watching Earth for a thousand years and is prepared to deliver its final verdict on the human race. Within the year the judgment will come. The shock troops of the divine invasion are already among us getting ready to wipe out the unrepentant.

The members of Gansvoort's pepperman cell, which police say has been responsible for at least six terrorist bombings in the last year, are convinced that Gansvoort is telling the truth. Since the visitation they have turned themselves in to local authorities and have been returned to the government Indigent Work Program.

"Better to heal than to destroy," said Martha Vetters, 63-year-old ex-bomb maker for the cell.

"They only want us to make a decision now and stick with it," Gansvoort said.

Still Time

The alien secret agent says that there's still time for those earthlings willing to see the truth and abandon Evil, according to Gansvoort.

To prove his kindly intentions the alien gave Gansvoort a mysterious metal token that has the ability to heal warts and maybe even cure cancer. Scientists at a famous western university who have examined the two-inch-long object, shaped remarkably like an ordinary door key, are mystified as to how it works. The head of the research team speculated that the Healing Key works by emitting Z-rays.

"It's on the cutting edge of technology," the scientist told HCR. "I don't see how Gansvoort could make up a thing like this."

World scientists have speculated for decades that space may be inhabited by intelligences vastly more powerful than our own. The universe contains more than one hundred million galaxies.

The story set an ache in George's chest. It made some kind of sense. A messenger. A misleading appearance. A promised judgment. He sorted through the other clippings, trying to find connections.

After four days they unhooked him from the machine. After a week he could not understand why he was still in the hospital. Lucy talked about taking him home. A reporter for the *New York Times* called and asked him questions about his reporting team. Lucy showed him an article about him in the media section: "HCR Puts Special Projects on Hold."

Richard was quoted as saying George was feeling strong and impatient to get back to work. At least that was true; George had never felt so much like he had things to get done and no time to do them.

One day, while Lucy sat in the room reading a magazine, glancing up from it from time to time to watch him when she thought he wasn't looking, George realized that his wait for a Sign was going to be a long one. Life was a more complex matter than Life after Death. George was being tested, or he was being punished, or he was being rewarded. But the test, the punishment, the reward, was going to be a subtle one. He feared that he might not be able to stand it.

Finally the doctor told him he could go home. Lucy and Richard came for him.

"My friend, Abramowitz is pressing." Richard sat in a chair while Lucy helped George dress. "I've had to put downers in Levine's cream of wheat to keep him from grabbing a camera and interviewing the cleaning lady. Seriously." Richard winked at him. "He's been talking to Jeff Pack and I'm afraid they'll go to Abramowitz over my head."

"We'll go out the side way, George," Lucy said, buttoning his shirt. George found it difficult to keep from embracing her. He wanted to rest his head on her shoulder. He shivered.

"I feel cold," he said.

Richard was irrepressibly cheerful. "You're fine, George. You're going to live forever. Have a little faith in the medical profession."

"Richard," said Lucy. "Perhaps you should get the car."

"I don't think so. You'll need me to do CPR on George again when he sees the bill. We don't want to lose him, do we?"

Lucy looked up briefly at George, then lowered her eyes and began knotting his tie. "We don't," she said quietly.

Lucy helped him on with his coat. They put him in a wheelchair and wheeled him, laden with wilting flowers and boxes of candy, down the hallway under the fluorescent lights, to the outpatient exit. He signed a form. They smiled at him; he got out of the chair and walked out between his wife and his friend. The parking lot was almost empty: it took people like Richard to find the gasohol to run a car. A blustery wind buffeted George's face, bringing tears to his eyes. There was weather after death. Or maybe it was life. Richard unlocked the Mercedes and held the door open for him.

Lucy sat with George in the back seat and Richard drove. When they stopped at the booth at the end of the lot, George watched the young blond woman punch their ticket; he heard the time clock stutter out the printing on the back of the card. The girl had her hair pulled back in a pony tail; she gave Richard his change, but her "thank you" was drowned out by the roar of a tractor trailer from beyond the chain-link fence. They pulled out of the St. Anthony's lot and into the imitation world.

June

The human mind is not a dignified organ.

—*E. M. Forster,* Aspects of the Novel

3: FRIDAY, JUNE 4
....
Lucy eats a Sandwich

George had become obsessed with something; Lucy was not
sure what. He pulled mirrors off the walls to look behind
them. He soaped over the hand mirrors and crept around
the apartment like a terrorist. She often caught him spying
on her. Now he wouldn't leave his workroom long enough
to eat.

Lucy hesitated outside his door, balancing the tray on her
left hand, began to knock, then checked herself. The tray
wobbled. She could hear the babble of three different televisions competing for his attention. She started to knock
again, stopped again, and set the tray on the table beside the
door. She pictured George as they had found him: slumped
forward, deathly pale, a tangle of amber gibberish glowing
at the bottom of the screen because his head had fallen on
the keys. She wondered if he was still alive in there now.

She knocked lightly on the door. "Lunch," she said

quickly, then retreated down the hall without waiting for an answer. She went into her own study. An inmate, knifed in a fight at the state prison, had filed a *pro se* lawsuit charging negligence by the nurse in the prison infirmary. Lucy's notes on a motion for summary judgment were spread across her desk. It was typical of the seventy active cases she was juggling for the Attorney General's regional office, nothing particularly tricky. But she could not concentrate. She had taken the job defending employees of the Department of Corrections with some reservations: her sympathies more naturally ran with prisoners than with guards. She told herself that prison guards, doctors and administrators were people too, doing a hard job for too little money, but lately that had not kept her from feeling bad about her role in the system. It was hard to avoid admitting that the whole structure was rotten; still worse, that no legal structure could compensate for the deterioration of the society which fed both prisoners and guards into the meat grinder. Day to day she did her best and tried not to think. She was turning numb, and did not like it.

Meanwhile, what was she worrying about? George's welfare, George's friends, George's state of mind, George's career, George's feelings about her—George's lunch!

She put aside the plaintiff's affidavit, moved to her armchair, and leafed through a copy of *Vanity Fair,* more aware of her hands holding the magazine than of the words on the page. A bruise marked the base of her index finger, the same place where ten years before there had been a callus. She'd thought she was beyond that, but apparently she was wrong. On the page beneath the finger was an article on discrimination against the revived.

George had always been an advocate of revived rights, even though the official position at HCR was that "Zombies" were an abomination. "When you're dead, you're dead," George said, "So bring the poor sons of bitches back." Would his attitude change now that he had been brought back himself? More to the point, what would the Attorney General think if he found out that Lucy had arranged for that revival? At best her career would be over. At worst she would be filing her own *pro se* lawsuits from the state prison.

Lucy flipped through the magazine and looked at the pictures. Escape to the Virgin Islands: the beach at Megan's Bay looked up at her. A tanned woman wearing next to nothing stood thigh-deep in tourmaline water. She was very slender. She held her finger to her lips. Lucy wondered whether there was a callus on it. The woman's eyes were opened wide and her full lips pouted. Her whole attitude spoke of innocence, arrogance, self-confidence. Lucy tried to remember the word that described such an attitude. She knew there was a word for it. She had a very large vocabulary.

The phone rang; Lucy picked up the screen from the table. She thumbed the corner and Richard Shrike appeared.

"Lucy, how are you?"

"I'm fine. How are you?" Lucy felt as if she were talking to him from the bottom of the ocean.

"Listen, how is George?"

"George is alive and working. You can't talk to him now."

"I have no desire to talk to him, Lucy. I want to talk to you."

"Speaking."

Richard did not answer. Lucy looked at the phone's electronic imitation of Richard's face, listened to its electronic imitation of silence. The screen's resolution was poor, and she could hear the tiniest hiss.

"Are you all right, Lucy?"

"What do you mean?"

"You know what I mean. I know you don't trust me. You've never trusted me."

"Why do you say that?"

"I don't know. I just opened my mouth and out it came." Lucy looked at the woman in the ocean.

"So why not tell me why you hate me," Richard said.

Insouciant. That was the word. "Richard, what's going on

with the doctors? You've got Evans in your hip pocket and
I can't get any straight answers."

Richard sighed. "I wanted to keep you out of it. Your
boss doesn't like his assistants bribing clinics to break the
law."

"Don't patronize me. I'm in this as deep as you are. It
was my idea to revive him."

"And we did. And he's alive. What's your complaint?"

"It's this crazed secrecy. You act more like a spook than
George's friend. Can't you be straight with me for once?"

Lucy could hear the electrons jostling through the screen.
"I'll be honest with you," they told her in Richard's voice.
"This is a confusing situation. Whenever I am confused I try
to leave as many options open as possible. I do that by
keeping my own counsel."

If he was so close-mouthed, why was the rumor mill at
her office already churning out stories about George and
revival? Knowing Richard, there was no way she would get
very far with that question. "I'm his wife, Richard. You're
just his boss."

"I wish you'd abandon this moral tone. I've known
George a lot longer than you have. I have his best interests
at heart." The electrons duplicating Richard's face made a
genuine appeal. As if you could ever tell whether Richard
was any deeper than the screen on her lap. "Your interests,
too, believe me."

"You seem more worried about his work than his
health."

"I'll admit it. I stand to lose points if George doesn't get
back to work. But I wouldn't bring a man back to life just
for that. That wouldn't be cost effective."

"You still should have let me know what was going on."

"Of course. But you were distraught. I didn't think it was
a burden you needed just then. Why should I get your
hopes up when three times out of four the dead man stays
dead? So I did my negotiating with Evans, who I don't
mind saying was pretty nervous about the whole business.
And I bore the added expense myself. Okay, I expect a
main-menu report out of this. But I also get to keep a

friend, and spare the feelings of a woman I've come to re-spect."

"Sometimes, Richard, I don't think it's my feelings you respect."

"I respect your body, too, Lucy. Don't get me wrong. But if I wanted to plunder your fertile valley it would be to my advantage to have George out of the way. Am I wrong?"

She felt twisted around. "No."

"Fine. So I admit it; I didn't think about you, and I'm sorry."

"All right," said Lucy finally. "If you called to talk to me, what did you want to talk about?"

"I'd like you to do something for me."

She wondered if the screen were shooting hard X-rays through her skull. "Yes?"

"I bet George is having trouble getting back into it. Am I right?"

"I don't look over his shoulder, Richard. He seldom talks about his work."

"Now who's being evasive. You've lived with him for years. He's been home a month. He stops in the office two days a week and mumbles at me. His eyes are lit up like he's doing six kinds of speed. The staff is still waiting on him. Levine is chomping at the bit; I saw him talking to Abramowitz yesterday and now I hear they're sending him and Jeff Pack down to interview Gilray tomorrow."

"I'm sorry to hear that."

"HCR is down three points against Reuters. We've lost some subs. Compunet is thinking of signing on *Revelations Grapevine* as a replacement, and Abramowitz wants something besides UFO reports and teen suicides to carry us through the summer." Richard looked off camera, as if contemplating his soul. "Personally, I like teen suicides," he said, "but Abramowitz is a true believer. That means the heat's on Special Reports to get this religious story. And George is out to lunch."

"He's been spending all his time working on it—working on something, anyway. If it were up to me I'd stop him.

HCR doesn't do anybody any good. It was a good joke once, but George is not well now."

"I'm not forcing him to do anything he doesn't want to do. He started back to work of his own free will."

It was true. She could protect George from HCR, even from Richard, but she couldn't protect him from himself. "You said you wanted a favor. Get to the point, Richard."

"This is precisely the point. At the very least we need to watch him. He was dead for at least an hour. Sure, they pumped him full of SOD and Dr. Pepper, but he probably lost a ton of brain cells; we're lucky he's not a vegetable. Even if his head's okay, revival is number one on the Stanford Stress Analysis Profile. He could easily go wonky on us. So the first thing I want you to do is keep him diverted until we know he's okay."

"Maybe we can play Monopoly."

"That's not funny, Lucy. He's been traumatized. You can't see signs of that?"

"Yes."

"I thought so. The other thing I want you to do is monitor his work."

"Sure. I'll get a court order and we'll tap his phone."

Richard ignored her. "What I suggest you do is copy his notes. We can look them over and have some idea of how this is progressing. And if he seems to be getting too wrapped up in the project, to the detriment of his health, we can lead him away from hurting himself."

"And just incidentally, you can sandbag Levine and hold off Abramowitz. Right, Richard?"

"Certainly. But what I'm suggesting here is ideologically correct. It benefits George; it benefits you. I never sell dog food that isn't 100% beef."

"Why are you trying to sell me anything?"

"Look, Lucy. I'm George's best friend. I got him this job when nobody in New York wanted to hear his name. I might be your friend, too, if you'd deactivate the Peace Shield for a minute. If I were really the vicious sleaze some have made me out to be, I would add that it's your insecurity that makes you feel used. But I'm too kind to say that."

"I appreciate it."

"So think about this before you decide anything. I don't want you to do anything that you think will harm George. Okay?"

Lucy looked at the picture of the woman in the magazine, lying open on the table beside her. The holo made it look like the woman was lying in a niche set into the tabletop, decorated with motionless waves and a crystal sky. A tropical coffin. She thumbed the screen off, and Richard's face dissolved into matte gray. "All right," she said.

Lucy took the tray back from the table outside George's study to the kitchen. He had not touched it. The BLT was cold. She lifted off the top slice of toast. It was covered with mayonnaise. Bacon cost a fortune, lettuce almost as much. Standing at the kitchen counter, she plucked out the stiff strips of bacon and ate them, then the lettuce, tomato and toast. It didn't take a minute. When she was finished her fingers were smeared with grease and mayonnaise, sticky as blood. She wiped them on a dish towel, shoved the plate into the dishwasher. She shook some soap into the compartment, slammed the door and turned it on, then fled to the living room.

The last month had been among the worst of her life. The heart attack had only been the culmination of George's deterioration. She wondered whether she should have realized what he might turn into when she first met him—but back then she had been very young.

The ink on her diploma still damp, Lucy had gone to work for the State Insurance Commission. She was helping write a position paper on the revival technique that Han had developed at the University of Houston Medical School. When he came into their office, George was a little-known free-lance journalist researching an article. Their first meeting was all business. He called later to ask some followup questions, and she agreed to meet him for lunch.

George was forty-one then, and she was twenty-four. He was like a big, dour bear. Dark beard and shaggy hair, prematurely gray. His cowlick stood up like an eight-year-old's, and he wore a herringbone jacket ten years out of date. At the same time his ingenuous questions put Lucy at ease, she recognized his considerable intellect.

He was so poised between cynicism and idealism. She liked his deadpan humor, and everything he said was tinged with a fatalism that she found endearing. When he introduced her to Richard, the combination of Richard's penetrating nastiness and George's unworldly intelligence left her in fits of laughter. Even though she could not compete with Richard in cynicism, she was admitted to their magic circle, while the rest of the absurd world was left out. Richard never used his nastiness on her, perhaps out of respect for George, and George seemed to appreciate her more after spending a few hours with Richard. The darkness of their humor did not seem wrong then.

Lucy was impressed by George's passion, his fundamental decency. She was wary of men. She had let herself be used too many times: she had spent most of her undergraduate days desperately unhappy, dieting and bingeing, worried about what her current boyfriend thought of her. But George's attraction to her seemed to be more than a matter of hormones. Not that their sex life hadn't been good: in fact, because they had shared more than a bed, it had been great. During those first years together Lucy had found passion in herself that she had not known existed. George cared for her implicitly. She cared for him. His occasional obsessiveness had not mattered.

Though they had ideals in common, they argued over methods. Lucy was committed to the law. To her it was more than a way to make money, it was her chance to preserve what was worth preserving and change what needed changing. In practice the law was as full of sexism and hypocrisy as the society that created it, but Lucy saw another law, a potential law, a law where reason and persuasion counted for more than your sex. It wasn't there yet, but any sane person could see that was what the law was supposed to be.

The trouble was that everyone was not sane. Society only

worked when people accepted the rules, when they did more than the law obliged them to do, and less than it allowed. It required faith. In the last decade, for more and more people, that faith had broken down. This was a bitter pill for Lucy to swallow. At first she tried not to, insisting that the irrationality that ran through society was an aberration that would eventually be cured. But the years went by and the world got crazier. Lucy felt like the Dutch boy trying to hold back the flood, except that for every hole she plugged a dozen more sprang open. And worse, too many people around her—lawyers, politicians, preachers, broadcasters, Jason Abramowitz, Richard Shrike, even George himself—instead of helping, were busy drilling new holes.

George's deterioration had been the bitterest pill. Only gradually did she realize that he was full of insecurities: he insisted on being fair out of a desire to avoid guilt, was lucid because he was terrified of being misunderstood. His passion for political change veiled a fear that politics could not change because people could not change. George himself was his own chief example of someone unable to change. Since life was all you had, he maintained, and death was a black hole, George's growing inability to believe that anything could get better left him with nothing. His career stagnated. He became quietly obsessed, more and more unable to believe that anything he did made a difference. His last free-lance articles alternated between strident appeal and plain despair. Then Richard got George the job with the *Hemisphere Confidential Report,* and George vanished beneath the waves of the nut news. He was a great success. HCR had set him on the slide toward his heart attack, and Lucy had been unable to pull him back.

Lucy could feel the tug toward irresponsibility. She loved George. She needed his help. She hadn't hesitated a moment to risk her career in order to bring him back—but except physically, he had not come back. She held on, hoping that she could wake him up to reality. Instead he looked at her as if she were a plastic replica of his wife, and their conversations became a tennis match in which he would not return serve. They had not made love since before his heart attack. Instead George stayed shut up in his room with the TV on.

Lucy sat on the sofa, staring out of the window at the sun declining over the opposite side of the courtyard. She heard a noise in the hall, and George came into the room carrying a printout in his hand. He was wearing his red bathrobe and an old pair of docksiders. His hair was grizzled gray peachfuzz, and the lines at the sides of his mouth were deeper than she ever remembered them. Bright eyes rimmed with red, he looked like a sixty-year-old alcoholic. "We need to talk," he said.

She felt some hope. "I think that's a good idea."

"Things have been different since I came back," he said slowly.

"You didn't tell me but I guessed."

"I've been thinking about it a lot. I've realized what's important now."

"Yes?"

He would not meet her eyes. "Did you ever notice how all the things on television fit together?"

"Not lately. What things?"

"Little things." He paused. "We're living in a religious age. But people are killing themselves. Does that make sense?"

"A lot of people are out of work. The prisons are full. I see it every day. It's all the more reason for us to stick together, George."

He glanced at her, then quickly looked away again. "I don't think there are any accidents," he said to the corner of the ceiling.

Lucy shivered. "What do you mean?"

"Look at this." He came over and showed her the printout.

It was a map of North America covered with colored dots: blue, red, yellow, black, green. Numbers and slashes were written in beside them—the numbers were dates. The dots were connected by a tangled network of lines. The whole thing looked like a child's connect-the-dots picture. Except there was no picture, only chaos.

She tried to conceal her fear. "Yes, George?"

"You see the pattern?"

"No."

He looked at her for a moment, and the animation seemed to drain out of him. He sat on the window box and looked across the courtyard. After a while he said, "Nice view, huh?"

They were in trouble. "If you like bricks."

"We used to sit here at night just after we moved in," George said, as if he were talking about some previous wife. "We'd look across and make jokes about the people in the other apartments. That was a long time ago."

"Less than two years."

"Everything's different now. Who was on the phone?"

Lucy was startled. "When?"

"A while back there was a phone call. Was there any message for me?"

"It was Richard. He didn't want me to disturb you while you were working."

"What did he want?"

"He just wanted to know how you were doing. He's worried about the service. I told him you didn't have to work if you didn't want to. You're not well enough yet."

"This is work I'm doing. The most important I've ever done. It could mean the end of the world."

She couldn't take it any more. "The end of the world, George? You've run that story three times in the last year. Which version is it this time?"

He started to hold up the map, then crumpled it in his hand.

"George, I don't think it's a good thing for you to get wrapped up in this again so soon."

"The next time Richard calls with a message for me, let me talk to him myself."

"He didn't have any message for you—"

"How do I know that?"

It was an effort for Lucy to go to him. The setting sun, just above the roof of the building now, shone full into George's face. He squinted against it but would not lift his head to look at her. She touched the fuzz growing back at his temples. "George?"

"What?"

"George, he didn't have any message for you. He wanted to talk to me. He's concerned about how both of us are taking all this."

"What does he want?"

"He wants moronic news stories. That's all he cares about."

"It is?"

Lucy stopped stroking his hair. She put her arms around him, resting her head on his shoulder. At first he relaxed, but after a moment she could feel his muscles tense.

He looked from the window to her. "What do *you* want?"

"I want peace on earth and my husband back. But I'll settle for the husband. Please. Forget about HCR. We're more important than a bunch of hysterical lies."

She looked at his face and saw a determined stranger. He turned to the window again. "At first I thought the sun was brighter than it ought to be," he said. "But it's not."

He placed his palm flat against the glass, testing it as if to reassure himself that it was really there.

George ate supper and went to bed. Lucy cleaned up the kitchen, nibbling at his leftovers. Why was she cooking meals for this man? Didn't she have her own life to worry about? The more she thought about it, the angrier she grew.

Lucy didn't want to do Richard's spying for him. She couldn't stand to go back to the Corrections Department brief. God help her, what she wanted was to get into bed with George, slide up to him, put her arms around him and feel the warmth of his body. She could convince herself that he was alive and that she was not alone.

She went to the bedroom and got undressed. George lay with his back to her side of the bed. She switched on her reading lamp. His broad shoulders, once dark with curly hair, were smooth as a young boy's. As a little girl Lucy had been entranced by a television show about a backwoods family that had a pet bear. Every week the bear would rescue a family member from a bobcat, warn them of a forest fire, or perform some other act of loyalty. From the beginning, in her playful moments, Lucy had thought of George as her own bear. He could be that affectionate, as considerate and perceptive as the miraculous television bear. She turned off the light and slipped into bed beside him, thinking that if she ever stopped believing that bear was still inside of George, despite his depression, death and revival, then she could not stay with him anymore.

She slid her arm around his waist. His breathing was steady and deep and she could feel the regular beat of his heart. That heart had stopped for seventy minutes. The thought terrified her. George stirred slowly, as if still asleep, turned onto his back and pulled her to him. He was not fully awake. She felt his erection against her thigh. The unconsciousness of his response was inexpressibly comforting, and she rested her cheek beside his.

George jerked suddenly. His eyes glinted. She felt him shudder. He drew away from her, turned his back, moved to the edge of the bed. Even in the dark she could tell that he was trembling.

"What's the matter?" she asked.

"Alive," he said. "I'm alive."

She waited.

"George?" When she touched his shoulder he flinched.

That was more than enough; it was too much. Without flipping on the light she got out of bed, put on her robe and left.

She went to the living room, turned on the television, turned up the volume, then went to her study and found a package of blank disks. She stepped down the hall to George's workroom.

The place was full of charts and hard copies. The HCR wordline was scrolling silently across one of the desk screens; the three wall screens were blank rectangles. Lucy found his data and video disks. Four of them were marked "Millennium." She booted up and copied them, put everything back where she had found it, and went back to her study. She hid the copies in the space at the back of her bottom file drawer where she kept the candy, fig newtons and granola bars. She closed the drawer and sat down in her reading chair. She picked up the *Vanity Fair*. It opened to the picture of the woman on the beach.

Lucy sat there for a few minutes, then got up and opened the drawer where she had put the disks. She ripped open the fig newtons and ate one as she went to the kitchen, where she got a glass of water. She went back to her study and ate all of the fig newtons, one after another, one at a time. She ate three Milky Ways and drank the water. She could hear laughter from the TV in the other room. Her stomach hurt.

She got up and started down the hall toward the bathroom, stopped and went back to the living room to turn the TV still louder. In the bathroom she locked the door, kneeled over the toilet and shoved her index finger down her throat until she gagged, biting down hard on the bruise, and threw up.

4: SATURDAY, JUNE 5
....
The World Crashes into George's Study

People he didn't even know, and who didn't even know him, were trying to drive George crazy. He was brutalized by television.

"*Here's* the question," the Reverend Jimmy-Don Gilray whispered, and it was as if he were there in the room, about to confide in George at last. "—Here's the question they never ask because they *can't* ask it." The organ voice was stopped down, held in check for the crescendo that was coming. "—Here's the question that strikes like God's burning spear of truth at the heart of their so-called 're-vival': what soul would come back from paradise?"

"Zapadoolah!" George moonwalked around his study in time to the music in his head. The other two TVs challenged the Reverend's appeal. One of them was tuned to the Reuters *Insideline*—HCR's chief competitor—and the other to a countdown of the top 100 videos of the twentieth century. Number 43 was "Degauss Bop" by The Weird Girls With Problems. The videosynthed VJ was eating his fingers while he hyped the next hour's playlist.

George zoomed in on the *Zion Tribulation Hour* until Gilray's face filled the 90-centimeter screen. He studied the Reverend's chiseled features, his spiky silver hair, his flaw-less skin, his sharp gray eyes. The Reverend's eyebrows, sil-ver too, were like the wings of a furious angel. He moved like a popstar, with edgy, spectral intensity. Out on the street they called him "The Rev."

George cut the sound from the music station and the newsline to the point where they became whispered coun-terpoint to the Rev's message.

"The answer, good friends, is one that any child could give," Gilray said. "The number of souls that would come back from heaven is: *zero!* If the Just have gone on to their reward, then they *could not be* called back."

"Free World scientists charge space aliens run Sin-gapore," the *Insideline* anchor whispered.

The VJ spat out a fingernail. "Ricardo Rot of Dada Alert will marry revived Porn Princess Di Downstroke in a cere-mony to take place on the group's current video tour. The time and place will be determined by computer conflation of Western Hemisphere skin cancer rates and the Tibetan *Book of the Dead*—"

George's hard copies littered the floor like leaves from electronic trees, his time line stretched across one wall of the room, his maps covered every tabletop, dots and lines like snapshots of his developing mind. He surged out of the swivel chair, singing. "Degauss me honey, I'm burning up!"

"—what are these revived? They are nothing new. God shoots us an early warning in Revelations. Chapter 13, verse 13—but those numbers are an accident, right?"

The congregation, as if on cue, shouted, "There are no accidents!"

"No accidents! The Antichrist, 'Worked great miracles . . . it was allowed to give breath to the image of the beast.' Christ raised Lazarus—so too the Antichrist, in strict fulfillment of the prophecy of John, will seem to raise the dead. Who are these Dead?"

"Zombies!" the people shouted back.

"—Triple Economy forces one third of the indent population into sex slavery—" Vid of a tired-looking woman in olive fatigues talking to a social worker. "Correspondent Roger Insider reports from the Bureau of Indentured Labor—"

A naked woman on a pink neon pogo stick, insistent synthesized drums of the Wild Seeds:

"I know that secret
You know that secret
They know it too—"
It spirals round your genes like smoke
From Indonesian ovens
And when the light comes up again
You're spread like lampshade skin across the floor

"—the Undead!" the Rev shouted. "Baldies! Zombies! Animated corpses! Tell me: how can you animate a corpse—except by infesting it with a demon!"

"—the spunky Seppuku Club prexy told police in New Jersey that if they thought they had the right to keep her from offing herself then she had a .38 caliber Israeli Surprise for them—" Vid of an orange-haired woman in a print dress, face like a cinder block, brandishing an automatic weapon.

"They slide a new soul into these dead bodies the way I slide a program into my computer. But there's only one vendor for used souls."

George zeroed in on the Reverend. He didn't want to be teased and left wondering—he needed to know the answer. "A multinational vendor! With outlets all over this wretched world! *Hell, Incorporated!* Open twenty-four hours a day, seven days a week! Full of legions of damned souls, aching to get out. They've got plenty of souls ready to infest the dead! To trick you, to suck you in, to drag you down to high-tech perdition!"

George cut the Reverend's sound halfway and turned up the music station:

> What will you name your child?
> Rover, that's rad
> It's been done before
> But honey what hasn't?

> What will your gun name you?
> Kimberly or Don?
> Kim's hot as a pistol
> Don's a zombie dream.

> Don't give me no static, hon
> Or I might cling
> Boop, boop
> Zapadoolah!

When George had first arrived home he had wasted a lot of time running reality tests. To keep from being spied on, he covered over the mirrors. He took the legs off the chairs looking for a hidden memory chip. Nothing. Thinking that perhaps Lucy could tell him the truth, he tried sneaking up and surprising her. She simply acted surprised.

Idly at first, as he pored over his pre-death notes, he turned on the television—and discovered the painful truth. TV was the conduit. Why? Because it infuriated him with its irrelevance. Because it never stopped. George spent hours watching, dazzled by surmise, overwhelmed by reality, terrified. Finally, the source of his distress emerged. All the images which came over the TV to dance before him were images of real people. All the words they said were real words. Yet no image connected with any other, and every word was meaningless. Tummy troubles?—try Nulining. Ninja terrorists raid satellite bioweapons stockpile. At Raoul's, your gratification is our pleasure. ATM Security Systems knows what your children mean to you. A simple lemon juice solution removes those stubborn pet odors.

Near despair, he had gone back to his notes. It was only then that revelation came. "Don't give me more static, hon—" George wailed, "—Or I might cling. Boop, boop—Zapadoolah!"

He fumbled through the papers scattered over his desk and plucked out one of the hard copies, from the HCR *Crimeline,* a couple of months before:

PLAY-FOR-PAY GIRL SAYS JESUS MADE HER DO IT

Denver—Mar 19—CLN—A woman charged with solicitation has told police that she took up prostitution as a result of a conversation she had with an angel of the Lord.

Mary Benzell, 37, was arrested Tuesday at the Museum of Natural History after soliciting off-duty police officer Otto Eisenhauer. When interrogated, Ms. Benzell told Eisenhauer she had quit her job with the State Motor Vehicles Bureau at the beginning of the month and had spent most of her time since then in various public buildings "turning tricks for the Lord."

Benzell said she became convinced that she would die within the year unless she quit her job and took up streetwalking, police reported. "She said she got this idea from another woman at the Lutheran

Church," said Eisenhauer. Ms. Benzell claims that the woman was one of God's Archangels sent to convince her to change her way of life.

Police have been unable to locate any woman fitting the description given by Ms. Benzell.

Ms. Benzell, an attractive brunette (37-27-35, address available to CRIMELINE PRIME subscribers) said she had attended the Good Faith Church for the past seven years. She told reporters that she had never seen the woman before they struck up a conversation at the March 13 sunrise service.

"She read my soul," Ms. Benzell said. "She gave me a sign that a human being could not give. She carried the good news."

The Reverend R. Finnerly, minister of the church, was unavailable for comment. The accused was released on $1000 bond.

Other stories littered his desk: "Pittsburgh Millworker Eats Himself." "Foxhole Fad Sweeps Midwest." "Unarius Temple Firebombed." "High School Valedictorian on Sex Rampage." "Jehovah's Witnesses Torn by Schism." "High-Tech Pioneer Founds American Atheist Party." "Saucer Men Land at Fatima."

George had cut the deck all possible ways, sorting the stories by category, by place, by date. Ranging back as far as three years, George had culled out all that contained at least three of his five core characteristics: A disguised being. An encounter. A threat or actual act of violence. A judgment. An emotional revolution.

He then plotted the incidents according to date and place: red crosses for murders, blue for suicide, orange for other violence, yellow for religious conversions, green for total losses of faith, black for miscellaneous. They made a pattern in time and space. A pattern that implied an agent. A creature of mystery and deception. A disruptive force moving among them. The Alien.

It had started around the first of the year in Phoenix. A

rash of UFO reports and the first of the encounters—this one reported as a dispute between Father Edouard Mendoza and the bishop of the Catholic Diocese of Phoenix over the doctrine of original sin. Phoenix was where the Alien had landed. George had a couple of other stories from the Phoenix area during January. Then the Alien had taken to the road in the first of the rapid movements he was to make at two to three week intervals over the next few months. Two stories from Carson City on January 31, one datelined Salem, Oregon, concerning three bizarre suicides on the evening of February 1 in McMinnville. The next day, a man shouting that the Rapture would occur in days had disrupted the state legislature in Olympia, Washington.

Phoenix, Carson City, Salem and Olympia were all state capitals. They lay on a rough line northwest from Phoenix.

For the first half of February the Alien stayed in the Washington state area. George had stories from Tacoma, Yakima, Walla Walla. Then, in mid-February, another lightning traversal. Incidents in Boise on February 13th, Salt Lake City February 14th and Austin February 20th, with a probable in Santa Fe on February 16th. When he plotted these on his map, George felt the air in the room quiver with meaning. Olympia, Boise, Salt Lake City, Santa Fe and Austin, state capitals all, lay on a northwest-southeast line of almost mathematical precision.

The Alien. The key to the truth. Perhaps this discovery was the reason for George's continued existence—for George was convinced that only he had followed this path of flawless reasoning. Only he had come to this flawless conclusion. He could close his eyes and see, standing before him, in vague but ever-increasing detail, the Alien.

First, his arrival, in any of a multitude of disguises, in a state capital. Next, his encounters with average citizens. Some sort of challenge to their perceptions, some threat of destruction—a threat that was as often as not fulfilled in violence. Those who did not die were irrevocably changed. Third, a period of consolidation in which the Alien's effects on the region spread rapidly, like a local infection. The entire county, eventually the state, would become feverish with

sightings, personal disasters, changes. Finally, just as suddenly as he had appeared, the Alien would shoot away
across America, stopping briefly to infect intervening capitals before landing in a different city. There the process
would begin again.

January in Phoenix. The first two weeks of February in
Olympia. Late February in Austin. A trip north through
Oklahoma City, Topeka, Lincoln and Des Moines; three
weeks in St. Paul in March. A loop west through Pierre and
Cheyenne. Two weeks in Denver. A straight shot east to
Jefferson City, Missouri. Stop-offs in Kansas City and St.
Louis in mid-April. Nashville for the rest of April; May in
Atlanta.

But now it was early June. Time for another movement.
There were two possibilities—up the eastern seaboard by
way of Columbia, Raleigh, Richmond, Annapolis and Trenton—or north to the Great Lakes, through Lexington, Indianapolis, and Lansing.

George swept a pile of printouts onto the floor, then
gathered together his most recent map, a list of names and
addresses, his notebook and microdisk videocamera. The
phony gasohol ration card Richard had gotten for him. He
knew that his chances of success were slim, but he was determined to keep at the hunt as long as necessary. He would
put himself in the way of this creature, and trust to chance
or further design to bring them face to face. He would file
reports back to HCR via digital burster. In this way George
would liberate himself.

He punched up Interrail on his computer and booked
himself coach on the evening train to Philadelphia in the
name of George Hynek. He billed it to Mr. Midas, his secret account, then reserved a seat on the midnight train
from Philadelphia to Chicago, by way of Columbus and Indianapolis, for George Sagan. Coach was good enough. It
was cheap and anonymous. While he waited for the confirmation he glanced over a hard copy beside the terminal.
It was a news story from Kansas City about a woman who
claimed to have been tattooed, against her will, by her husband. The husband was in Chicago at the time.

The confirmation came back: the tickets would be available at Penn Station. George printed up a hard copy, crammed it and the other papers into his briefcase, and went to the door. Behind him, the three televisions were still going. On the middle the trashcaster was voicing over a vid on the mishap at the Prometheus solar microwave transmitter, which had lost its fix and for three hours irradiated Tucson. The picture showed a deserted street whose few pedestrians were dressed in aluminized mylar clothing. On the righthand screen was a classic video of Mick Jagger back before he'd had all his media appearances vidsynthed. On the farthest left, the Rev was finishing his appeal. He danced with nervous energy, a half-smile on his face, as if he and George were in on some secret that no one else could grasp.

"The Devil is clever. We don't call the Antichrist the Antichrist just because he's the opposite of Christ, but because he has the power to imitate Christ. Jesus multiplied the loaves and fishes. The Antichrist turns stones into bread. Go into your supermarket! There it is in your food counter—what do they call it?"

"Vitabulk!" the congregation shouted.

"Plastic food!" The Rev rushed up to a young woman in the front row, leaned toward her and opened his jacket as if to sell her a filthy picture. "Offer you some tree bark, miss?" The crowd roared.

"Christ caused the stones to speak. The Antichrist makes statues walk—what does he call it?"

"Artificial intellience!"

"Did ever a term more accurately describe the fraud it was designed to cover up? Artificial intelligence. AI. AI from the AC. Of course that's just an accident."

"There are no accidents!"

"Christ raised the dead. And the Antichrist raises the dead. He calls it revival—"

The congregation roared its derision.

"Just another accident, right? Revival! For hundreds of years God's servants have been using this word to describe spiritual rebirth. But now, the Antichrist calls his parodies of humanity the revived—

"—when everyone knows they are the Dead."

George closed the door behind him. He went to the living room. "Lucy?" he called.

She was not there. She hadn't been around much lately. She had not listened when he'd tried to explain to her. She was not interested.

George tried the kitchen. Empty. He knocked on the door of her study, and when there was no answer he went in: open law books, empty box of granola bars. He went into the bedroom and pulled the small bag down from the closet shelf. He threw some clothes into it, got underwear from the dresser. Lucy came out of the bathroom wearing a robe, a towel wrapped around her head. She had the hair dryer in her hand.

"What are you doing?" she asked.

"I just need to get some things," George said. "Don't let me disturb you." He slid past her into the bathroom and pulled a drawer open. The air smelled sweetly of soap. "Didn't we have an extra tube of toothpaste?"

"Where are you going?"

George found the toothpaste. He put it and his razor into his shaving kit. He turned to leave the bathroom. She stood in the doorway.

He was sweating. They were crowded up against each other in the tiny room. "I'm going—I'm doing some research. I have to make a trip. I don't know how long it's going to take."

"What about HCR? And Richard?"

"I was going to ask you to talk to them for me."

She didn't reply.

"I don't know why you're always bringing up Richard," George said.

Her lips tightened. "He's your friend."

She seemed to struggle with something, then spoke more calmly. "George, listen to me." She took his elbow and pulled him to the bed. They sat next to each other. Her eyes, filled with worry, were all the time on him. "You're not well. You need to stay home. *I* need you to stay home."

"I'm sorry. But this is too important. The country's in trouble. Maybe the world."

"Another story on bigfoot isn't going to help it any. But *we're* in trouble, too. Do you understand what I'm saying?"

George felt the urge to drag her out and shove his charts in front of her face. It was all so different since he'd woken up. He saw her more clearly. They had made an unconscious deal at the beginning of their relationship, where Lucy would take care of the practical side of their lives and he would do the long range thinking. George loved her passion, but her passion was for personal things. Lucy didn't care enough about the large, impersonal forces that would grind them into a powder—along with the rest of the world—unless somebody did something.

He grabbed her by the shoulders. "Look, Lucy, I want you to think a little bigger for once. You know I love you, but there are things going on that make love pretty insignificant."

"George, you're acting crazy! I promised I would never leave you if you were in trouble. I took a huge risk having you revived."

"Do you regret it?"

"Of course not! But I've got problems too. If you walk out now, you're on your own."

"I can take care of myself."

The look of frustration on her face almost made him stop. He tried to hug her. She twisted out of his grasp and went to her dresser. She unwrapped the towel from her head, took up the hair dryer and began drying her hair. He watched her tilt her head, brush her hair out as she directed the air at the nape of her neck. She moved with unconscious grace, the muscles of her arms sliding beneath her skin in self-contained beauty. He went to her. He wanted to hold her, but he was afraid that if he did he would not be able to let go. "Lucy," he said. He touched her shoulder.

"What?" Her voice was defiant, but she did not pull away. He tried to think of something to say. She turned off the dryer, lay her head on his shoulder and began to cry. He smelled her fragrant hair, felt the warmth of her body. He kissed the top of her head, wanting to cry himself, but instead swept up in a wash of desire.

He pulled her onto the bed, surprised at his own strength. He had not felt so strong in a long time. He remembered falling down the imaginary rabbit hole at the medical center, unable to move anything but his eyelids. He kissed her cheek; she turned her head away. He pressed her down against the pillows, tugged the robe from her shoulders. The light in the bathroom was still on. Water dripped in the shower. Lucy unbuttoned his shirt. Her face was shadowed, grave. He closed his eyes and rested his head on her breast, embraced her hips. Outside the atmosphere orbited alien starships controlled by intelligences as far beyond theirs as theirs were above the insects. George would push hard against Lucy, push until she understood that the world was infinitely strange, full of babble, teasing him toward meanings he feared were illusions. It had killed him and brought him back. In the street people played Christian music on boom boxes. Lucy drew her legs up to hold him. She reached down and laced the fingers of her hand in his. Distant thunder, rain on the window. They made love without words, and it was as if George had died again, and the world with him.

When he awoke it was night. Lucy lay asleep, her face inches from his on the pillow. She looked like a child. From another room of the apartment he heard voices, whispering, excited. After a moment he realized they came from the televisions in his study.

He slipped out of bed and put on his scattered clothes. Lucy stirred as he was closing his bag. In the kitchen he ate an apple and a piece of bread. He got the microcam, pulled on his jacket and took the elevator down to the lobby. Curtis, the security man, nodded at him through his bulletproof glass booth. Two boys in monk haircuts loitering on the streetcorner looked him over. "Hey, Zombie," they called, and jerked their codpieces at him. George hailed a moped. The driver buzzed the lock; George climbed in back and spoke into the grille to the driver's compartment, "Penn Station."

5: SATURDAY, JUNE 5
··

Answers are offered to many Serious Questions

"Death isn't cruel," the Reverend Jimmy-Don Gilray said. "Death is the natural end of life. Life without death is a meaningless extension of our misery. 'A little while, and you shall see me,' Christ told us. But if we are too cowardly to take that step—that small step—from life, across death, to eternal life—then we doom ourselves to Hell here on earth. This is what revival means.

"The Lord holds out one hand ·in invitation. In his other he holds raised the flaming sword! Anyone who needs a reminder—look at San Francisco! The sodomite has learned, the harlot is learning, and the atheist will learn!

"Time is short, brothers and sisters. The holy Father Ship is on its way. When it lands, and the Prince of Peace comes forth in all his glory to rule the reborn world—you'd better hope you're ready. May the grace of the Lord Jesus Christ be with you in these terrible Last Days."

He lowered his head, dropped his arms to his sides. The entire congregation was silent. Then the music came up and the chorus began to sing. The cameras pulled back; a moment later the red light went off and the TV lights cut down to half intensity. Gilray raised his arms to the people, to the cripples in the front row and the old black men and to the girl with a nest of blond curls who had been trying to get an hour alone with him for a month now. The chorus still singing, the congregation on its feet, he strode off the platform.

"Looked good, Rev," one of the cameramen said.

"Thanks, Ed," Gilray said. He looked over at the men who had been watching from just offstage throughout the broadcast: a tall one who carried a microcam and the slender, bearded one who was Stanley Levine. One of Eberhart's flunkies. Felton, beside them, looked as if he were standing guard over a couple of prisoners.

Marianne Bellereve came up to him with a clipboard. "They're waiting," she said.

Let them wait. The Lord knew that Gilray had spent years waiting. He felt the twinge of pain in his bladder again. "Give me fifteen minutes and send them into my office."

He left Marianne and went backstage, through the rear door, down the corridor, through the lobby to his office. In his bathroom he stood for some minutes at the toilet trying unsuccessfully to urinate. *Lord I am not worthy, help me now in my unworthiness.*

Gilray's penis was very large. It was the source and sign of his power. Other people looked at him and saw a righteous testifier to the glory of Jesus and the life to come, but the Reverend Jimmy-Don Gilray, standing there waiting for the relief that he hoped the Lord would vouchsafe him, knew himself a sinner striving for grace and possessed of God's holy instrument, which he held in his hand and shook a little in the hope of encouraging.

Often, when listening to some member of the congregation confess his own sins, Gilray wondered at the mildness of the accusations these sinners made against themselves. If they deserved to be the dust beneath the feet of the Lord, then how much less did *he* deserve—to be less than dust—to be, for the bottomless depth of corruption in his heart, bound to the lowest place in hell. That was God's paradox. For it was his own unworthiness that convinced Gilray of the glory of God. He had felt, through the rod he held in his hand, the power of the Lord. Like the Rose of Sharon on the bridal night, he had lain in the dust, waiting to be ravished by Christ's holy love. It was only the infinite grace of God, rising to an infinite height of fullness and glory, that could pierce down to the bottom of such an abyss as the soul of Jimmy-Don Gilray.

Every time he felt the ecstasy of the body, he knew how infinite God's mercy was. That was why he kept himself chaste. His body belonged to the Lord. With it, he could bring any woman to the physical ecstasy that was a shadow of the ecstasy with which, at any instant, God could fill the soul. He could impregnate any woman through a single congress: nothing could stand in the way of the grace of God. Another man might presume to take the credit to himself, but Gilray knew that any success he had was an undeserved gift.

He awaited only the special woman who would be sent by the Lord to complete the age and usher in the Millennium. He had denied himself for years, waiting. He had doubted. Perhaps this latest difficulty was some sign.

Suddenly, miraculously, like the breaking of the sun over the rim of the old world each morning, one more assurance of God's grace came—there in Gilray's bathroom at the End of Time Institute—the sudden release, the warm, powerful rush, the hiss, like so much applause, against the inside of the bowl. Gilray sighed. He shook the last few drops away, flushed the toilet, washed his hands. He brushed back his hair in the mirror. He felt renewed, reassured that judgment would be postponed another day.

When he stepped out into his office they were waiting for him. The cameraman paced about, talking about angles, and Levine sat in the visitor's chair. They stopped talking when he came in. Levine stood.

"Reverend? I'm Stanley Levine, from HCR." He held out his hand.

Gilray took it. "Pleased to meet you." The cameraman ran a battery check and put the headpiece on. "This is Jeff Pack," Levine said. "Enough light, Jeff?"

The tall man nodded. "Okay."

Gilray and Levine sat down on opposite sides of the desk. "I thought Mr. Eberhart was going to do this interview."

Levine's thin nose hooked like a carpet knife. "Mr. Eberhart is still recovering from his heart attack."

The cameraman slipped a disk into the shoulder pack and dropped the sight down over his eye. The red light at his temple went on.

"You'll tell him we're all praying for his speedy recovery."

"I'll pass that on. Can we get started?"

After a few preliminary questions, Levine got down to cases. "You've got this crusade against revival stoked up pretty high. Now nobody likes zombies, but aren't there circumstances where revival is justified—in the case of murder victims, for instance?"

"I'm against revival under any circumstances," Gilray said. "Even atheists should be able to see that revival is just a way for the rich to keep from *ever* giving up power. It's not for the average man, despite the promises of the scientists in the pay of the government and big business."

The cameraman's lens rotated, zooming to closeup. Gilray looked directly into it.

"But that's trivial compared to the morality. First, look at the method. In order to revive a dead person the scientists have to alter the genetic structure of the cells. To do that they use 'seed DNA.' And where do they get this DNA? From aborted fetuses. What's happening here is that we're killing an unborn generation in order to preserve one that's properly dead. God sets the limit to a man's life, and these revivalists attempt to escape that limit. The doctors play the saviors, bringing down life from on high. It's blasphemous."

"Who cares, if it's the end of the world coming?" Levine asked.

"There are still souls to be saved. 'There will be false saviors in those days.' What is revival but the falsest of saviors? It tricks people into thinking they can escape God. Men are mortal. They are born and they die, and their souls are taken up to await final judgment. Why do so few revival attempts succeed? Why do so many of the revived seem changed? It's simply this: they have no souls, or the spirits that inhabit these revived bodies are sent from Hell to deceive. Satan is subtle. There is no end to his tricks."

Levine licked his lips. "The revived are demons from Hell?"

The town atheist, the secular Jew, looking to mock him. Gilray wondered if Levine would be among the 144,000 Jews to convert before Armageddon. "I'm saying that the souls of the dead pass on to await a judgment from which they can't be recalled. What's left is trash. To bring that trash to life again violates so many fundamental laws that the result can be nothing but evil. You can see it happening in the world today."

"What are you going to do if the Supreme Court strikes down the state anti-revival laws?"

"It won't matter what the Supreme Court says if a dozen more states ratify the ARA."

"What if they don't?"

"We'll fight it. The people will be heard."

"You can't go against democracy. Sixty-two percent of the people support revival."

Gilray picked up his Bible and waved it at Levine. "*This* is democracy. This is the Constitution of the United States."

"That's a pretty immoderate statement."

"Moderation in rooting out evil is no virtue. Moderation is what got us into this mess. It paralyzes people when they ought to act."

"You sound like a politician."

"Politicians avoid the truth; it's too offensive."

"You can't deny that you have a lot of political power in this state."

"Some of my followers do."

"Like Charles Duke Sumner."

"I know Mr. Sumner."

"And your Institute holds the contract on one of the largest private prison systems in the country." Levine checked his notes. "In the last year you've taken the rehabilitation contracts on prisoners from sixteen different states. Governments from all over the country are pawning their inmates off on your farms."

"That's because we have a recidivist rate under ten percent. It's the power of prayer."

"And nembutal." Before Gilray could protest Levine went on. "What about all these security guards? You have a separate barracks for them. Some people have accused you of forming a private army."

"That driver of yours, Felton," broke in the cameraman. "He told me he was a Green Beret."

"That's right. Felton saved my life when a man pulled a gun on me in Dayton. I've faced three assassination attempts. I need the security."

"You don't need an army."

"By the end of the year we may all need one. I want to be here to see the face of my redeemer in the flesh. I didn't want to be a preacher—"

"—until your software biz went belly-up," Levine said.

"I was *called* to do this work. I speak only because God allows me, blind as I am, to see a little of His light. The scales will drop from your eyes, friend. They'll drop at midnight on December thirty-first."

"Thanks for the warning. Let's talk about the end of the world. UFO reports have doubled in each of the last three years. Are the Saucer Men preparing to invade the earth with the coming of the new millennium?"

"I'm a minister, not an expert on flying saucers."

Levine thumbed his notepad and read. "Last October on one of your broadcasts you said, 'UFOs are signs. Christ is coming. The New Jerusalem shines on our radar screens.'"

Gilray smiled. "This is Christianity, not a UFO cult. It's true that flying saucers may be another evidence of the Last Days."

Levine worked a remarkable amount of incredulity into his voice. "Do you mean to tell us that flying saucers were predicted in the Bible?"

"There is nothing about these last times that isn't. Interpreting these messages from the past is hard, but I can give you just a few examples. One of the chief prophets on whom we base our reading of the End Time—Ezekiel— 'saw the wheel way in the middle of the air.' What was that wheel? In the Book of Revelations, it says "I saw a star that had fallen to the earth." That star could be a vehicle from space. John goes on to call the star 'he' and predicts it will have a key to open the shaft of the abyss, letting out a great smoke that will blot out the sun. How can a star be a person with a key? Is some creature from space coming to start a war that will bring on the nuclear winter?"

"An alien from space is going to start a nuclear war?"

"I didn't say that. I am not interested in UFOs other than as one of the many signs that were predicted to preceed the Tribulation. God's like any other businessman: He sets signs to attract people's attention. Many people are coming to Jesus now, some of them because of these UFO signs. Any reason is a good reason. Time is short, and all good Christians need to be ready."

"And the New Jerusalem? You've called it the 'Father Ship.'"

"Look how Revelations describes it: a titanic cube a mile on each side fashioned of jewels and metal. It has twelve gates or doors. It shines 'like a stone most precious.' And it descends out of the sky, from God. It *is* the Father's ship. And it's coming. I'm just putting it in modern terms."

"What about the other prophecies you say have been fulfilled?"

"They have been fulfilled. That's how we know we're in the Last Days. The Bible predicts that certain events will happen: the Jews will return to Israel—they have been there since 1948. A burning star named 'Wormwood' will fall upon the earth and poison the waters, killing many men—in 1985 a meltdown occurred at the Chernobyl nuclear plant in the Soviet Union. 'Chernobyl,' in Russian, means 'wormwood.' The Roman Empire will be reinstituted in a ten-headed beast—in 1997 the European Community established a ten-person commission to fight the worldwide depression. The nation of Gog and Magog will come from the north to fight a war in the valley of Armageddon—we see the Soviet Army bogged down in a stalemate in the Middle East today where, among other territory, they currently occupy the valley identified in the Old Testament as 'Har-Magiddo.' The soviet premier, an avowed atheist who has forged an economic union with the U.S., bears the Mark of the Beast on his forehead.

"Revelations said the Antichrist would cause everyone to be branded with such marks, 'and no one was allowed to buy or sell unless he bore this beast's mark, either name or number.' In your wallet, Mr. Levine, you have your universal credit card. Many people, eager to be on the government dole in these depressed times, have their UCC. There is a number on that card that says you are owned by the state. Whatever that number may be, it is really 666.

"Open your eyes! War in twenty places around the world, terrorist diseases, Japan and Brazil in league against us, Chinese factories decimating our economy, four hundred percent inflation, the hoarding of food in the face of mass starvation! The Four Horsemen are galloping around the world. The Abomination of Desolation has begun."

Levine listened with visibly increasing impatience. When Gilray finished he turned off his notebook, leaned back and looked at the cameraman. "You might as well save the disk space, Jeff. This is old news. Reverend, you Bible thumpers have been singing this same tune for thirty years. What makes you think anyone wants to hear it any more?"

"You came to me."

"Sure we came to you. We thought you had something new to say. But we turn on the cameras and you do a traditional folk dance. Our readers are interested in science, not religious hype. Science has been explaining these old myths since Galileo. Who's to say that Jesus wasn't just a shipwrecked ET with a heart of gold? He crash lands among a bunch of savages who can't keep up with the video input. He drops a cap into their wine and they think he's multiplied the loaves and fishes. He receives a few messages and they think it's prophecy from heaven. He dies and a couple of CPR specialists shoot down to save him. Hell, we do it now. The confused natives call it resurrection. We call it revival. And *we* don't get all wet between the legs about it."

Gilray forced himself to stay calm. Even Christ could not cure the soul hardened against him. "It always amazes me

how easily you so-called 'skeptics' will accept any silly explanation as long as it has some hint of 'science.' You're total
materialists. Revival isn't resurrection. It's a fraud."

"I bet you wouldn't say that if you were terminal yourself."

As if to remind him, Gilray felt a twinge from his bladder.

"I can't persuade a godless bigot."

"Get this, Jeff. The man sees atheists under every rock."

"It's the easiest place to find them."

"I'm wounded, Rev. Let's get back to the UFO reports.
Lots of highbrows are on your side. The kraut psychologist
Carl Jung said flying saucers were signs of the end of the
world, too." Levine switched on his notes again. "Listen to
this. Jung said he had to 'prepare those few who will hear
me for coming events which are in accord with the end of
an era.' How about that? Sound familiar?"

"Jung was no Christian."

"Don't bet on it. He said the world situation was just
right to goose people into expecting a redeeming, supernatural event. The only thing keeping them from having visions was that we were supposed to be a scientific culture.
So people have the visions anyway. They project them out of
their sick minds. They see 'space ships' and 'extra-ter-
restrials' only because today that's easier to believe than angels in flaming chariots."

"Don't patronize me, Mr. Levine. I know about this
book. It's the same old story. Jung was a secular humanist.
His psychology was just another 'scientific' explanation that
helped him keep God out of the world."

"He said UFOs are a sign that ours are the Last Days of
the West," Levine said.

Gilray crossed his arms over his chest. "Was he born
again?"

"Not that you'd notice."

"Then that settles it."

"Anything that keeps you from answering the tough questions, huh, Rev? Can God make a rock he can't lift? Did
Jesus ever have a wet dream?"

"You're pitiful, Mr. Levine. I offer you bread but you

prefer manure. You don't care about Christ's message; you just want to know about his sex life."

"That's the ticket. What about his sex life? Why was he always hanging around with prostitutes?"

Gilray stood. "This interview is over. If you think I'm going to sign your release forms now, you're out of your mind."

Levine's sneer faded. "I thought the office already arranged that."

"They did not."

"You mean none of this is on the record? Somebody slipped up!"

"There are no accidents."

But as he spoke Gilray felt a sudden weakness sweep over him. It was as if plugs had been pulled in his heels and all his blood drained out through them. His vision clouded, then cleared. The weakness settled in his thighs. The door opened and Marianne came into the office to remind him about the nonexistent appointment he had that afternoon. She saw them facing each other like a freeze-frame from a prizefight. "Reverend? Your appointment."

Gilray leaned on his desk until the nausea passed. "Thank you, Marianne."

Levine was sweating. Had Gilray not felt sick, the man's desperation would have been comic. "Do you take any responsiblity for the violence against the revived that's taken place in the last few months?"

Gilray came around the desk and held his hand up toward the camera's eye. Pack flinched. The red light went off.

"Is it true that three drug deaths have occurred on your voluntary farm in the last year?"

Gilray ignored him. "Marianne, it's time for these men to leave. Make sure they don't talk to anyone on the way out."

"We have reports some of your followers have formed paramilitary units in South Carolina," said Levine.

"Stan," Pack said. "We need to get the answers before I can shoot the questions."

"First you need to get the questions right," said Gilray. He stood in the open doorway. "You need help, Mr. Levine," he said as he pushed them out.

"Yeah, well—"

Gilray leaned out and said, "Marianne, get Felton." He closed his door on them.

His knees felt as if they would fold at any moment. But he did not think his trembling was visible as he went over to the window, leaned on the frame, and looked out at the pines across the lawn. He ought to have known better than to try to reach anyone through the trashnews.

A squirrel stood frozen at the edge of the wood, and then, taking itself to be safe, began to nibble at an acorn. One of the boys rode by on a lawn tractor. The squirrel scampered for the woods, then froze again at the base of a tree. Sudden change from stillness to motion to stillness again. When the squirrel ran, that meant it was afraid, Gilray thought. When it stood still, that meant it was terrified.

The feeling of weakness subsided.

Jesus was the only man who ever really raised the dead. Gilray wondered what it was like to be revived. Did the revived feel themselves in the grip of some demonic force? Did they have minds at all?

His groin felt like it had turned to paper. He turned to the desk and touched the intercom button. "Marianne? I want you to schedule a doctor's appointment for me."

6: SATURDAY, JUNE 5

Fun with Drugs

Richard was returning from an evening of serious alterations. He had lost track of the different psychotropic substances he had consumed, inhaled, drunk and rubbed into his skin. Things were not going well at work. He had started at three in the afternoon and was well into a night of Game-playing by the time he reached his apartment.

The Game was Richard's own invention. The rules were deceptively simple: first you got very twisted. The bigger the twist, the bigger the challenge. Then you tried to act normal. That was the whole game, on a microchip. But it was a very tricky game, with subtleties that only became apparent once you were well into the play. Everything you did became a test. Can I carry on an intelligent conversation? Can I ride the subway? Can I pick up a pencil?

In order to win the Game you had to perform a completely successful, unbroken string of totally convincing actions, so that anyone observing could not tell that you were out of your mind. To play the Game well required vast amounts of self-control. So far Richard had never won, because he had inevitably lost consciousness somewhere during the play.

This time, however, he had been doing very well. By the time he got home he had ordered, eaten and paid for a meal at Guido's in the Village, used the men's room while politely declining an interesting offer from the man at the next urinal, and walked home through Washington Square Park having only to buy a bottle of cheap Moet from the park's Central Committee. He popped the cork and drank from the bottle as he walked up Broadway. It tasted awful. Once home he found the right key, remembered the proper lock code and punched it in without fumbling. He had just closed the door behind him when he was completely undone by his telephone.

"Answer me!" it shrieked in the voice of Margaret Hamilton from *The Wizard of Oz*. Richard had programmed the phone to speak with the voices of his favorite movie stars.

He dropped the bottle, which rolled away from him, pumping champagne across the hardwood floor like blood from an artery. Richard tried to catch the bottle, slipped on the wine and banged his knee against his Bauhaus coffee table. Game One was over.

"'Auntie Em, Auntie Em,'" the phone taunted him, "—if you don't answer me, you'll never see your Auntie Em again!"

Richard reached behind him for a chair, missed and fell back, soaking the sleeve of his jacket in the wine. He felt a headache coming on. Good. One more factor to deal with in Game Two.

"Hurry up, Pilgrim." Now the phone was John Wayne. "I'm gettin' tired of waitin'. I'm gonna count to three."

That meant it was a priority call. Richard wondered what the bad news was. His legs did not want to work; finally he gave up and crawled. He hit the answer stud as Wayne hit "three," before William Demarest could begin to read him the riot act.

"Hello?" Richard said.

The screen did not light. "Richard? It's me, George."

Richard pulled himself onto the sofa. Normal, he thought. I'm very normal. "What's the hurry, friend?"

"I've got to make a train. I just wanted to tell you that I'm going to be out of the office a while longer."

"Why won't you let me see you?"

"I'm in an old pay phone. Look, Richard, I've only got a minute. I'm onto a big story, the biggest ever. I want you to keep the Gilray thing on the back burner for awhile."

"Can't do it. Levine interviewed him this afternoon. He butchered it. Abramowitz is furious. It will be all I can do to keep him from firing all of us."

"Okay," George didn't sound disappointed. "Do what you can. But Gilray is way off. It's not like he says. You let me catch this thing and I'll guarantee you main menu for a month."

Richard's head felt like a quartz watch running slow. The seconds pulsed in his temples. "Catch what thing, George?"

"The Alien."

"What?" No, Richard thought. I sound too surprised.

"Listen, I can't go into it over the phone. Talk to Lucy, she'll explain it. This UFO craze is not just silly season stuff. There is at least one alien creature loose in the U.S. right now, maybe more. I'm onto his trail and I'm going to catch him."

"Right."

"He makes boundless promises with prophet-like conviction, Richard. In a rootless, desperate society where norms are disintegrating."

It felt like someone had inserted a needle behind Richard's left eye. Cancer for sure. "Are you talking about the Rev?"

"Not the Rev, Richard. The Alien."

He had it now. The needle was not behind his eye—it was George needling him, stringing him along to see how much he'd swallow. George must have heard about the Levine interview. He must be feeling more normal: it was one of the roots of their friendship, to goof on each other like this. George wasn't really at Penn Station. That was why he wouldn't use the video.

"Cosmic," said Richard. "A great idea. It will go big."

"I thought you'd understand," George said.

"Any dead people in this one? Weeping spouses? Ash heap the human interest stuff—stay lean and mean."

"I'll be good, Richard, but I want you to do me a favor."

"What's this alien's name, anyway?" Richard massaged his eyeball.

"He doesn't have a name." George sounded irritated. Advantage, Mr. Shrike. "He may not even be physical."

"Not physical! He's a ghost, then. Can he get us an interview with Elvis?" The bottle of Moet had stopped emptying, but the flood now crept toward Richard's Greek Revival area rug. Still massaging his temple, Richard tried to roll up the rug, but the coffee table was sitting on it. When he pushed the table, the rug only slid with it across the floor. The champagne reached the corner and began to soak in. It turned the classic blue pile a brilliant cobalt.

"This is serious, Richard."

It sure was. The damned rug had cost him a month's pay. Richard touched it and held the damp finger to his nose. "I'm serious," he managed to say through the haze of intoxication. "No metaphysics this time. The operators can't spell it and the readers don't know what it means. *I* don't know what it means."

"Richard, keep an eye on Lucy for me."

"Certainly. You just bring him back alive, George."

There was silence at the other end. Richard was congratulating himself on having played a brilliant match when in that silence he heard, low but distinct, the sound of a PA announcing the departure of the next train for Philadelphia.

Suddenly the Game collapsed. George *was* at Penn Station. He wasn't playing, he was serious. He had finally gone truly crazy. Richard's head ached as he tried to switch gears, but he seemed to have stripped them all. "George—"

"Goodby, Richard. I've got to go."

"George!" The phone beeped off. "Bloody Hell!"

What to do? Lucy. He punched the autodial button. The phone had rung for a full minute without answer when there was a knock at Richard's door. He gave up and went to answer it. Through the fisheye he saw the beautiful, androgynous face of Jake. He opened the door.

"Jake. What are you doing here?"

She glided past him and threw her woolen cloak on a chair, stepping carefully in high-heeled sandals past the wet spot on the rug. She stooped gracefully, righted the champagne bottle, and sat down on the sofa. "You haven't called me since I did your income tax."

Jake had piled her hair high like Helen of Troy, and the camisole top of her dress showed her square white shoulders to advantage. She claimed to have started life as a male, but Richard had never been able to tell whether or not she was lying.

Richard closed the door. There was nothing he could do about George right now; he would get on it in the morning.

Time for Game Three.

"I've been very busy," he said, stepping over to the sideboard. "I think my best friend has gone insane. Drink?"

7: SATURDAY, JUNE 5

....

Sandy Ellison disputes a Judgment Call

Bottom of the first, no score, Dutch on first, Simonetti on second, two outs. In the bar afterwards, Sandy replayed it in his head.

Sandy had faced this Louisville pitcher maybe twice before: decent fastball, good curve, enough so he'd gotten Sandy out more than his share. And Sandy was in a slump (3 for 20 in the last five games) and the count was 1-2 and the Louisville catcher was riding him. Ump waiting to signal the big K, fist punching the air but it might as well be Sandy's gut. It was hot. Sandy's legs felt rubbery.

Pilot Stadium was quiet. No more than 1,500 people there, tops; Louisville was leading the American Association and the Bisons were dead last. Overcast, heavy wind snapping the flag out in left center, but hot for Buffalo, even for June. People were saying the climate was changing: it was the ozone layer, the Japs, the UFOs, the end of the world. The pitcher crouched over, shaking off signals. He went into his stretch.

Then something happened: Sandy knew he could hit this guy. The pitcher figured he had Sandy plugged—curveball, curveball, outside corner and low, then high and tight with the heater to keep him from leaning—but suddenly Sandy *knew* where the next pitch was going to be. And there it was, fastball inside corner, turn on it weight back *bye-bye baby!* Sweet crack of the ash. Sandy watched it sail out over the left field fence toward the Thruway upramp. The pitcher, head down, kicked dirt from the mound (you might could miss the bigs after all, pal) while Sandy jogged around the bases feeling perfect. He was going to live forever. He was going to get laid every night.

In the top of the second he made a shoestring catch in right center and in the sixth he threw out a runner trying to go from first to third. He went four for five, bringing his average back up to a tantalizing .299. And number five was an infield bouncer that Sandy was sure he'd beat out, but the ump called him out. A judgment call. The wop pud-knocker.

Aronsen, the Sox' general manager, was in town to take a look at the Bisons in the hope of finding somebody they could bring up to help them after their bad start. He came by the locker room. He glanced at Sandy's postgame blood panel. Sandy played it cool: he was at least 0.6 under the limit on DMD, not even on the scale for steroids. Sandy should get ready right away, Aronsen told him, to catch the morning train to Chicago. They were sending Estivez down and bringing him up. They were going to give him a chance to fill the hole in right field. Yes sir, Sandy said, polite, eager.

Yes sir, he'd thought as he walked down Swan toward the tramway—goodbye Buffalo. Now it was a few hours later and Sandy was having a drink with Dutch and Leon at the Ground Zero. He'd already stopped by a machine and withdrawn the entire three thousand dollars in his account, called up the condo office and told them he was leaving and not coming back. Sandy paid for the first round. He had it figured: you paid for the first without hesitating. People remembered that much better than how slow you were on the second or third, so if you played it right, when the evening was done you came out ahead on drinks. Sure enough, Dutch paid for the second round and Leon for the third and then some fans came by and got the next two. Sandy's day. Only one thing was needed to make it complete.

"Killer," Dutch shouted over the din of the screen behind the bar, "you haven't played that well in a month. You go crazy on the day Aronsen's in town. You lucky sonofabitch."

They called Sandy "The Killer" because of the number of double plays he hit into: Killer as in rally-killer. "He was going to take me anyways," Sandy said. "But it doesn't hurt to do your best for the boss."

Dutch stared at the screen, where a faggot VJ with a wig and lace cuffs was counting down the Top 100 videos of the 20th Century. Most of them were from the last two years. "Wouldn't do my any good," Dutch said. "They've got two first basemen ahead of me. I could hit .350 and I wouldn't get a shot at the bigs."

"Playin' the wrong position, man," said Leon. His high eyebrows always made him look innocent.

Dutch didn't have the glove to play anywhere but first. Sandy felt a little sorry for him. At eighteen Dutch had been a pretty hot prospect, a first baseman who could hit for average and field okay. But he didn't have any power, so he'd taken HGH in order to beef up. He'd beefed up all right, to six-five, 230, but in the process his reflexes got shot to hell. Now he could hit 20 home runs in triple-A, but he struck out too much, his fielding was mediocre and he was slow. And the American League had abandoned the designated hitter just about the time Dutch went off the drug.

"You ought to work on the glove," Sandy said.

"I got to piss." Dutch said. He headed for the men's room.

That burned Sandy. A real friend didn't bitch at you when you got called up. "Sometimes Dutch ticks me off," he said.

Leon leaned back against the bar, elbows resting on the edge, his gnarled catcher's hands hanging loosely from his wrists. Leon had grown up in Fayetteville, not ten miles from Sandy's Dad's farm, but was ten years older than Sandy and the wrong color. Sandy always felt like blacks were keeping secrets that he would just as soon not know.

"Got to admit, Killer, you ain't been playin' that good

lately," Leon said. "You been clutched out. Been tryin' too hard."

Sandy finished his bourbon and ordered another. "You don't win without trying."

Leon just nodded. "Look at that talent, there."

Sandy looked. At the table, alone, sat a woman. She had microshort blonde hair and a heart-shaped face. Blue lips. Dark eye makeup. But what got Sandy was her body. Even from across the room he could tell she was major league material. She wore a tight blue dress and was drinking something pale, on the rocks.

As Sandy watched her she locked glances with him, and he was overwhelmed by a vivid memory, a flashback to something that had happened to him long before—

—It was the end of the summer of his junior year of high school and he was calling Jocelyn from the parking lot of the Dairy Queen on highway 401. Brutal heat. He tapped his car keys on the dented metal shelf below the phone. Jocelyn was going to Atlantic Beach with Sid Phillips and she hadn't even told him. Five rings, six. He had to get the news from Trudy Jackson and act like he knew all about it when it was like he'd been kneed in the groin.

An answer. "Hello?"

"Miz James, this is Sandy Ellison. Can I talk to Jocelyn?"

"Just a minute." Another wait. The sun burned the back of his neck.

"Hello." Jocelyn's voice sounded nervous.

"What the fuck do you think you're doing?"

A semi blasted by on the highway, kicking up a cloud of dust. He turned his back to the road and held his hand over his other ear.

"What are you talking about?"

"You better not fuck with me, Jocelyn."

"Slow down, Sandy. I—"

"If you go to the beach with him it's over." He tried to make it sound like a threat instead of a plea.

At first Jocelyn didn't answer. Then she said, "You always were a jerk," and hung up.

He stood there with the receiver in his hand. It felt hot

and greasy. The dial tone mocked him. Then Jeff Baxter and Jack Stubbs drove up in Jeff's Trans-am, and the three of them cruised out to the woods near Ft. Bragg and drank a six-pack. "Bitch," he called her. "Fucking bitch—"

—And he was suddenly back in the bar. The woman still stared at him. She didn't look at all like Jocelyn. Sandy broke eye contact. Dutch had come back, had been back for a while. Fucking Jocelyn.

Sandy made a decision. "One hundred says I plug her tonight."

"Green or red?" Leon asked.

Sandy had taken his withdrawal in new currency. He pulled the wad of bills out of his shirt pocket and laid a red one hundred, a third of all the money he owned in the world, on the bar. Leon regarded him coolly. Dutch snorted. "Gonna pull down your batting average, boy."

"Definitely a tough chance," Leon said.

"You think so? We'll see who's trying too hard."

"You got a bet."

"You hold it, Dutch. I'll get it back tomorrow when I pick up my gear." Dutch stuffed the redbuck into his shirt pocket. Sandy picked up his drink and went over to the table. The woman watched him the whole way. Up close she was even more spectacular. "Hey," he said.

"Hello. It's about time. I've been waiting for you."

He pulled out a chair and sat down. "Sure you have."

"I never lie." Her smile was a dare. "How much is riding on this?"

He couldn't tell whether she was hostile or teasing. He went with the pitch. "Two hundred—new style. That's a month's pay in triple-A."

"What is triple-A?" Her husky voice had some trace of accent to it.

"Baseball. My name is Sandy Ellison. I play for the Bisons."

She sipped her drink. The shortness of her hair made her violet eyes enormous. He would die if he didn't have her that night. "Are you a good player?" she asked.

"I just got called up to the majors. Monday night I'll be starting for Chicago."

"You are a lucky man."

The way she said it made Sandy think for a moment he was being set up. But Dutch was too dumb to pull some elaborate practical joke. Leon was smarter, but he wasn't mean enough. Still, it would be a good idea to stay on his guard. "Not luck; skill."

"Oh, skill. I thought you were lucky."

"How come I've never seen you here before?"

"I'm from out of town."

"I figured as much. Where?"

"Lexington."

"Kentucky? We just played Louisville. You follow the Cards?"

"Cards?"

"Our game today was against the Louisville Cardinals. They're in town on a road trip."

"What a coincidence." Again the smile. "I'm on a road trip, too. But I'm not following this baseball team. I came to Buffalo for another reason, and I'm leaving tomorrow."

"It's a good town to be leaving. You help me celebrate and I'll help you."

"That's why I'm here."

Right. Sandy glanced over at the bar. Leon and Dutch were talking to a couple of women. On the screen was a newsflash about the microwave deluge in Arizona. Shots of emergency workers in the streets wearing aluminized suits. He turned back and smiled. "Run that by me again."

The woman gazed at him calmly over her high cheek-bones. "Come on, Sandy. Read my lips. This is your lucky day and I'm here to celebrate it with you. A skillful man like you must know what that means."

"Did Leon put you up to this? If he did the bet's off."

"Leon is one of those men at the bar? I don't know him. If I were to guess I would guess that he is the black man. I'd also guess that you proposed the bet to him. Am I right?"

"I made the bet."

"You see. My lucky guess. Well, if you made the bet with Leon then it's unlikely that Leon hired me to trick you."

This was the weirdest pickup talk Sandy had ever heard. "Why do I get the feeling there's a proposition coming?"

"Don't tell me you didn't expect a proposition to pass between us sometime during this conversation."

"For sure. But I expected to be making it."

"Go ahead."

Sandy studied her. "You northern girls are different."

"I'm not from the north."

"Then you're from a different part of the south than I grew up in."

"It takes all kinds. May I ask you a question?"

"Sure."

"Why the bet?"

Sandy considered. "I just wanted to make it interesting."

"I'm not interesting enough unless there's money riding on me?"

He smiled. "I just like to raise the stakes," he said. "But the bet is between me and Leon, to prove a point. It has nothing to do with you."

"You're not very flattering."

"That's not what I meant."

"Yes. But we can make it even more interesting. You think you can please me?"

Sandy finished his bourbon. "If you can be pleased."

"Good. So let's make it very interesting." She opened her clutch purse and tilted it toward him. She reached inside and held something so that Sandy could see it. It was a straight razor.

"If you don't please me, I get to hurt you. Just a little."

Sandy stared at her. "Are you kidding?"

Her gaze was steady. "Maybe you're not as good as you tell me. Maybe you'll need to have some luck."

She had to be teasing. Sandy considered the odds. Even if she wasn't, he thought he could handle her. "It's a deal."

"You're sure you want to try this?"

"I know what I want when I see it."

"You already know enough to make a decision?"

He came around to her side of the table. "Let's go," he said. She closed her purse and led him toward the door. Sandy winked at Leon as they passed the bar; Leon's face looked as surprised as ever. Once in the street Sandy slipped an arm around her waist and nudged her over to the side of the building. Her perfume was dizzying. "What's your name?" he asked her.

"Judith," she said.

"Judith." It sounded old fashioned. There was a Judith in the Bible, he thought. But he had never paid attention in Bible class.

He kissed her. He had to force his tongue between her lips. Then she bit it, lightly. Her mouth was strong and wet. She moved her hips against him—

—Sandy was twelve. He was sitting in the Beulah Land Baptist Church with his mother. She was a pretty woman with blonde hair, putting on a little weight. His father didn't go to church. Lately his mother had been going more often and reading from the Bible after supper.

Some of his classmates, including Carrie Ford and Sue Harvey, were being baptized that Sunday. The two girls rode the bus with him, and Carrie had the biggest tits in the seventh grade.

The choir sang a hymn while the Reverend Foster took the girls into the side room, and when the song was done the curtains in front of the baptismal font opened and there stood the Reverend and Carrie, waist deep in the water. Carrie was wearing a blue robe, trying nervously not to smile. Behind them was a painting of the lush green valley of the Promised Land, and the shining City on the Hill. The strong light from the spot above them made Carrie's golden hair shine, too.

The Reverend Foster put his hand on Carrie's shoulder, lifted his other hand towards heaven and called on the Lord.

"Do you renounce Satan and all his ways?" he asked Carrie.

"Yes," she said, looking holy. She crossed her arms at the

wrists, palms in, and folded her hands over those tits, as if to hold them in.

The Reverend touched the back of her neck. She jumped a bit, and Sandy knew she didn't expect that, but then she let him duck her head in the water. He held her down for a long time, made sure she knew who was boss. Sandy liked that. The Reverend said the words of the baptism and pulled her up again.

Carrie gasped and sputtered. She lifted her hands to push the hair away from her eyes. The robe clung to her chest. Sandy could see everything. As she tried to catch her breath, he felt himself getting an erection.

He put his hand on his lap, trying to make it go away, but the mere contact with his pants leg made him get even harder. He shifted uncomfortably, and his mother looked at him. She saw his hand on his lap.

"Sandy!" she hissed. A woman in front of them looked around.

His mother tried to ignore him. The curtains closed. Sandy wished he were dead. At the same time he wanted to get up, go to the side room and watch Carrie Ford take off her wet robe and towel herself dry—

—He felt the warmth of Judith's lips on his, her arms around his neck. He pushed away from her, staring, the memory fading. What was happening to him? She bit her lower lip. He had an erection after all, either because of the memory or Judith; he felt the embarrassment and guilt that had burned in him at the church. "Listen," he said. "Let's go to my place."

"Whatever you like." They walked down the block to the tram station. Sandy lived in one of the luxury condos that had been built on the Erie Basin before the market crash. He had an expensive view across the lake; it cost all his salary. Sun-belters moving north to escape the drought were keeping prices high, but Sandy wanted first class whether he could afford it or not. He inserted his ID card and punched in the security code. The lock snapped open and he ushered her in.

The place was wasted on Judith. She walked through his

living room, the moon through the skylight throwing triangular shadows against the cathedral ceiling, and thumbed on the bedroom light as if she had been there before. He found her standing just inside the door. She began to unbutton his shirt. He felt hot. He tried to undress her, but she pushed his hands away, pushed him backward until he fell onto the water bed. She stood above him. The expression on her face was serious.

She knelt on the undulating bed and rested her hands on his chest. He fumbled on the headboard shelf for the yohimbine. She pushed his hand away, took one of the caps and broke it under his nose. His heart slammed against his ribs; his lips were dry and the tightness of the crotch of his jeans was agony. Eventually she helped him with that, but not before she had spent what seemed like an eternity making it worse.

The sight of her naked almost made him come right then. But she knew how to control that. She seemed to know everything in his mind before he knew it himself, responded as he needed, precisely, kindly. She became everything that he wanted. She seemed hooked into the sources of his desire: his pain, his fear, his hope all translated into the simple, slow motions of her sex and his. He forgot to worry about whether he was pleasing her. He forgot who he was. For an hour he forgot everything.

It was dark. Sandy lay just on the edge of sleep with his eyelids sliding closed and the distant sound of a siren in the air. The siren faded.

"You're beautiful, Sandy," Judith said. "I may not cut you after all."

Sandy felt so groggy he could hardly think. "Nobody cuts the Killer," he mumbled, and laughed. He rolled onto his stomach. The bed swayed; he felt dizzy.

"Such a wonderful body. Such a hard man."

She slid her hand down his backbone, and all the muscles of his back relaxed, as if it were a twisted cord that she was unwinding. In the back of his mind was a tiny alarm, like the siren that had passed into another part of the city.

"Now," said Judith, "I want to tell you a story."

"Sure."

Lightly stroking his back, Judith said, "This is the story of Yancey Camera."

"Funny name." He felt so sleepy.

"It is. To begin with, Yancey Camera was a young man of great promise and trusting nature. Would you believe me if I told you that he was as handsome as the hero in a black-and-white movie? And he was as smart as he was handsome and as rich as he was smart. His cock was as reliable as his credit rating. He was a lucky young man.

"But Yancey did not believe in luck. Oh, he gave lip service to it; when people said, 'Yancey, you're a lucky boy,' he said, 'Yes, I guess I am.' But when he thought about it he understood that when they told him how lucky he was they were really saying that he did not deserve his good fortune, had done nothing to earn it, and in a more rationally ordered universe he would not be handsome, smart, or rich, and his cock would be no more reliable than any other man's. Yancey came to realize that when people commented on his luck they were really expressing envy, and he immediately suspected those people. This enabled him to spot more than a few phonies, for there was a large degree of truth in Yancey's analysis.

"The problem was that as time went on Yancey forgot that he had not done anything to earn the good looks, intellect, wealth and hard cock that he possessed. In other words, Sandy, he came to disbelieve in luck. He thought that a man of his skills could control every situation. He forgot about the second law of thermodynamics, which tells us that we all lose, and that those times when we win are merely local statistical deviations in a universal progress from a state of lower to a state of higher entropy. Yancey's own luck was just such a deviation. As time passed and Yancey's good fortune continued, he began to think that he was beyond the reach of the second law of thermodynamics."

The second law of sexual dynamics. First you screw her, then she talks. Sandy thought about the instant he had hit the home run, the feel of the bat in his hands, the contact with the ball so sweet he knew it was out of the park even before he had finished following through.

"This is a sin that the Fates call hubris," Judith was saying, "and as soon as they realized the extent of Yancey Camera's error, they set about to rectify the situation. Now, there are several ways in which such an imbalance can be restored. It can be done in stages, or it can be done in one sudden, enormous stroke.

"And here my story divides: in one version, Yancey marries a beautiful young woman, fathers four sons and opens an automobile dealership. Unfortunately, because Yancey's home is built on the site of a chemical waste dump, one of his sons is born with spina bifida and is confined to a wheelchair. This child dies at the age of twelve. One of his other sons is unable to compete in school and becomes a drug dealer. A third is brilliant but commits suicide at the age of fourteen when his girlfriend goes to the beach with another boy. Under the pressure of these disappointments Yancey's wife becomes a shrill harridan. She gets fat and drinks and embarrasses him at parties. Yancey gets fat too, and loses his hair. He is left with the consolation of his auto dealership, but then there is a war in the Middle East in which the oil fields are destroyed with atomic weapons. Suddenly there is no more oil. Yancey goes bankrupt. A number of other things happen which I will not tell you about. Suffice it to say that by the end of this version of the story Yancey has lost his good looks, his money, and finally his fine mind, which becomes unhinged by the pressures of his misfortune. He even loses his hard cock, and dies cursing his bad luck. For in the end he is certain that bad luck, and not his own behavior, is responsible for his destruction. And he is right."

Sandy's eyes were closed. "That's too bad."

"That is too bad, isn't it." Judith lifted the hair from the back of his neck with the tips of her fingers. It tickled.

"The other version of the story, Sandy, is even more interesting. Yancey Camera grows older and success follows him. He marries a beautiful young woman who does not get fat and fathers four completely healthy and well-adjusted sons. He becomes a successful lawyer and enters politics. He wins every election he enters. Eventually he becomes the President of the Entire Country. Everywhere he goes people gather to meet him, and when Yancey departs he leaves two groups of citizens behind. The first group goes home saying, 'What a fortunate people we are to have such a handsome, smart and wealthy president.' The others say, 'What a smart, handsome and wealthy people we are to have elected such a handsome, smart and wealthy leader.' Like their president they assume that their gifts are not the result of good luck but of their inherent virtue. Therefore, all who point out this good luck must be jealous. And so the Fates or the second law of thermodynamics deal with Yancey's nation as they dealt with Yancey in the other version of this story. In their arrogance Yancey Camera and his people, in the effort to maintain an oil supply for their automobiles, provoke a war which destroys all life on earth including the lives, good looks, wealth and hard cocks of all the citizens of that country, lucky and unlucky. The end.

"What do you think of that, Sandy?"

Sandy was on the verge of sleep. "I think you're hung up on cocks," he mumbled. "All you women."

"Could be," Judith whispered. Her breath was warm on his ear. He fell asleep.

He woke with a start. She was no longer beside him. How could he have let down his guard so easily? She could have ripped him off—or worse. Where had he put his money? He rolled over and reached for his pants, poked his index finger into the hip pocket. It was empty. He lurched out of bed, began to haul on the pants. He was hopping toward the hallway, tugging on his zipper, when he saw her through the open bathroom door.

She turned toward him. The light behind her was on. Her face was in shadow, and her voice, when she spoke, was huskier than the voice he had heard before.

"Did you find it?" she asked.

He felt afraid. "Find what?"

"Your money."

Then he remembered he had stuck the crisp bills, fresh

from the machine, into the button-flap pocket of his shirt. He found the shirt on the floor. The money was there.

When he turned back to her, she was standing over him. She reached down and touched his face—

—He was fifteen. He sat at the chipped formica table in the kitchen, sweating, eating a peanut butter sandwich and drinking a glass of sweet tea. The air was damp and hot as a fever compress. Through the patched screen door he could see the porch, the dusty, red-clay yard, and a corner of the tobacco field, yellowish green, running down toward the dark line of trees along the bend of the Cape Fear that marked the edge of the farm. The air was full of the sweet smell of curing tobacco. Even the sandwich tasted of it.

He was wearing his high school baseball uniform. His spikes and glove—a Dale Murphy autograph—rested on the broken yellow vinyl of the only other kitchen chair. He was starting in right, at two o'clock, in the first round of the Mid-South 4-A championships, and afterward he was going out for pizza with Jocelyn. His heart was pulling him away from the farm, his thoughts flew through a jumble of images: Jocelyn's fine, blonde hair, the green of the infield grass, the brightly painted ads on the outfield fence, the way the chalk lines glowed in the summer sun, the smell of Jocelyn's shoulders when he buried his face in the nape of her neck. If he never had to suffer through another summer swamped under the sickly sweet smell of tobacco it would be all right with him.

He was washing out the glass and plate in the sink when he heard his father's boots on the porch and the screen door slammed. He ignored the old man. His father came over to the counter, opened the cupboard and took out the bottle of sour mash bourbon and a drinking glass. Less than an inch was left in the bottom of the bottle. He poured the bourbon into the glass, then drank it off without putting down the bottle. He sighed and leaned against the counter.

Sandy dried his hands and got his glove and spikes.

"Where you going?" his father asked, as if the uniform and equipment weren't enough.

"We got a game today."

His father looked at him. The old man's eyes were set in a network of wrinkles that came from squinting against the sun. Mr. Witt, the coach, had the same wrinkles around his eyes, but his were from playing outfield when he was with Atlanta. And Mr. Witt's eyes were not red.

His father didn't say anything. He took off his billed cap and wiped his forearm across his brow. He turned and reached into the sugar canister he kept in the cupboard next to his bottles. Sandy tried to leave but was stopped again. "Where's the sugar bowl money?"

"I don't know."

"There was twelve dollars in here. What did you do with it?"

Sandy stood in the door, helpless. "I didn't touch your money."

"Liar. What did you do with it!"

Pure hatred flared in him. "I didn't take your money, you old drunk!"

Sandy slammed the screen door and stalked over to the beat-up Maverick that he'd worked nights and weekends saving up to buy. He ground the gearshift into first, let the engine roar through the rotten muffler, spun the tires on the dirt. In the side mirror he saw the old man standing on the porch shouting at him. But he couldn't hear what he was shouting, and the image shook crazily as he bounced up the rutted drive—

—Sandy flinched. He was crouched in his apartment with the woman standing over him. He still shook with anger at his father's accusation, still sweated from the heat; he could even smell the tobacco baking in the sun. How he had hated the old man's suspicion. For the first time in years he felt the vivid contempt he'd had then for his father's smallness.

He backed away from Judith, shaking. She reached out and touched him again—

—It was a few minutes earlier. Sandy was in the bedroom, leaning half out of the bed where he'd just gotten his ashes hauled better than he had in his entire life, in order to stick his finger into a pocket to see whether he'd been robbed. On the day that he made the majors, on the day he played better than he ever had, on the day he played better than, in truth, he knew he was really able to play. Sticking his finger into his pants pocket like a halfwit sticking his finger up his ass because it felt so good. A pitiful loser. Just like his father—

—Sandy jerked away from her. He scrambled toward the bed, terrified.

"What's the matter, Sandy?" She stepped toward him.

"Don't touch me!"

"You don't like my touch?"

"You're going to kill me." He said it quietly, and as he spoke he realized it was true.

She moved closer. "That remains to be seen, Sandy."

"Don't touch me again! Please!"

"Why not?"

Cowering, he looked up at her, trying to make out her face. It wasn't fair. But then something welled up in him and he knew it *was* fair, and that was almost more than he could stand. "I'm sorry," he said.

She wrapped her arms around him and said nothing. She stroked his hair.

After a while he stopped crying. He wiped his eyes with the corner of the bedsheet. He sat on the edge of the bed. "I'm sorry," he said.

"Yes," she said. Then he saw that in her other hand, the one she had not touched him with, she held the straight razor. She had been holding it all the time.

"I didn't realize I might be hurting your feelings," he said.

"You can't hurt my feelings." There was no emotion in her voice. There was nothing. Looking at her face was like looking at an empty room.

"Don't worry," she said, folding the blade back into the handle. "I won't hurt you."

It was a blind voice. Sandy shuddered. She leaned toward him. Her body was excruciatingly beautiful, yet he stumbled back from the bed, grabbing for his shirt, as if the pants weren't enough, as if it were January and he was lost on the lakefront in a blizzard.

"You don't have to be afraid," she said. "Come to bed."

He had to get out of there. She was insane—fuck insane, she wasn't even human. He looked into her cold face. It was not dead. It was like the real woman was in another place and this body was a receiver over which she was bringing him a message from far away. If he left now he would be okay, he knew. But if he did, something that might happen to him would not happen, and in order to find out what that was he would have to take a big chance. He looked up at the moon through the skylight. The clouds passed steadily across it, making it look like it was moving. The moon didn't move that fast; it moved so slowly that you couldn't tell, except Sandy knew that in five minutes the angle of the shadows on the wall and chair and bed would be all different. The room would be changed.

She was still in bed. Sandy came back, dropped the shirt, took off his pants, and got in beside her. Her skin was very smooth. He slept.

When he woke the next morning he was alone. The clock read 8:45; he would have to hurry. He felt good. He got his bags out of the closet and began to pack. Halfway through, he stopped to get the shirt he had left on the floor. He picked it up and shoved it into his laundry bag, then remembered the cash and pulled it out again.

She had left him twenty dollars. One ten, two fives.

He pushed the shirt down into the bottom of the bag and finished packing. He called a cab and rode over to the stadium.

On the TV in the cab he watched the morning news, hoping to get the baseball scores. The Reverend Gilray declares the Abomination of Desolation has begun, the Judgment is at hand. Reports the Israelis have used tactical nukes in the Djibouti civil war. Three teenagers spot another UFO at Chestnut Ridge.

When he got to the park Sandy gave the cabby a five to hold him, went directly to the locker room and cleaned out his locker. As he was getting ready to leave Dutch showed up to take some hitting before the Sunday afternoon game.

"Looks like I underrated you, sport. Just like on the field." He hauled out his wallet and began to get out the bills.

"Keep it," Sandy said.

"Huh?" Dutch, surprised, looked like a vanilla imitation of Leon.

"Leon won the bet."

Dutch snickered. "She got wise to you, huh?"

Sandy zipped his bag shut and picked up his glove and bats. He smiled. "You could say that. I got to go—cab's waiting. Wish me luck."

"Thought you didn't need luck."

"Goes to show you what I know. Say goodbye to Leon for me, okay?" He shook Dutch's hand and left.

8: SUNDAY, JUNE 6

....

Anecdotal Evidence of Reality

George sat in a crowded coach on the late train from New York to Philadelphia, across the aisle from a thin Hispanic woman and her two children, a chubby boy of about eleven and a large-eyed little girl with black pigtails. While her mother slept, the girl watched George with a fascination he could not fathom. The coach's air conditioning was out, and the vent rattled as it blasted hot air down on them, shaking the pages of George's newspaper.

The woman awoke, looking exhausted. "Mia. Don't stare," she said, tugging on the girl's shoulder. The girl sat back on the seat, whose upholstery had been ripped up so many times that it was now almost completely covered with duct tape. She stretched her legs out in front of her and stared at her crossed ankles for a few seconds, then squirmed around to peek at George again. He smiled at her. She turned away, demanding her doll, which her mother pulled from a Bloomingdale's bag on the floor beside her. The boy woke up and asked for gum.

In front of George, on the corner seat that faced back into the coach, slept a black man wearing dirty camouflage fatigues. His shoulder still had the red-and-white subdued unit patch of the 91st Central American Division. The man looked as if he hadn't shaved since the war ended and smelled as if he had been drinking ever since.

A conductor came by and checked their passes. The woman fumbled in her sisal purse and came up with the green passports that marked her and her children as transient aliens. Half of New York were transients, with no permanent address. Whenever they were on the point of establishing eligibility for social services the State would round them up and ship them to the next state, which would either pass them on or, if they needed workers, billet them in a camp until it was time to shove them along again. Despite the unemployment problem, deportation of illegals was politically impossible. The government had created the conditions that made them refugees in the first place, and too many businesses had avoided collapse in the last five years only by hiring indentureds.

The condutor raised an eyebrow when George handed him his blue card. Blue meant next to unlimited travel rights. It had cost HCR plenty. The Interrail man studied the picture on the card and compared it with the hairless man in front of him. Slowly a light dawned on him. "I saw you on the cable—"

"That's right," George said in a low voice. "I'm in disguise."

The man ran the magnetic strip on the ticket through his canceling machine. "Finding out what it's like to be a zombie? Pretty sick."

The conductor moved off. The coach lurched as it ran across a particularly bad stretch of the ancient roadbed. It had taken them four hours to get to Princeton and even though they were going to bypass Trenton it would probably be morning before they reached Philly: Interrail couldn't keep the Northeast corridor open for a week before one terrorist group or another ripped up the tracks.

The little girl looked over the back of the seat at him again. Her mother pulled her back and whispered a line of rapid Spanish. The boy smirked. George raised his paper higher. It was a copy of the Louisville *Courier-Journal* he'd had printed at the Penn Station newsstand. He'd selected for national news, space news, local news and sports. He looked for some event that would show the Alien had been at work in the Ohio Valley. It could be Lexington, or Indianapolis, or as far north as Lansing, but the only reader-selected edition available at Penn was Louisville.

The *Courier-Journal* was a conservative paper struggling to keep to the traditions of respectable journalism, which meant that the editorial slant was slightly less jingoistic, sex-ridden, and trivia-obsessed than HCR. It refused to print photos of half-naked women unless they had been murdered. The front page had twinned stories on the triple economy and the prospects for the Democrats to mount a serious challenge to the President in the next election. In the second story Senator Harper said a Democratic administration could bring Economy I unemployment below 20 percent while keeping the Economy II rate steady at nine. In the first the Treasury Department said that the latest devaluation of the dollar would be the last of the year. Inflation over the last twelve months had dropped to 36 percent, stabilizing the dollar at roughly one tenth of its 1990 purchasing price. The jump line said the stories were continued on page sixteen, but George didn't read past the first page.

In space news, the Energy Administration reported the microwave beam alignment problems on the Prometheus I solar power satellite had been solved and the plant would be reactivated in one week, despite threats from environmental groups across the southwest to stage demonstrations at the beam target. Some units of the Arizona National Guard had been called back from Mexico City to cordon the area.

George quit reading that one after three graphs and turned to the local news. He found most of his leads there anyway. First he read a feature on the sharp increase in attendance at Kentucky churches as people anticipated the coming Millenium. Conservative theologians expected a corresponding dropoff after the first of the year, but the radicals said there wouldn't be a first of the year. George read the whole thing even though he realized halfway through that this was just the standard pre-millennial piece that had been appearing in papers for six months or more. He read about a man who had been killed in a fight outside a bar, but there was nothing unusual about the circumstances. A couple of Peppermen were arrested for attacking the director of the city shelters. The Peppermen said the shelters were "bandaids" to keep people from confronting the plight of the aged. The paper printed the report right next to an ad for a Seppuku Club: "Tired of Pain?" Someone doing layout had a sense of humor.

He gave up and turned to the sports page. The Louisville Cards' winning streak had been stopped at nine when the Buffalo Bisons beat them 7-2 Saturday. The Bison right fielder, a kid named Ellison, had gone 4-for-5 and was being called up to Chicago. George had been a crazed White Sox fan back in the sixties, when he was a college student in Evanston. You could always count on the Sox—they still had the worst hitting in the league.

George could remember all such details about his predeath life now, but that life still seemed as if it had happened to someone else. He remembered meeting Richard back in 1980, when Richard was a philosophy-obsessed punk rocker in London and George was an economics editor for UPI who liked to hang around the clubs. He remembered the drunken year they had spent together, before Richard went back to school and George back to New York by way of Paris. George remembered reams of futile political journalism. He remembered walking into the State Insurance Commission office on a wet spring day in 1991 and seeing Lucy. He remembered falling in love, and how for a time, with her, his despair had been held in check. That didn't last.

When Richard got George a job at HCR, it had seemed a sort of last-ditch effort. George could not figure out how Richard persuaded Jason Abramowitz to hire him: George was legit journalism and the *Hemisphere Confidential Report* was a drug-crazed fantasy. Richard said it was because HCR wanted to expand into legitimate markets. George was just the man he needed to head up the Special Reports team.

Richard persuaded Abramowitz to give George autonomy. When Richard was on, he could do almost anything. He had the ability, without offending, to insult you in one sentence and flatter you in the next. If you spent enough time around him you began to wonder why you didn't talk, dress, even breathe the way Richard did. You could never tell whether he believed anything he said, so that when you tried to figure out his motives you ended up filling him up with your best guess. Lucy said this personality vacuum would get Richard in trouble some day, and George supposed that it might, but he knew Richard better than she did. Even at his most outrageous, inside Richard was a core of humanity. This humanity, George was convinced, was the fuel behind the games Richard played. It was the cement that bonded them. George had seen it that first night in an East End club, when Richard came down off the platform to smoke a cig during a break and they'd struck up a conversation. It was there still. George was Richard's safety valve, the one person to whom he could, occasionally, reveal his emotions. It was a role George was glad to play.

At HCR Richard got George to do more consistent work than he had done on his own. For the wordline George produced trash news with a twisted logic that took it to the top of the menu on Compunet. For the videoline George did call-ins. His ursine good looks struck some chord in a populace jaded by a decade of smoothly hollow "commentators." Although his following was still small, he had already been dismissed by a worried article in the *Columbia Journalism Review*. George's reports staff respected his intelligence. His lack of personal ambition didn't hurt him because he had Richard to play the political games necessary to keep an operating space open. The reports on the Texas Gene Meltdown and the Black Plague helped boost HCR into second place among Compunet news services.

He folded the paper and stuffed it into his clothes bag. The sleeping vet snored loud enough to rival the air conditioning. Through the window George watched the lights of the opposite shore glinting off the oily surface of the Delaware as the tracks descended the ridge to run along the riverside. He wished he could open the window. The air was thick. He looked up at the ceiling. Smoke boiled out of the air conditioning vent.

An indentured worker, an Interrail cop and the conductor trotted up from the back of the car. The conductor and the workie carried fire extinguishers. The door at the front of the coach was jammed. The smoke thickened. People were coming awake throughout the coach. The Hispanic woman was getting agitated. The vet was still asleep. Through the window in the door George could see that the space between the cars was full of smoke. People beat on the door from the other side.

The conductor cursed and the door swung open. Three coughing people stumbled in. The conductor and the men with the extinguishers moved into the forward car. "What's going on?" George asked.

One of the passengers, a teenage boy carrying a Bible, said, "Car's on fire. It's coming from under the floor."

"Why don't they stop the train?"

The boy looked at him as if he were crazy. The passengers who were awake acted like this was a daily occurrence. A few moved back to another car, but when they saw there wasn't any more room most came back. George peered ahead. The workie had smashed open the forward car's windows to let out the smoke. He and the conductor were hanging out of one of them, spraying the underside of the coach with the extinguishers.

Eventually the smoke coming out of the air conditioner diminished. George sat back down. The vet was still asleep.

"Watch your sister," the Hispanic woman said to her son.

She moved along the jolting coach back toward the rest rooms. As soon as she was gone the boy called the girl a "buttface" and took away her doll. When she tried to grab it back he slapped her. The girl began to cry. Something in George snapped.

"Cut it out," he said to the boy. The boy flipped George off, and a rage swept over him, quite as real as the ones he had gone into before his heart attack. He tried to pull the doll from the boy's hands. The kid would not let go. George yanked; the doll's arm tore off and white stuffing spilled across the floor. The girl screamed loud enough to wake the Nicaraguan vet, who came out of his dream fumbling for a weapon that wasn't there. George tried to hold the doll so that the beads of styrofoam would stop flowing. "I'm sorry," George said, trying to give the doll to the girl.

The girl howled. Her brother threw the torn arm down and ran toward the back of the car. The restroom door flew open and knocked him on his ass.

"Maria!" the woman shouted, throwing herself toward George. Before she got there something crashed into the back of George's legs. The vet.

By the time George managed to untangle himself the woman was towering over him. She had her daughter by the arm, pulling her up so only one of the child's feet touched the floor. The boy, nose bleeding, tried to talk, but the woman drowned him out. George attempted to get up. She kicked at him and backed away. "Police!" she yelled. "Help!"

The cop hurried back from the burning car. "Listen," George started, but before he could explain the vet was shouting at the cop: George had tried to hurt the little girl, then bloodied the boy's nose when he tried to defend her. The cop poked his gun at George. "Spread 'em, Baldie."

George faced the wall and spread his arms and legs. The cop felt under George's armpits and grabbed his crotch. He fished George's passport from his jacket and flipped through it without saying anything.

"All right, turn around. What happened?"

Everyone started talking at once. The little girl began crying again. "Quiet!" the cop shouted, and turned to the woman. "You first."

George waited while the woman explained, in halting English, how George had been watching her daughter since they'd boarded the train and started the fire with his evil eye. He had been withered by the Devil. The cop looked tired. He asked the vet for his version and got the beginning of a tale of U.S. foreign policy in the 1990s. The cop cut him short. Then George told his story. "I've been undergoing chemotherapy for cancer. I was trying to stop the kids from fighting."

"Anyone else in here see what happened?" Nobody said anything until the cop picked on a pale woman wearing a cheap tunic that made her look pregnant. "The guy grabbed the doll from the boy and it broke," she said.

The cop turned to the mother. "Look, lady, there's not much I can do based on your say-so. This guy doesn't look like any kind of geek to me."

"He's a Zombie!"

George tried to stop her. "Listen, I am not—"

The woman fell back a step, crossed herself. *Madre Dios!*

"Calm down," the cop said. "I got other things to worry about. This guy just got old a little early, looks to me."

"Please, help," the woman said. It was clear that she was close to cracking under the weight of the disasters that had led her to share a third-class coach with one of the Undead. "Help us."

"Trust me, lady, I wouldn't—" the cop started.

"Trust you! Trust you! *Calabaza!*"

The cop got mad. "Okay. I want you to sit down with your kids and shut up. Fix your kid's doll, why don't you. And you—" he pushed an index finger against George's chest. "You sit down, too, and keep out of trouble. Go to sleep. Pretty soon we'll be in Philadelphia." He handed back George's ID.

"What about me?" the vet asked.

The cop's expression was infinitely pained. "You compose yourself a letter to your congressman. Maybe he can get you on the cable news." He waited until all of them sat down again, then sat down himself in the front corner seat.

The woman got out a handkerchief, licked its corner and used it to wipe her son's face. George felt sorry for her. He was very tired. He leaned his head against the window and tried to sleep.

He didn't know how much time had passed when he imagined he heard the far-away sound of fireworks, bringing him the vivid memory of a summer's night in Enid, Oklahoma—it must have been forty years before, 1960, earlier—when as kids he and Seth had lain awake listening to the Fourth-of-July celebration going on across town in the park. Seth had wanted to sneak out the window, shinny down the drainpipe and go see the fireworks, but George was afraid of their mom. George had always been afraid of her.

Seth had never been afraid of anything. He had died in 1972, electrocuted when a radio fell into his bathtub.

The distant explosions brought George fully awake. He looked out the train window. Across the river white flashes punctuated the darkness, followed seconds later by muffled concussions that were not fireworks at all but grenades, mortars or pipe bombs. Pale smoke drifted above lightless, geometric rows of burned-out houses. The Interrail cop still had his eye on George. "What's that?" George asked him.

"Suburbia," he said.

9: SUNDAY, JUNE 6
. . . .
Lucy's Career goes Up in Smoke

In the morning Lucy was awakened by a phone call. It was Mari Tokugawa, another lawyer from the Corrections office.

"I'm only telling you this because I like you, Lucy," Mari

said. "The A.G. knows you had George revived. He's worried about the political fallout, so he's going to make an example. Monday, when you come in the office, they're going to arrest you."

Lucy rubbed her gummy eyelids. "How did they find out?"

"Detweiler ran into Richard Shrike in the Village one night last week. Richard must have been twisted. He let something slip."

"Son of a bitch," Lucy whispered.

"Please don't tell anyone I told you," Mari said. She hung up.

Lucy sat up in bed. Could she fight it? Not likely. Detweiler was the A.G.'s political catamite. He had been sniping at Lucy since she came into the office, and this was just the club he needed to beat her to death. She looked around the bedroom. George was not there, and his overnight bag was gone. So much for protecting him from the lions. Who was going to protect her?

She showered and dressed, then made breakfast. The world was crashing down around her ears, and it was time for decisive action: eggs and bacon, pancakes with butter and syrup, a pot of real coffee. Instead of panic, she felt suicidally cheerful. Responsible Lucy. She had risked her career for George, and he had left her. She had trusted Richard and he had betrayed her. The most caring thing anyone had done was Mari's warning her, and Mari had concluded by asking not to get her involved. Fuck them all. Lucy's cheerfulness gained an edge, and by the end of her second stack of pancakes she had named it: rage.

She called Richard. The phone rang eight times. When he finally picked up the receiver, she simply said, "He's gone."

"Who's gone?" Richard sounded irritated. No video.

"Judge Crater. Who do you think, Richard?"

"Lucy. Do you know where he went?" He didn't seem particularly surprised.

"No. I don't much care, either."

"I'll be right over. Please don't talk to anyone until I get there."

"Don't worry, Richard. I can keep a secret." Lucy hung up. She poured herself another cup of coffee. She laughed.

She was still sitting there when the intercom buzzed. She had Curtis send Richard up, and after a few minutes there was a knock at the door. She took her time, so that when she opened the door his hand was poised to knock again. His eyes looked like they had been kept overnight in a bottle. "Are you all right?" he asked. "What happened?"

He was so smooth. So concerned. What did he really think of her? There was absolutely no way to tell. She wondered whether Richard even knew himself, and the possibility made her see him in an entirely new light. Maybe he even conned himself. That was how he could be so sincere while saying things that he knew were lies. For a moment she pitied him—but the moment passed. What would it be like to play Richard's role, to string him along? "I'm fine, Richard. Let's talk about what's important—George."

"I told you he was under pressure."

He didn't hear her mockery. "His overnight bag is gone and so are some of his clothes."

"He packed without you hearing him?"

She led him to George's study. All of the TVs were on. "I took a sleeping pill," she said. "I've had trouble sleeping since he came back."

Richard stood in the middle of the room and scanned the heaps of printouts, the three whispering TV screens. "What a bloody mess. Abramowitz called me yesterday to ask how George was getting on. He said he couldn't keep waiting with the wire operators threatening to strike. He sent Stan Levine to do the interview with Gilray."

"I'm sure Levine did an adequate job."

Richard picked up one of the maps and studied it. "He hashed it. He forgot to get a release. Do you know what this is?"

"No. What is it?"

The speed with which Richard suppressed his exasperation was a marvel. "I don't know what it is, Lucy. That's why I'm asking you. Did he ever talk about any of this?"

Lucy turned up the volume on the religious station. A

handsome man wearing a flannel shirt was chopping wood in what looked like a national park. He stopped and turned to the camera. "I'm an Opportunist," he said. Richard reached past her and turned it down again. "Lucy, listen to me. I think George is having a breakdown. We need to help him."

George was having a breakdown. "You're right," she said. "I'm sorry I haven't been paying attention. I guess I must be in shock."

"Let's go into the living room and talk this over." Richard carried the map out with him. He put it down on the coffee table and went over to the bar. "How about a drink?"

"Scotch." She sat on the sofa.

Richard brought over two scotches. He spread the map on the table and used his glass to keep the corner from curling. "Look at this. He seems to be plotting out some sort of itinerary. He never showed this to you?"

"He did, once. We were right here, sitting just as we are now. I wish I could remember what he was saying, but it was so confused." She looked at him and smiled. "I was high at the time."

Richard's exasperation threatened to break out again. "Try."

She furrowed her brow and let him wait. "I can't remember, Richard. Do you think it would help if we got twisted?"

"Go ahead if you think so."

"I wouldn't feel comfortable unless you joined me."

She got two sticks of THC gum from behind the bar. Richard took one. She imagined him wearing black leather, behind the keyboard, twenty years old. Corny punk hair. Lucy had not felt this good in months. She popped a stick into her mouth. Spearmint with a trace of burnt rope.

"Okay," he said. "What did George tell you?"

"He was after something," said Lucy slowly. "You know all those violent news reports he had? I think he had figured out that some religious agents were behind it."

"Religious agents?"

Lucy made it up as she went along. "Gilray was using mass hypnosis. The Reverend had cadres of psychological shock troops working on the electorate. I think George said something about them being paid by Brazil."

"Why didn't you tell me this before?"

A little truth, to nail it down. "I didn't trust you, Richard."

Would he buy that?

He did. "This is bad news." Richard got up and began pacing in front of the window, back and forth like the target Jap in a video game. "We've got to figure out some way to handle this." He stopped to look at her. Blam!—if she'd had the joystick in her hand she could have plugged him.

"We'll have to hire a detective," Richard said. "Have him start at point 'A' on the map."

Lucy wondered if Richard remembered telling Detweiler about George's revival. She decided it was probably just a mistake. Most of the things that were turning the world into a sty were mistakes, done with the best of intentions. Richard was just a little crazier than most.

"And we better not let on to Abramowitz for as long as possible," said Richard. "No, that won't work. I'm seeing him tomorrow and there's no way I can stonewall." He turned to Lucy. "George's camera! Doesn't he have a microcam around here? Did he take it with him?"

"I don't know. He keeps it in the closet in his study."

Richard rushed back to the study. "It's not here!" he called.

"He might have brought it back to the office. He never uses it."

"No." Richard came back into the room. "George took it with him. That's our story. I'll tell Abramowitz that George went off on a hot lead—that's it. I can lay it off to his enthusiasm. 'He's come back stronger than ever. He always was an emotional guy. That's what makes him so good.'" Richard seemed satisfied. "That will work while we hunt him down. Hell—it may even be true." He looked at her again. "You're sure you have no idea where he was going?"

Seeing the wheels turn in Richard was a revelation. Did

he care so little for George? Lucy had reason to be fed up with George; what was Richard's excuse? For the first time ever she felt contempt for him. She would humiliate him. "I haven't looked around the bedroom yet," she said.

"Let's look, then."

She followed him to the bedroom. How gracefully he bounced along, like a boxer closing in for the knockout, the toes of his Korean shoes barely touching the carpet. She played with the jewelry on her dresser while he yanked the drawers out of George's chiffonier and scattered clothes across the bed. "How about the bathroom?" she suggested when he slowed down.

He went into the bathroom and started opening drawers. He was really into it. Lucy worked hard to keep from laughing. As silently as she could, she took the chair from the dressing table. She pushed the bathroom door shut and wedged the chair under the doorknob. The knob rattled. "Lucy?" Richard called.

"Yes, Richard?" She got her purse.

"Lucy." His voice was calm. "Let me out of here."

Something about his voice really got her. He had no business being calm. She would show him.

She ran to the kitchen, found the can of lighter fluid and a box of wooden matches. Back in the bedroom she piled the camisoles and French panties from her underwear drawer on top of the clothes Richard had thrown onto the bed. She pulled the cap off the can and squirted lighter fluid over the underwear. Richard wasn't even trying to force the door.

"Lucy, what the bloody hell's the matter?"

"I think the basic problem, Richard, is that God is dead. Everything started to go wrong after that."

"Are you all right?"

"Except for the fact that human beings are beyond hope, I think so."

Richard laughed. The ruefulness of it almost made her open the door. "That's a pretty large reservation," he said.

"We like it. We've been living on it for years and we like

it much better than the real world." The can sputtered and was empty.

The doorknob rattled again. "Lucy, open the fucking door!"

"If you get bored, Richard, try to remember the conversation you had with Ralph Detweiler last week." She struck a match and tossed it into the pile of lingerie. The fabric smoldered and flamed up. The black smoke was acrid.

"Ralph Detweiler?"

She grabbed her coat and purse and took the elevator down to the lobby. Curtis nodded to her as she walked by his booth. "A cab, ma'am?"

"No thanks, Curtis." She had a thought as she was about to step out the door, and went back. "Did you see Mr. Eberhart leave here last night?"

"Yes ma'am."

"Did he say where he was going?"

"He didn't say."

She started to leave again but couldn't. "Curtis," she said. "You'd better call the fire department." She walked out.

When she hit the street the shock hit her. If her legal career wasn't over before she'd touched the match to her underwear, it was undoubtedly over now. She felt both frightened and liberated. She was outside the law now. It was as if she were a new person. At least working at Corrections had taught her a few things that might come in handy.

Gramercy Park swarmed with people. The mayor's crusade to keep indigents out of the residential neighborhoods was not working, and the Sunday joggers dodged bag ladies and beggars. She started south, crossed East 14th and walked through the East Village, past dusty shops and up-scale boutiques, among young people parading in Greek togas or New Enlightenment frock coats and powdered wigs. Rows of run-down apartments alternated with refurbished houses. Fanlights rose over large oak doors full of leaded glass; spear points jutted menacingly from wrought iron fences.

On the corner of East 2nd and 1st Avenue she found the

diner she was looking for: The Tropic. Around the room
ran a Rousseau-like mural full of dark panthers, orange ti-
gers, brown women in blue robes carrying masses of ba-
nanas on their heads. At the end of the counter an Oriental
woman whispered to a man wearing a caftan. The man
laughed.

"I need to speak to someone," Lucy said to the counter
waitress.

The woman pointed to a booth at the back. While Lucy
waited she ordered the $80 special: soyamelt, French fries,
coleslaw, kosher dill, with artificial coffee and banana cream
flavored pie for dessert. She listened to the latin-rhythmed
music on the diner's stereo.

It was an old song. She knew she'd heard it before, a long
time ago—high school, Tenafly, New Jersey. Tenth grade,
when she dated Vince Carvaggio. Vince was a senior; he
drove a Fiero and played sexy music on the deck. His family
had money and Lucy's didn't; her mother was a pothead
and her father was out of work. By the age of sixteen she
was paying the bills and buying the groceries while pulling
straight A's in school. She had gone out with Vince for a
year before she realized she didn't really like him. They had
nothing to talk about and he never listened to her. But she
remembered riding in Vince's car, how good he looked with
his short, dark hair ruffled by the breeze, how good she'd
felt to be out with him to a movie or a party. Warm summer
nights, sun down but the sky still lit orange and purple and
the lights of the street just coming on. That was sixteen
years ago. The mid-point, the center of her life—riding in
that car with Vince.

Lucy heard a siren in the street and an emergency truck
flashed by the window. Her food came. She ate it all. She
looked at the crumbs on her fork. She looked at the bruise
on her finger. Never again. But what the hell was she going
to do now?

A tall black woman entered the diner. The waitress spoke
to her, nodding toward Lucy. Lucy watched them. She was
in their world now. If she hadn't revived George her life
would still be secure. But she hadn't wanted to face the
world without him. She hadn't realized that, even before
he'd died, George was checking out. Maybe when she was a

little more used to being on the street, she could laugh at the irony.

The woman sat down across from Lucy. She was very thin. Her hair stood up in spikes, and her broad mouth twisted in a grin that showed a missing incisor. Irony Number One: Lucy had made a career arguing against the rights of people like this woman.

"Ida tells me you want to talk to me."

"Yes," said Lucy. "I need a new identity."

10: MONDAY, JUNE 7
....
Is this the Goal of Modern Medicine?

"You can wait here," Dr. Vance's receptionist said, ushering Gilray into the office. "The doctor will be in to see you soon."

Gilray sat down in a leather armchair across from the desk. He was miserably uncomfortable. He stared across the room at the wall.

The wall of Dr. Anthony Vance's office revealed all one needed to know about the man. B.S., University of Oklahoma. M.D., Johns Hopkins. NSF Commendation. A photograph of a slightly younger Vance, in a mylex suit with a helmet under his arm, standing with several other men in a litter of electronic gear on a rocky seashore. Gilray could imagine the brightness of that day, the blue of ocean and the dazzling white of spindrift. In the background stood the double dome of a nuclear reactor. That would be San Luis Obispo after the earthquake. Strange that the day should look so beautiful when the radiation levels at the time the photo had been taken were probably only slightly below lethal. This, too, had been predicted: "The dragon grew furious with the woman, and went off to wage war on the rest of her offspring . . . He took his stand on the sea shore."

Gilray picked up a copy of *Life* from the table beside him. The cover was a photo of one of the UFOs in the recent Clanton, Alabama sightings. He leafed through the magazine until he chanced across a picture of himself, then put it down again. He looked at his watch. 6:45—he was still on Eastern time. He looked around the room again. The place looked the same as it had the last time he had been here, a year before.

Only Marianne knew that he had gone to see the doctor. He wanted to keep it as quiet as possible. Many people waited to take advantage of any weakness he might show. The secularists didn't have the nerve to face him openly, so they resorted to character assassination. It was part of his burden. Christ had said, "Behold, I send you forth as sheep in the midst of wolves: be ye therefore wise as serpents." In the world of wolves it was best to bleed in secret. And that was why Gilray's personal physician was in Lexington, Kentucky, instead of Raleigh.

Gilray had never trusted doctors. As a boy he had suffered from asthma. He remembered a summer spent undergoing an endless series of scratch tests that never led to any relief, sitting bare-assed, wearing a flimsy robe, on a cold plastic chair while decrepit Dr. Kinbote poked at his chest with a knuckle so swollen that it looked deformed.

And then, when he turned fifteen, his allergies had disappeared as suddenly as they had appeared. Gilray had been lying alone in his room, trying only to breathe. The lights were out and sunlight slanted in through the curtains above his bed. In the hot Tennessee afternoon, near to despair, he spoke aloud, saying over and over, "Let me breathe, let me die, let me breathe, let me die," almost as if he were offering God a pair of options. But he didn't believe in God then. Suddenly a jet of cool air shot down from the ceiling. It passed directly through his breastbone, pinning him like a butterfly in a box. It was not death. It was life. He inhaled deeply, and it was as if he were freed and flying around the room. The air was cool and pure. He was charged with energy. He had an erection a mile long.

It was only later that Jimmy Gilray realized that, in that moment, he had been ravished by God. He had found his calling. It was a miracle, his mother said. A spontaneous cure, the professionals called it. "Profession" was an accurate word for medicine: doctors professed to understand things that were beyond their understanding. They took credit for improvements they had not caused and shirked responsibility for disasters they had. They were unwilling to admit their fallibility. They would rather be mysterious priests than servants of God's nature.

Yet he was back at their mercy again. Had he been a laughing man, he would have laughed.

The events of the last thirty years, that had taken him from poverty in Memphis to the television ministry in Raleigh, had not done much to improve his opinion of doctors. They had cured diabetes with an engineered microbe. Treated mental illness with designer drugs. They sold male oral contraceptives, and the rumors of resulting birth defects were, they said, greatly exaggerated. And since 1995, a number of people who would formerly have been declared certifiably dead, had been brought back to a semblance of life.

The door opened and Dr. Vance came in. "Reverend Gilray."

He shook Gilray's hand. Vance was a horse-faced young man, no more than thirty-five. His curled hair, neat beard, and white tunic showed he was on the Greek Revival bandwagon. The beard and the lantern jaw made him look dour, like Gilray's image of Jonathan Edwards. This clerical aura only annoyed him more. The only interest Vance had in religion was to press Gilray to let him visit Raleigh for a few weeks to do research on faith healing. It galled Gilray to have to submit his body to such a judge.

Vance had the credentials, he had the upbringing, he had the money. Of course he was a humanitarian, too, as long as he didn't have to have any contact with the recipients of his charity. Occasionally he would fly into Houston or Chicago in a government plane, swooping down like an archangel, to perform a gene alteration on some child of destitute parents, leaving behind a tearful mother and a brace of telelink reports on the multitalented surgeon and internist. He served on the AMA's governing board, one of the youngest members ever. He was warm and rational and efficient. His smile was a machine of polished chrome.

But now something was different. Instead of hurrying to get the desk between them, Vance sat in the other armchair, tossing the folder he'd carried into the room onto the desk as if it did not matter.

"How have you been getting on?" Vance asked. Earlier that afternoon he'd only poked at Gilray's groin, had his assistants take vials of urine and blood. Now his soberness was tempered by an almost palpable sympathy. Gilray had the feeling he was being softened up for something.

"I've felt fine."

"You haven't felt weak, sitting here? No pain?"

Gilray studied him. "No."

"And since your last visit what about your sexual performance?"

"You'll have to tell me why you're asking this."

Vance settled back in his chair. "I wanted to take this opportunity to ask some questions. I've always been a little intimidated by you, you know."

"What about the tests?"

"Don't worry about them," Vance said. He hesitated, then said, "I've heard speculation that in heaven, the souls of the blessed copulate endlessly. That's why it's called heaven."

Gilray could not have been more surprised if Vance had turned into a parakeet. "What are you talking about?"

"I only mention this because you seem to have a bigger investment in your sexuality than most preachers I've had the opportunity to treat. Than most men, for that matter."

Gilray started to get out of the chair. "I don't have to listen to insults—"

Vance reached out to touch his arm. "Hold on, please. I mean no insult. I'm sorry if I offended you. But I'm a scientist. I'm talking about simple facts. You have a penis that, statistically, falls in the upper two percent for size in the population. You must have realized this since junior high school, at the latest. I'm only suggesting that this physical attribute must have had some effect on you."

Gilray sat. "Nothing happens without the will of God."

"I put my faith in science. Science is the way we determine the answers to the big questions."

"Science has never answered a single question that was worth asking."

Vance smiled. "So God gave you that big crank, then? Or did it simply happen independent of God, though he knew of it and allowed it to happen?"

Gilray stared at him. "It doesn't surprise me that you would blaspheme like this. I realized—"

"You've never speculated about the cause?"

"God does not give us any ability unless he intends for us to use it."

"Okay. If you don't mind, I'd like to pursue that. I mean, He gives us the ability to rape, steal, murder. He gave Eve the ability to seduce Adam and Adam the ability to succumb. For centuries Christians have argued that he gave us certain things to test whether we had the will *not* to use them."

"You're twisting the language. The ability to rape is not a true ability. It's the misuse of abilities that God gave us— physical strength, for example—for other purposes. Man invented rape, not God. What's the purpose of this quiz?"

"Catechism. I wish to discover what you believe, and the basis on which you believe it."

"It's none of your business what I believe."

"People's beliefs affect their health. I wrote a paper on it. There is a physiochemical basis for thought, and this accounts for the way beliefs affect people's bodies. The Hindu fakirs, for instance, and their ability to walk over hot coals. Or the Christian sects who handle poisonous snakes in their rites. I narrowed this down to some tiny cellular clusters in the pineal gland. If I were a bolder scientist, I would have identified this as the seat of the soul."

"You're crazy."

"You doubt my results? I can show you the paper—"

"I don't need to see your paper. And if you don't mind, I'll be leaving now. You're a joke. How can you expect to heal someone without giving anything of yourself?"

"I seldom really heal anyone. I make my living by cutting things out."

Gilray felt a needle in his groin. Vance was taunting him, trying to get him to leave without having to reveal what he had found out. He sat back down. Vance waited. "Tell me the results," Gilray said.

"Urinalysis has shown the presence of cancerous papillomas, which are an indication of early bladder cancer."

Gilray stared at him. Vance's brown eyes were cool.

"In addition, during the physical examination I detected a lump on your testes. I'm afraid that suggests that the growth may have metastasized."

Gilray remembered sitting in Kinbote's office, waiting for him to scratch his back again. "What does that mean?"

"The cancer has spread from its original source to more than one area of the body. Here's what we can do: we'll get you into the hospital tonight and operate in the morning."

"Operate on what?"

"We'll have to remove whatever we can of the growths in the bladder and the testes, then start you on chemotherapy."

It was all too fast. "How much?"

"The expense should not be a consideration—"

"I mean—how much are you going to cut."

"As much as is necessary." Vance stopped. "I can't lie to you. The bladder cancer looks to be in the early stages. The testicular—well, is more advanced. We're going to have to—"

God was testing him. "Can't I get a second opinion?"

"Certainly. But time is wasting. If we're going to use conventional treatment, we need to get to this soon. 'If thy right hand offend thee, cut if off, for it is profitable for thee that one of thy members should perish, and not thy whole body.' "

"Be quiet!"

The doctor paused. "I hesitate to suggest this to a man of your convictions, but there is another, more radical possibility."

"What."

"Do you know anything about the Han process?"

"It is the method of reviving the dead." Sickness in his gut. This was some test. There are no accidents.

"Right. But its potential goes well beyond that. I've done research that suggests that the Han virus, if applied to cancer cases of this sort, can effect a complete cure." Vance leaned forward, clearly excited.

"Han himself spent his early years in cancer research. It was an accident that he discovered revival, and it's distracted researchers. The Han process, you see, is something like a viral cancer itself. It works by what we call 'transduction.' Han was trying to tailor viruses using genetic material from animals. What he came up with is a virus that carries information from the animal cell to another animal cell. The initial animal genes are incorporated into the chromosome of the infected cell by recombination."

They that are whole need not a physician, but they that are sick. He was sick. God knew it. Gilray forced himself to listen.

"In revival," Vance went on, "the recombinant virus is constructed from the genes of the clinically dead person, and this virus is injected back into the patient. Meanwhile we're flushing the body with enough chemicals to jump-start a Mack truck. If we're lucky and we've got a dead man whose cellular resistance to hypoxia is in the top ten percent of the population, the virus asserts itself over enough of the newly dead cells so that we get a return of function."

Mack truck. Return of function. Vance looked at a man and saw an automobile. Neatly cut beard, Jonathan Edwards, mocking him. Why was this happening? Saved at fifteen only to be exterminated at forty-eight? Shot full of chemicals and returned to life as a zombie? Vance's skin was perfectly smooth, his voice earnest as that of a TV chef describing the latest fad entree.

"In this new treatment, we use an analagous process on the cancer. We create a virus using genetic material from undamaged cells. We infect the patient, the kluge virus latches onto the cell receptors and counteracts the runaway DNA in the cancer cells. You're back to normal replication. Cut out the residual tumor and you're completely cured. There's only one problem."

Only one problem. There was a message here. If only Vance would shut up and let him think, he knew he could read it. "Yes?"

"The reason why I asked all those questions about your beliefs is this: for the Han cure to work, the patient has to be already dead. I'm afraid we'd have to kill you first. Or else we can go the conventional route and just cut your balls off."

The despair swept up from his soul. Gilray fought it. He wanted to run out of the office.

Vance watched him. "Have a little faith, Reverend. They tell me it's moved mountains. I'll leave you alone now so you can make your decision." He left the room so silently that Gilray was not sure he was gone.

It was a judgment on him. He had failed in some way—even before he had stepped into Vance's office he had known, at some level, what was at stake. Vance was the messenger. His voice was the voice of Satan, but like Satan he was doing the Lord's work. It was up to Gilray to accept that judgment. So why did he feel devastated? Why was he so afraid of losing that which was central to him? That was what death was for—to take away all you falsely valued, in order to give you back what was truly valuable. But it hurt. Gilray looked at the folder on the desk. He began to cry.

The door opened and someone came in. Still weeping, Gilray sat up in the chair. It was Vance again. The doctor stared at him with deep embarrassment. Bastard. He had probably enjoyed the whole interview; he'd enjoy the cutting and the bleeding, too. Gilray rubbed his eyes and met

the doctor's stare with one of his own. "What are you looking at?"

"Nothing," said Vance. He looked at the desk. "There it
is," he said with annoyance. He sat down, opened the
folder. "I'm sorry to have kept you waiting."

"I won't go through this revival farce," Gilray said. "I
know that's what you want. You think I'm a hypocrite.
Well, you can cut whatever you want off me and you won't
shake my faith."

Vance looked confused. "I can't imagine what you're
talking about."

"The Han method is out. I'd rather undergo the cancer
surgery."

The doctor raised an eyebrow. "That would be fine with
me if you had cancer. What you have, however, is a urinary
tract infection."

Gilray felt his heart beat like a quiet machine. He felt the
strangest combination of anger and hope.

"What was all that talk earlier? Did you want to see how
I would react? Unless you've got a pretty good explanation,
doctor, you're going to be hearing from my lawyers."

The mention of lawyers seemed to focus Vance's attention. "Reverend Gilray. You have a urinary tract infection
and a slightly inflamed prostate." He placed his hand, palm
down, on the folder. "Here are the test results, which I'll be
glad to go over with you once you stop talking about lawsuits. Now if someone in this clinic gave you the notion that
you have cancer, I would like to know who it was."

"You did. Not ten minutes ago, in this room."

"I've been with another patient until I walked through
that door. This is the first time I've spoken with you."

"Then who was it who was here before?"

"That's your problem."

11: MONDAY, JUNE 7

Richard risks Entrapment in the Filthy Jewel

A tired man in a video sandwich board paraded back and forth in front of the Daily News building in the rain. Water dripped from the brim of the man's shapeless fedora. TOP CARTOON STRIP OF THE TWENTIETH CENTURY, the board read, and then, TOP FEMSTAR OF THE TWENTIETH CENTURY, and then . . .

Top Humiliation of the Twentieth Century, Richard thought. Top Ludicrous Misjudgment of Character of the Twentieth Century.

By the time he had smelled smoke and broken through the bathroom door, the bed was in flames. He almost collapsed from the fumes but had the sense to crawl out of the room, hacking and wheezing, eyes full of tears. The firemen arrived as he stumbled out of the building.

A day later Richard's eyes still were not right; he had to blink rapidly to keep away tears. Some chemical in the smoke. He had not felt so humiliated since 1979. It was not so much that he had been fooled, but that he had let down his guard for so long. It showed that Lucy had gotten to him in some way that a woman had not gotten to him in years. Perhaps it was the gum.

He entered the building and crossed to the security desk. The big globe in the middle of the lobby needed care: dust covered the chipped surface of North America, and the blue

Pacific was dingy gray. The guard caught him looking at it. "The original isn't doing too hot, either," she said.

"You keep up with it more than I do." He rested his hands on the edge of the desk and leaned toward her. She had cropped her ash-colored hair, but her eyes were still the softest brown. "How are you, Sally?"

"Chipped and faded." She touched the switch that unlocked the elevator, and he rode it up to Abramowitz's office.

Abramowitz's style was imitation Vanderbilt—polished mahogany paneling, dark green plants, indirect lighting, Greek sculpture on Roman pedestals, tesselated black-and-white marble floor, Persian rug, female receptionist in conservative gray. The receptionist's name was Polly. She did not joke. "Good morning, Mr. Shrike."

After a minute the man himself came out. "Hello, Richard," he said, giving him that man-to-man stare.

Jason Abramowitz looked like an ex-wrestler. He wasn't six feet tall. Barrel chested, he had raised the firm handshake to an art, combining it with a manner so hearty you expected him to break into a lumberjack song at the least provocation. Despite the fact that Abramowitz half-believed the wildest stories HCR put out, he was the shrewdest man Richard had ever met. Abramowitz made a great show of being the paterfamilias; he never raised his voice, he never argued in public and seldom in private. But the mangled careers of those who had crossed him littered the corporate boardrooms. He had made the *Hemisphere Confidential Report* into the third-largest information service in North America, had brought trashnews on the telelink to the point where even religious smoothbrains like Jimmy-Don Gilray were taking HCR seriously. He was the major corporate sponsor of the last mayoral election, had friends in Singapore and Sao Paulo, and his favorite seafood was broiled piranha with lemon. And Richard was going to have to lie his way out of a jam with him.

But lying was not so hard once you realized that there was no truth. At seventeen Richard had grasped this, and the ensuing years had given him no cause to change his mind. When he was fourteen his father, a monetarist economist at the University of Chicago, capped off the spring term by drinking a can of drain cleaner. Richard's mother, a Keynesian who ascribed her husband's advocacy of a gold standard to penis envy, decided to do her mourning at the London School of Economics, where she secured an appointment for the fall term. Richard had never heard her speak about his father's death since.

Richard was crushed by the suicide. He had worshipped his father, and his self-destruction raised Richard's fatalism to a level of quiet hysteria. Richard's grandfather had also killed himself. No one seemed to notice the coincidence, but when the geneticists discovered what had been suspected by sociobiologists for years—that the propensity for suicide was inherited—Richard was not surprised. It did not bode well for his future. But the future was overrated.

Richard liked London. It was the late seventies. England was wracked by unemployment and unfocused social rebellion. Richard had studied classical piano since he was seven, and while still in public school, started a rock group. Very punk. They called themselves Six Million Jews. In honor of his father Richard adopted the name Gene Lethal. They played a lot of clubs in London and eventually got some following—including a wire service editor, ten years older than any of them, named George Eberhart—but they never got a record deal, mostly because the others thought that was incompatible with the music. If you were sincere you couldn't let yourself be swallowed by the Beast. Richard disagreed. His notion was that you should get inside the Beast and slice its guts up from within, slice and keep slicing until the thing collapsed, preferably destroying you with it. They fought, the group broke up and, four years late, Richard went to Cambridge.

At Cambridge he read philosophy. For fun he wrote imitation Peter Handke novels. At twenty-six he received his bachelor's degree. He paid a visit to his mother, who by this time had remarried (to an Austrian marxist who combed his hair carefully over his bald spot) and was living in Vienna. Richard spent a year kicking around Europe. The Crash caught him six months into his tenure as janitor of a sleazy *pension* in Milan. Clearly it was time for a change. Back to New York, where he rented a loft in Soho with a conceptual artist and a drug dealer while he tried to write another novel. The conceptual artist got AIDS, the drug dealer got busted, and the novel never got written, but Richard managed to get a job with Reuters, first as a copy editor, then as a news editor. That was when he met up with George again.

In the beginning, Richard had been suspicious of George. All that ex-hippie earnestness. But George had a sense of humor that could turn bitter, and eventually Richard recognized him as another person who did not care what happened to himself. Maybe he wasn't as ready to give the engines that were going to destroy them all a little push, but his suicidal tendencies were still well developed. He had the lethal gene.

Richard theorized that the gene had mutated in the eighteenth century, just about the time of the Industrial Revolution. Until then it had been a recessive. Now it was a dominant, associated with the genes for mechanical ingenuity. So as the world ascended the technological slope during the next two hundred years, self destruction became a growth industry. That was why there was coming to be a Seppuku Club next to the health spa in every shopping mall. That was why the human race was getting ready to off itself.

George would object. Suicide had been fashionable in certain cultures throughout history, he would point out. The Romans. The Japanese. Richard countered that the gene for suicide was probably Asian and had only spread widely in the West after the rise of colonialism. George said the current difficulties were simply signs of the latest round of premillennialism. Richard would turn up the music and draw George a diagram of the principles of Creative Nihilism. "Are you always going to be a conservative, George?

There's nothing left to conserve. Off yourself now; avoid the rush."

The advent of Lucy complicated the relationship, but like the third leg of a stool, provided stability. Lucy became Richard's rival for George's affections. It came as a surprise to Richard that he had affections for George. He would never admit it, and he might get annoyed at George's deliberate innocence (which amounted, in Richard's mind, to something close to hypocrisy), but he needed George.

Richard got hired away from Reuters when Abramowitz got the idea of putting HCR on the telelink. Richard hired George. At HCR Richard found his calling. When they lacked copy he invented stories, and his inventions turned out to be no more absurd than reality. He didn't care about the truth. The world was going to be destroyed soon. This was evident to even the stupidest of its inhabitants, who reacted with the erratic behavior that only brought the crash closer. Nothing could be done to stop it.

Richard knew that all action was useless, and this made it possible for him to act. It made anything possible. To go from Gene Lethal to Richard Shrike? From leather and studs to Brooks Brothers? From radical anarchism to radical conservatism? No problem. Naked opportunism? The Libertarian revolution?

Absolutely no problem. Richard loved free enterprise. People with clean hands and blue eyes and marvellous haircuts, people who believed with constipated intensity in the bottom line. How they labored to bring forth gnats. How much easier for Richard, who believed in nothing. There was a purity to Richard's vacuousness that made it more genuine than the media-drugged, THC gum-chewing masses' professions of faith in art, God or ideology. He was the Kant of cynicism, the Picasso of appearance. Nuke the Hawaiian separatists! Shroud of Turin Speaks! Brazilian Zombie Armies infect America with AMPS!

But sitting on the commode in Lucy's bathroom, he realized that something had gone awry. The stability he'd built with George and Lucy had broken. He was getting old. He remembered how it had felt to play, late at night in some East End club, he and Nick and Cotton and Stu on the risers in the corner of a smoky room, coked up, sweating, deafened by the noise. He would turn up the farfisa and lean on the keyboard, the music would scream through his too-clear brain, and he could see the whole world as if it were captured in a crystal ball, a filthy little jewel that he would smash to pieces with sound. He was Frankenstein's monster, abused and rejected, transfixed by one hundred thousand volts of electricity, spasming out rage through his fingertips.

So he had failed to save George. He was party to an illegal revival, which fact he had apparently let slip to a man from the Attorney General's office. He had tears in his eyes from the smoke of a fire set by a woman who had made a fool of him. He supposed he had been a fool back in London too, when the set was over and the lights came up. But that was twenty years ago, when he was connected to no one.

Abramowitz thought they were playing for high stakes; he didn't know that Richard had already lost everything. The amazing thing was that, against his intentions, Richard had ever accumulated anything worth losing. But he had an ace in the hole, if he needed it, a way out that would in the process set up the most intriguing version of the Game Richard had ever contrived. A brilliant pre-millennial challenge. He almost hoped Abramowitz would push him to it.

Abramowitz led him through the wireroom. The place was deserted; a couple of reporters from George's team were manning the datanet terminals and the copy desk was being run by Penny Stalkowitz from personals and burned-out Victor Dunn, who wrote the "Dr. Fate" advice column. Richard was surprised. "The operators went out!"

"If you'd been anywhere I could get hold of you last night you would know they went out," Abramowitz said. "We talked until five and got nowhere. Until we agree to cover Alzheimer's in the medical plan they're off the job. I said no way."

They reached his office. Abramowitz closed the door behind them. The walls were covered with mounted blowups of front pages from HCR's supermarket tabloid days: ZEN MYSTIC EXPLODES ON TV, PUPPY FROM HELL TERRORIZES FAMILY, SCIENTISTS PROVE ELVIS REINCARNATED AS PORPOISE. A large window showed the mist-shrouded upper stories of buildings across 42nd Street.

"They were willing to settle for medical coverage?" Richard said. "Jason, you should have signed. Cathode brainrot is pure hysteria—there's nothing to it. You wouldn't have to pay a single claim."

"How do we know there's nothing to it? Just because some doctor says so? The doctors said there was nothing to Computer AIDS, too."

"There wasn't, as far as people went. It was a software virus, it only affected information. Nobody gets Alzheimer's from working at a VDT."

"Spend some time with a twenty-year operator. Most can't tell the difference between shit and buttered toast."

Had Richard not been able to picture Abramowitz in an SS uniform, with little lightning bolts on his collar, he might have been flustered. Abramowitz took a copy of *Death* from his desk and waved it at Richard. "Have you seen this review of the election? It's by your friend Thompson." He assumed an effiminate lisp and read: " 'The recent HCR-sponsored mayoral race hits a new low. The candidates pranced through their tired paces with no sign of a definable context, their keepers as cheerful as an Indonesian Truth Squad marching clients to the furnace. If this keeps up we'll be praying for a return to public financing.' "

"He's a Green, Jason. You have to expect it."

The rain ran down the window behind Abramowitz. "The only 'definable context' Thompson knows about happens when he's on his hands and knees in a Turkish bath."

Richard smiled. "Critics are the price you pay for getting

taken seriously. Once the bourgeois intellectuals discovered HCR it was only a matter of time before the critics moved in. Thompson's as hooked as anyone. He spends his nights plugged into the screen."

"Yeah. But the horny kids were easier to please." Abramowitz sat on the corner of his desk. He seemed satisfied. "So, Richard. Where's George?"

"George is on the road."

Abramowitz tilted his head as if he were listening to some ticking from within the desk. "Isn't that going to interfere with his work? People like George. Levine doesn't suit the Baby Boomer image of itself. Friendly. Soulful. You know what I'm talking about, Richard?"

"Vaguely. But I think you shouldn't be short-sighted. George is only good because he's original. He's original because he can't be controlled."

"I'm not paying him to be out of control."

"He's not out of control. He's on a trip west. He took the 9:30 train to Philly Saturday. He's going to be bursting me stories by phone."

"What about this Gilray investigation? We're already running promos. Gilray walks Levine around the park Saturday without even giving him a kiss. Then I find out somebody failed to get a release."

"That was Stan's responsibility."

"Yes. Well, Stan is going to be taking a little sabbatical. And I want George back here."

"You've got to realize, Jason, that George is like the goose that lays the golden egg. You can't go poking into his guts too much or he's useless."

"I'm not going to poke him. But he's under contract, he's out of the hospital for a month now, I don't know what he's been doing in all this time, I don't know when we're going to get him back, we've lost six rating points and now I don't even know where the guy is? This is not the way we do business. So first, I want you to tell me where he's going. Then I want to know why. And I want to know how you're keeping tabs on him. I assume you know better than to let him go without keeping tabs on him."

"Of course. George has a gasohol card that I got for him. I can follow him using that."

"You said he took the train."

"He also has a secret credit account that he thinks is secure. It isn't. I can have it voided in an instant, but I'd rather use it to keep track of him. I know George. I have a hunch he's going to come up with something that will be big news, and I don't want to spoil it by busting in on him before he's gotten anywhere. Look, did you think he'd catch on like he did? Of course not. You tried him because you trusted me."

"Actually, I don't trust you."

"Right. But I know how to sell news. So we'll keep track of George, and if the stuff he sends is no good we cut him off, send out a man and pick him up. Or don't pick him up, for that matter. It's that simple. We let the situation ride for awhile. But you have to take a chance sometimes."

Abramowitz considered it. The silent bomb he heard in his desk seemed to absorb all his concentration. He closed his eyes, and a thin line of white showed between his not-quite-shut lids, instantly negating his look of rude health. It made him look like a drowned man. He opened them again. "Okay," he said. "You give me the account code. And I want a detective on his trail."

"I already have someone in mind."

"Good. So what's George after, Richard?"

This was it. Time for some really creative nihilism. "It's come out of the millennialism series. He's got evidence that the increased UFO reports, the revival clinic bombings—maybe even the plagues—are being done by religious zombies, people who have been taken possession of by spirits while going through charismatic church services. George suspects Gilray is behind this."

"Possessions?"

"I don't know what George's evidence is. Gilray could be using some new drug on them. George's notes show he was looking into instances of religious violence. But this has big political overtones."

Abramowitz wanted to be sucked in, Richard could see it.

But he resisted. Despite himself, Richard began to sweat. "How long are we supposed to wait for him?" Abramowitz said. "When we don't even know exactly what he has and where he's going? And what am I going to do about this Gilray situation in the meantime?"

Richard could see Abramowitz in the jewel. George was in there too. He might have to smash it. "How much time do you think we can give him?"

"Two months, tops. And if it doesn't look like anything is happening within one, I am going to have to cut my losses."

It was time for Richard to play his ace. "It won't come to that, Jason. I'm going to get to Gilray myself."

"He's not going to let us interview him after that session with Levine."

"I don't mean interview. I'm going to go to work for him."

Abramowitz stared. His eyes narrowed.

"I can do this, Jason. He's gearing up for the end of the world. He wants to reach the maximum number of viewers. He's got UFO connections and the trashnews fascinates him. It's a perfect setup. Here's what we do: you put it out that you've fired me because of the botched interview. You're furious. I'll go to him. I'm a convert, I'll say. I'll worm my way in. Meanwhile, George is bursting stories to me by way of my private telecode. I process them, add my own stuff, and send it on to HCR. The Rev doesn't know a thing about it."

"How will you persuade him?"

"He needs me more than he needs an interview. He's a religious fanatic. He'll want to believe."

Abramowitz looked at Richard with an expression that might have been respect or revulsion. "Why not just have a detective find George and bring him back?"

"No. We have him followed, but we don't want him back. We want his stories."

"What about his health, Richard? I thought you were friends."

"I'm not his keeper, Jason. He'll take care of himself."

Richard listened to his own voice. How coolly he betrayed his best friend! He had smashed it all to bits, now. For what? He had no clue how he was going to persuade Gilray to trust him. He had no reason to let George go. The whole thing was a beautiful, glittering absurdity.

And Abramowitz was buying it. "Nobody's got a guarantee," the publisher said. "Sometimes I don't feel so well myself."

"Me, I feel fine," said Richard.

They made some further arrangements. Richard left. Riding down the elevator, he wondered what Abramowitz thought of him. Did he have contempt for the easy way Richard sacrificed George to save his skin? Or did he admire Richard's ruthlessness? It was an interesting ethical problem, one that, in his school days, Richard might have subjected to mathematical analysis. The elevator opened onto the lobby. The faded globe greeted him. Sally watched him cross to the revolving doors. It was still raining. He paused, watching the man with the videoboard: LATEST SURVEY OF U.S. RELIGIOUS BELIEFS.

Abramowitz might think better of Richard if he knew that George wanted to die. That frantic afternoon in April, while Lucy bribed the emergency squad and Richard called Dr. Evans from George's study to arrange the revival, Richard had found a vial under George's desk. It was an empty bottle of barbiturates; George must have taken them all. He'd actually done what they'd always talked about. Richard had not suspected a thing. He felt genuine surprise. And envy.

But to introduce George's death wish and Richard's envy into the equation would complicate the ethical mathematics, perhaps beyond solution. SEVENTY PERCENT OF AMERICANS SAY JUDGMENT AT HAND. Richard supposed that meant that he didn't have to solve the equation. He turned his collar up against the rain and pushed out past the man into the street.

12: MONDAY, JUNE 7

....

George meets an American

George took the train west from Philadelphia to Columbus.
He got off, shouldered his bag and walked to the Grey-
hound station, where he bought a ticket for Louisville. It
was drizzling. *Thirteenth Straight Day of Rain!* the Columbus paper shouted. A new storm system blanketed the
Northeast and some guy in Athens was building an ark.

George could have stayed on the train until Indianapolis,
but he had the hunch that he would have a better chance to
pick up the trail in Louisville. He had found two news items
that were potential contacts in Lexington, none in Indianapolis; that meant the Alien was in the middle of one of
his traversals, starting in Atlanta and heading north. His
next stops were probably Indianapolis and Lansing.

While George waited in the station, a USTS semi pulled
in. The driver yelled something through the vent door behind the cab while the crew chief hopped down and went
back to unlock the rear doors. Out stumbled twenty or
thirty workies in army drab, fresh in from Dayton, Cincin-
nati or Cleveland, about to be reassigned within the East
Central Economic District. They huddled under the eaves of
the station while the work officer went over the roster with
the crew chief. Then the officer mustered the men and
women on the sidewalk and they shuffled off downtown
through the rain.

George might have rented a car, but the contretemps on
the train from New York to Philly had convinced him he

needed to get a feel for how things were going in the heart-land. He had been thinking in a vacuum. His ideas about HCR viewers were mostly speculation. How could he save people from the destruction sown by the Alien unless he knew what moved them? Did they prefer cheese sandwiches to noodle cups? If the world were to end tomorrow, would they have any regrets? Late at night, in deserted parking garages, how many of them heard voices?

He had more than an hour until the bus left. He needed to counteract the zombie problem. He stowed his bag and the microcam in a coin locker and went looking for a barber shop. A block from the station he found "Hair Today." For a redbuck the stylist gave him a monoxydyl massage; for another ten George bought a toupee. He still looked pretty unlikely, but he didn't look dead. After that he went to a bank terminal and withdrew another fifty from Mr. Midas. Back at the bus station snack bar he had a cup of coffee, some fried tofu and a stale Danish. He ate at a formica standing table sticky with coffee rings. The station was busier than he would have expected in a time when few could afford to travel unless the government was sending them.

Still twenty minutes to go. He wandered over to the main entrance. The drizzle had become a downpour. People dashed out of cabs, dragging baggage behind them, jackets pulled up over their heads. The wind blew gusts of rain in under the overhang so that even the porters stayed inside the entrance, smoking cigarettes. The only person left out there was a man dressed in a navy blue swallowtail coat over red and white striped trousers that were too long for him. Their soggy cuffs lay bunched around his ankles. He wore a top hat painted like an American flag. With his white beard and hawk nose he looked like a run-down Uncle Sam. He sold pocket calculators from a plastic tray slung around his neck. He had no takers, but he stood there still as a thought, staring through the rain that bled his sign: "Gen-uine American Calculators, Five Old-Style Dollars." The man looked so miserable that, on impulse, George went outside. George went over and put a redbuck into his cup. "Keep the change," he said.

"Don't you have some real currency?" the man asked.

"This is real."

"Depends on your definition," the man grumbled. He picked through his merchandise until he found a choice one for George. He had a voice like a photograph of Abraham Lincoln—hard, bony, with a hint of wit. "My merchandise is of the best. Genuine product of the United States of America. Not clever forgeries."

Nothing at all about the calculator was clever. Credit-card sized, six functions; probably manufactured by some prison factory in Pikeville or Paducah, you could buy ten of them out of a catalog for a dollar. "Hard for an amateur to tell," George said.

The man peered at him from beneath the dripping brim of his hat. "You can tell. Quality speaks for itself."

"I wish I were as sure."

"I know values," the man said. "I used to be a literary theorist."

George didn't say anything. Uncle Sam tried to give him change, but when George refused he did not insist. George slipped the calculator into his pocket. "Why don't you come in out of the rain?" he said.

"I taught at Chicago," the man said.

The rain was flying into George's face. He squinted; water collected on the tips of his eyelashes. "What happened?"

The man looked George over. His china blue eyes had a psychotic intensity. "I figured out the truth about texts. The truth was that there was no truth."

"Texts?"

"You know—language. Social structures. Flower arrangements. Everything. The whole world was a text."

"I thought that sort of thinking was out of style."

"Style! Exactly. Look, you go into a diner and order a hot dog, usually you get a hot dog. But sometimes you'll get a polish sausage dog. Or you'll get a hot dog with sauerkraut and you didn't want sauerkraut. But the waitress thought when you said 'hot dog' you meant a kraut dog—that's what everybody else wants when they say 'hot dog.' It's no use your getting pissed off. You're lucky you didn't get a custard pie."

"They're not going to give you a custard pie if you order a hot dog."

"How do you know? Do the words 'custard pie' have anything in them that signifies that they should refer to the object we commonly associate with them, when they could arbitrarily refer to the object we commonly call a 'hot dog?' Of course they don't." The man snorted. "Forget Chomsky. That's what I told them."

George imagined the man at thirty, at a lectern, exposing each of his students in turn to a withering trendiness. He wore a leather jacket and an earring. In the front row sat a girl with orange hair and fishnet stockings. "Forget Chomsky," she wrote in her notebook.

"Who's Chomsky?" George asked.

"Exactly. The word is insufficiently specified. Ask any politician. What does 'triple economy' mean? Or 'your tenure rights are suspended'?"

George was cold. "So what happened?"

The man looked at George as if he had just spoken in Turkish. After a moment he seemed to remember what he was about. "I had a powerful tool. I could strip away all pretense. First I showed how the canons of literary criticism were full of assumptions whose validity could not be established. I gave papers on the topic. I began to write a book."

"That must have been good for your career."

"I never finished. Before I got past chapter four I realized I would have to rewrite the whole thing. I was guilty of latent logocentrism. An unexamined mode of discourse. Then I realized that my method left me with nothing to stand on. There was nothing I could say that I could be sure of. Everything was a text. What was the rock that sat by the side of my front steps but a text? What were the wind, the air, my wife? All texts. The problem was how to interpret them, and I had realized that interpretation is dependent on the code. All relative."

"That must have been disturbing."

"Not necessarily. I decided that it merely meant that I was constructing plausible fictions, and that these fictions were as true as anything else. Joyce came home one day and she had changed her hairstyle. You remember those bouffant jobs? Teased up like a rat's nest. I couldn't figure out what she was up to."

"Did you ask her?"

"She said she just felt like getting in style. Well, what was I to make of that? What did she mean by 'style'? What did she mean by 'felt'? She spent more time in the bathroom. How was I supposed to read that?"

"A good question."

"It all depended on the context. I got very interested in contexts. Read history: historians are no different than literary critics. All sorts of assumptions, resulting from and revealed in the language they use. History is written by the winners; the truth they assert is simply a device to show that their own position is justified. The idea of an impartial search for historical truth is merely a device used to justify the economic and cultural biases of the historian. Racism, sexism—the traffic laws!"

"Traffic laws?"

"I took them apart like an Indonesian watch. By then I had started on my Marxist phase. Tell me—who creates the traffic laws?"

"I—"

"The automobile driving class structure! They say an impartial study of traffic patterns proves that efficiency will be increased seventeen percent if we pass a right-turn-on-red law. Transparent! Just ask yourself who benefits from right turns on red, and it all comes apart in your hands. Didn't I expose their self-serving justifications! I started driving on the left side of the road. It was too much for them. Their fascist goon squads brought me in—more than once! I explained it to the prosecutor. Did he listen? Language is a club the powerful use to beat the powerless. The most charitable thing I can say about the State is that it is too caught up in its mode of discourse."

Something extraordinary had happened to this man. George's meeting him was no accident. "Have you ever had an encounter with an unusual stranger?" George asked.

Uncle Sam ignored him. "The State couldn't allow me to challenge their self-interest."

"Someone who looked normal, but challenged your idea of reality?"

"They put me out of the universe of discourse."

"Familiar, but threateningly different?"

The man tilted his head toward George. Water dribbled off the brim of the top hat. "They took away my license."

"Aliens took your license?"

"What aliens? The State!"

"Kentucky?"

"Where?"

"Here!" George indicated the bus station, the rain-slick street.

"I had them!" The man jerked back; his top hat wobbled. "I could penetrate their hypocrisies! They would tell me that my analysis was wrong, and I would show with mathematical logic how their impartiality was a sham used to buttress their class interests. I order a hot dog, and they give me a custard pie! So I threw it back in their faces."

"I don't doubt it."

"Doubt everything!"

George was staggered by his vehemence. Uncle Sam lowered his voice. "Everything not American, anyway."

"American?"

"That's when I realized it. I was in service to a foreign ideology. A true Marxist would be the truest of Americans. What, after all, could be more American than to question all assumptions? What was America but the blank slate on which mankind—and womankind—I was no sexist, sir!— had written its texts? Who was I but yet another contributor to the greatest text of all, America? Not a critic—an artist!"

George would have to let him tell his story in his own way. "What did your wife have to say about this?"

"That bitch? Dumber than a ball peen hammer! Completely under the sway of the texts she had learned at her scheming mother's knee! I had lost her way back at structuralism. She was sleeping with the department chair. I bet he inscribed a few new legends on her slate!" The man cackled.

"What happened then?"

"Didn't I have them buffaloed! Didn't I twist their smarmy little texts around their own necks!" He smiled so broadly that he looked to be in pain; drops of water ran down his gaunt cheeks. "The curriculum committee was at a loss. The chair couldn't move a piece of business past us without me having my way with it—all in the service of America, mind you! Not a bit of ego was involved! Then came the Crash. Tenure was no defense. Oh, they had learned. They rewrote the text. So impartial! Circumstances beyond their control. A new mode of discourse. Economic crisis! Temporarily straightened circumstances! Lighten the load! Words! Words are whores. They spread their legs for the fascist power brokers. Before I knew it I was out on my ear. You know how I fought them, you know what I showed them to be."

The man seemed to calm down. "I'm better off here," he said. "And my merchandise is of the best—I can validate it! Try one."

George was moved. The cold had numbed his hands. He imagined the old man standing out here into the night, then going back to sleep in the cashier's booth of some deserted self-service gas station. On the wall would hang a smudged poster for Michelin radials and a certificate from the Modern Language Association. Aliens would watch him from the yawning garage bay. They would beam microwaves into his skull. Forget Chomsky.

"You look vaguely familiar, sir. An American, are you?"

"Born and bred." George fumbled in his pocket and pulled out another redbuck. "I'll take one," he said.

The man picked through the calculators until he found one to his liking. "There you are. You hold onto this. It will come in handy some day. Hermeneutically speaking."

"Right." George slipped the calculator into his pocket

with the first one and backed away. He bumped into some-one—a woman towing a surly two-year-old. She scowled at him and pushed into the terminal.

George had to get away. He couldn't save Uncle Sam. He hurried back inside, following the woman. One of the porters smiled at him as he walked by. "Ain't he a pistol?"

George shoved the second calculator at the porter. "Give this back to him," he said. "Tell him you found it on the sidewalk." He looked back over his shoulder as he headed for the gate. Uncle Sam stood out in the rain, his face stony, his eyes flicking back and forth as if trying to anticipate the next attack.

13: THURSDAY, JUNE 10

Lucy gets Arrested

"Come the New Age, won't be many lawyers left," Luz said.

"I'll say," the short woman wearing the gauze mask muttered. "Keep stirring that gel," she said to Lucy. "Don't let the temperature get above sixty-five or below sixty."

Lucy stirred. The thermometer that hung over the side of the beaker read 61° C. She nudged the knob of the Coleman stove up a bit. The concoction stank. In four days she had gone from cooking for her husband to cooking for a couple of women she had never seen before. But she wasn't exactly cooking, and the feeling was entirely different.

The woman from the Tropic was named Luz. She had refused Lucy's offer of money, would not bargain. She had listened to Lucy, then made her come back to the women's room in the diner. There she had grabbed Lucy's wrists, pushed up her sleeves and examined her arms. Luz had very strong hands. The veins on their backs stood out in blue relief against chocolate skin. She inspected Lucy's eyes like a vet examining a sick cat. "No more drugs," she said, and took her home.

The woman with the gauze mask was Concepcion. She and Luz lived in a railroad apartment on East 128th Street. A computer, its plastic monitor sprayed bright green, was hooked into the phone line. They had no gas and the water that came out of the kitchen tap was orange, but the electricity worked and the place was clean. They didn't use the tapwater anyway; one of Lucy's jobs had been to carry up bottles of water from a case that had appeared in the alley. Luz kidded Lucy when she collapsed onto the broken-backed sofa after the fifth trip. "Best be maybe you go home, now."

"I can't."

"You left a body in the kitchen?"

"In the bathroom."

"Let me guess—husband in the bathroom, and you burn the house down."

"My husband ran away."

"Good riddance. So who's in the bathroom?"

"My husband's best friend."

"Explains everything."

Luz took Lucy's cash and her credit cards. "Got the Mark of the Beast on them," Concepcion told her soberly. "We'll pray them clean, trade them off. A woman can't carry that trash into the New Age."

They cut Lucy's hair short and took her picture. On Sunday night Luz worked at the computer while Concepcion went out. She came back and gave Lucy an I.D. card. Her new name was Hester Palenque. They told her she could earn her new identity by working. Lucy didn't ask any questions and they offered no answers. Aside from a few simple chores they let her do what she liked as long as she stayed out of the room behind the metal door at the back of the apartment. The door had a rubber seal around the jamb. Lucy felt uneasy. She ought to leave. She looked out the windows, walked around the apartment and tried to come up with another option. Silk-screened posters covered cracks in the walls. Brightly colored, they bore simple figures of beasts and people above nursery rhyme slogans that were both familiar and disquieting:

> Whales in the Sea
> God's voice Obey.

and

> Xerxes the Great did Die
> And So must You and I.

Lucy slept on the sofa; for a pillow she used a stack of old magazines, *Science* and *ChemE News* and *Biotechnology Newswatch*. On Monday morning they gave her some bib overalls and a T-shirt printed with the slogan, "Fish Cannot Carry Guns." They took her coat and clothes away and came back in an hour with a box of bottles and white plastic containers. They gave Lucy an old hundred-dollar bill. "'Cep got over a thousand old style for your coat," Luz said. It had cost Lucy two thousand, and that was three years ago.

Luz and Concepcion spent most of their time in the back room with the door shut. They came out only long enough to eat, use the computer, or run out to various pay phones to make calls. They gave Lucy the job of preparing agarose gel on the LPG stove they used in place of the useless Tappan in the kitchen. Lucy would add what they told her was an ampicillin solution to the gel, then transfer it to sterile test tubes.

The apartment grew stifling during the day, and despite the rain Lucy opened the windows. Whenever the door to the back room opened, air from the rest of the apartment would be sucked in. Luz or Concepcion, wearing dirty aprons like short-order cooks, would take a rack of tubes from Lucy and retreat behind the metal door.

Monday's *Daily News* had an article about the apartment fire: six people had been treated for smoke inhalation and Lucy was being sought for questioning. Nothing about George's revival. That night she lay awake wondering what to do. It was hot; Lucy wore only the T-shirt and panties yet still she was sticky with sweat. She had been embarrassed by her expensive underwear, half expecting them to take those from her, too. Through the street windows she heard kids talking, rattle music, the whine of a bus on Lennox Avenue, a man and woman arguing in the apartment on the other side of the top floor.

Luz and Concepcion were bootlegging microbes. The Pandora's box had been opened when biotech was deregulated in the mid-nineties in the effort to shrink the balance of trade deficit. Once the recombinant genie got out of the bottle no crackdown had been able to put it back. Anybody with a couple thousand dollars and a library card could set up a lab in his bathroom. Profits were high. So were risks.

If they were busted for bug cooking, the revival charge Lucy had fled would seem like jaywalking. The only sane thing for Lucy to do was to leave, and not look back.

On the other hand, since she had torched the apartment and fled, Lucy had felt a freedom she had never experienced before. She was a different person. A woman could walk out of her personality as easily as Lucy had walked out of her apartment. For the first time in her life she felt the exhilaration that came from breaking the rules, and she could see that it could become as addictive as any drug. The prison inmates must feel that. The psychotic must feel that. Anything was possible, because nothing was determined.

Yet her impression of Luz and Concepcion was not of two sociopaths. The very way they moved indicated the assurance of women who knew what they wanted, knew they could get it through their own efforts, and were working rationally toward a goal. What goal? That was not clear, but Lucy was convinced that if she hung around long enough they would tell her. She felt the pull of that goal, whatever it might be. Why not wait and find out? She fell asleep staring, in the dim light from the street, at an orange-and-red poster of a little bearded man in a robe being clubbed by a big bearded man. Below was the slogan,

> Job Feels the Rod
> Yet blesses God.

She was awakened Tuesday morning by some kid on the street practicing martial arts yells with bloodcurdling conviction. She stretched some of the knots out of her back. The smell of frying soyabulk drifted in from the kitchen. Concepcion peeked through the door. "Time to eat."

Lucy rubbed the circulation back into her leg and pulled on the overalls. She was ravenous. There were two plates on the kitchen table. "Where's Luz?" she asked.

Concepcion poured them water from a plastic jug. "She'll be back soon. She told me you really are a lawyer."

Lucy couldn't place the tone in Concepcion's voice. "I am."

"What kind?"

"I defend the Department of Corrections against civil lawsuits brought by inmates."

"You protect jailers?"

"I did."

Concepcion chewed her soycake. "How can you stand it?"

"It's the law."

"Laws made by men. Made for men."

"Unless women get involved they'll always be made by men."

"Only way women get to make laws is if they think like men. Left-brain. What about the right brain? The music side?"

"Very mystical. Are we going to exchange mantras now?"

Concepcion smiled. "Not mysticism. Biology."

Lucy sipped the room-temperature water. The martial

arts kid had moved down the block, still yelling. "Why did you let me come here?"

"I didn't. It was Luz's idea."

"If you get caught I can't help you. I'm in trouble already."

Concepcion's gaze followed Lucy's hand; Lucy realized she was looking at her wedding band. The dark woman's eyes flicked upward to lock on Lucy's own. "The world is not well arranged," she said.

"Terrorist diseases aren't going to fix it."

"I'm not a terrorist. I'm a microbiologist. Getting ready for the New Age."

"The New Age. Sure. Which New Age are we talking about?"

"Better living through biology. I've a virus back there—" she pointed at the gray metal door, "that could make people grow fur like rabbits. I'm thinking about one that lets you eat tree bark. And I'm maybe making one that'll scramble men's brains up like blood pudding."

"Men's brains are already scrambled." Lucy thought about George. "You make me one to unscramble them and I might buy it."

"I'll make it for free," said Concepcion.

Concepcion's calm scared Lucy. "This is crazy, Concepcion. There's no New Age coming—just jail, if you keep it up. You're just breaking things down faster."

Luz came in through the hall door. "That's the point," she said. She set her canvas bag on the counter, turned a kitchen chair around and straddled it. "Been talking politics, Concepcion?"

"No talk that ain't politics."

"We got a customer. Thursday at three."

Concepcion picked up the dishes and took them to the sink. "Where?"

"The hospital."

Lucy stared across at Luz. "I've got to go now," she said.

"The door is over there."

Lucy didn't get up. "Why did you bring me here?"

Concepcion turned to them as if she was interested in the

answer. Luz crossed her arms on the back of the chair. "You asked for help. I want to help."

"I'll bet."

"World's going up in flames, if I see a woman looks like tinder, I help."

"Some help. This is a bug house."

"Mercy! Hear that, 'Cep?"

"Chilling."

"What gives you the right? If everyone follows their own ideas of right and wrong you get chaos—look around you."

"You're in an untenable position to act holy, Lucy. Jail's waiting for you, too."

Lucy felt hot. "I broke the law to save my husband. I'm not proud about it."

For the first time Luz looked angry. She slammed the back of the chair against the table, spilling Lucy's water. "Proud! You're full of pride! You look around *you*! Law only works when it's fair. Is it fair now? You don't want to die like a dog on the street you're going to have to get straight. Men been bringing it on for six thousand years, but their time is *up*! Woman's time coming now; the train is leaving, 'Cep and me we're giving you a help up on board and you're fretting about the ethics." She waved her broad palm at Lucy, a gesture of disgust. "You been a lawyer too long."

"What's wrong with ethics?"

"Ethics is for people with full bellies."

"If people really cared nobody would go hungry. That's what ethics is."

"True," said Concepcion.

"Right," Luz said. "But people got to change. In their hearts—"

"—In their heads," Concepcion said.

"We been heading for the Big War some time now," Luz continued. "It gets to be full-time work to ignore it, but most people got no other work. We're gonna wake them up."

"You're making illegal microbes. How's that going to help?"

"People got to see the old politics don't work no more. Need to have a total breakdown before the Millennium."

"That's pure fantasy, Luz. You sound like Jimmy-Don Gilray."

Concepcion laughed. "Gilray's talking the Old Age. The Very Old Age. But you got the idea."

"I told you she was smart," Luz said. "One world, Lucy. And the only thing's gonna bring the people together is when their problems get too big to handle by themselves. Men been heading us that way already; we give them a push. We sell them bugs that do more than they expect. White man, for instance, gonna have trouble keeping the Black man down when tomorrow he could turn black himself. So—Acquired Melanin Production."

"You started AMPS?"

"We help it along," Concepcion said.

"That's Step One. Step Two is organization, ideas, education. We're ready with organization to help pick up the pieces."

"Don't be ludicrous. You can't take over the world."

Luz grimaced. "That's a male idea. We put out the information, organize the neighborhoods. Everybody lives in a neighborhood. Whole world's made of neighborhoods. When the top comes tumbling down, the bottom's got to be ready to build the New Age."

"It's more likely to top is going to take the bottom down with it."

"Maybe. Could be the Big War wipes us all out. We're walking the knife edge. Could be maybe the whole human world smashes like Babylon. But it's a pretty good bet it comes down anyway if we don't act."

Two women in Harlem talking about saving the world. With plague germs. It would make a great HCR story. "What do you want from me?"

"Nothing. We give you a place to live. Maybe you listen to us. If you think after awhile we're not crazy, maybe you help us. You tell us what you think. Whether you sign up or not, you maybe get busted and sent to prison."

"Get raped by one of your prison guards," Concepcion said.

Lucy looked at both of them. "I'll think about it."

"Sure." Luz got out of the chair. "Meanwhile we got to fix a package."

Luz and Concepcion retreated to their lab for the rest of the day. At night, after they'd eaten, they sat with Lucy and took up the conversation again. Talking seemed to be their main form of entertainment. Lucy liked that. She told them about growing up Italian in Tenafly, about law school, about George. Concepcion described how she'd gotten kicked out of graduate biology at Berkeley. Luz told a dozen scary, funny, angry stories about staying alive in Jamaica, Haiti, and Ft. Lauderdale. "Ft. Lauderdale," she said, "was the worst."

That night, after they had gone to bed, Lucy had a nightmare. She was back at Rutgers, walking home at night from the library to her dorm. There was a rapist loose on campus, and she had stayed too late. How could she have been so stupid! It was well after midnight, midwinter: heaps of snow lined the footpaths and the campus was deserted. Lucy became lost in a maze of sidewalks. She was freezing. In desperation she walked faster, took turn after turn. She heard steps behind her, but when she stopped there was nothing.

Just when she thought she would never find it, she saw the dorm ahead. A man awaited her in front. He stood at the edge of the circle of light thrown by a streetlight; a tall man wearing a slouch hat and a pea jacket. He looked familiar. Lucy's heart raced. With the inexplicable certainty of dream knowledge, she knew she would be all right if she didn't look him in the face. Everything depended on her acting as if she wasn't afraid. The thought made her terror unbearable. Her boots squeaked on the crusted snow. Her breath clouded the air. He waited. She tried not to look, but she could not help herself. As she came within an arm's length, she peeked at his face. Beneath the shadow of his hat, she saw a face carved out of ice. His frozen eyes glittered.

She hurried toward the door. He stepped forward and seized her arms.

"No!" she said. "I'm not afraid!"

His grip was cold. "You are. You looked. You saw me."

"I didn't!" Lucy struggled, crying for help, not wanting to look again. He grabbed her jaw—his hand of ice burned her cheeks—and made her face him. It was George.

"Lucy," he said. "Lucy, I'm cold."

She awoke, panting. Luz crouched beside her. "It's all right," she said. "It's all right." She lay her hands on Lucy's shoulders. "It was just a nightmare."

Lucy trembled; she propped herself on one elbow. She could not speak. Luz pushed the hair away from Lucy's sweaty brow. She gave her a glass of water.

Lucy drank. Her dream faded. "Thanks," she said. The room was quiet. "I'm sorry."

Luz sat on the edge of the table. Her dark skin glistened in the light from the street. Lucy noticed for the first time how tired Luz's face looked.

"This must be hard for you," Luz said.

"It can't be easy for you, either. This life."

"I'm used to it."

Lucy understood something then. "You're afraid, too."

Luz's mouth broadened into a grin. "You're not supposed to see that."

"It's not so hard to see."

"Not many bother to look. Let it be our secret, then, us three. The League of Frightened Women."

Luz leaned forward, kissed Lucy on the forehead, and left.

Thursday morning it stopped raining for the first time in weeks. Lucy went downstairs and sat on the front stoop. She had still not come to any decision. The sky above the street was gray; bits of trash and oily scum floated in the gutters. Barrels blocked either end of the street, making it into a kind of communal living room. Lots of people were out on the stoops.

The old man living in the basement came up to talk with

her. "Louis Akal," he said. "Let me guess your name. Your name is—"

"Hester Palenque."

Louis Akal had greasy gray dreadlocks and wrinkled lips. He acted as if he knew all about her staying with Luz and Concepcion. She was probably not the first to pass through their world; she wondered what had happened to the others. She asked him what the slogan on her T-shirt stood for.

"It's a secret," he said.

"Tell me," said Lucy.

"Fish have no hands," he said.

"That's true," said Lucy. She liked his cracked earnestness.

Three girls walked by, wearing kosodes decorated with views of Sugar Loaf and Rio's Guanabara Bay. One of them nodded to Lucy.

"The fish stands for Jesus," Louis said.

"But Jesus had hands."

"Yes."

They chatted. As the morning warmed toward noon the clouds broke and the sodden street steamed in the sun. After awhile Louis Akal hobbled back into his stairwell and returned with a picture of the promised land he was painting on a piece of masonite. Tiny black, yellow and white figures soared above a landscape of green fields, jagged mountains and gleaming, futuristic cities. Lucy asked him questions and Louis explained how God had taught him to paint. By noon Lucy realized that she liked being Hester Palenque. She felt happier than she had in months.

She went back up to the apartment. To her surprise Lucy found Concepcion and Luz sitting in the front room. On the table between them were a half-full bottle of wine, two glasses, and a credit-card sized calculator.

"I'd like to stay—for now," Lucy said.

Luz wove her knotty hands behind her head, her elbows spreading out like wings. She smiled. "Another lawless woman."

"Are you prepared to change the world?" Concepcion asked.

"I think so."

"You ready to destroy it?" Luz asked. "Destroy yourself, too?"

"I'm already destroyed."

"No you're not. Not yet." Luz picked up the calculator. "Got a virus in here. No threat unless you swallow it. We're gonna sell it to a man later today thinks it'll turn his cells into little endorphin factories. Thinks he's gonna get naturally high any time he likes."

Concepcion laughed.

"What is it really?" Lucy asked.

"You want to know?"

"Tell me."

Luz put the calculator down on the table. "It's the end of the Male World. The latest, the best. The end of philosophers and economists and scientists—"

"—Marxists and Capitalists—" said Concepcion.

"—Platonists and Existentialists—" Luz said.

"—and lawyers," said Concepcion, pointing at Lucy.

"—and microbiologists," said Luz, pointing at Concepcion. They laughed.

Lucy laughed too, nervously. "You'll kill all the men?"

"Don't need to kill a man if you can change his mind." Luz said. "We're gonna change men's minds."

Lucy sat down.

"Problem with revolutions in the past was too much theory, not enough soul," Luz continued. "All the revolutionaries were full of principles. Abstraction instead of reality. Hard ideas that turn into swords—"

"The letter killeth, the spirit giveth life," said Concepcion.

"—and pretty soon somebody's getting beheaded. You know how hard it is to talk to a real male. But if you alter the brain chemistry—different story. Make the logical one creative. The male one female."

"Men aren't all bad," said Lucy.

"Sure," Luz said. "I knew a man once who was kind but not patronizing."

Lucy felt a pang. "So did I," she said. "I don't want them all dead."

"We're not killing anybody."

"Oh," said Lucy. "You won't kill them. You'll just change them into women."

"Don't be so literal minded, girl."

"It'll work on women, too," Concepcion said. "Depends on their testosterone levels. Changes the left-brain, right-brain balance. Hard to tell how much. Ain't tested on humans."

"Isn't this kind of risky?"

"People dying every day," Luz said. "Desperate circumstances."

Lucy picked up the calculator. It felt perfectly normal: cheap plastic, six functions. She tried to imagine so much change, in so small a package. She knew she ought to be repulsed, but a thrill ran through her. To have power, and to use it. "You're going to give this to somebody who doesn't know what it is?"

"Yes. A surprise."

The end of the male world. Lucy punched a few keys on the calculator, and the numbers showed up in the LCD window. She looked up. "Why are you trusting me?" she asked. "I could be a narc."

"You want the truth?" Luz said. "Because we got the same name. Real logical, huh?"

Uncertain, Lucy put down the calculator.

At two o'clock they left the building. The sun had turned the streets into a sauna. They walked up Lenox Avenue past the gutted Goodfrey Nurse and Harlem houses. On one of the cross streets west of Harlem Hospital they stopped at a deserted tenement. Concepcion stood lookout in the street while Luz and Lucy entered. A pile of rags rotted on the black and white tile of the vestibule; wallpaper peeled from the hallway. Luz slipped in through a wedged-open door and they moved to the back bedroom of a deserted apartment. A glassless window gave onto the fire escape. Luz stationed Lucy on the sill. "Tell me if you see anyone," Luz said, and sat down on a mattress in the corner. "Shouldn't be long."

Lucy leaned out so she could get a better look at the empty alley. A dog was nosing through some trash. Lucy wondered what the dog would do if all the men died. But that was paranoia: Luz and Concepcion had talked about brain chemistry, not genocide. They wouldn't murder half the human race. That would be insane, and despite their millennialist talk Luz and Concepcion were not insane. Still, suppose they made a mistake? The more she thought about it, the more crazy it seemed.

Lucy turned around. Luz watched the doorway, her eyes intelligent and calm. She did not look crazy. She was one of the most centered women Lucy had ever met. But watching her, Lucy realized that it would take more than abandonment by her husband and the threat of jail to change a lawyer into a revolutionary. A woman couldn't just walk out of her old life after all; at least Lucy couldn't. She was still the girl who paid her father's traffic tickets for him. She needed to tell them, go home, and turn herself in.

"Luz—" Lucy started.

A huge man entered the apartment from the hall. Luz shushed her and stood by the door. "Here," Luz said. The man came back.

He must have been six feet eight; his chest was an assault on the small room. He glanced at Lucy, then sat on the mattress with Luz. He took a fat envelope out of his hip pocket, unfolded it and laid it on the stained fabric. He pushed it toward Luz with a finger as thick as a broom handle.

Luz picked up the envelope and thumbed through the bills inside. She reached into her bag, got out her wallet and slid the calculator from it. She ran a fingernail along the edge and it split in two. Inside was a square of clear plastic with a red spot in its center. "Mix it with some orange juice, swallow it dry, even rub it on the inside of your cheek. Don't open it unless you mean to use it."

The man smiled. "I'm no fool."

No, thought Lucy. She felt panic.

"How long before it works?" the man asked.

"It don't work at all unless you activate it. Just drink a Dr. Pepper before you exercise." Luz put the square back inside the calculator and sealed it. She handed it over to the man. If Lucy was going to stop him, she had to act. "Wait—" she started.

Before she could speak there was the sound of a scuffle in the hall. Concepcion shouted, "Get out!"

Luz kicked the man in the stomach and shoved Lucy out onto the fire escape. A truck roared up the alley from the Avenue, hitting the dog, which yelped in agony. Lucy jumped to the ground and Luz landed beside her. They ran down the alley away from the truck. Behind them Lucy heard tires squeal, the doors slam open. "Police!" a man shouted.

Luz stopped; Lucy ran into her. Ahead, another cop was pointing a shotgun at them.

Two cops ran up from behind, knocked them to the pavement and made them spread their arms and legs. The big man came down from the apartment and searched them for weapons. He seemed to take particular pleasure in groping Lucy's crotch. Lucy lay with her face in the wet grit and listened to the whimper of the dying dog.

14: THURSDAY, JUNE 10
....
George gets Arrested

Louisville was a bust. George spent two days disking interviews with gunshot victims in hospital emergency rooms and discovering that no Alien was involved. He decided to move north to Lansing.

The rain had kept up all week; the train was late leaving because of doubts about the old bridge over the Ohio. Eventually they took a chance: the bridge did not collapse and the train labored through hilly southern Indiana without mishap. George dozed in his seat. Some new problem delayed them in Indianapolis through the night; George ate in the station and slept in the lounge. By the time they continued he felt as if he had been living in a dumpster for two days.

Back on the coach George sat facing a large black man a few years older than he. The man wore a neatly pressed suit, steel-framed glasses, and smelled of cologne: on the shabby coach he stuck out like a hard news story on HCR. When they pulled out of the station water started seeping in around the edge of the window beside them. "Looks like it's never going to stop raining," George ventured.

"I like the rain," the man said. "Hasn't rained in Wichita in three months."

"People say the climate is changing."

The man laughed. "They say more than that."

George introduced himself. "I'm George Valee," he said.

"Langston Burdock," the man said.

"So, where are you going?"

"Lansing. Business."

"What business is that?"

Burdock smiled. "Chinese agent, right?" He settled back in the threadbare seat in the leaky coach as if he were in a suite at the Plaza.

"Actually, I'm a reporter," George admitted. He rested his hand on the microcam bag beside him. "I'm on the road."

Burdock examined George. "Your name's not Valee—it's Eberhart! The nut news. My wife watches you all the time."

George found he was not dismayed at being recognized. "What do you think?"

"I think you should get a better hairpiece. Is this a disguise?"

"Not exactly. Let's just say I'm on the lookout for improbable things."

"I'm in aerospace," Burdock said. "I believe in a lot of improbabilities."

"I thought aerospace was dead."

"Just resting. In fact, that's why I'm going to Lansing."

A gust of wind through the crack in the window sprayed cold droplets of water into George's face. Burdock handed him a handkerchief. It was very clean.

"Thanks," George said, handing it back. "Riding the train is an adventure."

"I like it," said Burdock.

"But you want to put it back out of business."

"Yep."

"What will you use for fuel?"

"Fuel's no problem if you get the engine efficiency high enough. You can use alcohol. Mash up some corn, tree bark, weeds—any vegetable matter."

George kept to himself his opinion of making corn into fuel in the light of the equatorial food wars. "What other improbable things do you believe in?"

Burdock's clear brown eyes were on him. "Racial equality," he said.

George smiled. "I guess that qualifies you as an optimist."

"That qualifies me with the UFO nuts. You ought to put me on TV."

"People would rather hear about flying saucers."

"I know," Burdock tapped the back of his fingers against the window, looking out at the soggy fields. "I saw a flying saucer once."

"When?"

"Thirty years ago. At Fort Bragg. We were out on maneuvers, bivouacked in the woods one night. I was woken up by this big light overhead. I thought it was a flare and there was going to be an attack. But it wasn't a flare."

"What was it?"

"A bright silvery ball, maybe twenty meters across, hovering just above the treetops. It made a sound like a big transformer. Made the hair on my arms stand on end, though that could have been because I was scared."

"Did anyone else see it?"

"The whole platoon did."

George considered what he was willing to tell a stranger. "You know, not all the stories on HCR are invented."

Burdock looked skeptical. "Rain of Frogs in New Mexico? Garden of Eden Located in New Jersey? You must make up those UFO stories, too."

George leaned forward. "The Dogon."

"What?"

"An African tribe. They knew about the existence of the companion star of Sirius before European astronomers. They had contact with space aliens before recorded history."

"I think I heard about it." Burdock adjusted his glasses. "But didn't some astronomer explain how they knew?"

"He had to twist the facts more than HCR ever did. And what we ran was just the tip of the iceberg. Why would the contact have to have been prehistoric? Why couldn't it have come recently?"

"Wouldn't these Africans have more details?"

"Not if the aliens erased all details from their memories."

"Why would advanced aliens contact a primitive tribe?"

"Who's to say what an alien would consider advanced? The Dogon are a stable hunter-gatherer society. They have no crime. They're in balance with their environment. No poverty, no psychosis, no social maladjustment. It might seem to an alien that they were the most advanced society on earth. Especially if the aliens were black."

"Black aliens!"

"Why not?"

"So what are these aliens doing now?"

"They don't want to contact a society founded on racism. They want to make some adjustments first."

Burdock looked skeptical. After awhile he said, "AMPS?"

"Exactly," said George. "What better way to prepare the ground than to sow a little blackness? Soften up the white locals for the New Order."

"You're saying they're using biological warfare?"

"Mr. Burdock, if I told you all I suspect you'd think I was crazy."

"Right." Burdock looked like a man in a burning theater checking for the exit. George realized he was squandering an opportunity. The Aliens might be very interested in the aerospace industry. If an alien was in Lansing, Burdock might act like a magnet to draw him in. George ought to be using him, not putting him off with talk about UFOs.

"Don't bother telling me any more," Burdock said. "I don't buy it."

"Actually, neither do I," George said hastily. "I'm just working on our next series and now and then I'll try something out. You're a good sounding board."

"You don't mean any of this stuff?"

"The basic Dogon story is true. I'm just seeing how far I can take it."

Burdock smiled. "I have to admit, it would explain a few things."

George breathed a little easier. "That's one of our principles. All our stories explain things."

Just then the train lurched. The brakes squealed and the passing scenery slowed to a halt. The drumming of the rain on the roof rose out of the background. Passengers peered out the windows as if staring at the fields could tell them what was going on. Eventually a conductor passed through the coach and assured them that they would be on their way shortly. Burdock excused himself and went up the aisle toward the front of the train.

George resisted the impulse to follow him. He stared out the window. He had babbled like an idiot. If he didn't get his act together, any alien he met would laugh at him.

The rain let up and the setting sun broke briefly through. Water in the ditch along the roadbed caught the light and flashed it back like molten lead. He thought about Lucy. Fifteen minutes later the coach jerked into motion, and soon after, Burdock came back. He flopped into the seat opposite George, took out a large cigar, stoked it up and raised a newspaper between them like a wall. Clouds of smoke billowed over the top of the paper. George read the front page: "Asian Cooperative Completes Space Platform," "Flooding Spreads Along Wabash," "Baby Anne Declared Human," "Missing Persons Reports Soar."

George imagined Lucy waking and finding him gone. The scene rose before him like a vision. She reaches across the bed and touches only the crocheted afghan his mother gave him for Christmas during the hard winter of 1972. Her eyelashes tremble. She strikes his pillow with her fist, not hard but with finality. The sun creeps in the window; Lucy stares at the African violets on the sill. Then she showers, shaves her legs, dresses, showing no emotion, her heart ripped by the hot iron of betrayal. The televisions whisper in his office. Flooding Spreads Asians. Space Baby Declared. Missing Persons Soar.

George felt shame sweep over him, so pure it was physical, each returning hair on his body standing on end the way Burdock's hair must have stood when the alien craft drifted over his platoon, charged with electromagnetic energies of unknowable magnitude. Lucy drinks black coffee. She calls Richard. She demands explanations and does not listen to the answers. She cleans the mirrors, studies her face. She polishes her shoes at the kitchen table. On the counter lies the spiral peel of a tangerine, still holding its shape although its insides have been torn out and swallowed. At night she dreams about auto accidents, falling elevators.

There was nothing mechanical about George's image of her, no hint of a delusion, a trick. He should have tried to explain, but she hadn't wanted to listen. Too many barriers, too many laws. I do not reveal my hopes and you do not reveal your fears. When telling stories, you emphasize adjectives for effect; when listening, I assume a pose of intelligent interest. When we are close, you must want to be closer and I must run away. I buy the groceries. You pay the bills. Laws.

Now he had no laws at all.

Burdock burst into a racking cough. He bent forward, gasping for breath, then hawked and spat on the floor.

"Are you all right?" George asked.

"Never better." Burdock stuck the cigar back in his mouth and drew on it until the tip glowed. He folded the paper in his lap. "So why don't you tell me how these space aliens are poisoning us. How they're getting their bugs into our soup?"

George wished he had kept his mouth shut. "They can make themselves look human," he said.

"I thought you said they were black. Don't black men look human?"

"They aren't necessarily black. That was just one of my ideas. They could be any color."

"Black people aren't smart enough to make space ships?"

He was paying for deserting Lucy. "Of course they are. But their color is irrelevant. I figure these aliens couldn't do all the things they're doing if they are just one kind of being. They must be able to assume a variety of human appearances."

"Say what?"

"They can change shape."

Burdock grinned crookedly. He puffed on the cigar. George became aware of an unpleasant smell. The man's suit was no longer neat; he looked as if he had slept in it.

"Change shape?" Burdock said. "How do they manage that?"

"They're biologically different from us. They're *aliens*."

"They ain't got no bones?" Burdock said loudly. Several of the other passengers were watching them.

"How should I know? They could be anything. They're from another solar system."

Burdock blew more smoke at George. "I don't care if they're from California, Eberhart, they've got to follow the laws of thermodynamics. I'm an engineer. Any creature that changes shape is going to have to take some time to do it, and it's going to cost a lot of energy. Gonna have to be eating every minute of the day and sleeping any time it ain't eating. Not much time left over for invading the earth."

"How do we know how their metabolism works? Maybe they run on batteries."

"Very large 'D' cells."

"Look," George said, "I'm sorry I brought it up. I didn't mean to antagonize you."

"First you treat me like some dumb nigger and now you want to back off when I blow your cover. How slow do you think I am?"

"Believe me, I'm not trying to insult you."

"You're just so good you do it without trying. Or maybe you're just a paranoid schizophrenic."

George felt trapped. "I'm sorry! Look, let's change the subject."

Burdock kept grinning. George couldn't get over how bad he smelled. He wished he could open the window. They were coming into a town; the train crossed a river and slowed as they passed through a block of warehouses. Burdock folded his paper to the sports page. "You follow baseball?"

"Some."

"I saw a game the other night. Young kid just got called up to the Sox. Mark my words: he's going to be good."

Burdock's brown eyes studied him; he seemed amused. Before George could reassemble his wits the train drew into the station. "Fort Wayne," the coach's speaker said.

Burdock jumped up, grabbed his bag and headed up the aisle. The train squealed up to the platform. With relief, George watched him hurry into the building. He decided to stretch his legs and shoot some background. He got out the microcam, made sure he had a new disk, put on the shoulder pack and lens headset and went into the station. He shot some of the vagrants, all the time wondering about Burdock's sudden transformation from genial businessman to aggressive skeptic, almost as if he'd been replaced on his visit to the men's room.

George stopped, the camera focused on nothing. *Replaced.* The way Burdock had taunted him. His smell. The thing had dared George to guess, and he had been too dumb to notice! He scanned the station. An Interrail cop stood by the message kiosk.

The cop was a skinny kid no more than twenty. His uniform, compulsively neat, hung on shoulders narrow as a wire hanger. "What's with that outfit?" he asked.

George flipped the lens up onto his forehead. "Home movies. Look, have you seen a big black man get off the train? Rumpled suit, glasses, maybe smoking a cigar?"

"Who takes home movies of the Fort Wayne Interrail station?"

George held his temper. "I'm with a news service. I think this man may be a fugitive."

The cop folded his arms across his chest. "I ain't seen nobody."

George gave up. He flipped down the lens, thumbed the switch on the shoulder pack and headed for the men's room. RECORDING, said the display in the corner of the viewfield. An old man at the urinals stared as George entered—his red face looked as if it had been boiled and his hair was like dirty straw. He left quickly. George checked the stalls. Two of them were closed. He peeked in the gap along the edge of one of the doors and a man gaped back at him. He slipped down the line toward the other closed door, at the end of the row. George stood back a ways, stooped down and looked under the door. Two feet in brown shoes, ample trousers piled around the ankles.

George slipped as quietly as he could into the adjacent stall, climbed onto the toilet, one foot on each side of the unsteady bakelite seat. He still couldn't see over the wall. He shifted to one arm of the seat, stood on tiptoes, and peeked over the top.

He was looking down on the balding head of a middle-aged black man. The stink was overpowering. George held his breath. It was hard to tell, but the man looked to be in a trance of some sort. His face was slightly upturned, and the eyes were half-lidded in concentration. Was he communicating with others of his kind—with some craft that even at that moment hovered in geosynchronous orbit 22,000 miles above their heads? Messages. Commands. Contact the earthman Eberhart. Rip the fabric of reality apart, reveal to him the sweet white noise behind everything. George felt his calves tremble; a month out of the hospital, he was in no shape for a confrontation with forces from outer space. As he strained to keep his balance, wondering what to do next, the door of his stall slammed open.

"What the fuck do you think you're doing?" the cop yelled.

George's foot slipped. His chin came down hard on the top of the stall and he almost bit through his tongue. His leg plunged into the toilet. The cop had his gun out, trained on George. In the next stall he heard the rattle of a belt buckle.

"Don't let him get away!" George sputtered. His mouth was bleeding.

"Come out of there!" the cop yelled. "You all right, buddy?" he called to the other stall.

"You don't understand! He's not human!" George lurched out of the toilet. The cop almost fell over backwards trying to get out of the way. The knuckles of the hand gripping the gun were white. "Don't shoot!" George gasped, spraying drops of blood.

Burdock came out of the stall and lumbered toward the exit. The man in the stall down the row was out already; George had a nice shot of the guy's ass as he stumbled away, pulling up his pants as he ran. "1847 CDT," the read-out below the recording indicator read. George was getting it all. If the cop didn't shoot him this would be main menu for sure. George pointed at Burdock. "That man isn't real. You've got to stop him."

The cop looked worried. Burdock tried to get by him, but the cop backed off farther. "Hold it!" he said.

"What's going on here?" Burdock asked.

The cop looked as if he thought that was a pretty good question.

"Officer, this man is an imposter," George said. "He's taken the place of a real man I met on the train."

"He what?"

"Look, give me a chance and I'll explain. At least hold him for questioning."

Burdock looked at George as if he were the alien. "I've got business in Lansing. This man is crazy; I'm not going to stay here and help you figure it out." He headed past the cop.

"Don't let him go!" George pleaded.

"Shut up," the cop said. "Lie down on the floor."

Burdock was almost out the door. George leapt past the cop and grabbed the big man around the back. They fell hard to the floor, struggling. Just before the cop put out his lights with a blow to the back of his neck, George realized that the man he was wrestling didn't stink after all. He smelled of cologne.

15: THURSDAY, JUNE 10

More Fun with Drugs

Richard's train arrived in Raleigh by noon and he was checked into the Brownestone Inn by one. His appointment with Gilray wasn't until four. He made sure the switchboard had his satellite relay code, jacked his Mitsubishi portadeck into the phone and turned on the TV.

Around the channels. For ten dollars Richard could punch into a magazine station with interactive stories. The old networks were running soaps, the first set in a hospital, the second in the Pentagon, the third in Gay Nineties New York. He found "The Lord's Tinderbox," a Christian variety show, on which a black man and a white man joked about the floods in the North. Richard kept turning. Twelve newsnets including HCR. A shopping station pushing Braun home water distillers. The seven basic music networks. Movies around the dial—in a quick scan Richard recognized "The Searchers," a Blondie movie, and on the public station a rerun of episode nine of "Jesus: The Miracle Years." When Richard found himself coming back for the

third time to John Wayne tearing up the southwest in search
of Natalie Wood, he turned off the set. He hated to admit
it, but he was nervous. He decided to take a walk.

The sun was bright, the day hot; the men on the talk
show were right about the difference from New York. A
student ghetto surrounded the hotel. On the side streets the
houses needed paint; their porches sagged and duct tape
zigzagged across cracked windows. The yards were weeds
and red clay. Generations of faded leaflets plastered the
telephone poles: Ban the Klan! competed with Kill the
Pope!

Richard walked downtown on the main street, past the
YMCA, another hotel, and big old houses that had been
converted to offices. A line of pickets marched in front of
one labeled, "Raleigh Women's Center: Green Party Headquarters." Men in white shortsleeved shirts and women in
skirts the bright colors of five years ago carried signs reading, "Feminism is Satanism" and "Greens are Reds." Their
faces wore looks of dull certainty, of simple fatigue—and of
spiritual exaltation.

A bus approached. Richard got on in front of an I-Hop
and rode downtown. The fare was only three dollars. He
crossed the street and walked around the grounds of the
state capitol, an old Georgian building whose columns,
dome and porticos were indistinguishable from public archi-
tecture anywhere in America. The grounds were rife with
memorials: to the Confederate dead, the Spanish War dead,
the Great War dead, the Vietnam dead. A statue of George
Washington, leaning on a cane, stood inside a wrought iron
picket fence and bracketed by cannon. In the rotunda of the
capitol sat a more remarkable version of Washington: reclin-
ing on a throne, dressed in a tunic and leather battle dress,
he held a tablet in the crook of his left arm and quill poised
effeminately above it in his right hand. The Founding Father as Caesar. The South as abode of patrician civilization.

On a downtown pedestrian mall Richard found a Christian tag-team testifying before a knot of onlookers. When
one preacher wore out another would take his place; a ban-
ner across the top of the storefront read, "BEFORE MY

EYES WAS A DOOR OPENED IN HEAVEN." Richard stood in the back of the crowd and listened to the usual about the signs that the Millennium was at hand. Inside the store helpers dispensed glasses of iced tea and sausage biscuits. Men and women passed back and forth between the spiritual and physical food. From the looks of the crowd they were preaching to the already converted.

"How many of you haven't had a regular job in a year?" the current speaker asked. A forest of raised hands. "Two years?" At least half the hands remained raised. "Three!" Still a third. The man smiled grimly. "How many of you know somebody that died in the last year from one of the plagues?" More hands, a few shouts. "How many of you *right now* are suffering from an incurable disease?" A few hands, some sobbing from a woman in the front.

"I know, I know," the speaker said. "There's nobody that hasn't been touched by pain in these Last Days. But you walk across Capitol Square to the legislature and, if you can get their paid cops to let you in, you take a good look at the fat men sitting on their consciences there, eating off the backs of good Christians.

"Go a mile down Hillsborough. You see those kids hanging around there, you don't know whether they started life white or black, man or woman! They're taking drugs didn't exist two years ago. Spreading sex diseases like rats on a sinking ship. Talking Red revolution. They smell like a Tennessee outhouse, but their teachers smell worse. Where do these teachers come from? How many of them from North Carolina? How many of them saved? When the Rapture comes, they're not going to have to hire any new faculty. They're not going to lose any to speak of!"

Nervous laughter, some shouts.

"So you ask yourself how God could stand to let that go on? You ask, how can the Lord let the Devil work his ways so plain in the face of His Law?"

More shouts.

"I'll tell you why the Lord is waiting. You got a boll on your neck, before you lance it you got to let all the poison gather, till it seems that the pain of it is about to make you weep. But you can't do it any sooner. The evil times are part of the Plan, but the time is about run out. It's coming time to lance that boil that sits there across the mall, that festers in Chapel Hill and Durham and down the other end of Hillsborough St."

More of the people shouted; others nodded. It was a good line; Richard could appreciate a good line when he heard one. He bought a newspaper from a display box and turned to the job listings as he walked back up the mall. It was a wasteland. No data processors, no real estate, no sales reps, no technical editors, no apartment managers, no accountants. Ten years ago the area had been one of the high-tech wonderlands; now it was barely alive.

On the way back to the hotel, Richard stopped in the shade of a huge oak, opened his pillbox and took an amphetamine and half a tab of one of the new psychedelics. His head was already buzzing from the heat, and the white line in the street glowed with more than natural brightness. He watched his reflection in the black glass of an office front. He pushed the mood along, anticipating the rush. Raleigh could be fun. It was more volatile even than New York: high-stakes religion, the end of the world, disease and unemployment, technological potential banked down far below capacity. Highly educated people out of work who had been used to living well, regional and racial resentments than went back two hundred years. Flying saucers and nihilist socialists. If he could persuade the Reverend to take him on, they could stoke up quite a bonfire before they were done.

At the hotel a message waited: Felton McRae, Gilray's driver, would be out to get him in an hour. Already flying, Richard went down to the lobby to wait. At 3:30 a poker-faced man with a military haircut arrived and they drove out in a brutally air-conditioned 1994 Lincoln to Gilray's headquarters in what had once been Research Triangle Park. Rumor had it that Gilray had built his Institute in the middle of the high-tech mecca as an affront to the computer company that had once employed him. He wanted to assert his desire to use the tools of the twenty-first century against itself. Richard liked the ballsiness of that, and at the same time was wary of the pathology it suggested. Maybe Gilray had a problem with authority.

McRae drove silently, erect as a Marine guard. Richard suddenly recognized him.

"Felton McRae!" he exclaimed. "You're the one who saved the Rev's life. You broke that assassin's neck like a matchstick."

"Attempted assassin," said McRae. In the rear-view mirror all Richard could see of McRae's face was his mirrored sunglasses. Richard was so tripped out that he thought he could see his own microscopic image in the mirror's reflection of the lenses' reflection of the back seat of the car.

"Right," he managed to say through his haze. "You look out for the Rev's life."

"I protect him from people like you."

A side road took them past more pine forest and demure signs announcing corporate facilities: Sumitomo, Mitsubishi, Glaxo Incorporated, The National Humanities Center. They turned down a winding drive that gave out onto a complex of low buildings and well-kept lawns. The Institute included offices, a TV studio, a media research lab and an attached complex of apartments where Gilray and some of his associates lived. The road looped around a fountain to the entrance. In the center of the fountain stood a white marble statue of Christ, arms outstretched, ascending into Heaven. Or maybe He was descending to rule the reborn earth. A kid with a thatch of blond hair was mulching the azaleas.

In the glass-walled atrium a young woman, Gilray's aide, greeted Richard. She led him to the Rev's office. Gilray was not there; he kept Richard waiting for half an hour, then entered suddenly. "Mr. Shrike." Without shaking hands, he sat down in the chair on the other side of the mahogany table. "You've got three minutes."

"I may need more than that."

"Anything worth saying can be said in three minutes."

"You sound like a broadcaster."

"How would you know? I wouldn't call what you broadcast news."

Richard actually felt as if there were something riding on this. "There are a lot of people who wouldn't know what to do without HCR. We give them a way to look at the world—just like you."

"That's the problem. You give them lies when they need truth."

"We never print anything that isn't true."

Gilray merely stared at him. Richard felt some well of rage lurch open inside him—why, it was a gaping pit! It burned, it stank like Lucy's flaming underwear. It was very sweet.

"Don't stare at me that way," Richard said. "You're no different. You think you know the truth—"

"Why are you here?"

Richard tried to get a grip on his story. "I've been fired by Jason Abramowitz. Because of that interview fiasco last weekend. The bastard blamed me. I'm a free man. So I thought I would get him by coming to help you."

"What possible need could I have for help from you? You're not even saved."

"Whether I'm damned or saved doesn't matter."

"It matters a lot. It's all that matters."

"You can't save me. I don't need saving." Richard was losing control, surprised at the bitterness in his own voice.

Gilray got out of the chair, took one measured step toward Richard, drew back and slapped him. Richard was so unprepared that he took the full force of it. His cheek stung. "Don't lie to me," Gilray said. "I can smell lies."

Richard touched his cheek and came away with blood on his fingers. "I'm here to work for you."

Gilray sniffed. "And Abramowitz fired you? That's a lie."

Richard licked his bloody fingers. He tasted the salt, imagined the blood cells sliding into his stomach, feeding him. The Rev was better than he had had any right to hope. "You're right. I set this up with him. He thinks I'm going to ingratiate myself with you so that I can get dirt for HCR. Let him think that. I'll work for you. You don't tell me anything you don't want me to know. You don't do anything you don't want to do. We'll feed him stories that will

get you the support you're looking for. The minute I do
something you don't approve of I'm out of here."

Gilray studied him. "You're a confused man, Mr. Shrike.
How am I supposed to figure out what you want?"

"I may be confused. You don't have to worry about that.
I came here to offer you a proposition. You need a pub-
licist."

"I don't need you."

"You don't have anyone who understands the popular
mind like me. You have a message and it's not getting out."

"We're reaching millions of Christians."

Richard felt suicidally sharp, as sharp as he'd felt since
the breakup of Six Million Jews. He let his rage fuel him.
"Sure. I've watched you; you're good. You've got some of
that videostar nerve. Despite the cornball setup you already
get some people you shouldn't expect to. I don't know
whether you're aware of this, but you've already got half the
flash addicts and codpiece wearers in Manhattan believing
it's the end of the world. Now you need to turn it up.
You've got to tell them what's in their own best interests,
point out the people who are standing in their way."

"I'm already doing those things."

"You're doing it the same way it's been done by every TV
preacher in the last thirty years. It's old news. HCR is new
news. The UFO connection is a start. But don't soft-pedal
it: give them more than vague connection—spell it out.
Give them a place to go."

Gilray sat back on the desk and played with the ring that
had cut Richard's face, turning it about his finger. "But you
don't believe any of it."

"I don't have to believe in it."

"Why should I trust you?"

"You don't have to trust me. I'll let the results speak for
themselves."

"I'd like to know your motives."

Richard laughed. It hurt. He felt the trickle of blood running down his neck into his collar. The fucker had slapped
him. For that alone he deserved the truth. "You're predict-
ing the end of the world."

"The beginning of the New World."

"I don't believe in that," said Richard. "I just want to see this one go out. I want to help it."

Gilray tapped his fingers on the desktop. "What has that got to do with working for me?"

"You're helping to bring it on. I think you're out of your mind. UFOs, the Second Coming, the Abomination of Desolation, the Rapture."

"I differ with a lot of people about the Rapture."

"Who cares? It's all rock and roll. People are ready to die for you. Some of them to kill. That fellow Felton, for instance. The whole scene's bloody cracked."

"The pharisees thought Christ was crazy."

"Charles Manson's one of your biggest fans. That's the kind of fact that gets to me. You could unscrew your foot and stick it in your ear and it wouldn't matter to me, as long as I can help you bring on the crash."

Gilray actually smiled. "A nihilist. If I were to give you a job my people would think I was crazy."

"This isn't a job. It's an adventure."

Gilray pulled a tissue from a box on his desk and handed it to Richard. "Here. You're still bleeding."

"Thanks." Richard dabbed at his cheek. "I don't understand my motives. I want to do this. I've never had the chance to work for someone who had the guts to hit me."

"You're headed for hell."

"Here's your chance to save me."

"You fool even yourself, don't you? You need to be slapped more often."

"And you're just the man to do it. Well, how about it?"

The Rev stood up, turned his back to Richard, looked out the window. The blond gardener had worked his way around to the back of the building. After a minute Gilray turned. "Did you ever hear the one about the man who jumped off the skyscraper, Mr. Shrike?"

"Not lately."

"As he passed each floor on his way down, he was heard to say, 'So far, so good.'"

Richard smiled. "I don't see the relevance. I know we're headed for a crash."

"So far, so good. I need to think your offer over. For now, let me take you around to meet my staff."

It would be worth staying alive until the end of the world if only to study up close the cool glow of absolute faith in Gilray's eyes. As they left the office Richard realized that he would do almost anything to keep generating that spark for as long as he could.

Later, back at the hotel, he tried to decide how much of what he had felt that afternoon had been genuine. He had lost control. The rage had flared as hot as it had when he was twenty. Richard hadn't even known it was still there. In the bathroom mirror he studied the mark that Gilray's ring had cut on his cheek. It looked like it might leave a scar.

When he came out of the bathroom he noticed that the red light was flashing on the phone. He had received a call keyed to his remote code. He hit the playback. George's face came onto the screen. Haggard, eyes red, he wore an impossibly ugly hairpiece.

"Richard, this is George. Good news! I'm in a police station. It's stopped raining. I can only talk for a minute. I've got a story to burst on the end of this. The Alien! He's black! Actually, it wasn't him I caught but the man he replaced. You'll have to clean up the video."

Holding the phone between his ear and shoulder, Richard checked the Mitsubishi. Sure enough, there was something on disk.

There was no telling what it was. "Got to go Richard," the recording said. "What are you doing in Raleigh? I think he's hunting engineers. I had a hard time getting through. Maybe these plagues have something to do with it. Tell Lucy I'm sorry; I'll make it up to her somehow.

"I'll keep in touch. I feel great. They're going to feed me now. I'm on the trail!"

The image flicked off. The digital birdsong of George's report coming over the line followed, then silence.

Richard played George's story back through the room's TV. He watched a jerky chase through a train station that climaxed with an overhead shot of a man on the crapper and ended with a lurching dive of the camera into the broad canvas of the man's fleeing back.

Richard thought it needed some editing.

16: THURSDAY, JUNE 10
. . . .
A Computer-Assisted Revelation

By the time Shrike left it was evening. The Reverend Jimmy-Don Gilray retired to his rooms in the residential wing of his Institute. Mrs. Walsh had his supper waiting. He set the security alarm, tested the food for toxins and ate. Afterwards he went to his bedroom. He took off his tie and shoes. From the drawer in the bedside table he took the Bible he had found in the trash heap behind a hardware store when he was sixteen. He sat down before his computer and slid the Bible into the slot he'd made for it between the CPU and the VDT. He booted up the Bible randomizer he'd written himself back when he'd worked for IBM, asked the Lord for guidance, and hit the return key.

The screen went blank, and a second later a verse appeared, glowing amber:

Jeremiah 10:23: O Lord, I know that the way of man is not in himself: it is not in man that walketh to direct his steps.

Gilray read the words several times. He had been directed to Jeremiah, familiar territory. A book that foretold the apocalypse that was upon them even now.

But why this particular verse? ". . . the way of man is not in himself . . ." It was a reminder that men could not know the purpose or outcome of events, that all was ordered by God. And Shrike? "It is not in a man . . . to direct his own steps." That was the troublesome, glorious liberation of faith. One had to surrender his will to the Lord. Shrike's arrival was no accident. It made no difference that Gilray distrusted him, that Shrike considered himself an atheist; it made even less difference what Shrike's intentions were. He might think he was going to work for Gilray in order to humiliate him—but his steps were directed by God.

Gilray turned off the machine and went over to the full length mirror in the dressing room. He unbuttoned his shirt. He had returned from Lexington in confusion, unable to get any satisfactory explanation from Dr. Vance. He had not even tried to find out how he had been tricked. What was significant was that the source of his power had been questioned—by supernatural means. Gilray was given his physical gifts for a purpose, and the deceiver had ridiculed those gifts. Could that deceiver be an agent of the Lord? He took off the shirt, then unzipped his pants and stood naked in front of the mirror. Just a man. Flesh. In His Image. Did God look like this? Did He have a mirror?

He put on his pajamas and got ready for bed. Christians could be attacked by Satan, and Satan was subtle. He could take on any form. He could pose as a doctor. He could pose as a slick media man with a touch of a British accent.

Yet the Lord directed their steps. Gilray would not give in to doubt. He could help Shrike if he desired faith, he could understand him if he desired power. He could listen carefully to Shrike's counsel and study his actions. There were only months left before the end, and there was much work to be done. The world had to be made ready for His coming. Shrike could be useful. The important thing would be to see that Shrike did God's work, whether he knew himself to be doing it or not.

Gilray was troubled by the prospect that he might not be

able to tell what moved Shrike. He would have to act in the space between uncertainty and faith. But when had it ever been different?

He turned off the light and slept. That night, for the first time in what was to come to be, over the next months, an endless, fascinating ordeal, Gilray had the dream. He was alone on the roof of a building. A city was in flames around him. In the sky above shone lights of religious significance. And through the smoke came a woman with gray eyes and hair black as the midnight sky, the terrible woman who was promised to him and whose coming would bring on the end of everything and the beginning of nothing. She reached out, and he held her in his arms, and it was like falling from a very high place to one very low.

17: FRIDAY, JUNE 11
....
Wes Purcell maintains his Credibility

"Point eight!" Wes could barely hear Harry's shout over the keening that filled the lab, even though they were separated from the engine by the wall of the test chamber. On the monitor the prop was a disk-shaped haze. Its thickness decreased as the blades pivoted; their circular velocity was approaching Mach 2. It looked as if, if you reached out to touch it, it would be yielding yet firm, like a good pillow. Cool and dry against your cheek. But that was crazy. Lean your cheek against the prop and your head would explode into a mist of blood and minced bone.

"That's enough," Wes said. Harry looked at him as if he had not quite heard; Bob Eliott and Stan Curtis were so intent on the board that they didn't respond at all. Wes reached past them and cut the power. "Enough," he repeated. As the whine of the engine faded, the whine of a guitar blasting out of the lab stereo rushed back. A real oldie: Hendrix, "Let me Stand Next to Your Fire." Number 1600 in the top 2000 of the twentieth century. "We all know it works," he snapped. "We're just wasting fuel."

It was a good enough reason. The turboprop had passed six hundred hours of lab tests: the stall/flutter qualities were excellent, fuel efficiency was fifteen percent higher than the NASA/Lockheeds, fifty-five percent above the old Pratt and Whitneys. But the truth was that Wes just could not stand watching it anymore; it had been whirling in his mind long before they built it, so that the engine itself was only a shadow of the years-old dream. He needed a rest, he needed to stop whirling himself. But he had at least another day of spinning to do.

Eliott made a show of turning off the monitor, the disk recorder and the stereo. Curtis leaned against the board and popped an antibiotic lozenge into his mouth.

Harry turned to him. "So what now?"

"I think we ought to send everybody home. Do you want to meet Burdock?" he asked Curtis. Curtis sucked on his lozenge. Curtis was as hypochondriac as a spinster aunt, but with his curly red hair, lean face and western shirts he looked like the Marlboro man. He liked baiting Wes.

Before he could answer, Harry broke in. "The point is, Wes, that Burdock will want to meet him."

"He has all the specs he needs."

"He's not here to see specs. He's here to see us. He's not going to advise that they invest deep money on the basis of specs."

Wes looked at the blank monitor screen. "All right. Bob, Stan—find something to do until this guy shows up. Harry, let's talk." He headed for the door and Harry followed, out of the lab and across the damp concrete toward the quonset hut office that crouched against the side of the hangar. It had finally stopped raining. The air was hot and thick as crankcase oil and smelled about as good. The sunlight seemed to be coming from about a hundred yards above their heads; it threw their muzzy shadows onto the cracked apron. Wes had bought the space at Capital City cheap when he started Purcell Aviation. Airport space was a bargain in 1996, when the only things running down the centerline stripes were skateboarders.

Wes grimaced when he saw the battered black Chrysler Harry had rented baking in the sun beside the office. "Is the car's air-conditioning working?"

Harry shrugged. "I was more worried we'd need pontoons."

Wes had a sinking feeling in his gut. "We should have rented a better car."

"No. You've got to understand the venture capitalist mind, Wes."

"Burdock's going to sweat his ass off in that car."

"No problem. He wants to know that we need the money. When he sees the car, he'll be sure we do. Believe me, if you try to act rich, they figure you must not be able to deliver the goods. At dinner, you let him pick up the tab. That lets him think he's in the driver's seat. And he is."

Wes gritted his teeth. Didn't Harry understand that that was the whole problem? Harry yanked open the side door of the hangar. Inside, Wes paused to look over the plane. They had already mounted one of the turboprops into the wing engine cowling; the eight curving blades looked like slender tangerine sections. The airlines had gone belly-up by mounting props in the tail, as pushers, to keep the noise down. That cut fuel efficiency too much. Wes's design was quiet enough to put up front. He could see his and Harry's reflections in the polished fuselage, stretched taller by its curved surface: a tall thin black man and a tall thin Jew.

Wesley had got FAA permission to test and a brand new flight registration number. The bureaucrats were happy to have anything to do. Although they still maintained that the days of massive air travel were not over, nobody had told that to the Army of God in the Middle East.

"Hey, I almost forgot," said Harry. "Molly told me that Burdock was in Vietnam back in the sixties."

Wes stared at his reflection, reached out to touch it. The hand of the distorted reflection reached out to meet his. He ran his fingertips along the metal. "No kidding," he said. "When was he there?"

"I don't know. 'Sixty-seven, 'Sixty-eight. This is the thing: we show Burdock the layout and he looks around, but what he's really here to do is check out you and me."

"I know that."

Harry looked annoyed; he turned his back on the plane, faced Wes. "All I'm saying is you should use this Vietnam connection. You're both vets. Talk old times. That could make a difference."

"No one cares about Vietnam anymore," said Wes.

"This guy does. Apparently he's into it big time."

Wes drew his hand back and rubbed it on his trousers. "My stomach is acting up. I'll be in my office. When you going to pick him up?"

Harry looked at his watch and broke into one of his looks of mock horror. "Right now."

He left. Wes retreated to the bathroom. He took two Alka-Seltzers. Watching the tablets fizz in the crusted glass he kept on the sink, he had a vivid memory from more than thirty years before. He'd been a freshman at RPI, a scared kid from Rochester who had never been away from his mother for more than a day in his life. Studying for his first physics test tied his stomach into knots. His roommate, a Jewish kid from Port Washington, gave him some Alka-Seltzers. Wes didn't know that you had to dissolve them in water first. He'd swallowed them, and heaved his guts out for the next half hour.

He had felt like a fool. He had wanted to go home. But his mother was making up rooms at the Ramada Inn and working a second job nights to keep him in school. So he stayed.

Looking into the mirror now, Wes saw the sweat standing out on his forehead. He poured some bottled water into the basin and splashed it into his face. His reflection did not look so distorted as the one in the plane, but, watching his brown eyes rimmed with red, he thought about that scared kid and knew that most images were illusions.

The lie had started simply enough. It was remarkable how the events that came to rule your life began so simply. They might have been the matter of a half hour some afternoon except they touched some nerve deep inside you that went back to who knew where—to the womb, probably, or the DNA threaded like a secret message in your cells. And there you were, caught.

Wesley had graduated from Benjamin Franklin High School in 1966. At that time nobody took Vietnam seriously. Maybe in Berkeley they did, but not in Rochester. Some of Wesley's friends, expecting to be drafted, had even enlisted. Wes got accepted to fill a minority quota in aeronautical engineering at Renssalaer. By the end of his sophomore year everybody was talking about the Tet offensive, the big troop shipments, Johnson abdicating, King and Kennedy. Wesley got caught up in the protests, the rallies, the strikes. It was as if the white world had suddenly discovered that it needed Wesley; a black man gave your position credibility. Wes remembered meeting a couple of radical white girls back when making it with a "spade" was a badge of cool. At some level Wes knew they were phonies, but he was confused, too. He wanted them to like him. He wanted to get laid as much as the next twenty-year-old. "Let me stand next to your fire." Sure. They all liked Hendrix and Sly and The Temps. They liked Wes, too.

When he thought about the black men his own age who were dying in Vietnam it was only to pity them. Most of the time he was more worried about keeping his marks up. When the lottery started he pulled a high number. After graduating he got one of the last jobs available with Bell Labs before the collapse in demand for engineers when NASA cut back after the moon landings.

And then the war was over. Wesley felt a twinge of conscience when the POWs were released and there was a lot of talk about the plight of the vets. He didn't feel guilty about not going over there and dying—black men killing yellow men for the white man—but still, they had taken it and he had not. For the first time in his life he had been spared one of the ordeals that came with being black. Except he *was* black. Something was wrong.

He didn't realize how much until he cut his heel in his back yard. For a week he was limping around the office. When one of the new draftsmen asked him how he'd hurt himself, out of Wesley's mouth popped, "Vietnam."

He did not know why he said it, but he remembered it. When his mother died in 1979, Wes took a new job in Lansing. He was a blank slate to everybody in the Midwest. When people asked if he had served in Vietnam, he simply said, "One tour."

It didn't seem like much. He didn't owe them the truth anyway. But in saying it he had opened the floodgates, and the deluge washed over him. At first idly but then with increasing interest he started reading about the war. He bought a VCR in 1982 and got hold of videotapes of TV documentaries. He made friends with a sound engineer at the local ABC affiliate and got some dupes of network file footage. Within a year he was sitting up in front of the tube until well after midnight, stumbling to bed bleary-eyed to dream about fire fights and napalmed villages and Hispanic soldiers with their legs blown off by claymore mines. He talked to vets at Fort Benjamin Harrison. He studied the 196th Light Infantry, in the period of 1967 and 1968, Task Force Oregon in Quang Ngai Province. If he had been drafted right out of high school, it was a good bet that was where he would have ended up.

From the research it was a small step to concocting a history. In order to obtain some of the documents he wanted to look at, he claimed he was a member of the 196th. After he started telling lies it was easier to tell more than to admit the truth. Then he had to invent more lies to support the original ones. He had to refine them, come up with the details that would make the story credible even to experts.

Wes bought himself an M-16 through a weapons dealer in

Flint, a scary man named Huey who was getting ready for the race war that would end the world. Huey just stared as Wes handed over the cash, as if he could see the future better than he could see what was going on in the basement storehouse where he did his business. Wes set up a shooting range on his farm outside Moddersville. On weekends he would drive up there, dress in his combat fatigues, strap on the ammunition belt, pouch, canteen and pack, stuff the earplugs into the case he carried in the left front pocket of his fatigue shirt, put on the helmet with its camouflage cover and crawl through the woods above the Muskegon River. But the Michigan woods were not jungle. So he went down to Guatemala for a vacation. Rebels were fighting in the hills, but Wes avoided that—instead he spent two weeks in the jungle by himself, imagining himself part of a platoon humping into the hills above Thanh-Phuoc, walking into an L-shaped ambush like ducks in a shooting gallery just so they could call down an air strike and napalm Charlie into barbecue.

He got real good with the M-16. Then he asked around, carefully, under a phony name (by now he had learned to do all his research through a post office box, under phony names—William Dietrich, Walter Bucknell, Sam Esperanza, T.C. Walsh—Wes had a lot of names; he was a whole platoon all by himself). From a dealer in Las Vegas he bought an M-60 machine gun. "The Pig." He learned to haul its twenty-four pounds and a full pack without tripping on the ammo belt. When you pulled the trigger on the Pig it was like someone was punching you in the gut with a jack hammer. You had to lean on it just to keep it from leaping up in your hands and spraying the treetops. But if Wes was going to be a vet, he wanted to be something hard, the man who was the target for the VC in any ambush because he carried the serious firepower for the platoon.

An absorbing game, even though it was a lie. But no one seemed to want the truth, anyway. By the late eighties the country had buried the truth in a sediment of lies that turned into facts: that the war had been a noble effort. That the U.S. had been there at the request of a democracy, to protect it against Communism. That we would have won if the army had not been held back by a timid government and a bunch of disloyal agitators. There were a hundred other half-truths, outright fabrications, sudden and convenient bouts of amnesia. Wes's lie fit right in. His was small, human-sized. After awhile it fit him well, like the fatigues. When, in 1989, he managed to bribe a Spec 4 in the Pentagon to falsify some records for him, placing Wes in Bravo company, 196th Light Infantry, from May 1967 to March 1968, it felt more like correcting a mistake than lying.

In the meantime his career prospered. He loved engineering. In a computer simulation, on a test stand there were no colors. Only the numbers counted, and though it was a tricky game to control them, at least you had a chance. It was only away from the CAD screen that you had to be a politician. Wes learned what it took. The eighties were the decade for blacks who were willing to do what it took to get ahead. Wes could spot a racist a mile off, and he used their racism against them. The easiest kinds were the ones who pretended not to even notice his color. Whenever he saw that, he knew he had them. He would play them along, then mention something about the 'Nam and watch their guilt level double. He let them indulge their fantasies that they had a black friend. He could imagine them undressing at night in their bedrooms, fat men telling their dull wives, "That Wes Purcell, he's okay. He's not looking for a free ride. He respects us."

He knew that he got some consulting jobs simply because he was black, and he shoved it back into their faces by doing an impeccable job, on time and under budget, so that their condescension might fester inside them. But they didn't fester. They didn't even look uncomfortable. For all he could tell their consciences were milk-white as mashed potatoes. On weekends he would drive out to the farm and fire the pig until his shoulders ached and his hands blistered and the ringing in his head drove away all other sound. He would rip a hole in his plywood target big enough to walk through, and then he would walk through it. He would haul another sheet out of the barn, nail it up to the four-by-fours and shoot a hole in that one, too. After three or four sheets of plywood he would feel okay.

Eventually he didn't need Vietnam, but by then Wes was one of the best known vets in Lansing. The world needed him, the black vet who made good. The minority capitalist. Worried about being exposed, he declined to talk about the war. He was already old to be floating a new business. It made it that much more important that he not slip up. But then Central America took some of the heat off. Vietnam became the last generation's war. The man you found sleeping in the bus station, wiped out on combat drugs, had gotten his habit in Choluteca, not Danang.

Now he was going to have to face this Burdock, a man who had been in the 'Nam for real. Wes had met all comers so far without defeat; he was the heavyweight champion of misleading appearances. It was all old news anyway. The odds were against Burdock having been in Quang Ngai in 1967.

But Wes's house of cards had gotten stacked pretty high over the last twenty-five years.

Burdock settled into one of the armchairs across from Wes's desk. "Let me ask you, Wes: what are you after with all this? Suppose your machine goes into production and all of a sudden people are flying all over America again. What will that mean to you?"

"It means we'll be rich," Wes said.

Burdock was maybe fifty, the same as Wes, but unlike Wes he had let himself go to fat. His white shirtfront sagged over his belt. His breath was like a trash fire and he had a bad smoker's cough. The fluorescent lights glistened off his high brown forehead and steel-rimmed spectacles. One corner of his mouth quirked higher than the other, making him look as if he were about to deliver a sarcastic comment at any moment.

Harry headed for the cabinet where they kept their bar. He had stocked up on some pricey booze; his desire to look needy did not extend to the alcohol budget. He looked over his shoulder. "Drink?"

"Scotch on the rocks," said Burdock. "Does the money matter that much to you?"

"Money doesn't matter to Wes," Harry said. He poured two glasses of Chivas and gave one to each of them. Wes sat down behind the desk, near the air conditioner.

"Money isn't the real reason," Wes agreed. "It's just the way you keep score. If Aerodyne comes through, that tells me that my design work is good. It means strangers are willing to bet big money on my work."

"Not just on your work, Wesley," Burdock said. "There are a dozen firms working on engines like yours. If Aerodyne bets, they're betting mostly on you."

"Maybe that's what I want."

"That's the line to take." Burdock gulped scotch as if it were the water of life. "We might have to stand you up in front of some of the men in New York. Three-quarters of this business is making a good impression. You got to learn to lie like a nigger, and smile."

Harry laughed nervously. Wes forced a smile. Burdock grinned with half his mouth, a twisted smile at once savage and vastly amused. Wes realized that the crooked expression was not just habit—Burdock's face was disfigured. The nerve on one side of his mouth was frozen.

"You've played that game, Wesley?" Burdock asked. Before Wes could answer Burdock burst into a racking, tubercular cough, ragged with phlegm. Wes half expected him to cough up a wad of bloody sputum and spit it on the carpet. Instead of concern, Wes felt repulsion. With a wheeze, Burdock finally caught his breath. "Have you?" he repeated.

"Sure. Sometimes. I don't usually go out on the limb and say so."

"I always go out on the limb. You can see farther from out there." He produced a silver case from his pocket and took from it a ludicrously big cigar. He lit it with the lighter from Wes's desk, leaned back in the chair and exhaled a cloud of smoke. "In 'Nam, the guys that played it safe were the ones that came back in bags. You're caught in an ambush, the only way out is to charge them head-on."

Wes got out of his chair and went for the liquor cabinet. "How about a refill?"

"Absolutely."

Harry stood up. "I'm going to call Alice and tell her where to meet us." He left the office. Wes tried not to look relieved. He would survive if Harry kept his mouth shut. Tomorrow he would go out to the farm and load up the Pig. Burdock heaved himself out of the chair and ambled over to the window.

When Wes approached him with two more glasses of Chivas, Burdock was looking across the airfield toward the old control tower. He tasted the scotch, smacked his lips. Even over the sound of the air conditioner Wes could hear the man's clotted lungs laboring. "Remember when you could fly everywhere?" Burdock said. "The sky was full of planes. They burned the old JP-4 like there was no tomorrow. It wasn't so long ago."

Wes sipped at his scotch. "That's what makes an opportunity for us."

Burdock looked at him. The twisted mouth twitched. "Are you an Opportunist?" Burdock said. "One of these all-American boys?"

"I know how to take advantage of a situation."

"Men like us, Wesley, the way things are made, we should be against the system. We fight all our lives. But the Man's too strong. So we go underground, we tell lies. We make up our whole lives for them." Burdock picked up the purple heart Wes kept on his desk, ran the pink pad of his thumb over the silk ribbon, the wooden frame. "You were in the war."

"I don't talk about it."

"Why not? I do. If I hadn't gone to the 'Nam I would have been just another dumb nigger. The 'Nam made me."

"I don't like to talk about it."

"So why the medal on the desk?"

"That's for business. It's not for me."

Burdock raised one eyebrow. Wes was getting irritated. Was Burdock serious? The 'Nam? The Man? He talked like a bad TV actor.

"Vietnam ruined guys." Wes said. "It didn't make them better."

"Depends on the man. Look at these Nicaraguan vets. Bunch of lazy eunuchs. The media shed tears for them like Niagara Falls. There were lots like that who came back from the 'Nam, but not as bad as these guys. Hell, they won their war, pumped on combat drugs, full tactical support. They come back clean as a schoolmarm's privates. What do they have to complain about?"

"Some of them got gene damage."

"Some of us got Agent Orange. It's a war, not a pig pickin'."

Wes finished his drink and went over to the cabinet for another. The panic he had felt about whether Vietnam would come up was just edginess. He poured three fingers of scotch. Something was working in him. He wanted to spit in the eye of this fat blowhard.

"Are you telling me that because men get killed in any war, then it's okay?" Wes said. "If the brass didn't lie to the men, maybe you'd be right. But what grunt ever knew why the hell he was fighting? In Vietnam, who ever got sent out to the boonies with a sensible strategy? They were just meat for the grinder."

"All I'm saying, Wesley, is that you got to expect bullshit from the Man. You just feed the lies back to them. That's what they want to hear."

"I don't care what whites think."

Burdock looked amused. "So you are against the system after all, Wesley. Good."

Wes stared at him.

"I was wondering whether I ought to back this idea with Aerodyne. Your work looks good in the lab, but I wasn't sure about your guts. But now you got some credibility."

"What are you talking about?"

"Credibility. Business runs on it. Trying to swing a deal without credibility is like trying to run one of these engines without fuel."

"Are you saying—"

"Why do you think they fought the damn war? To kill

VC? To save South Vietnam? Credibility! They didn't think they could use the bomb against the Reds, so the only way they could show the Russians and Chinese that America wasn't pussy was to feed those soldiers into the 'Nam."

"Bull. Look at what they did in Cambodia after we left. They exterminated the place. We were there to prevent that."

Burdock gave him that half smile, as if he were examining a fly caught in his screen door, waiting for it to pause long enough for him to squash it. "Wesley, you're my man. You got the party line down pat. You were made to stand in front of the VC."

Wes's nervousness was back. "What?"

"The venture capitalists, Wes. You'll put it over. Look: when you're living in prison, how do you keep from getting screwed? You kick some ass whenever you have to, and people know not to mess with you. You maintain your credibility."

"Sure," Wes said. He loosened his tie.

"It's like when you're humping the Pig. You seen the guys who get handed the Pig and you know they can't handle it. All they're thinking about is how they're the target. It's like they got a big bull's-eye on their chest, and they're looking to run before there's any reason to run. So the first time there's a fire fight, they're on their face in the mud while the brothers are getting killed around them. You remember Bo. If Sarge hadn't taken the Pig away from him and given it to you, we wouldn't be here sucking this booze today. Everybody in the platoon knew it, it didn't take any brains."

Wes stared at him. Burdock's steel glasses glinted. They shone so brightly that Wes was blinded.

Burdock flopped back into an armchair. "Now you remember me. I wondered how long it would take. Don't worry about what I tell Aerodyne." He reached out the brown hand holding his empty glass. "Refill?"

Wes handled the glass gingerly, as if it might explode. "Sure I remember. But I thought we were talking business."

"Business? I am talking business, Wes. I'm talking about balls, and that's business. You've got credibility. You proved that a long time ago. You only need to prove it once with me. It's like being saved. Once you been saved then you're washed in the Blood. Doesn't mean you can't fuck up. But it means the Man listens when it comes time for you to explain."

Wes poured Burdock another glass of scotch. He moved in slow motion, a scuba diver, deep underwater. His mind worked furiously. Burdock couldn't possibly remember Wes. If he was lying, it must be some kind of test. Either he expected Wes to crack and admit he had never been in the war, or he expected Wes to brass it out.

Or maybe Burdock had mistaken Wes for a guy who really was in the 196th. Maybe Harry had said something to him and when Burdock met Wes he just filled Wes into some hole in his memory. Christ, it was thirty years ago. Who remembered what happened when they were eighteen?

Or else Burdock was pretending to know Wes because *he* was lying, too. Because he had never been in Vietnam either. Maybe a little offense was the best defense.

"How's the wound?" Wes asked him, handing him the glass. "Ever bother you?"

Burdock touched the twisted corner of his mouth. He started to speak and instead started coughing again. It took him a full minute to catch his breath, and when he did his face was an unpleasant liver color. "This? Hardly know it's there. Dead nerve never grows back, you know."

"You think about it a lot?"

"Almost never. How about you?" Burdock's smile was a sneer. "I'm not saying I don't remember. I remember humping along the Song Tram, it was about a million degrees out and Willie Estivez talking to himself with dysentery cause he drank some river water."

"He was pretty sick," Wes said leadenly.

"Sick? He crapped his pants till he bled. You had a piss-poor attitude, Wesley. Short-timer's disease. Remember that night Handjob sent us out to check on some noise he heard in the brush and you started firing at nothing, and we ran back and told them we'd got jumped by Charlie? And the

time in that ambush on the hillside you fired the Pig so long
you burned all the skin off your hand? Remember Duc
Tan? Pinned down for sixteen hours? Then when we got
out you plugged that girl in the love-hole with your
weapon—all the way up to the magazine? Lordy. I guess I
might remember that, too."

Wes sat down in the other armchair. He didn't say anything.

"Still got the trophy box? I remember when Sarge tried
to take it away from you in Chu Lai, when he found you
with Madame Whoopie. You had it open next to the bed
and were trying some stuff out on her. Stank to high heaven.
I wouldn't talk about that either, if I was you."

Wes tried to catch his breath, but all he inhaled was a
lungfull of sulfurous air. Sometime during his monologue
Burdock had let an enormous, silent fart.

"And how we were all brothers, then. The guys come in
from all over the States, but after six months in the boonies
there's no more black and white. You're all going to die or
live and the only way you're gonna live is to stick together.
And then you come back to the World and it's business as
usual. Yessir. I wouldn't want to remember that either. Too
much irony."

Wes roused himself. "What are you talking about?"

Burdock relit his cigar, talking between puffs. "Hate
irony." Puff. "Kills people." Puff.

"Stop it," Wes said, and he was surprised at the steadi-
ness in his voice.

Burdock's face was innocent as the moon. "Stop what?"

"I never did those things."

"Don't worry. I know when to keep my mouth shut."

"Stop it!" Wes gripped his glass until his hand shook,
spilling scotch on his trousers. "You know I wasn't there."

"Wasn't there?" Burdock raised an eyebrow. "What do
you mean? Where did you get this Purple Heart, then?"

"I bought it. I made it up, you son of a bitch!"

"If you weren't there, Wesley, then how come I remember you?"

Wes stood up, shaking. "Because you weren't there, either!"

"No sir. I could mail you my discharge papers. 'Langston H. Burdock' it says up top." Burdock drew on the cigar, coughed a little. "We were both there, Wes. Vietnam made us."

"You're not Burdock."

"Langston H. Burdock." He flapped a hand at Wes. "In the flesh. Go ahead, touch me."

Wes recoiled. "You're crazy."

"Doesn't that just burn you up, Wesley, the way they say that about all us vets?"

The door opened and Harry came in. "Sorry I took so long. All set. She'll meet us at the Buttonwood at seven. You guys get it all figured out?"

Wes stared at Harry. He carefully set his glass down on the desk. Langston H. Burdock got up, smiling. "We were just talking over old times. Did you know Wes and me were in the same unit in Vietnam?"

"No kidding!"

"Yep. Wes here was something special. I bet he never talks about it."

"Not much."

"Modest." He looked at Wes. "Doesn't pay to be too modest, Wes." He set his glass down on the desk, beside Wes's. "Well, let's eat."

Burdock's hand brushed against Wes's, a light, quick contact, so slight as to be incidental. But it wasn't. It felt as if Burdock had smeared shit on him. Harry was walking out the door.

"Harry," Wes called to him, shuddering. "You take Mr. Burdock with you. I want to check something. I'll catch up with you."

Harry looked at him. Wes could tell he was worried that Wes had said something to queer the deal. "You'll have to take a cab. You'll be late."

"I'll be there," Wes insisted.

"Okay, Wes," Harry said grimly.

Burdock stopped. "Wesley, come along. There's more we should talk about. You worry too much."

Wes stared at Burdock, and for the first time saw that Burdock had two faces. It was like a drawing Wes had seen once that from one angle looked like a young girl, and from another like a withered hag. The twisted expression on his face wasn't necessarily sarcasm. It might be pain.

In another instant the impression was gone, and Burdock's face held only sardonic amusement.

"I can't come with you," said Wes.

"I'll be around for awhile," Burdock said. "We'll see a lot of each other. Just like old times."

"No," said Wes quietly. I can't, he thought.

After he watched them climb into the Chrysler, Wes crossed the apron to the lab. The brutal sun was setting. His mind was like a lump of hot wax, melting; his face felt flushed. The bloods in Vietnam must have felt this hot as they stumbled through the boonies, waiting for their time to run out. The short-timers—the ones who were going home soon—they were the most nervous. Wes did not feel nervous at all.

In the lab, he powered up the board and turned on the prop. On the screen it began to revolve, slowly at first, so that you could count the individual blades—but within a second or so they were a blur. The pitch of the engine's whine rose to a high keen, then stayed there. Whirling, whirling. He remembered when it had been just an idea, a very good idea. How hard it had been to make it real. The problem he had had to solve was that when the engine got going too fast, the stresses on the blades became too much for the metal, and the prop would tear itself apart. But he had solved that problem. So far his design had withstood every test. Wes checked the board one more time, then opened the door to the test chamber.

October
····································

*Whenever a true theory appears, it will be its own
evidence. Its test is, that it will explain all phenom-
ena. Now many are thought not only unexplained
but inexplicable; as language, sleep, madness,
dreams, beasts, sex.*

— *Ralph Waldo Emerson,* Nature

18: SUNDAY, OCTOBER 10

....

Showing that the Days of the Samaritan have not Passed

The back of George's throat was scratchy and his ears buzzed. He fished the plastic water bottle from the refuse piled in the car. About an inch was left. Keeping his eyes on the deserted highway, he tilted his head back and squirted some into his mouth. It tasted of sulfur. His throat didn't feel much better and the heat was still impossible. He focused on the road and tried to think.

The '90 Hyundai he drove supposedly had air conditioning, but that was a fiction that George estimated had not had any relation to reality for at least five years. Discovering tread on the tires was a triumph of nostalgia. The man in Providence who'd sold it to him claimed it had been up on blocks in his garage since the second ration cut in 1996, and that the 42,000 miles on the odometer was a reliable figure.

George had been in a hurry. The car had already broken down once, outside of Wilmington, Delaware, and just the other night in D.C., Dadaist punks had broken in and installed an expensive stereo. The interior smelled of gasohol from the twenty-gallon cans George had crammed into the back so as to use Richard's phony ration card as little as possible. A hot wind blasted through his window. On the passenger's seat a battered 1992 Mobil Travelguide lay open on top of his microcam. He estimated he was forty or fifty miles south of Richmond and might possibly make the North Carolina line before dark if he didn't come across another place where I-85 had rotted into unusability.

As if thought had conjured up reality, a line of orange barrels emerged out of the heat mirage. George stopped in the middle of the right-hand lane, beside an exit ramp, thirty yards in front of the barrels. He peered down the road. There was no telling whether the detour was a holdover from some fantasized repair project or a prank by local kids or even a trap set by secessionists. He couldn't waste time; he should have been in Tallahassee before the beginning of the month. A little scared, George got out of the car and walked on past the barrels.

The ramp peeled off to his right among the acid-scarred pines. Ahead, weeds shot through cracks in the asphalt. The setting sun threw shadows of the trees across the pavement. The map said he wasn't far from Lake Gaston. Maybe the road across the water was gone. Maybe a sniper waited in the woods. He was about to turn around and go back when he saw something lying on the pavement some way ahead. From a distance, in the slanting light, it looked like the crumpled sleeve of a jacket, but when George drew closer he saw it was a dead cat.

It had not been dead long. A few flies had gathered. The tail looked as if any moment it might flit into agitated life, but the legs were flung out in four different directions and the body was strewn a yard or more across the line in the center of the road. The cat's skull was intact but pushed flatter than normal. Its eyes and mouth were closed. Death had written an expression of resignation on the cat's face. "Look what you've done to me," it said.

Oto, George's Siamese, had been killed like this fifteen years ago, in the road outside his house in Valhalla, New York. Oto was chocolate brown, darker than this cat. He was very smart. George would come home from work in the city and find that Oto had opened the cupboard, dragged out the tupperware box that held his food, opened it and helped himself. He had to get a child-proof latch for the door. When George found him mangled in the road he didn't believe it. Oto was too smart to do such a stupid thing. Angrily, he had dug a grave in the back yard, but as soon as the last shovelful of dirt was on it he had broken down and cried.

Nine years later, the first laboratory revivals had been performed—on cats.

George stared at the animal. Such things shouldn't happen anymore, with hardly any cars on the roads. He wondered who had been driving along so recently and where they had gone after they hit the cat. He wondered if they'd even bothered to stop. Christ, you'd think it would take more than one car to do that much damage. George considered getting his tools and burying the cat. He didn't have a shovel, but he could dig a hole with the tire iron. But then he'd have to pick it up, and for that he didn't have anything but his hands. The thought made him sick. Besides, it was stupid to get sentimental about dead animals when people were dying daily. Night was coming on. He stumbled back to the car, feeling even more that he was being watched. The engine rattled and he inched down the ramp to old U.S. 1. Whether or not the interstate was intact, he didn't want to have to drive past the carcass—yet he could not escape feeling guilty at leaving the cat lying on the empty highway.

In the months he'd spent pursuing the Alien since his week in the Ft. Wayne jail, George's ability to gut things out had worn thin. The first stories he'd filed to HCR were full of ideas. His theories expanded. Maybe the alien invasion was happening all over the U.S. at once. Maybe the idea of an alien invasion was too single-minded an explanation for a metaphysical phenomenon that might be arising out of the millennial *zeitgeist*. UFO reports continued through the summer, but if a pattern persisted he could not discern it. As time passed without another encounter, the revelation that had seemed so stunning to George in New York began to seem more and more unreal. Doubts grew. The Burdock he'd trapped in the men's room was probably the same as the one on the train, only a man and nothing more. You didn't need to resort to malevolent aliens to account for people messing up the world.

As his spirits flagged, George's health failed. His beard had grown back in patches but the fuzz on his head would never convince a diehard anti-revivalist. Worse, by the end of July the Anti-Revival amendment had been ratified by 41 states. Legal revival had vanished. The legal status of the already revived was in some doubt; there was a case pending before the Supreme Court, where the aging conservatives still held sway. It did not look good for people like George. He still wore his toupee.

More than once he considered giving up and going home. He tried calling Lucy: at first he got no answer, and then was told their number was out of service. When, during their next teleconference, he told Richard he was worried about her, Richard revealed that Lucy had changed her number and didn't want to talk to him. She had sworn him to secrecy, Richard said, but Richard couldn't keep a secret from his best friend. Richard assured George that Lucy was all right—working away at the Corrections office—but angry. He said she needed time to get over George's leaving. George didn't blame her for being mad, and he respected her need for privacy. They'd always had that kind of relationship. So he took Richard's advice and stopped trying to call her. Instead he relayed print messages back and forth through Richard.

I love you Lucy.

I know you do George.

I have to do this. Please wait for me.

Find your alien, George. Don't come back until you're ready.

She was a remarkable woman, Lucy, to understand. George pushed on. One way or another he would see an end to it. He hoped there would be some answers when he got there.

George turned on the Dadaists' radio and scanned through the FM band for news, but all he got was country western and gospel. He encountered few vehicles on U.S. 1; in one fifteen-minute period only a bus and a state tractor trailer, both headed the other way. He was hungry, but he didn't want to stop in any small towns.

Night had fallen, and he had just passed a sign announcing "Welcome to North Carolina" when he was startled by a figure waving frantically in the middle of the road. He slammed on the brakes. The car shook like a paint mixer and jerked to a stop, slewed halfway onto the shoulder. His headlights showed two women beside a big car. George sat trying to get his heartbeat to slow, thinking about Oto dead in the road.

He got out of his car. The woman he'd almost hit shaded her eyes and squinted against his headlights. The other leaned, arms crossed, against the side of their old Buick. They both wore T-shirts and blue jeans.

"What's the problem?" George asked.

The woman who had waved him down said, "Our car broke down."

"Do you have a cigarette?" the other woman said.

"I'm sorry, I don't smoke."

"I can't believe this," she said disgustedly.

"What happened?" George asked.

The first woman looked at him in confusion. She had bleached blond hair cut in a pageboy. Her eye shadow made her look like a vampire. "The car broke *down*," she repeated.

"He's a blind man," said the other.

"I mean, how did it happen? What did the motor sound like? Will it turn over?"

"It just stopped."

"Does anybody have a cigarette?" the second woman asked again. Her T-shirt had an arrow pointing to her left, and beneath it, "HIS." Off in the direction of the arrow loomed dark trees smothered by kudzu, like figures out of a child's nightmare.

George opened the Buick's door and tried the ignition. There was not even a click. "Sounds like your battery's dead. I've got jumper cables."

The blond looked worried.

"I can't believe this, Bets," the other said. "I paid fifty dollars for this car."

George tried to be sympathetic. "I'm sorry. I'll give you a jump."

"Listen," Bets said. "We have to get this car running because we have to get to Zion. Charlene's husband is going to beat her if she doesn't get there in time for the meeting."

Charlene didn't look too worried about it. George refrained from pointing out that Charlene's husband couldn't beat her if she didn't ever show up.

"I'll pull my car around." He moved the Hyundai around to face the Buick bumper-to-bumper, tugged the cables from under the gas cans and opened the hoods. The Buick's motor was hot; a wisp of steam came from the radiator. George wondered where they'd gotten the gas to run it. He shone his flashlight on the hoses. They looked intact. The women did nothing. He hooked up the cables. "All set," he said.

The women didn't move.

"Does anybody have a menthol?" Charlene asked.

"Try starting it," George said. He stepped on the Hyundai's gas pedal; the motor raced, the lights brightened.

After staring a moment Bets finally got into the Buick and tried the ignition. The engine turned over sluggishly but did not start. George went around to try it himself a few times, with no better luck. He got back into the Hyundai and turned off his engine. The sudden silence was filled by the sound of insects.

"I can't *believe* it." Charlene stood with her hand on her

hip and an expression on her face that could sterilize. George wondered what sort of meeting they were going to.

Bets came over to stand beside him in the tall grass by the ditch. She wasn't more than twenty-five; neither of them was. "Couldn't you just push us to Zion?"

"My car is pretty small. Yours is big."

"But yours is running."

"How far is Zion?"

"Zion—you know—Raleigh?"

"I can't believe this!" Charlene shouted. She kicked the side of the Buick with her sneaker.

"That's eighty or more miles," George said.

"Why don't you just push us there?"

George tried to keep his wits. "I'll give you a ride to the nearest phone. You can call for help. You can tell her husband what happened."

"Won't matter none to Buddy. Buddy's got the Call."

George smiled. "He'll have to hang up sometime."

The joke died pitifully. Charlene, who had quieted down enough to listen, snorted.

"Ain't you been saved yet?" Bets said.

"Look, I'll drive you to a phone," George said. "You can call home."

"We don't have any phones. We don't have anybody to call."

"Doesn't anybody have a menthol cigarette?"

George looked down the road. A couple of hundred yards ahead, part way around the bend, stood a deserted gas station. Maybe he could get some water for the Buick's radiator. He took one of his empty gasohol cans and walked down the road. The station was an old two-pump country special, vintage 1940s. Beside the door a battered ice machine gleamed in his flashlight. A faded, flyspecked poster for "Pepsi: Pride of the Carolinas" still stood in the window. Next to it was a white cardboard sign with black hand lettering:

CLOSED UNTIL KINGDOM COME

Around the side of the building George found a washtub filled with rainwater. He dunked the can until he had a good amount and lugged it back toward the cars. The can banged against his leg and his arm ached. It really ought not to have been that heavy; he had lost a lot of weight. The women were leaning against their car. Charlene looked unhappy. George wondered if she had been drinking. He thought wistfully about the liter of scotch in his gym bag. He poured the water into the radiator, splashing it on himself. "We got to get out of here," Bets kept repeating.

"Try it now," George said.

"Why don't you just give us a push?" said Bets.

Charlene snorted again. "He's driving a Jap car, Bets. Don't want to touch no American car."

George got into the Buick and tried the ignition. The motor labored but nothing happened. After repeated tries he stopped for fear of running down his own battery. He sat behind the wheel, exhausted, breathing shallowly. He listened to his own lungs labor until they settled back to something like calm, then realized that there was other breathing in the car. He felt a warm breath on his neck. In panic he jerked himself out of the Buick, ready to scream.

A dog sat in the back seat. Nicely groomed, expensive—a Chou. It sat happily, patient, bright-eyed. It must have cost more than the car.

"Can't you fix it?" asked Bets.

"What?" George felt dazed.

"He doesn't know any English, Bets," Charlene said with exaggerated emphasis. "No speak *American*. Too busy trying to grow *hair*, Bets."

Bets stared at George's toupee. "You ain't a *zombie,* are you, mister?" Charlene snickered.

"You think I'd stop if I was?" George wondered whether he'd better get lost before they began to think about that.

"Lordy, it's dark here," Bets said. "They was a flying saucer report up here just last month. I hope they don't come back. You think it's the end coming?"

George shook his head; it felt like his brain was rattling around inside. He needed a drink. "I can't wait here. Won't you come along to the next town?"

"Give us a push."

"That doesn't make sense. I can't push you. My car's barely running."

"I can't believe this car doesn't work. I paid fifty bucks—"

"Look, will you get in the car?"

Charlene turned on him. "Listen. I don't mean to be rude, but why don't you just fuck off."

George stumbled back. He picked up the gas can, threw the cables and flashlight into the back of the Hyundai. His hand was shaking as he turned the ignition; the starter wound sluggishly and for a horrible moment he thought the motor would not start. It caught and rattled to life. He backed the car around, across the two-lane road, his headlights fanning away from the women and their dog and their car. Charlene was leaning against the fender again and Bets was already back in the middle of the road preparing to flag down the next car. Lights flared in George's mirror and he saw a pickup truck approach, slowing to a stop. He put the Hyundai in gear. In the mirror he could see Bets leaning in the window of the truck.

19: MONDAY, OCTOBER 11
....
A Desperate Character

The problem with people was that you could not tell when they were lying. The desk clerk in the Federal Arms Hotel, for instance. Twenty minutes after Frances Delano Roosevelt Amassa checked in, the clerk rang up to the room and told Delano she would have to move to another because the distilled water system for that floor had been contaminated.

Contaminate the water on a single floor? Right. The clerk
tried to move Delano from room 777 to room 666. Delano
wouldn't put up with that; she made them give her 101. Let
them try to figure out what that meant.

Delano knew that the clerk was a Vietnamese agent, despite
her red hair and freckles and California teeth, because she had
Vietnamese eyes. HCR had reported about the Caucasoid
virus the southeast Asians were using to alter racial characteristics, enabling them to infiltrate every level of American life.
But you couldn't hide Vietnamese eyes. Vietnamese eyes were
fanatic. Devious. Worse even than Chinese. Bred into the
genes through two thousand years of alternating hegemony
over Southeast Asia and domination by the yellow colossus to
the north. Any white person unable to grasp the Vietnamese
character was doomed to fall prey to it, though grasping it was
like grasping a thistle in your bare hand.

But that was Old Business. In room 101 Delano got back
to tracing Eberhart. She jacked her terminal to the phone
and punched up the Library of Congress. Once she was into
the catalog she used an orthogonal scalpel to exit the library
for a little fishing expedition into the Department of Energy.

There were only a couple of ways to get enough gas to run a
private car. The obvious ways were to be rich or have influence. The rich had influence and most who had influence were
rich. Eberhart was not rich, and his most obvious source of
influence was HCR. Richard Shrike had not told her anything
about Eberhart having access to gasohol through HCR, but
Delano had experience enough with Shrike to know he was a
liar. So she had taken the precaution of inspecting Shrike's
own finances before setting off after Eberhart.

The DOE system was ten years out of date, and forty
minutes later Delano managed to work her way past the
defenses into the ration records. She cross-checked Shrike's
personal credit numbers against her best guess of Eberhart's
movements around New England in the last two months.
Bingo. Cross linked with one of Shrike's accounts she found
a gasohol ration card number. Charged to this number she
found a series of withdrawals from the U.S. Strategic Gasohol Reserve: on June 28 to Gerald Konstantis of Provi-

dence, Rhode Island; on July 19 to John A. Kunen of Quincy, Massachusetts; on September 1 to Leo Ennis of East Brunswick, New Jersey; and on October 6 to Susan Lawrence of Wilmington, Delaware. Clearly, all these people did not hold the same ration card. Yet the pattern they followed was consistent with Eberhart's movements. Shrike must have given Eberhart a card containing a magpie routine that drew on the authorizations of random citizens. Such cards were hard to come by and completely illegal.

And Shrike had told her nothing of this.

Delano turned off the portable and stretched. Shrike might lie, but technology did not. It was two o'clock and she had not eaten. The Federal Arms bragged that it was still air conditioned, but they were running at a nominal eighty-five because of the power rationing, which meant, during the current heatwave, ninety or higher. She played with the locker key, rolling it across her fingers like a coin. She had a couple of hours to kill before she could pick up her package in Union Station. She went into the bathroom, washed her face and shoulders from the distilled water tap, pulled her white jacket over her T-shirt and headed out. Though she had no faith in the hotel's security, she slipped her card into the slot and set the door to lethal. Anyone who wanted to check her out would at least have to give the maid ten bucks. Delano had been a maid once, and she knew they could use the money.

She walked down Pennsylvania toward the White House. At Washington Circle she bought some fried tofu and lemonade from a vendor. Since the last time she'd been in D.C. the cops had given up trying to keep the street people away from the commercial districts. Washington Circle offered cripples and AMPS sufferers, a schizophrenic talking to someone who wasn't there, and a man squatting on the sidewalk playing the harmonica. His cap had a few coins in it; his sign read, "I'm from California: Help Me." The Twits and Twists on their way to and from their offices wore designer surgical masks. They might have money but were not rich enough to desert the microbe-infested air of the city for the country. At Pennsylvania and 17th a knot of national guardsmen lounged around a tank on the sidewalk in front of the Executive Office building, smoking and eyeing the women. They didn't give Delano a second look. She smelled the tent city on the Ellipse before she even got there, an odor of mildewed canvas and porta-toilets. The occasional scent of cooking could not conceal the fact that most of the protestors were starving.

Delano crossed 17th and passed between the tents. The protestors, confined to one side of the sidewalk because the Dornan Law allowed the guardsmen to shoot anyone crossing, looked at her with indifference equal to the soldiers'. Away from the sidewalk thin men and women sat beneath the overgrown trees. The Ellipse had long since lost its grass; now it was baked earth that turned to muck whenever it rained. At the center, in a cleared space a hundred yards across, a splinter group of the Reverend Jimmy-Don Gilray's followers had marked out a cross in stones: the landing pad for the advance ship the hopeful expected to arrive any day now bringing the Message that would save them all.

At one end of the clearing stood a wooden platform. A woman and a couple of men were sitting on the edge listening to a radio, recuperating from their noon ceremony. At first, from the sound of the crowd noise coming over the radio, Delano thought they were listening to a religious rally, but when she got closer she realized it was a baseball game.

"What's all the cheering about?"

"It's sarcastic," the woman said. She wore a faded yellow shirt and jeans with the knees worn through. She sweated profusely.

One of the men, wearing a crusted T-shirt on which the blood of his latest flagellation had not yet dried, said, "Senators just blew a two-run lead. That kid Ellison hit one out for the Sox."

Delano hoisted herself onto the platform, crossed to the back and pulled herself up on one of the two-by-fours supporting the sign that read, "The Fact that He has not Destroyed us is Proof of His Love." She looked across the tops of the tents, across E Street, past the tanks and troops to the White House. They were almost done reconstructing the

East Wing where the suicide plane had crashed. She wondered if the President, looking out the windows of the Blue Room past his helipad, could see her. I'm here, Mr. President, she thought. I'm ready when you need me.

Delano had always felt a connection to the President. Not with any one president, but with whoever the President happened to be at the time. She often got messages from him. He sent them secretly. He had to. Considering the way things were going now, it was amazing that the country hadn't fallen apart completely. Sometimes the messages would come by way of single lines in the news reports— mostly over HCR—and sometimes, especially when the President had something he wanted to convey that he had to keep secret from the CIA, they'd be much more subtle. The way her toothbrush had been moved slightly overnight, pointing toward the spot on the wallpaper. The stray dog that would look up from nosing in the trash of an alleyway just as she passed. And there the message would be: "Don't eat dairy products." "Old people are dangerous." "The next person who hires you is our agent."

There was no sign from the White House. She had not really expected one.

"Sister, you need some help?"

Delano reached for the police .38 at the small of her back. She looked down at the skinny man on the platform. The others there were looking at her too. The man was feverish. His skin was peeling and the fresh skin below it was decidedly darker. He was turning black. No wonder he was living with the flagellants, praying for help. He should have worn a condom.

Delano hopped down from the sign. "What time is it?" she asked.

The man stared at her stupidly.

"Three-thirty," the woman in the yellow shirt said. The woman had AMPS, too.

"Thanks," said Delano. She got off the platform on the side away from them and walked off south toward the Washington Monument.

Delano had been trailing Eberhart since June. Her contact

was Richard Shrike, but Jason Abramowitz had to be pulling the strings. Before she had even gotten properly started, Shrike was in Raleigh and working for the Reverend Jimmy-Don Gilray. The juxtaposition of HCR and the Reverend's ministry was too significant to be ignored, especially when stories by Eberhart continued appearing on HCR during the last four months, while Delano was chasing him around the Midwest and Northeast. These stories had all passed through Shrike's hands, but Shrike had insisted to her that Eberhart had scrambled his burster signal so that he could not be traced. For all she knew Shrike had originated the stories himself. And no one seemed at all interested in the disappearance of Eberhart's wife, Lucy Di Paulo.

Shrike had sent Delano off with a vague recollection of the map he had seen in the Eberhart-Di Paulo apartment before it had been torched that Sunday in June. The fire had destroyed Eberhart's notes. So Delano had been on her own, the reason for this chase never made clear to her. The fact that Eberhart was using Shrike's gasohol card was only the latest evidence that she had not been told the truth. There was a plot afoot; the President had told her. Eberhart had either killed his wife and Shrike had covered up for him, or Shrike had killed both Di Paulo and Eberhart and orchestrated a clever chase to distract attention from this fact, or Di Paulo and Eberhart had run off together. But what about the "heart attack" that Eberhart had suffered only weeks before his disappearance? What about the terrorist attack on Mt. Rushmore that had taken place on the day Eberhart disappeared? What about the White Sox climbing from sixth to first since that date? What about Gilray's founding of the City of Zion immediately after Shrike's move south?

If Eberhart had already killed he could kill again. If others had killed him then Delano would be killed too if she came too near the truth.

Or perhaps the President himself had set these events in motion. Perhaps he had done it all simply to get Delano Amassa's attention. The President was a lonely man. The burden of power in a country where peaceful polity was eroding had fallen upon his gentle shoulders, and there was no woman beside him to help him carry that weight. He needed a woman schooled in harsh reality, one determined to do whatever was necessary to ensure the survival of the republic. A woman who would act according to conscience rather than expediency. People could see that Delano was such a woman, and they did what they could to keep her from coming to a full understanding of her powers.

She only wished she could comfort him more.

But no one said her job would be easy. Whatever happened, she would be guided by the truth. When the conflagration came that would purge the United States for the next thousand years, there would be at least one true patriot ready to face down evil with a pure heart.

The Mall was quiet. The ranks of the NRC Disaster Insurance Army, waiting for the reparations that would never come, had been swelled by numbers of other protesters. Still others were bums. If you had asked them, most would have called themselves "tourists." Too aimless to take on politics or religion, they probably weren't sure exactly why they hung around the Mall. They wanted to see the sights. They were out of work and had nothing better to do. They wanted to be able to tell their never-to-be-born grandchildren how they had been in the nation's capital on the eve of the new millennium. They heard they could score some wide-spectrum antibiotics there. They wanted to disk some pictures of Susie and Tommy at the Lincoln Memorial, and the weirds in body paint living by the Vietnam Wall, and hear, shouted from the platform where Delano had just stood, the words of the letter the flagellants said they had gotten from God.

Each no doubt had his or her reason, just as each lemming undoubtedly had his own reason to join the rush to extermination. If there were such things as lemming camera crews, they would send a remote down to interview the lemmings; Mr. Arthur Lemming would pause a quarter of a mile from the sea, the salt breeze blowing back his whiskers with the scent of his waiting annihiliation, and tell the furry reporter about his family, about his career, about his interest in lemming sports and lemming sex and lemming politics. And then he'd turn for the cliff.

Delano walked down Constitution Avenue past the mile of public buildings, by the ruins of the IRS building to the Capitol. Lemming Central. There was no place more out of tune with the technological realities of the twenty-first century. No faith in human invention or anything else. She turned up toward Union Station. The cavernous hall was busy, supplicants coming in, officials and their bodyguards going out, squads of soldiers keeping track of them both. The clock above the ticket windows read 16:25. Delano went up to one and booked a compartment on the late evening Sunliner for Tallahassee. She then sat down and watched locker 325 on the chance that the delivery had not yet been made. Nothing happened. At five o'clock she went over to the locker. She took out the camera bag she had left there when she'd arrived that morning. No corner of the station was out of the reach of security cameras, so despite her desire to check it she slung the bag over her shoulder and took the metro to Foggy Bottom. She got off and walked back up to Pennsylvania.

Washington Circle was changing from day to night. The vendor was gone. Dealers were out hawking drugs and cures. The diseased beggars had moved. The schizophrenic had fallen asleep on one of the benches; the street musician had a few more coins in his cap but had stopped playing. Delano crossed back over Rock Creek to the hotel. Time to dress and have an expensive dinner, on Abramowitz. She disarmed the door. The room looked the same. That didn't mean it hadn't been searched. But it didn't smell changed either. She decided to splurge; she found a five-dollar coin in her purse and took a real shower. She put on her white riding pants and was admiring how the blue steel of her gun worked with her best cobalt blouse and titanium ear rings when the phone beeped. She turned off the eye and answered. Shrike appeared on the screen.

"Francie?" he asked. "This is Richard."

"I can see that," she replied. He looked like he had just returned from Mount Olympus, stunned by divinity. She assumed an attack stance, aimed the .38 at the camera, and flipped on the video. Bang.

"Nice gun," he said. "Matches your shirt."

Delano slipped the gun into the holster beneath her jacket. "What do you want?"

"Want?" He seemed to think about it, then remember. "What's the latest on George?"

"He's headed south. He might be in Raleigh right now, for all I know."

"Zion. We call it Zion, now. He's coming here?"

"If you were right about that map, I think he's just passing through on his way to Florida. Have you had any more contact with him?"

"That's why I'm calling. He hasn't filed anything for almost a month. We aren't getting enough to make continuing this chase worthwhile."

She decided to cut through the bullshit. "I know you've got his credit number. Cut off his money and you'll have him."

Shrike stared at her. "Something could happen to him. I just want you to close on him as fast as possible. When you catch up with him, call me before you make a move. We may have to bring him in."

He didn't even acknowledge that he'd lied to her. And did he really care what happened to Eberhart? Delano didn't buy that. Maybe Shrike wanted her to be so worried about Eberhart she would get careless and let herself be offed by him. Shrike had never cared much what happened to her.

"Sure," she said. "So, how are you, Richard?"

Shrike's pupils were like pinpricks into the void. "Doing the Lord's work. There's a lot of it to do. I'm thinking that I may have to make a trip to D.C. soon."

"A lot of people are doing that."

"How are things up there?"

Delano thought about the President. What would he want her to say?

"Things are going according to plan."

Shrike hesitated. "Good." he paused again. "Look, I wouldn't want you to hurt George."

"I won't hurt him unless it's necessary."

"You don't think it will be necessary?"

"What does the Reverend say?"

"The Reverend isn't into this. He doesn't know George."

"And the Commandante?"

"I don't know what you're talking about."

Delano sat down on the bed, out of the center of the phone's eye. She picked up the camera bag and put it on her lap. "I was just teasing."

Shrike searched for her. He looked lost, a look she hadn't seen from him since the time they'd slept together. "I've got to go. Call me."

"Right," she said. The screen went blank.

Delano wondered what the call was all about. She was fed up with lies. She unzipped the bag. Her ten thousand dollars was gone. In its place was a flat package wrapped in an ace bandage. She unwrapped the bandage and found a folded sheet of paper and a packet of thirty capsules. She had been seeking it on the street for six months. The technological solution. She unfolded the paper, a single laser-printed sheet, and read:

TRUTH

One cap only, seekers. Inhibits left temporal lobe language receptivity, stimulates right lobe tonal & attitudinal receptivity. Global aphasia of six to eight hours duration.

You will be unable to understand spoken language during that period; your sensitivity to tone of voice, body language, inflection, nonverbal cues will be simultaneously enhanced.

The Tyranny of the Word is broken. Enjoy. Just don't try to talk too much.

Delano broke the seal on the packet and examined a cap. The stuff was so hard to get that she'd been willing to take the chance on getting burned with the blind locker dropoff.

The powder inside was yellowish white. It could be powdered sugar. She got some water and swallowed one. She wondered how long it took. She turned on the TV and watched the cable news. During a review of the Bogart/Gable remake of "The Man Who Would Be King," Delano realized that, although she could understand what the director was saying, his words had turned into gibberish. She smiled. "God damn," she said aloud.

At least that was what she thought she said.

As she walked to dinner through Georgetown, Delano was followed. To make sure she made three consecutive right turns and stepped into an alley. She stood against the building and watched the sidewalk. A small figure appeared there. Delano took one quick step, grabbed the kid by the arm and jerked him into the alley. She clamped her hand over his mouth.

"Are you following me?" Delano said. The words came readily to her lips, but she heard them as if she'd spoken a foreign tongue.

The boy stopped struggling and answered in a brief rush of words. Delano felt his tense muscles, heard the fear in his voice, saw the flick of his eyelashes in the dim light. Whatever his words were he was saying he wasn't following her. And he was lying.

He wore a green work shirt and patched jeans. She found a knife strapped to his leg. "What's this?"

The boy was trying to think of a way out; Delano could feel it in the twist of his shoulders. Another flight of words, superficially calmer, but with an edge of calculation. Some kind of excuse.

"Who do you work for?" Delano found that, if she didn't think about what she wanted to say, but simply let the words flow, it was easier to talk. The sounds she produced still didn't make sense, but she decided she could tell what she'd said by the boy's reaction.

The boy spoke more words, clearly no answer. *Let me go, please.*

He was as easy to read as a billboard. A feeling of power swept through Delano. The .38 slipped into her hand like a touchstone, cool, heavy. "Who do you work for."

The boy knew he was in trouble now. His reply was less defensive. It might not be the truth, but it wasn't a lie either. An equivocation.

"The CIA?"

No. Truth.

The kid was too evasive. He might be a mugger, or a religious nut sent to follow Delano from the Ellipse, or a spy for one of the President's enemies, or Eberhart's agent. Delano poked the gun between his shoulderblades, shoved him toward the back of the alley.

His eyes were wide. Vietnamese eyes. His hair was red, like the desk clerk's, but cropped short. Delano made him get down on his knees with his hands behind his back. In the darkness she could just see his chin tremble. From the street came faint sounds of passersby.

"You wired?" Delano asked him.

The boy shook his head, swallowing. Afraid. Of dying for the cause? Of being found out? Delano couldn't tell.

She shot him in the back of the head, then went to dinner. She had some trouble understanding the waiter, but the menu was no problem.

20: MONDAY, OCTOBER 11
....

Richard, at the Piano, has a Religious Experience

"What I want to know," asked the woman in the white dress with the shocking red slash down its side, "is—what's the Reverend really like?"

"Loving," said Richard. "He's the most loving man I've

ever met." He sipped his champagne and looked at her, eyes wide as he could manage, over the rim of his glass. The drug was kicking in. They called it "Lips": he could read the fissures of the woman's lips like a relief map. She exuded a haze of pheromones. God, how he loved North Carolina!

Charles Duke Sumner's pre-election party was in full swing. The babble of voices, the cigarette smoke, the clink of champagne bottles against glasses in the crowded rooms of Sumner's fine southern home had grown over the last hour and a half until, closing his eyes, Richard could imagine he was in an East End club during the break. The accents even sounded a little like the Brits, if you were twisted enough. Richard was.

"Have you read *The Samurai Magnolia* yet?" the woman asked.

The latest southern regionalist best seller. That was choice. If he could keep from being sick he was going to enjoy this. "Southern Literature?" said Richard. "Don't make me puke."

"You don't like our writing?"

"Writing's extinct: fossil wing of the Smithsonian."

"You're from the North," she said coquettishly. "You don't have a tradition. But Southern fiction is alive and well; it's still in touch with values. With The Land."

Richard laughed. "What land? It's history! All you've got left is a bunch of scribblers serving up the same old incestuous caricatures so they can sell to a New York audience that wants its prejudices confirmed. Hoping for the movie deal. And you're flattered by it! You think you're special. You're too busy taking pride in your accents to see you're just the same venal, hypocritical narcissists as the rest of Americans."

The woman blanched. Perhaps, he thought, he had overstepped the bounds of circumspection. He held up his empty glass, smiled, and fled to the verandah.

Round one of the Game had ended upstairs in Sumner's bedroom when Richard had forgotten what Charles was saying because he had become too fascinated by the confused stew of dementia and two-year-late trendiness in Charles's appearance—ruddy tan, plucked eyebrows, waistcoat, knee breeches, shapely calves accented by white stockings. Charles Duke Sumner came from old money. His mother's family had been prominent in North Carolina back to the War Between the States; his father had fought desegregation with genteel tooth and well-manicured nail. Charles rebelled. He went to the University of California, majored in engineering instead of liberal arts. In the early seventies he came back to the piedmont, went into real estate, and made a fortune in the transformation of the Raleigh-Durham-Chapel Hill area into the South's answer to Silicon Valley. By the time of the second crash Charles was a millionaire many times over. Then it was politics. He ran unsuccessfully for senator. He had friends in the legislature; in the mid-nineties he was a voice of moderation when plans were floated to imprison indigents or fire half the state university faculty. Despite the fact that he was fundamentally as conservative as his parents, he'd acquired a reputation as a liberal.

As his bank account grew, that liberalism twisted into sybaritic mysticism. His personal life was a mess. He conducted several untidy affairs concurrently, had sampled every recreational drug to come to popularity in the last ten years, could no longer manage his own finances, and could not be said, Richard thought, to have any sure grasp on reality. But he put up a good front. His handshake was firm, his complexion good. He took multivitamins and kept his weight down. His direct way of speaking disguised the fact that his mind held only tenuous contact with the material world.

When the Reverend Jimmy-Don Gilray came to Raleigh, Charles announced that he had seen the truth and the truth was that Jimmy-Don Gilray was the prophet of the Millennium. At first people thought this was Charles's joke, to while away the idle days until his bank account hit bottom. But Sumner was sincere. Maybe at the beginning he thought he might use Gilray for his own purposes, but the Rev soon was using Charles to solidify his own political power. The two became confidants. Gilray overlooked Charles's sexual and chemical escapades: Charles gave Gilray a secular power base.

Until Richard had appeared on the scene, they'd worked on a small scale. It was Richard's idea that they use Sumner's connections to take over the largely powerless Triangle Regional Planning Commission, then push for new city and county elections in Durham and Raleigh, justifying them by the economic crisis and the Green Party riot. If by ballot and intimidation they could get the municipalities to invest decisionmaking in the Planning Commission, they would have effective control of the entire region.

Within a week after beginning work Richard had fostered a dozen rumors of Commandante followers in the city and county government, irregularities in the District Attorney's handling of the grand jury investigation of the riot, collusion between the mainline Protestant churches and the state SBI, and microbes in the drinking water at Falls Lake. The mayor and D.A. resigned. A special election was scheduled. Richard suggested Charles run for mayor of Raleigh; Charles wanted governor but was willing to settle. The summer passed in a torrid uproar; many people left the state, the Reverend's flock moved in. There were some ugly incidents. The Reverend started dormitories and kitchens for the immigrants. Charles's agency found homes for those who could afford them and some who couldn't. He ran on a platform of taking Raleigh "Nearer to God." They started referring to the city as Zion.

Richard got maybe four hours of sleep a night. He ate little or nothing. He was buzzed on amphetamines and power and had never felt so good in his life. By midnight Tuesday they would control the Triangle and the decks would be cleared for the next step: goose the Reverend up into a frenzy and marshal his followers into cadres for the coming destruction of the world. The only problem was George. Richard didn't need George's stories anymore; he didn't care what Abramowitz or HCR did. But Delano was out of control, and Richard couldn't think of any good way to bring George home without admitting he'd lied about

Lucy, that he didn't know where she was, and that he'd set a possibly insane private detective on George's trail.

Richard wandered around the verandah, which ran around three sides of the house. Through French doors he saw people talking and drinking, and a wall screen tuned to the Reverend's station. While he stood there he was accosted by Charles's wife Marie.

"Richard Shrike. The man with a plan."

"I have no plan, Marie. I'm learning as I go along."

Marie's lips were pale and glistened. She radiated a southern charm about as authentic as the pillared porticos they built onto the front of white clapboard houses in order to make them look like Tara. It took a lot of effort to maintain such a false front, and even when well kept it was out of proportion. Marie, however, wore hers with a playfulness that made Richard wonder what kind of house she really was. He liked that. Rumor had it she was saving herself for the Second Coming.

"I talked to one of the flagellants from the mall today," Marie said. "She said they need new whips."

"So ungrateful," said Richard. "We give them everything else: a place to stay, a stage where they can expiate themselves in front of millions on TV, a uniform, songs."

"Oh, she seemed happy enough," Marie said. "The flies were living on her scars, but she smiled. She said that when she saw herself reflected in the shop windows she looked like the bleeding Christ." Marie snagged an hors d'oeuvre from a passing servant.

"What does the bleeding Christ look like?"

"He looks like someone who can't afford his own whip." Marie touched the tip of her tongue against her fine teeth. She watched Richard from beneath long lashes. "I, however, can."

Marie was wearing a high-necked, long-sleeved dress despite the continuing heat wave. "You use it to get nearer to Christ?" Richard asked.

"Time is short. The Rev says free the spirit."

"You should show me some time how it's done."

"How about now?"

He nodded.

"Five minutes. Second floor, west corner, end of the land-ing." She glided off, smiling soberly, through the crowd. She had excellent posture.

While he waited Richard strolled outside to the yellow-and-green striped pavillion in the side yard. He had his wine glass refilled by a black servant in a white coat. He spoke with Lucas Boston, who ran the Rev's federally franchised prison farm. He admired the tall white house. He studied the glossy green leaves of a magnolia tree so much like plas-tic as to appear rented for the occasion. Perhaps it was. He turned to go find Marie's room, but on his way in was cor-nered by a young man with a gold cross pinned to his lapel.

"Mr. Shrike? Thad Benzinger, *Evening Democrat*. Some comments on the election? What is the Reverend Gilray really like?"

Richard looked past him at the magnolia. "Rooted. Has his feet in the good red earth of the south, his head in the clouds, his eyes on his Maker."

Benzinger fished for information about Richard's connec-tions to HCR. In a minute Richard had him pegged: a J-school twit with a sense of moral superiority and half an education. Richard teased Benzinger and watched him try to control his temper. The champagne had gathered at the back of Richard's skull and was pushing on his occipital region. It was not unpleasant. When Benzinger asked what had happened to George, Richard said, "I don't work for HCR anymore. I was fired."

Benzinger lost it. "You don't care about the truth, do you. As long as you get at people. The Reverend's going to figure you out soon, and you'll be history."

"No need for hostility, Benzinger. I perform a service."

"So does the garbage collector. Only he doesn't feed it back to people and call it dinner."

"Oh, we have ethics, do we? HCR has a spot for you—commentator, maybe. You'll have to figure out some sort of costume: a geisha, maybe. Pluck your eyebrows, try to look inscrutable. They'll call it 'Comments by Lo Mein,' and give out your number to Prime subscribers."

"When the change comes, you people will be the first to go. You have every privilege America can provide, and you give back nothing."

"Except our garbage. I'm surprised you're so distressed. I'm just a consultant. I help the Rev get his message across."

"Expedient crap."

"Politics is the art of the possible," Richard said. "All media research does is turn the art into a science. I can write an equation that even accounts for you, Benzinger."

"I'll bet you can."

"The politician's job has always been to discern what is politically possible from what's impossible. But why depend on intuition when you can have science?"

"The Reverend's not a politician."

"Even the body of Christ needs good info. The Rev does a sermon and, thanks to me, fifteen minutes later he has a scientifically accurate poll based on a statistically significant cross section of public opinion. But that's nothing. Now we have the IRM."

"The what?"

Richard waved his glass at Benzinger, who dodged the wine that slopped out. "Information Response Module. We plant a chip right here—" Richard touched the base of his skull behind his ear, "—that's hooked into the logic center of the brain. Through a wrist cuff the person is tapped into the information net. Instantaneous feedback, at any time, on any question. We can do it without resorting to sensory input. We've got a crucial political decision to make—should Senator Kalikak get his eyes silvered?—we fire it out over the net to the people by way of the IRM, and we get back an instant answer. Yes, the people say. By all means, cover up those fishy things. There's stuff going on there we'd rather not see. So Senator K drops by the cosmetic surgeon and his ratings scoot up three points."

"So?"

"So the next step will be to tap the feedback from the IRMs right into the politician's brain. We get rid of the possibility Senator K might misinterpret the information: he just throws a switch and he becomes a mouthpiece for a scientifically sampled cross section of his constituents. Instantaneous representative democracy. The final perfection of our system of government."

"What does this have to do with religion?"

"Isn't it obvious, Benzinger? Religion is the most important kind of information. We can save a lot of souls if we can get Senator K online."

"And nobody ever has to think."

"Think?" Richard laughed. "Get online, brother! Thought is just resistance in the circuit. It slows things down, heats them up. It's not *necessary*. The easier the information flows, the less need for thought. How should Senator K vote? I give him the news. The only decision he needs to make—and the Rev can help him with this—is to set his priorities. After that we just run the program. No thought necessary—just act!"

Benzinger quivered like an animal rights activist at a steak dinner. Rad. But as Richard has ascended the ladder of his fantasy he had simultaneously become uncomfortably aware of the fact that Benzinger was made of flesh. Some side effect of the "Lips." Benzinger's eyes were balls of jelly suffused with warm, sticky fluids. Richard's stomach churned. He had to get out of there.

"Richard, Richard!" Charles Sumner rushed across the lawn. Richard felt a wave of relief. Then he remembered that Marie was waiting for him up in her bedroom with a whip. His mind flailed like a cat on ice. Before he could move, Charles grabbed him by the forearm. Beneath his tan, his face was bloodless. "Come see what's on the television," he said. "Hurry!"

Still shaky, Richard followed him into the playroom. On the screen was an alien from outer space. The face was greenish white, with a nose flattened to two tiny slits, huge eyes, a broad, hairless skull and pointed ears. It looked like a cross between a faun and Dwight Eisenhower.

"—decided to contact you in this way," the thing said in BBC English. "We have monitored your broadcasts from our mother ship in cislunar orbit for many years now. We have seen the dire straits that you have driven toward, and we are prepared to take a hand in saving you from yourselves, for it is clear to us that you are unable to do so without our help. This need not be a painful process."

The people in the room stared with varying degrees of awe. "It started a couple of minutes ago," said Charles. "Broke into the middle of the Rev's show."

"The first fundamental problem we propose to solve is the habit you earthlings have of dividing yourselves into classes. These classes have no basis in biology, and have been a major source of discord in your species." The alien looked out at them, as benign as St. Francis surveying a flock of pigeons.

"Fortunately, this problem admits of a simple solution," it said. "So simple a solution that, indeed, my gametes and I have wondered for many years why you have not come upon it yourselves. The first thing we must ask you to do is change your habits of dress. Clothing will no longer be used as a means of differentiating people from one another. You may decide for yourselves how you will accomplish this. For instance—" The image on the screen switched to a runway on which an impossibly thin alien with impossibly large breasts was striding, chin held high, twirling in the flash of spotlights. "—We prefer this simple one-piece jumpsuit, designed by Hunilla of Jupiter." The model was replaced by another wearing only a sequined g-string. "Or for more adventurous races, Terri here models the hottest in Venusian beachwear, perfect for those 700-degree nights!" The camera zoomed in on the thighs of the alien as she undulated past.

"The Commandante!" said Richard.

"Shut that thing off!" Gilray shouted. Someone rushed to do so, and a nervous silence followed.

"You see how far wrong a human soul can go," the Rev said. "He spits on our community of believers. But he can't touch us here." Gilray tapped his spotless shirt front. "He's more to be pitied than hated. But don't forget for a second that he's dangerous."

"Amen," said Richard. The party struggled to get back on track. All of Richard's senses were burning bright.

The excitement had taken something out of Charles. He looked like he'd crashed pretty hard. "I thought for a minute it was for real," he whispered.

"Maybe it was," Richard whispered back. He wondered if his own face looked as unlikely as Charles's.

Charles stared at him. "It was just the Commandante."

"Who's to say the Commandante isn't an alien from outer space? Nobody seems to be able to track him down. He gets on TV any time he likes. He's caused lots of serious problems."

"But that broadcast was ridiculous!" Charles waved at the blank screen. "Why would an alien play such an infantile joke?"

"He's an alien, Charles. Who knows how an alien thinks? Maybe he's an adolescent escaped from his parents. He's on a joyride in his dad's UFO, playing with the CB."

Richard would have traded a year of life for a picture of the expression of credulity that crossed Sumner's face. "Does the Reverend believe that?"

"The Reverend is imprisoned by God," Richard said. "He believes only what's revealed to him."

He spotted Bitsy Sumner weaving her way toward them through the crowd. She wanted something and whatever it was she wanted bad. Richard welcomed the challenge. He was sliding down a mountain of ice, shaky but still erect. God, how he loved North Carolina.

"Charles." Bitsy touched Charles on the shoulder and he jumped a foot. "There's a call from some woman. She says it's an emergency. You need to come down to the first precinct."

Richard suspected this was a code from one of Charles's women friends. The look of rage that passed between Bitsy and her brother told him more than mortal man was meant to know about their relationship. The first precinct. Richard imagined a scene with sheep and black leather. Charles hurried off.

Bitsy's close set eyes, combined with her fervent religiosity, gave her a chilling intensity. Richard could not remember ever seeing her blink. "You look upset, Bitsy."

"I get upset when I see my brother bound for Hell."

"A lot of us are bound for Hell. We can't always tell which ones by looking."

"Very clever, Mr. Shrike. I know you. You talk."

"I listen, too."

"You don't listen very well if you can't see Charles is a dead man."

"Jesus revived the dead. The clock hasn't run out yet. That's what the Reverend's all about."

Bitsy's tight forehead tightened further. The tip of her nose moved when she talked. "I wouldn't count on the Lord letting me live long enough to repent. Better to get right with Him now."

"That's why I'm here."

"I'll bet."

"Don't be hostile, Bitsy. Make sure your anger is righteous. It's true Charles is made out of clay. But you know, in his innocence he thought that TV broadcast was a real message from God. He's more ready to be saved than most. Even in his corruption he's innocent."

"Innocent!" Bitsy's voice was loud enough that several people looked at them. "That's not innocence, it's arrogance. To think that God's going to forgive you because your heart's in the right place. To act as if your sins just sort of collected on you, like dust. Charles wants the benefits of sin without the consequences. He's damned."

"Calm down, Miss Sumner." It was Gilray. He put his hand on hers, looked her in the eye. "Mr. Shrike doesn't want to judge. Who can blame him? The real Judgment will come soon enough."

"That's what I mean—"

Richard looked for his exit. He saw the huge Bosendorfer, shiny as obsidian, that filled the corner of the room. "How about some music?"

He lurched toward the piano like a leper for Lourdes. "A spiritual!" he said. "A celebration!"

He sat down, pushed up the fallboard and tried a chord. It was in impeccable tune. He had just started in to a rumbling baseline with his left hand, getting ready for "Down by the Riverside" when Marie Sumner slid onto the piano bench beside him.

Oops. Richard tromped down on the sostenuto pedal and launched into the song. People moved in from the verandah. Richard smiled weakly at Marie. She was wearing a different dress. Her look would wither a cactus. Her lips looked like dead slugs. "What happened?" she hissed.

The music wasn't going to work. He needed some other way out. His mind was a total blank. He played louder, more furiously. The chords slammed against his eardrums. The keys felt slippery, and his hands worked independent of his mind. The pressure on the back of his skull had become an electrical fire. He began to sing, not the words of the song (which he didn't know anyway) but whatever words came into his head.

> "Gonna lay down my Burdens
> Down by the wrecking ball
> Inside the bloody hall
> Ignore the feeble Paul—"

More people came in. Some tried to sing along. Richard sang louder, went from singing to a shout. He could feel his vocal cords go hoarse. People stopped. Marie slid away from him. He was shouting now, falling into a fit, shaking and spasming as if he were being electrocuted. That was it! It was working. They would never know what he was doing. He was possessed by the brilliance of his idea, by the force of his will—and they would think he was only possessed by the spirit!

> "Gonna blow up the antichrist
> After the seventh seal
> After the filthy deal
> After the crime's appeal
> Gonna drown in my loinfire
> Below the stolen war
> After the whore is dead!"

The bench rocked and the music desk quivered with the force of his playing and the surface of the wine in the glasses of the people danced in concentric, musical rings; the bubbles in the wine burst in time to the music and the discharges in Richard's brain. He closed his eyes and still he could see it all. Someone laid a hand on his shoulder. Richard twitched away, jerked his head, shook his hair, played. He bit his tongue and shouted through the pain. He could feel the saliva and blood trickling from the corner of his mouth. He opened his eyes and saw the pink droplets on the keys. People were rushing around.

The hand fell on his shoulder again; the Rev. Richard could see him but he couldn't hear over the screech of his own voice. He twitched and sang. He was beating them all! A perfect ruse. His vision clouded. More hands. They grabbed him and dragged him back off the bench. They laid him on the floor, twitching. He could still hear the music. He saw their stupefied faces, like dull animals. He bounced his head off the hardwood floor, shouting nonsense words, feeling the freedom and the white light. Free. A winner.

Why he had never thought of this escape before was a mystery to him.

21: MONDAY, OCTOBER 11
. . . .
On the Farm

Near the end of breakfast one of the matrons stopped by Lucy's table. "I'd like it if you would come with me, Hester."

The other women didn't look up from their oatmeal. Lucy put down her spoon and followed the matron to the security door at the end of the cafeteria. The guard in the bulletproof glass booth buzzed the lock, and the matron ushered Lucy through.

"Hey, Sharon," the guard said through the window facing the hallway.

"Hey, Mel," the matron said. "Too nice a day to be cooped up in here."

"Least I'm air conditioned," said Mel.

The matron made Lucy lead the way, guiding her by pointing the business end of her stun gun down the hall. They entered the staff lounge. She motioned for Lucy to sit in one of the wing-backed chairs. "Would you like some coffee, Hester?"

"No, thank you, matron."

The woman fixed herself a cup of coffee and sat down in another of the chairs. The matrons were nothing like the bull dykes of cliche; this one reminded Lucy of her third grade teacher, Mrs. Jackson. "I'm sorry to draw you away from your friends," the woman said. "And Heaven knows there's lots of work that needs to get done."

Lucy had learned to pick up her cues. "Heaven knows there is."

The matron allowed herself a smile so fleeting as to be little more than a twitch. "Your treatment has been coming along well, Hester. Considering how much you'd been hurting yourself before you came to us, you should be proud of yourself."

"I am proud, matron."

"Not too proud, though. The credit is God's."

"Praise be to Him."

The matron sipped her coffee. Lucy's nose began to itch; she kept her hands folded in her lap.

"I wish I could believe in your sincerity," the matron said.

"Please believe me, matron."

"I wish I could. Can you prove your sincerity to me, Hester?"

"How can I do that?" She knew what the answer would be.

"You can tell me who you really are. You can tell us

where and how your lab obtained the plasmid stock for gene reconstructions. You can name the other members of your movement."

"I don't know any other members. If I could tell you, believe me I would."

"How long have you been a leftist?"

Lucy remembered something Luz had told her the night before they were arrested, talking politics after midnight on the lumpy sofa while Concepcion, hunched over the microcomputer, pried DNA sequences out of a government database. "The Left and the Right got the same problem," Luz had said. "Can't fly with only one wing."

Lucy remembered the gleam of her smile in the dark. "I'm not anything. We were just helping each other."

The matron looked at her pityingly. She put down her coffee cup.

"What did you do with her?" Lucy said.

"With who, Lucy?"

"You know who." She was blowing it, but she couldn't stop herself.

"Why do you care about her if you didn't know her?"

"I got to know her."

"And now you are learning to forget her. The way you've apparently forgotten your real name."

Lucy didn't say anything. The matron stood.

"Okay, Hester. Let's go." But before they could leave the room the door opened. A well dressed man stood in the doorway; he looked Lucy up and down. His severe blue eyes and the puritan set of his mouth were contradicted by the shock of hair that swooped boyishly over his forehead.

"This is Dr. Kent," said the matron. She seemed unhappy. "We were just on our way out," she said to him.

Dr. Kent made them squeeze past him into the hall. His breath smelled of cigarettes.

Instead of rejoining the other prisoners in the sweatroom, where Lucy had spent the last three months sewing denim coveralls, they went back to the barracks. "Pack up your kit," the matron said. "We're transferring you to the Special Ward."

Lucy stuffed her few possessions into a duffle bag and they went down another hall to a barracks room identical to the one she had been living in: triple-decker bunks, fluorescent lights, a narrow aisle crowded with plastic trash barrels and picnic tables, framed pictures of Jesus and the Reverend Jimmy-Don Gilray above the doors at either end. The matron assigned her a bunk and watched as Lucy made it up. She gave her a new set of coveralls, white instead of gray, and made her put them on. A large red cross was stenciled across the breast. The matron pointed Lucy down another hallway and through a door out into a yard. It was already hot. The sun's hard glare threw their shadows ahead of them toward a field of soybeans where a squad of prisoners was at work.

"These patients are all receiving God's grace," the matron said. "He's given us this miraculous weather, so we're taking advantage of it to double-crop some beans. Except Satan's sent some vicious weeds. Maybe joining the battle against the Antichrist will make you more grateful to be alive, Hester."

They walked down the edge of the field toward a large red barn. Prisoners wearing white coveralls like Lucy's moved slowly up and down the rows of beans. Each had a plastic canister strapped to her back and was spraying weeds with a wand attached by a rubber hose to the canister. A couple of guards lounged in the shade of an oak.

Inside the barn, out of the sun, it was a little cooler. The air smelled of chemicals. From a rack against one of the walls the matron pulled down a canister and wand. She hooked her stunner on her belt for a minute, took the canister in both hands and gave it a good shake. "Enough for now." she said. "At the end of the day you fill it from that tank. It contains 2,4,5-trichlorophenoxyacetic acid. Don't get it on your hands or in your eyes." From a bin in the corner she pulled a pair of yellow rubber gloves. "Wear these."

The matron helped Lucy strap on the canister, took her back out to the field and introduced her to the guards. They wore mirrored sunglasses and carried single-barreled, pump-action shotguns. One of them called over a prisoner and told her to show Lucy how to spray the weeds and avoid the soybeans. After a few minutes of instruction she was on her own. The matron went back to the building.

Lucy spent the next few hours spraying weeds and swatting at the cloud of gnats that hovered about her head. The sun burned her neck and her back began to ache. She squinted against the brightness. Her hands, inside the gloves, became slimy with sweat. Occasionally she would stop for a moment and knead the small of her back; the other patients ignored her. None would make eye contact.

Why she had been taken out to do fieldwork was a mystery. This was God's Grace? Perhaps it was punishment for her non-cooperation, though Lucy couldn't see why it came now instead of earlier. Perhaps the matron meant what she'd said about fighting the Antichrist.

Lucy worked her way down a row near the chain-link fence that marked the end of the field, hardly lifting her head. A woman approached her up the adjacent row. Lucy caught her out of the corner of her eye, then did a double take: it was Luz.

In the month between their arrest and their trial, thrown into a stinking holding tank with twenty others, Luz and Lucy had become friends. At first Lucy suggested that they ought to try to cop a plea. Luz laughed. She had nothing she wanted to tell the prosecutors that they wanted to hear. Instead she said they should pray that the police not test the vial in the calculator and find out what it really was they were selling.

Luz suggested that Lucy turn State's evidence by herself in return for consideration on the arson charges. They talked about things Lucy could reveal that might work, and Luz assured her she would not hold it against Lucy. This time it was Lucy's turn to refuse. Why? The thought of prison, knowing what Lucy knew about prisons, ought to have made her frantic to escape. But something had changed her. It was Luz. Luz seemed to know who she was at all times. She recognized the forces stacked against her and still did not give in to rage, despair or alienation. Lucy could not leave her. So the days passed, and they were appointed a public defender, and still Lucy did not say the words that would save her own skin. Amazed at herself, strangely liberated, Lucy remained Hester Palenque.

The trial, in federal district court, lasted ten minutes: Luz got ten years, Lucy five. New York correctional facilities were at 200 percent of capacity, so they were contracted to a Christian rehabilitation institute in South Carolina. There Luz and Lucy were bunked with prisoners from sixteen states in a medium security barracks. Luz took it in stride. She told jokes and was punished for it. She got caught trying to organize a hunger strike—she had to have known that the room was wired—and was taken away. Lucy had not seen her from that moment until this.

As they came abreast of each other, Lucy hissed, "Luz! I thought they killed you."

Luz stepped forward quietly. "I'm fine," she said, and kept on down the row. Lucy looked over her shoulder. Luz pointed her wand at a weed near the base of a soybean plant and sprayed it. A guard was watching; Lucy quickly turned back to her work. She did not come near Luz again the rest of the morning.

The sun was past midday when one of the guards blew a whistle. Lucy followed the others to the bucket of water at the edge of the field. She unslung the tank and stretched her shoulders until they cracked. Luz and the others slurped water from the aluminum cup and exchanged a few words. Lucy drank her share, peeking over the rim at Luz. Luz glanced at her. Their eyes met for a moment, then slid apart.

Lucy went over to her. "Whales in the Sea, His Voice obey," she whispered.

"Amen," said Luz.

Lucy felt a profound relief. "Luz," she said. "How long have you been working here?"

"A long time," she said. "The work is good. I feel strong."

Lucy glanced at the guards. They weren't paying attention. "How can we get out of here?"

"We can be good."

"You? You can't be that good, Luz."

"We can never be good enough to deserve to be free," said Luz.

It was like icewater down Lucy's spine. "Are you serious?"

Luz looked at her. Her skin glistened with healthy sweat. Her brown eyes were clear and dark and warm. "I don't have time not to be serious. I was wrong. Now I'm getting right."

"But Luz—"

"All right," one of the guards said, "Back to work. This ain't Japan."

"Work with me this afternoon," whispered Luz.

They went back and finished the field of soybeans. They talked in snatches, telegraphic questions and answers, and the guards did not seem to care. Gradually Lucy became convinced that Luz was sincere. Her anger and sarcasm were gone. It seemed to Lucy that this new Luz was somehow less than the old, but when she said this Luz only replied, "That's your anger talking. Anger is a disease. I almost died of it. I'm glad that's over."

Lucy said nothing. She felt betrayed. Luz, the revolutionary, talked reconciliation while Lucy, the lawyer, felt only growing rage.

It seemed years later when the afternoon whistle blew. Lucy's stomach ground against her backbone. The patients formed a double file and headed for the barn, refilled and racked the sprayers, threw the gloves into a stainless steel bin. The guards seemed to loosen up. One of them teased Luz about how she was getting into shape. Luz smiled back. For the first time during the day, the other patients talked among themselves. Lucy felt lightheaded. She walked back toward the dormitories beside Luz and the guard. Luz's step was springy. She chattered on about the crop and the heat and the guard's severe black beard. It was as if she had done no more work that day than to go out for a pleasant jog. Eager, expectant, she was in the prime of health and spirits. Despite herself, Lucy was affected.

"You had a good time today, didn't you," Lucy said.

"I did," chirped Luz. "Didn't I?"

"You did," said the guard. "Don't worry, Luz. There's plenty of blessings to go around."

Just inside the door they stopped before a table. The patients crowded around edgily. At the table a smiling matron gave each of them a small glass of orange juice and a paper cup containing a capsule.

Luz shouldered her way in front of the other women. Lucy caught a glimpse of Luz's eyes as she took the paper cup in her trembling hand, placed the capsule on her tongue, washed it down with the juice. She stopped shaking. As she turned from the table she glanced at Lucy with no more interest than if Lucy were a cardboard cutout.

Lucy stood there until all the patients had gotten their capsules. The matron held out Lucy's blessing. "You're Hester, aren't you?"

The others were already on their way to the showers. "No thank you."

"You need this, Hester."

"I feel fine, really."

The matron put down the glass and the capsules. "You are a bad girl," she said.

"Fuck you."

"Would you like to come with me, Hester?"

"I'd like to rip your lungs out."

Hours later—after friendly persuasion, gentle warnings and sweet threats—after standing at attention, hot lights, endless repetitive questions—they showed Lucy the tape. Hunger had tied a knot in her stomach. Her head ached. She wondered why they did not simply inject the drugs and be done with her.

Dr. Kent was in charge. His hair was more disheveled than it had been in the morning. He explained to her that he was not a medical doctor; he was a penologist. Had it not been for his creepiness he would have been boring. It was late at night when he told the matron to take a break, leaving them alone.

"I'm going to show you a video, Hester, because your resistance to help is so firm." Dr. Kent touched a switch and a vid came onto the monitor on a shelf in the corner of the room. "PATIENT 999-97-9263. SESSION 6." the title gave way to a view of the same room they were sitting in. Luz sat in the chair Lucy occupied now. Behind her stood a matron, holding her stun gun behind her back. Across the table from Luz was Dr. Kent. Between them were an ash tray, a bright green book of matches and an opened pack of Marlboros.

Although Luz looked relaxed, almost insolent, something was wrong with her face. Her jaw was swollen. The corner of her mouth turned stiffly downward, as if numb. Occasionally she would reach up to touch the back of her neck.

"We're not here to punish you," the Dr. Kent on the tape said. "We're here to help you."

"You and Dr. Mengele," Luz said.

"You're angry," Kent said. "Anger is a disease, Luz."

"Government is the disease."

"I'm going to try to explain this one more time, because despite your sickness I think we owe you an explanation."

Luz pulled a cigarette from the pack and lit it, careful to avoid the swollen side of her mouth.

"Why do we imprison a man?" Kent said. The recorded voice echoed hollowly. "We imprison a man because he doesn't accept the values of society enough to act within the range of behaviors indicative of somebody who does accept those values. Am I making myself clear?"

"Barely," said Luz. She took another pull on her cigarette.

"We put the man in prison—"

"I'm not a man." Luz blew smoke at Kent. "But you know that already, don't you."

The matron looked very unhappy. Kent smiled. "We put the man in prison in order to separate him from the society whose rules he refuses to accept. Once he's in there we have two options: 'A'—keep him in prison indefinitely. 'B'—change the situation so that his behavior falls within acceptable norms."

"Keep her there till she rots." Despite the tape's poor sound reproduction Lucy could hear the weariness in Luz's voice. Lucy looked at Kent, but he was as absorbed in the tape as if it were a favorite old movie.

On the screen the matron started toward Luz, but a glance from Kent froze her. He went on. "Option 'B' admits an additional two options. B-1: change society's norms so that the prisoner's behavior, formerly criminal, becomes acceptable—"

"Sounds good to me—"

"B-2: Change the criminal's behavior so that it falls within the social norm."

"Do I get a choice?"

Kent actually looked at her then. His smile became very broad. "Of course not," he said. "Your opinions are outside the range of acceptable social norms. That's why you are here."

"I thought it was for cooking bugs."

The matron stepped up and discharged the gun against Luz's neck. Luz jerked like a startled cat and fell limp in the chair. The cigarette flew from her hand, hit Kent in the chest and rolled onto the table, coming to rest, still smoldering, against the ashtray. Kent scowled at the matron, who scowled back. He got out of his chair and felt the pulse in Luz's neck. He picked up the cigarette, took a long drag on it, paced the room until Luz started to come around, then sat down again and kept talking as if nothing had happened.

"Option A," he said, "is one to which traditional prison systems have often resorted—incarceration without parole for the so-called 'incorrigible.' Option B-1 has also been tried at various times in various societies—most recently in the wave of permissiveness that swept over America in the last thirty years—with disastrous results. The Christian Farm chooses option B-2. We change the criminal's behavior."

Luz stared at him dully.

"Do you hear me, Luz?"

"Sure."

"It would please us a great deal if you would take your pills. Is this clear?"

"Sure." She was coming back to herself. But the bravado was gone now. Lucy wanted to cry.

"You're never going to get better otherwise. Isn't that right, matron?"

The matron put her hand on Luz's shoulder. Luz jumped as if she'd been shocked again.

"You need your med'cine, Miss," the matron said.

"Sure," said Luz. She stared at the table.

Dr. Kent looked at her. The matron still had her hand on Luz's shoulder, her thumb playing with the hair on the back of her neck.

"Will you do that for us, Luz?" Kent asked. "Will you take your medicine?"

"Sure," Luz whispered.

The tape ended.

Kent turned off the machine. He faced Lucy as if he expected her to say something.

She stared at him. She was not afraid: she was furious. The world was not well arranged, Concepcion had said. No kidding. What Lucy could not understand was Concepcion's humor in the face of that hard fact. It was no laughing matter. If Lucy ever got out of there she would never laugh again. She glared up at the camera in the corner of the room. Her thoughts ran forward to some other woman, in a similar fix, who might be watching the tape of this session in the future. She hoped that her fury showed. Fuck them all, she thought to her potential compatriot at the other end of the camera. Defy them.

"You expect me to do what you want, now?" she asked Kent.

"You don't even know what I want, Lucy."

"You want me to take your drugs."

"Society wants that."

She would put her thumbs through his eyes. "You killed her."

"Nonsense. You spent this afternoon with her. Have you ever met a happier woman?"

He opened the drawer in the table and took out a credit-card calculator. "Do you remember this? It contains the virus that was used in evidence against you." Kent slid his fingertip along the edge of the calculator. "They tell me that this virus, triggered by the right activity, makes your body produce a flood of endorphins. Ten thousand times more powerful than morphine."

He didn't know what it was. The police must have assumed Luz was selling what she said she was selling. Lucy stared at the calculator.

"It's triggered by sex." she said. "It piggybacks on normal sexual response."

Kent turned off the video camera. "Is that the truth, Hester?"

"I know you want me," she said quietly. "Well, you can have me, if you'll just get me out of here. We'll take it together. I just don't want to end up like Luz."

"I'm no fool, you know."

Lucy let some desperation into her voice. It was not hard. "I saw Luz. She's dead inside. I can't face that."

"You'll do what I want?"

"Yes. But not here—somewhere else. I don't care where—a motel or something. I'll make it worth your risk."

Kent studied her. Lucy bit her lip and blinked until some tears came. She looked away from him at the ashtray on the table between them. Come on, you bastard. Take a chance.

The matron returned. Kent slipped the calculator into the breast pocket of his suit. "Matron, help Hester," he said, standing. "I'm going to run her up to Columbia for further psychiatric examination."

The matron looked angry. "Tonight?"

"Of course tonight." Kent's cheeks were flushed.

The matron pulled Lucy out of the chair, twisted her around and cuffed her hands behind her back. Kent opened a drawer in the table and took out a stun gun. "Come with me," he said.

They left the matron behind. Kent took Lucy down more corridors, through another security door. Suddenly they were outside. The night was humid and hot, more like August than October. Away from the buildings the fields ran down to the brightly lit road between the two chainlink fences that surrounded the prison. Lucy looked at Kent. She wasn't sure what she was going to do when the moment came, but her anger assured her she would think of something. He made her get into a car and they drove toward the front gate. "I know you're going to feel more secure away from the cameras, Hester," said Kent.

The guards did not question him. Once outside they drove along a narrow, two-lane road. The farther they got from the farm, the more Lucy felt like a weight had been lifted from her shoulders. The hot wind blew in through the window. She leaned back against her handcuffed wrists, watched the stars slide past the pine trees lining the road, and thought about Luz.

Kent pulled onto a dirt road between the trees. They jounced over chuckholes for a mile or more, then stopped in the middle of the road. Kent turned off the engine. The dry rustling of the woods sifted over them.

"What is this?" Lucy asked.

"This is the place."

"No. I want a motel."

"That's too risky. This will do."

Kent slid over on the seat and began to unbutton her coveralls.

"What about the virus?"

"Altering genes is a sin, Hester. I want to rehabilitate you."

Lucy tried to twist away. He grabbed her face in his sweaty hand and forced her to look at him. "Sin has troubled man since he fell from the Garden," he whispered. His voice was hoarse. His other hand fumbled with the buttons of her coveralls. His breath stank of cigarettes.

He gave up on them and ripped the coveralls open, then reached under her for her hands, manacled behind her back. "*Listen*, Hester," he gasped. "Every compassionate man who looks at history curses human folly. So many sinners, so many sins." He got hold of her wrists and yanked her hips against him. She tried to think. Control, she thought. I've got to get control.

"Yes," she said.

He seemed surprised. "Do you understand me, Hester?"

"Yes."

"Either you stand for this project, our rehabilitation method, or you stand with every ignorant soldier who burned the Library of Alexandria, who persecuted Joan of Arc, who crucified Christ."

She felt rage, despair, disgust. She held it in. "I know," she said. "Unlock my wrists."

"Now we're going to do something about it."

"Please. I'll help you."

Kent stopped. He pulled back, panting. He fumbled in his pocket until he had the key. He dangled it in front of her. "You want to get free?" he asked. "You don't deserve it yet."

Then he grabbed her thigh and pulled her legs onto the seat.

Later, when he had fallen asleep on top of her and Lucy had come back to herself, she felt something small and hard beneath her butt. She worked her fingers toward it. It was the key. As quietly as possible she scooted her hands over the edge of the seat. After an agony of cramped effort, of panicked fear that the key might slip from her fingers, she got the cuffs unlocked. She slid from under Kent and crawled out of the car. He stirred, his head hanging half out.

She slammed the door against his head, opened it, slammed it again. She didn't know how many times. After awhile she stopped and threw up in the road. Dry heaves. She felt a trickle of semen or blood inside her thigh. Coveralls down around her knees, she crawled back to the car. She pulled Kent from it, yanked off his suit jacket and rolled him into the ditch. He was still breathing. There was only a hundred dollars in his wallet. She spat on him, pulled on the buttonless coveralls and his jacket, stumbled back toward the car. She remembered the calculator. She took it out of the jacket pocket.

Trying not to think, she drove back toward the highway. The calculator, lying on the dashboard, reflected moonlight and a threat. She was tired of being jerked around. It could drive you crazy. It was as if that had become the purpose of her existence: to be driven mad.

The world was not well arranged. Tears in her eyes for Concepcion, for Luz, for herself, Lucy laughed.

22: TUESDAY, OCTOBER 12
Never Complain, Never Explain

"I can't tell anything unless you get him in here for some tests," Vance said. "I'm not inclined to speculate."

"Speculate," Gilray said.

"Well, it could be any number of things. Epilepsy caused by a brain tumor or some other sort of lesion. Or a result of long-term drug abuse. There are plenty of good doctors there in Raleigh who can figure it out for you. Or you could take me up on my offer and let me come there and do some research."

"You mean come and take a look at our freak show," Gilray said.

Vance frowned. "Not freaks—human beings."

Gilray told Vance he would get back to him and hung up.

In the aftermath of Richard's fit at the Sumner election party, Gilray had realized that some crisis was coming. Could Richard, against all evidence of his secular life, be one of the two witnesses Revelations predicted would prophesy for 1,260 days before their martyrdom would bring on the reign of the Antichrist? That would mean that

Richard had already been preaching for more than three years.

Few of Gilray's fellow Christians would think it possible. But they had been wrong about the Rapture while he had been right. They could be wrong about this as well. Even so, the chronology was confused. The Antichrist was already in full reign; the evidence was everywhere. It was not the Antichrist but the Redeemer himself who would come at the end of the year. That was the problem with Revelations. The truth had been revealed to John in a single blinding vision, in which time had been abrogated; for that reason the book was full of prolepsis, the describing of future events as if they had already happened. The order of John's vision could only be understood by an equal act of revelation.

It was enough for Gilray to know that he must prophesy. And that Richard was the other speaker. There was grim work to be done. No one would know the pain he would have to suffer in order to muster the ruthless will he would need to prepare Zion.

Marianne buzzed to tell him the car had arrived. In the lobby he found Richard talking martial arts with Felton. Richard looked subdued. He had not shaved, and his suit was uncharacteristically rumpled. They had taken him home from the Sumner party and put him to bed under the supervision of a nurse.

They walked out to the car. "How are you, Richard?" Gilray asked.

"I'm fine."

"You gave us all a shock."

Richard didn't say anything until they were inside and Felton had started the car. "It was a shock to me, too."

"You mustn't fight against it, Richard," Gilray said. "You've received a great gift. And a burden, too. You can't have one without the other."

"Thanks."

"It feels like a bitterness in your stomach—"

"I'll say."

"—but it is a sweetness in your mouth. I know."

"My mouth feels like the bottom of a reactor vessel."

"'Fire proceedeth out of their mouths, and devoureth their enemies—'"

"Sorry. I used a mouthwash."

"'—and if any man will hurt them, he must in this manner be killed.'"

"What a way to go."

Gilray gave up. If Richard was trying to avoid facing the truth, silence would do more work than persuasion. They drove until they reached the fire station that was their precinct polling place. A little crowd had gathered in expectation of their arrival. Gilray shook hands with a few of the people and left Richard to talk with them while he went in to vote. A photographer took his picture. When he was finished he came back out to find Richard holding forth on the lawn to one of the reporters, a young man the Reverend remembered seeing at the Sumner party.

"You think that was some sort of fit?" Richard said. He was talking louder than the Reverend could ever remember; the people stared at him. The reporter looked angry. Gilray stood in the doorway, where he could not be seen. "That was no fit. And that Commandante Jesus broadcast was no accident."

"What do you mean?" the reporter asked.

"Look at this juxtaposition of events: One, I show up here in Raleigh, and I get hired by the Rev. Me, not even a Christian. Two, within a month the Anti-Revival amendment gets passed. Three, UFO reports hit their peak since 1953. Four, Commandante Jesus steps up his broadcasts. Five, the climate changes: the flood stops and we get August in October. Six, plagues of locusts in the Midwest. Seven, the Green Party massacre. Eight, county and city decide on special elections."

"You don't need the supernatural to explain those last two."

"Don't be so sure. Take the odds against any one of those things happening. Some of them are pretty long. Then multiply them together. The odds against such a sequence are astronomical. I'm saying it's no accident."

Gilray heard the fire in Richard's voice. He recognized it.

"What is it, then?"

"The Rev says we're in the Last Days. I don't know anything about that. I'm a secular man. But these UFOs aren't just swamp gas. And Commandante Jesus isn't imaginary. What if he doesn't call himself Jesus just to annoy Christians? Suppose he's not just some crazy hacker? Suppose he's the head of an alien terrorist force already at work in the world? Suppose they've infiltrated all aspects of American life? Doesn't the Bible say that Satan will come in the guise of Christ?"

"You're saying Commandante Jesus is Satan?"

"Don't get religious on me. Maybe he's an alien with bat wings and hooves. Aren't people from another planet supposed to look different? Maybe they need our planet. Maybe they've been after it for thousands of years, trying to undermine the human race. Maybe there are benevolent aliens too, who look like angels and try to help us out now and then. Maybe we're a third-world planet caught in a struggle between the superpowers."

"What has this got to do with your fit?"

Richard didn't even pause. "A message. A telepathic message from the Good Aliens. They hooked me into their information system, their computer net or whatever. I wasn't ready, and the power surge almost shorted me out. But now I'm online. I'm ready to receive information that we can use to combat the bad aliens. I'm a terminal."

Gilray stepped forward. "He's a Prophet."

The crowd turned to him. Richard looked at him, aware for the first time that he was there.

"Mr. Shrike doesn't even think he is a Christian," the Reverend said, "Nor did Paul as he saddled up his horse to ride to Damascus.

"Some of you questioned my judgment when I hired this man. But I saw something in him, and yesterday afternoon it came to fruition. He talks of Good Aliens and Bad Aliens, and the Bible tells us of God and Satan. Mr. Shrike's mind has been twisted by a twentieth century education. But even a warped education cannot stand against the Truth that burns away error. There are no accidents. God steered him to Zion in time for the beginning of His Reign. Now He has breathed the breath of prophecy into his mouth. Even he has not grasped that yet.

"The results of this election will be another step in this 'series of coincidences.' We call them miracles. The time grows short. The apocalypse is coming. We need to get to work."

The reporter looked like he would die if he didn't make his office in time to meet the next edition's deadline. "You have all this on tape?" the Reverend asked him.

The man pulled a recorder out of his breast pocket. "Yes."

"Good. Write about it. On the first day of preparations for the coming of the New Jerusalem, let the papers tell the story."

Gilray motioned to Felton. The chauffeur headed for the car. Richard wore a dazed expression; he almost looked annoyed. Gilray smiled back at him. They might both be prophets, but Gilray understood that they would never be friends. The Lord chose His spokesmen for their particular characteristics. Some had an edge, like a chisel, for splitting things apart. Some, God's hammers, were blunt and strong. Still others were like augers that could bore into the heart of things and set a charge that would blow them to pieces. That was what it meant to be a tool. Gilray hoped that they would both be able to serve Him well. He knew, better than Richard probably ever would, the price to be paid. In a desperate circumstance, where impossible work was to be done, God's tools were in for some hard use. They might well break under the strain.

"You're going to be the Hammer of God," Gilray said.

Richard stared at him. "How much of what you said back there did you believe?"

"All of it. How much did you?"

"Absolutely nothing. I made it all up. It was a put-on."

"That's what you think," said Gilray.

23: TUESDAY, OCTOBER 12

....

George wises Up

The Gulf Breeze Motor Inn, an asphalt-roofed "H" of stucco and glass brick half a block from the I-10 offramp on Tennessee Street, had once offered its guests a seafood restaurant, a roller rink, and a miniature golf course. But the windows of the restaurant were boarded up, the roller rink had been turned into a bingo hall, and on the golf course the wings of the windmill no longer turned. Monday evening, when George pulled in after twenty-four straight hours of driving, a clot of retirees were queued up before the entrance to the bingo hall. George ignored them. He registered as George Shklovsky, staggered to his room and collapsed on the bed without even bothering to undress.

When he awoke fourteen hours later he could not remember where he was. He fumbled through the wisps of a dissipating dream about waking in a hospital. He tried to focus on the room. It wasn't a hospital. It was a motel. He was in Tallahassee. His travel alarm read almost noon but he felt no better for having slept through the morning.

George tried to get up; he fell to his knees. After a minute or two he braced his back against the bed and managed to push himself to his feet. His reflection in the dresser mirror was not pleasant. Were they still watching him? He swayed into the bathroom, splashed cold water into his face. The face in the bathroom mirror looked no better; its eyes were red and the skin of the cheeks was stretched thin over the bones. The battered toupee looked ridiculous. He wiped his face. The towel smelled of kerosene. He draped it over the bathroom mirror, took another back into the bedroom and hung it over that mirror, too. Whether or not they were watching, he would at least not have to look at himself.

He peeked through the blinds. Across the nearly empty parking lot the door of the bingo hall gaped like the entrance to a played-out mine. The neon sign above it glowed faint purple in the daylight. Two Hispanic boys in Hawaiian shirts leaned against the pink wall, talking to a woman in a white jacket and black jogging tights that showed every muscle in her athletic legs. George let the blinds fall and sat back on the bed.

George didn't feel hungry, but he supposed he ought to get something to eat. He found the liter of scotch in his gym bag and took a healthy swig. His normal routine was to settle down, get a feel for the area, and seek the pattern that might lead him to the alien. He was so tired. More to give himself something to do than with any hope of it leading to anything, he decided to do his laundry.

He stuffed his dirty clothes into a pillowcase and walked across the parking lot. His car was the only one there. The kids and the woman by the doorway glanced at him as he approached. The woman's eyes were so deep a brown that they were almost black. George stepped past them into the hall. He found a food machine near the men's room and bought a bar of soyabulk. He went back out, slung the pillowcase over his shoulder, chewed on the tasteless bar and walked down the street. He tried to let the hot, humid air soak through him, bring him back to life. Tennessee was one of those classic American strip streets dedicated to the automobile: car dealerships, auto parts stores, fast food restaurants, car washes, punctuated here and there by a laundromat, a video store, a voluntary suicide club. The date palms in the lots of the closed businesses looked hazy. The sky was milky white.

The laundromat shared a building with Charlie's Gym. A large poster of a musclebound man in red shorts separated the entrances of the two storefronts. Inside the laundromat a couple of old women folded clothes and an old black man in a T-shirt and Bermuda shorts slept on one of the plastic chairs. The women stopped talking when George entered. George emptied his pillowcase into one of the machines, bought some soap from a dispenser, and set the washer for an extra disinfect cycle. He stepped outside and bought a paper from the corner newsbox. From the open upstairs window of the gym came the staccato zap of rattle music. The hot breeze tasted of salt and smelled of dead fish.

It was last Sunday's paper. George sat in the heat of the laundromat and tried to analyze the stories, but the type kept sliding past his eyes and he would catch himself staring across the room at the clothes tumbling within the dryers' UV lamps. The slosh of the machines washed thought from his mind.

Eventually two kids came in wheeling an old shopping cart full of clothes. The old women left. The old man still slept. His eyes were sunk in wrinkles. George moved his clothes to the dryer. The rattle music from the gym was abruptly replaced by a series of barbershop quartets. The kids offered to sell George some meperidine.

"No thanks," said George.

"So, doctor?" the smaller boy said. "Ain't got no pains?"

"No pain," said George.

"You never know when you gonna need it," the other said.

"I believe you."

"Nice wig," the first boy said.

"Thanks."

The kids checked the pockets of the sleeping man, but he had no money.

By the time George got back to the motel he was exhausted. He searched the TV for local news, and flipping through the channels came to an HCR affiliate. For more than a minute he watched a spot on a mysterious church fire in Indiana that had been started by ball lightning, before he realized that it was grafted onto a vid that he had filed himself.

"—Indiana UFO investigators filed this captured video, found in the ruins of the burned-out Methodist Church, that they say was made by an alien surveillance team attempting to recruit an American citizen in the rest room of the Ft. Wayne Interrail station." On the screen flashed George's pursuit of Burdock across the Ft. Wayne station, ending with the attack in the men's room.

"Dr. Ivor Blossom of the American UFO Network says that the Columbia City church fire is only the latest in a series of attacks by UFOnauts on religious institutions throughout the Western Hemisphere." Switch to a talking head of Dr. Blossom speculating on the religious heresies of the space aliens.

The vid was George's, but the copy was manufactured. Someone had turned his story into the same old crap. George turned to the phone channel, read the instructions for making satellite calls, then punched Richard's code on the bedside telephone. He let the phone ring eight or nine times. He was about to hang up when Richard answered.

"Hello? George, is that you?"

George held the receiver to his ear and turned toward the TV. Richard needed a shave. "Richard," George said. "I just saw an HCR report that used some of my work, reprocessed. What's going on?"

"You know it's all reprocessed. Cheese food."

"This is important. I'm not just sending in trash. I'm trying to prevent a disaster. Who knows—"

"Disaster is our business. Disaster and miracles."

"Richard, what the hell's going on?"

"Don't get upset, George. You always were a looney. You're off on a wild tangent. It was a good laugh for awhile, but now I'm trying to steer you around to what's important."

"This is important—"

"I'm in the Belly of the Beast, here, George. I'm like this with the Rev." Richard held up his crossed fingers. "He thinks I'm a prophet. I'm hot, George. The car's racing down the mountain, it's dark outside, no moon, the sky is overcast, the headlights are out, the brakes are fading, the Rev is giving advice from the passenger's seat, the road is twisting like a thousand-dollar whore, I'm a little twisted myself, and I'm behind the wheel. *I'm behind the wheel,* George. I'm *driving.* It's rad, friend. I don't know where it's going to end up, but I'm going to enjoy the trip. Your stories are just part of the ambience. A little white noise, a little ancillary stimulation. You get me, don't you?

George didn't say anything.

"You have your own trip going, I can see that. But this one's more important. I'm putting your word out, George, and I appreciate the impetus you've given me. I didn't see the angle until you came up with this alien business. But the truth's a flexible thing. I bet you the truth is more twisted than either of us can imagine. Why don't you come back here and hop on? I can use you."

"Richard, you're talking crazy."

"Sorry. I know that's your department. Anyway, what makes you think I'm crazy? Just because I gave up my job to work for a religious fanatic who thinks I'm one of God's prophets?"

"What do you think about the stories I've been filing?"

"They're a fine starting point. I'm just helping them along a bit."

"Does Gilray believe in the Alien?"

"Gilray believes in God," Richard said. "You believe in the Alien. And I'm the intermediary. I don't believe anything. I just translate what you tell me into terms that he can understand."

"So the Reverend's into my theory?"

"He's into my theory. I don't think he worries about you. Give up this wild goose chase, George, and come work with me. It's good for a buzz."

George looked hard at the image of Richard on the TV. You could never tell with these low-definition monitors, but there was something eerie about Richard. TV was supposed to add flesh, make the thin man healthy, the normal man imposing. Richard looked exactly the way he had in New York. "I don't want to," George said.

"If there's one thing I've discovered, it's that when God wants you on his team, it doesn't matter what *you* want."

"How do you know it's God?"

"Don't be silly," said Richard. "There is no God. That's just a figure of speech."

"I mean, suppose it's these aliens? I've seen them at work, Richard. That's why I've been doing all this. The least you could do, even if you don't believe in it, is to help me out, not sabotage me—"

"George, that's exactly right. That's what I've been doing. I'm putting over the alien theory much bigger than you ever could. But I could use an idea man like you. You've always been hooked into the insane mind better than I."

"Suppose they're controlling you, Richard. And the Reverend. Suppose—"

"A conspiracy? Good idea. Like the Trilateral Commission. Or the Yeti Yellowstone guides. I like it. But you've got to get your ass in here, quit dashing about."

"If I'm going back anywhere it's to New York, Richard. I'm tired. And I'm tired of talking to Lucy through you. I want you to give me her new number. I'm going to call her and—"

"I can't do that, George." Richard's voice went flat.

"What do you mean?" George asked. He felt panic. "Has something happened to her?"

"Things happen to people all the time, George. We're all under stress—not just you. Except the rest of us are supposed to worry about your mental health, right? How we feel doesn't count."

"You've been lying!" George felt the room pitch like a sailboat. He sat on the bed.

"Fuck off, George," Richard said. "I've bent over backwards trying to understand you. It's not my fault if your marriage got out of control. You never paid her an ounce of real attention anyway."

"Where is she?"

"I can't explain this to you now. Come to Raleigh. Until—"

George hung up. The screen went to snow. He trembled. All this time George thought he had been talking to Lucy, Richard was deceiving him. He couldn't believe it. He tried to think. What could have happened? All he could come up with were images from a lifetime of television: Lucy in a hospital bed, cocooned in gauze like a victim of the Three Stooges. Lucy in her charcoal suit, defending herself against trumped-up charges before the Bar Association. Lucy barricaded in their apartment while latex aliens attempt to break in through the heating vents.

There was a knock at the door. George ignored it. It came again. "Yes?"

"Mr. Shklovsky?" A woman's voice, a little slurred.

He went over but did not open it. "Who is it?"

A long pause. "Patsy. Patsy Burroway. I work at the desk." The woman sounded drunk.

George opened the door a crack. It was the woman in the running tights.

"We've got a problem with your room," she said. "Come in?"

George let her in. He closed the door, and when he turned back she was standing by the bed. She looked as if she expected something. "Well?" he said.

"Make your move. Eberhart." she said.

She knew his name. "What are you talking about?"

"Don't be coy. I'm not really from the motel."

She pronounced the words perfectly, but her intonation was off, as if she could not hear what she was saying. As if English were a totally alien tongue. Another shock: she was one of them. He sat down on the edge of the dresser. "You found *me*," he said.

"Sure." She smiled. "Now you kill—or come with me."

"What do you want? What are you doing here?"

"My job. Bringing you back."

"Back where?"

"Home."

George imagined a UFO parked outside in the lot. "I won't go."

"So make your move."

"No. First you tell me why you've come to earth!"

The woman looked confused. She slid her hand from behind her back. It held a large gun. "Let's go."

"This is fantastic!" George said. "My mind can't grasp this. What are you trying to do here? Why are you tormenting us? Why don't you reveal yourselves?"

She looked at him as if she did not comprehend what he had said. Her pupils were dilated. She waved the gun at him. "Go!"

It was a close spot. George stood, and as he did, pulled the corner of the towel that hung over the dresser mirror. The towel slid off. The woman jerked the gun and shot the mirror. The report was deafening. George ducked into the bathroom and locked the door. The door rattled with the force of the woman's shoulder slamming into it. The lock held, but it wouldn't hold long.

"Come out!"

George tried the bathroom window, but it was painted shut. He pulled the towel from over the mirror, wrapped it around his fist. The woman beat on the door. He punched through the window, knocked out the four panes, ripped apart the cross in the center of the frame. The woman shot through the door; the bullet missed him by inches and sprayed shards of ceramic tile around the room. He got onto the toilet and pulled himself through the window. A sliver of glass tore his pantsleg. He fell to the ground.

Down the alley George ran, and across to the next street. The orange sun was setting between the buildings; streetlights were coming on. He zigzagged through several blocks, then forced himself to slow down. He gasped and wheezed; he had no wind at all. Walking down a side street, trying not to look scared, he passed the entrance of an old brick building, from which came voices raised in singing. The sign beside the door said: "Holy Martyrs." A Seppuku Club. George slipped inside.

At the other side of the little anteway a pair of doors opened into a large room lined with high, opened windows. About twenty people gathered in pews around a platform; on the platform several people were testifying. Most were old; a few were George's age. George sat down off to the side, between a woman in a threadbare dress and a bearded man in a shabby brown suit. He realized that he had lost his toupee. He crossed his leg over the tear in his pants and tried to look invisible.

"—and I was *prepared*," a woman on the platform was saying. "I was prepared to face that final judge. My time was come. I could taste the steel of the gun barrel, smell the sweat of my own fevered brow. But then it came to me, Brothers and Sisters, it came to me! I heard the voice of the Lord! 'Mary,' the Lord said, 'are you ready to check out without your friends? You been thinking on the Last Things—on Death, Judgment, Heaven and Hell—but what about your Sisters and Brothers? You just a little cell in God's Body. When that body goes to glory it got to go together!'"

"Amen!" someone shouted. George thought about leaving. In the back wall, beneath a burnt-out "Exit" sign, was a metal fire door.

"'—and you know how they been persecuting them that sees the need of a quick, painless death. They been trying to stop His Holy Martyrs when they got the knife raised above their breasts, ready for the glorious consummation. Mary, you got to think about somebody else besides yourself.'

"And so I took that forty-four out of my mouth and I brought it here with me tonight. Because, Brothers and Sisters, we got to get clean and die together to show we don't believe in the blasphemy of this twisted world, and we got to take the revived with us and show them that there ain't no escape from the Last Things." The woman held up a large purse and hauled out the gun she had been talking about.

"I got my ticket!" she said. "How about you?"

People around the room held up a forest of tickets to self-destruction: kitchen knives, a field of handguns, boxes of household poisons, a couple of ornamental oriental swords, bottles of pills.

"I ain't afraid to board that train!" the woman shouted. "Amen!"

The woman beside George waved her bottle of blue pills. "It's leaving now!"

George felt like he was going to be sick. He stumbled to

his feet and through the fire door. It was the processing room, full of buckets and body bags and old mops with rusty brown heads. The place smelled like a butcher shop that had failed inspection. George's stomach heaved. A couple of bored men looked up from the horse race on their TV. He pushed past them through the back door, and in the alley threw up against the brick wall. His head reeled. An abandoned car rested on wheel hubs a few yards away; he crawled inside.

As he lay there trying to catch his breath, the sound of the service inside floated faintly out to him. Someone else was talking now, a calm man murmuring about the surcease that was to be found in oblivion. George remembered then why he'd been in the hospital. It hadn't been a heart attack at all. It had been suicide. It had been the bottle of luminal he'd kept in his desk: he'd swallowed them all, washing the tablets down with orange juice, knowing that he had browbeaten Lucy so well that she would never enter his study to disturb him in time to prevent the escape he so devoutly desired.

24: TUESDAY, OCTOBER 12

Mrs. Shummel exits a Winner

The bingo hall at the Gulf Breeze was filling when Martha Shummel and her friend Betty Alcyk arrived. It was Free Central America night. To the right of the platform where the machine sat waiting hung the flag of Florida, to the left the tattered U.S. flag Pete Cullum had brought back from the Battle of Panama City. They said that the stain that ran along the edge was from the mortal wound of General West himself, the Savior of the Panama Canal, but although Martha did not question the story she always wondered how that could have happened unless he had wrapped himself in it. The rows of tables with "Gulf Breeze" stenciled on their centers were already half-covered with bingo boards; people leaned back and filled the hall with cigarette smoke and the buzz of conversation.

Martha liked to be early enough to get her favorite seat, set her boards in order, sit back and watch the people come in. She would chat with her neighbors about children and politics and the weather. It was like being in a club. You got together as friends, forgot how bad your digestion was or how hard it was to pay the bills or how long it had been since your kids had called. You took a little chance. Maybe when you left you still had to go back through streets where punks sold drugs on streetcorners, to a stuffy room in a retirement home, but for a couple of hours you could put that away and have some fun.

But Betty had not been ready when Martha came by. So instead of getting there early they got stuck in line behind Sarah Kinsella, the human cable news network. With Sarah you could hardly get a word in edgewise, despite the fact that the respirator she always wore made her voice sound like it was coming at you over a tin-can telephone. Her mask waggled as she told them about the UFO landing port beneath Apalachee Bay, about the Brazilian spies pawing through her trashcans, and about how well her grandson Hugh was doing at the University of Florida—starting linebacker on the football team, treasurer of his fraternity, and he was making straight A's. Martha and Betty had heard it all before. Finally they got to the front of the line. Sarah bought five boards and headed down an aisle. The two women sighed in relief.

"He makes straight A's," Betty muttered.

"Yes," said Martha. "But his B's are a little crooked." They laughed until their eyes were damp.

Ed Kelly, who sold the boards, smiled at them. "Come on, girls. Settle down. You're gonna wet those cute pants."

"Don't be fresh," Martha said. Boards were two new-style dollars apiece. "Six," Martha said, and handed over $150 of old currency.

They went inside. Betty's eyesight was failing, so she insisted on sitting close to the front where she could peer up at the number board. But Martha's eyes were fine—she could handle the twelve game panels on her six boards without trouble—and the people who sat in front were too eager for her. They made her mad when they shrieked "Bingo!" as if someone was trying to cheat them. Her own spot was over against the windows on the side, but when she got there a young man was already there. She started to say, "Son, this is my spot—" but then the boy looked up at her.

His touseled hair shone downy white, but he had the darkest eyes. He looked dazed, as if he had just awoken from being beaten senseless to find Martha gazing at him. His bruised eyes reminded her of David's. She stood there, holding the straps of her purse, neither setting it down nor picking it up.

Finally she managed to speak. "This is my spot," she said. "Please go someplace else."

The boy pulled a card and a stylus from the gym bag beside him. It was a magic slate, a film of plastic laid over a black background. Martha's children had played with such slates as kids. On the slate, before he pulled up the plastic sheet to erase them, she read the words, CHARITY NEVER FAILETH. The boy cleared the old message and wrote, then held the slate up for Martha to see: FUCK OFF BITCH.

Martha felt her heart skip a beat, then race. Before she could call one of the men over, the boy pulled up the plastic sheet and the neatly printed block letters vanished. She stood there lumpishly, listening to the gabble of voices in the hall, the scrape of chairs on the hardwood floor.

The boy looked at her. He sighed. Silently he slid his slate and his single bingo board to the opposite side of the table. He walked around and sat, facing her, with his back to the bingo machine.

Martha sat down. She'd be damned if she'd let some punk push her around, let alone a mute, retarded one. If you did that then pretty soon you were at their mercy. She spread out her boards, got the plastic box of chips and magnetic wand from her purse. She covered the free square of each panel with one of the metal-rimmed chips. When she looked up again the boy was staring at her.

He sat back in his chair, innocent and alert, his face cool as the moon on a hot night. His hair wasn't bleached, it was naturally white. She wondered if he was one of those neighborhood boys who could get your prescriptions filled cheap. Trying hard to ignore him, she looked around the hall. From the kitchen at the back came the smells of pizza and hot dogs. Men and women stepped back onto the old roller rink floor carrying beer in plastic cups and slices of pizza on paper plates with the grease already soaking through. The light was dying outside the rows of windows, and the mirrored globe at the center of the ceiling caught a wisp of sunset.

Martha could spot dozens of people she knew from the Paradise Beach condos. They were Italians, Germans, Poles, Blacks, Cubans, Vietnamese and Anglos, ex-New Yorkers and ex-Chicagoans and native Southerners, the newly wed and the nearly dead, Republicans, Democrats, Libertarians and even Hyman Spivek who preached a loudmouthed brand of Communism, men turned milk white by leukemia and women turned to brown leather by the sun, Baptists, Jews, Catholics, and Space Cases, some with money to burn and others without two dimes to rub together, tolerable people like Betty and fools like Sarah. Most were retirees scraping along on pensions, hoping to win the $250 coverall so they could put off for a little longer the last trip to a Seppuku club. As decent a crowd of people, Martha supposed, as you could scrape together in all the panhandle of Florida.

The mute boy couldn't be any more than fifteen, and he acted more like he'd grown up on Mars than in America. He was a total stranger.

It was almost time to begin. Tony Schuster fired up the

bingo machine: the board lit up, the numbered balls rattled into the transparent box and began to dance around like popcorn on the jet of air. "First game," he announced through the P.A., "regular bingo on your cards, inside corners, outside corners, horizontal, vertical, diagonal rows. First number—" The machine made a noise like a man with his larynx cut out taking breath, and sucked up a ball. "I-18," Schuster called.

Martha covered the number on two of her boards. One of them was an inside corner. "G-52." She had two of those, too, but they were on different panels from the first number. "G-47." Nothing. "I-29." Three covers. She looked up. Ed Kelly, now patrolling the aisles, was looking over the boy's shoulder: on his top panel the boy had covered the four inside corners. He sat silent. "Bingo!" Kelly called out, just as Schuster was about to announce the next number. The crowd groaned; Martha sighed.

"I-18, I-29, G-52, G-47," Kelly read aloud.

"We have a bingo," Schuster called. The room was filled with the clicking of chips being wiped from several hundred boards, a field of locusts singing. Martha ran her wand over her boards while Kelly counted out $20 in red bills to the mute boy. "Speak up next time, kid," Kelly said.

"He's deaf and dumb," Martha said.

"Can't be deaf, Martha—he's got his back to the machine. Whyn't you help him out?"

Martha said nothing and Kelly went away. The boy watched them both. Schuster began the second game, a series beginning with a $20 regular bingo and ending in a $100 coverall. Martha managed to get four in the "O" column before someone across the room yelled "Bingo!" She sighed again. In the followup, the inner square, she had gotten nowhere when a black woman in the front bingoed. While the attendant called out the numbers for Schuster to check, Martha glanced over at the boy's card. The inner square on one panel was completely covered.

She almost called out for him, but when the boy turned his face up to her she ducked her head to study her own boards.

Dumb luck, and the kid was too stupid to know it. Luck was like that. Who could say how the numbers would come: only yesterday she had lost $300 when the Senators lost the playoff to the White Sox on a wind-assisted home run by that rookie Ellison. Martha had been a baseball fan since the late fifties. She had met her husband Sam at a game in 1958, Yanks against the Athletics.

Sam was lucky about the Yanks—he had won more than his share of bets over the years—but not so lucky when the cancer ate him up at fifty-five. He had collected baseball cards. For fifteen years after his death Martha kept them. Sometimes she would take the cards out of their plastic envelopes and look at them, remember how Sam would worry over them and rearrange their vacations so they could go to swap meets where he might pick up a 1952 Phil Rizzuto or Eddie Lopat. She would sigh. Staring at some head-and-shoulders shot of a bulletheaded ballplayer wearing a baggy uniform, it would become all she could do to keep from crying. She would slide the card back into its envelope, stick the envelope in among the others, shove the collection back on its shelf in the closet. She would poke at her eyes with the wrist of her sweater and make a cup of coffee. It would almost be time for *The Strange and the Lovely.*

Of their three kids Robert, the eldest, was a CPA in Portland and Gloria bought clothes for Macy's in New York. Their youngest, David, her favorite, a beautiful boy—in some ways as beautiful a boy as this punk who insulted her in the Gulf Breeze—had died at the age of fourteen, in 1982. David had snuck off to Jones Beach one weekend with his friends. He did not have her permission, would never have gotten it if he had asked. Despite the fact that he had been a very good swimmer, he had drowned.

After that her life started to go to pieces. She and Sam had moved to Florida in 1990, and a year later he was dead too. Then the market crashed for good, taking Sam's pension with it. Inflation ate up everything else. Last year she had sold the baseball cards to raise some cash.

"B-9." She placed her chips, glanced up from her board and saw the boy covering the number on his own, completing the outer square, covering the complete panel as well. Schuster called three more numbers. The kid had all of those, too, on the lower panel of his board. With the fourth number came shouts of "Bingo!" from three spots around the hall. The crowd groaned. The boy just sat there. He didn't yell, he didn't sigh, he did not seem even to hear the babble of disappointed voices filling the room. The men checked the winners' boards and divided up the money.

"Now, for the coverall," Schuster announced. "I-22." Martha was so distracted, staring at the boy's board, completely covered with red chips, that she forgot to check her own. "O-74."

"Bingo!" a man shouted.

The boy tilted his board and all the chips slid off onto the table.

She tried to figure it out. He was trying to get to her. He had to have been cheating. That was why he had not called out—he knew that when the attendant came to check his board, they would find that he had not really won. Martha decided to keep an eye on him through the next game.

Schuster called five numbers. The boy had four of them, a clear winning diagonal that shot across the board like an arrow into Martha's heart. He remained mute as a snake, and somebody else won two numbers later. He had both of those numbers, too.

Martha sat there and, with an anxiety that grew like a tumor, watched him win the next five games in a row, none of which he called out. The room faded into the background until all there was was the boy's bingo board. Schuster would call a number, and it was as if he were reading them off the kid's battered pasteboard. The boy said nothing. He let other people take $170 that could have been his.

Martha had trouble breathing. She needed some air. But more than air, more than life itself, she needed that board.

By the time of the break after the tenth game, Martha's anxiety had gone from anger to fear. The boy had won every game and called out none. There was no way one card could win game after game unless the numbers on it changed, but as close as she watched Martha could not see them change. At the end of the last coverall, when two women, one of them Betty Alcyk, shouted bingo, the boy looked up at Martha. He pointed to her boards. She had been ignoring them. The boy wrote on his slate: DON'T YOU WANT TO WIN?

"Shut up!" she said. Some people at the next table looked over at them.

He ripped off the old words and printed something new. He held up his slate and his bingo board, scattering colored chips across the table. One of them rolled off into her lap. YOU WANT IT?

Martha bit her lip. She feared a trick. She nodded.

He wrote: COME OUTSIDE.

The boy got up quickly and went out the side door without looking back. After a minute Martha followed. She tried to look as if she was going outside for a breath of air; in truth the weight of the night and her losses had lodged in her chest like a stone.

Outside, in the parking lot, a few men and women were talking. Paula Lorenzetti waved to her as she came out, but Martha pretended she didn't see her. The boy stood under a street light. At first that reassured her, but then she realized it was only because he needed the light to use his slate.

When she got to him he held the bingo board out toward her. She took it. It seemed perfectly normal. A Capitol: dogeared pasteboard, two game grids printed black on white, a little picture of the dome of the Congress in each of the free squares. In the corner someone had written, in childish handwriting, "Passions Rule!"

"How much?" she asked.

He wrote on the slate: YOUR VOICE.

"What?"

YOU WILL GIVE UP YOUR VOICE.

Martha felt flushed. She could see everything so clearly it almost hurt. Her senses were as sharp as if she were twenty again; her eyes picked out every hair on the boy's arm, she smelled the aroma of food from the hall and garbage from the alley. Across the city somewhere a truck was climbing up the gears away from a stoplight.

"You're kidding."

NO.

"How will you take my voice?"

I DON'T TAKE—YOU GIVE.

"How can I give you my voice?"

SAY YES.

What did she have to lose? There was no way he could steal a person's voice. "All right," she said.

"Goodbye," said the boy: softly, almost a whisper.

He turned from her. The way he did this so reminded her of the way David used to defy her that she felt it like a blow—it *was* David, or some ghost come to torment her—and she almost cried out for him to wait, to please, please speak to her. In a moment he was down an alley and around the corner. She held the board in her hand. She felt light, as if at any moment her step might push her away from the earth and she would float into the night.

She remembered going with Sam down to the hospital, fighting the traffic on Long Island. Sam had urged her not to go; it was no thing for a woman to have to do, but she had insisted in a voice that even Sam could hear that she was going. The emergency room was hot and smelled of Lysol. The staff had wheeled David from a bay in emergency to a side corridor, left him on the gurney against the wall with a sheet over him like a used tray from room service. For the first time in her life she felt that her body was not her: she was merely living in it, peering out through the eyes, running her arms and legs like a man running a backhoe. There was David, pale, calm. His hair, very short except for the silly rat's tail in back that they had fought over, was still damp but not wet, beginning to stand away from his head. She touched his face. It was cool as a satin sofa pillow. Sam had to pull her away, trying to talk to her. It was a day before she spoke to him and then it was only to tell him to be quiet.

"Martha!"

It was Paula, come across the lot to speak to her. "Who was that boy?" She looked at the card in Martha's hand.

It took a moment for Martha to come back to reality. This would be the test. "Some punk kid," she said. "Hot night."

"It's that Commandante fellow. Messing up the air."

"It's always hot in October." Her voice flowed as easily as water.

"Not like this," said Paula.

Martha watched a man with a torn pants leg cut across the motel parking lot. He looked frightened. He jerked open the door of a parked car and drove away. "I like your blouse," she said.

"This thing?" Paula said. "It's cheap. If you don't like the pattern, all you got to do is wash it."

Martha laughed. They turned back to the hall. Inside, most of the people were already seated. Martha hurried to her place, put her other boards aside and set the new one directly in front of her. Mel Shiffman took over the platform to announce the rest of the games.

"Settle down, settle down," he said, like a homeroom teacher coming into class just after the bell. "Eleventh game, on your reg'lar boards, straight bingo. First number: Under the O, 65."

The room was silent. Martha had that number, on the lower playing panel—bottom right corner.

"B-14." Upper left corner.

"N-33." Middle top.

"N-42." No cover. Martha began to worry.

"O-72." Upper right. One more for the outer corners: B-1. B-1, she thought.

"B-1."

It was a flood of light, a joy that filled her, as if the number machine, Shiffman's voice, the world itself were under her control. "Bingo!" she shouted. The voices of the people buzzed in her ears. Ed Kelly came by and checked off her numbers. "We have a bingo," Mel announced.

Kelly paid out $20. The red bills were crisp and dry as dead leaves. "Inner or outer square," Shiffman called. The people settled down. "Next number: I-25." Both panels on Martha's board had that number. Shiffman called three more. Each number was on her board. All her senses were heightened: the board before her stood out like a child's viewmaster picture; its colors were bright. In the air she could pick out the mingled smells of pizza and cigarette smoke and a wisp of bus exhaust that trailed through the window. She heard restless crowd mutter, could almost identify the individual voices of her friends as they hovered above their bingo boards, wishing, hoping, to win. Except Martha knew that they wouldn't: she would. As if ordered by God, the numbers fell to her, one by one, and the inner square was covered. "Bingo!" she shouted again.

She heard the crowd groan, an explosive sigh heavy with frustration, and immediately after the voices: "Twice in a row." "She's lucky tonight." "I never win." "N-32; that's all I needed!" "She always wins." The last was Betty's voice, from twenty feet away as clear as if she were whispering in Martha's ear.

Kelly came by and paid out the $40. She could buy a new dress, buy a pound of real hamburger, get the toilet fixed. "Looks like your night," Kelly said. "Or maybe it's just this table."

"I never won like this before," she said.

"Don't act too guilty," Kelly said, and winked at her.

She started to protest, but he was gone. Something was wrong with her hearing. She heard too well. The next game began. She could feel the tension, and every sigh she heard as a number was called that was on her board and not on that of the sigher was like a needle in her chest. When the last number came, the one that both completed the outer square on her upper game panel and covered the entire panel, it was a moment before she could muster the breath to shout, "Bingo!"

The groan that came was full of barely repressed jealousy. Despair. Even hatred. She looked up and saw envious faces. Across the room she saw Betty's peevish squint. The crowd buzzed. Kelly read the numbers off her board. Someone shushed someone else. Shiffman announced that this was, miraculously, a valid bingo. Kelly paid out the combined prize of $160. She smiled sickly up at him. He counted the bills without comment.

It was all she could do to cover the free squares for the next game. Shiffman, so nervous now that his smile had faded for the first time in Martha's memory, began. The first four numbers he called ran a diagonal winner across Martha's board. When she stammered out "Bingo," it was with half the force that she had managed before.

Cries of dismay whirled around her. The hall seemed filled with envious voices. She tried not to take the money, but Kelly insisted. Each bill as it was counted out was like a blow, and when he was at last done she could not find breath to thank him.

When, in the next game, she saw that she had won again, she realized that she could not stand it. She didn't even put chips on the squares. At last another woman in the room shouted "Bingo!" The woman's triumphant screech was greeted by cheers.

Martha tried to leave, but her legs were too weak. She sat silently through the last games, watching her card, a lump in her throat. Had she been able to face her neighbors, she could have taken every dollar. At last it was over. She gathered up her markers, left the board on the table, and stumbled toward the door. Friends tried to talk to her. Betty Alcyk called her name. But the memory of Betty's voice among the others silenced her. She couldn't talk to Betty. Their friendship had been only a pact of losers, unable to stand the strain of one of them winning.

But there was worse. If someone else had had the magic card, even if that person was the dearest one in the world to Martha—Betty—Sam her lost husband—even her beautiful, lost son David—would her own voice have held that same hatred?

The people filed out. Their voices rang in her head. She had nothing to say to them, and she wondered if she ever would.

25: THURSDAY, OCTOBER 14
....
A Brief Rapprochement

Lucy peered through the brush, across the asphalt at the lights of a government gasohol station. Covered with chiggerbites, grindingly hungry, she wore bluejeans, a Georgia Bulldogs T-shirt and Dr. Kent's suit jacket. She had stolen the shirt and jeans off a backyard line outside of Canadys, South Carolina, where she'd abandoned the prison car. She kept to the woods, slept during the day in a tobacco shed, and crept up upon I-95 only after it was fully dark. All she'd eaten that day were some shriveled apples she'd found in an abandoned orchard.

Wind whipped the dry grass around her. The gasohol station was doing a pretty good business, considering, but Lucy had to wait a long time before she got the opportunity she was looking for. Finally a car pulled in next to a pump where the overhead fluorescent lights were out. The driver got out and went into the building. His shoulders slumped and he had trouble picking up his feet. Lucy dashed across to the car and wedged herself into the space behind the seats. The car was full of trash. She pulled a couple of empty gasohol cans down on top of her and prayed that the driver would be sleepy enough not to notice.

A minute later she heard someone running across the pavement. "Hey, buddy!" a voice yelled. The driver's door was yanked open and the man leapt in. He cranked the starter; the engine caught and the car jerked away from the pumps. Lucy held her breath. More shouts. The car bottomed on its shocks as they jounced back to the highway.

Once they hit the road and settled into steady motion Lucy almost fell asleep. She remembered riding in the back seat of her parents' car as a kid—back when they still took vacations, before they'd started drinking bad. On the way back from the shore she would lie down across the seat, her skin sticky with suntan oil and gritty with sand, her shoulders sunburn hot. The sun would slant lower through the windows until it faded entirely into twilight, then dark. She would listen to her mother and father talk. Lucy never paid much attention to what they said unless she heard her own name, but she was reassured just to hear their voices. Whenever they talked about her, Lucy knew that they loved her.

She remembered hearing her father complain once that Lucy was too sensible for a normal kid, too afraid to take chances. Well, Dad, look at me now. She felt in the pocket of Kent's jacket for his stun gun. It was still there, along with the calculator. But she couldn't zap the driver while they were on the road. Should she threaten him? Wait until he stopped again? Either way she would have to hurt him—maybe even kill. Lucy asked herself what Luz would do in this situation.

The driver turned on the radio and tuned across the band, pausing occasionally to listen. But inevitably he moved on. She heard snatches of a forties big-band, a barbershop quartet, a revivalist preacher, MOR rock. He paused on some politician talking about the ravages of crashflation on the Carolina economy, working up toward a secessionist argument, at which point the driver switched again until he stopped for a sports call-in show. People were discussing the prospects for the Braves vs. the White Sox in the World Series. When the broadcast broke for a commercial the driver switched yet again, moving in rapid fits and starts across the band. He settled on a old rock and roll program. In the midst of her plans to attack him, and despite herself, Lucy smiled. Listening to the man pan through the stations was like eavesdropping on his thoughts. His shifts bespoke impatience and a cranky boyishness.

The driver seemed to like the ancient rock and stayed there for some time. Midway through Elvis Presley's version of "That's Alright, Mama," he started to sing along, at first weakly, then at the top of his keyless voice. Lucy could not have been more surprised had it been Elvis himself.

"George!"

The man stopped singing. The car swerved. Lucy tried to sit up and was thrown against the back of the driver's seat as they skidded to a stop. The engine died. The song on the radio loomed larger.

The man pulled himself toward the steering wheel, twisting around to look at her. She grabbed the headrest and drew herself up. They faced each other, a foot apart, over the horizon of the seat.

"Lucy. Jesus Christ! Is it you?"

"Yes."

"How did you find me?"

She could hardly see his face in the darkness. His hair was in patches, his cheekbones sharper than she remembered. He looked old. "I wasn't trying to find you, George."

He didn't say anything for a moment. "Well, you did." He laughed. It was such a warm sound that she wanted to cry. He reached out and touched her face.

She pushed the microcam off the passenger's seat and, as George drove on, told him all that had happened to her since he'd run away. It was a relief to be able to talk. When she got to the night in the car with Dr. Kent she had a hard time going on. George asked her quiet questions until she told him. As she spoke the fury overwhelmed her. She was angry at him, too. It was trying to help him that had knocked her through a crack in reality into his crazy HCR world. Did he understand that? He kept glancing at her throughout her tale. He looked exhausted; when she finished he was silent for a moment. "The sons of bitches," he said. He reached over and held her hand. "I'm sorry, Lucy."

She gripped his hand tightly in both of hers. He told her how he had tried to contact her. "But Richard lied to me. He told me you were still in New York. He even faked messages from you—assuming it *was* Richard."

Lucy didn't ask him what he meant. After awhile she felt a little better. "Can we stop someplace?" she asked.

They found "Noah's Motel" in Manning, South Carolina. "Future launch site of the Revelation Ark," announced a portable marquee in the gravel parking lot. The place looked deserted. The motel was a "V" of tin-roofed clap-board cabins set up on cinder blocks. A big red brick farm-house sat out front. Above a side door a painted wooden sign said "Office." The screen door flapped back and forth in the dry wind. There was no one behind the desk. George and Lucy walked around the yard until they saw lights in an old barn a hundred yards back of the house. The wind kicked up dust devils as they walked back along a rutted clay drive. George stumbled several times. When they got close, through the half-open sliding door, they could see a flying saucer.

The thing was thirty feet across and filled most of the barn. It was made of strips of sheet metal riveted together; a hemispherical dome at the top had a single porthole of thick glass and was topped by a stainless steel cross. At several places around the rim other crosses were welded to the ship. A gull-wing door in the side, facing a workbench, was open, partially revealing the dimly lit interior. An extension cord ran from an outlet on a rafter into the ship. Lucy heard the sound of a drill.

George stiffened at the sight. Lucy stepped past him and knocked on the side of the ship where a couple of Greek letters were painted. "Is anyone here?" she asked.

The drilling stopped. A thumping came from inside and a old man in coveralls backed out the door. He straightened up slowly and faced Lucy. "Yep. What can I do for you?"

"We'd like to rent a room."

"Who's 'we?'"

Lucy turned around. George was gone. She turned back to the man. "My husband and me."

The man's mouth worked for a second and he spat out a wad of tobacco. "Cost you one hundred dollars, old style."

"Okay."

"In advance."

Lucy's stomach growled. "Will you throw in a meal or two?"

"All right." The man wiped his hand with a rag from the bench, then extended it. "Noah Barnes. Where's your better half?"

Lucy shook hands. She peered out the barn door toward the house. "He must be getting our things."

On their way to the office Lucy's curiosity got the better of her. "You're building a saucer?"

"Somebody's got to," the old man said.

"Will it fly?"

"God made the birds to fly, and the wasps, and the dandelion seed. He won't let us down."

"You designed it yourself?"

"God designed it, through his prophet John. It's all there in the Bible. You got your chemistry, your philosophy, your carbon arc welding—but the Book of Revelations beats Einstein to blazes. You just got to know how to read it."

George was standing by the Hyundai. He looked like a dog faced with the return of a master who had delighted in beating him.

"Mr. Barnes here is building a flying saucer."

"Ark," said Barnes.

"Is that so." George's voice was flat. "What kinds of animals you going to take with you?"

"My dog Jake. My cat Amos. The rest'll be frozen gametes."

"How you going to incubate them without mothers?"

"The Lord works in mysterious ways."

George went round to the back of the car and took out a gym bag and the camera. "I don't suppose we can argue with that. What cabin are we in?"

Barnes thought for a moment. "Number nine. At the end of the row."

"Nine it is," said George. He started back toward the cabin. Barnes stopped him.

"One hundred dollars."

George put down the bag. "I don't suppose you'll take a card."

"Nope."

George pulled a red ten out of his wallet.

"Thank you," said Barnes. "Be by in a few minutes with some supper."

Cabin nine was neat but musty. Knotty pine paneling, a double bed, rickety pine desk with an old clock radio. The bathrooms were in a separate building. George slung the bag onto the bed and dropped the camera on the desk. His lips were tight. Lucy was surprised to see his anger after so long. At one time she would have been intimidated, waiting for the explosion that probably wouldn't come because Geroge could make her feel worse by brooding. Now he looked so scrawny the whole scene was comic.

"What's the matter, George?"

"Somebody cut off my credit. And my gasohol card's been invalidated. I almost got arrested back at that station. Now, thanks to you I'm left with maybe ten bucks. I wish you'd let me do the talking."

Lucy laughed. "You had your chance. You ran away. You acted like that man was going to bite you."

"That saucer spooked me. I thought it was real."

"It looked pretty real."

"I thought he was one of them. They almost killed me in Tallahassee."

He looked completely serious. "You were lucky to get away, then. What kind of weapons did they use?"

"A gun. Police .38. Almost blew my head off."

"But you got away from him?"

"Her. It looked just like a woman."

Lucy remembered her conversation with Richard just before she'd locked him in the bathroom. "It probably was a detective, George. Richard told me he was going to put one on your trail."

"This was no human. It couldn't speak English. If you'd seen only half of what I've seen in the last few months—"

If she'd seen what *he'd* seen. She'd like to take him to visit the Farm. "You didn't do a very good job of explaining this to me before you left, George. How about spelling it out for me now?"

"You wouldn't believe it."

"Try me."

"Well, first I thought it was just aliens from outer space. All the UFO reports. There was no way they could all be hallucinations or frauds. There were aliens loose in the U.S., and they were disturbing people's lives. You saw all my clippings about that."

"They were all burned up in the fire."

"Oh—right. Well, I've been filing all these stories by satellite linkup through Richard. But he's gone to work for the Reverend Jimmy-Don Gilray."

"What! How did that happen?"

"At first I thought it was some scheme he cooked up with Abramowitz. But he's been acting strangely. The Reverend—or someone—has been warping him."

George was about the worst judge of whether anyone was crazy Lucy had ever seen. "If I know Richard, it's more likely he's warping Gilray."

"This Gilray is up to something. Have you paid attention to what he's been doing in the last few months?"

"I've been in prison, George."

George paced. "The Reverend is getting his followers hyped for a holy war when Christ shows up to lead them against the Antichrist. He's got people all over the world expecting some savior from the skies. They're parachuting portable TVs into the Amazon, Borneo, Tibet! Global propaganda! It fits right in with my HCR reports: he's explaining UFOs in religious terms. Now an alien shows up and tries to kill me. Do you see? This is no coincidence."

"I don't see anything."

"I was lucky to get out of Tallahassee alive. I had to sneak back to the motel and snatch my car."

Lucy felt her old exasperation. But less patience. "George—"

"If you were an alien planning to take over the earth, wouldn't it make sense to play into our superstitions? So when you show up we'll welcome you with open arms, even join up with you to conquer any resistance? Wouldn't it make sense, if you could take on human form, to send an agent to do this work for you? And if you were that agent, wouldn't it make sense to get a smart media type like Richard on your side?"

"Gilray's obsessed with God, not aliens."

"So? Maybe it is God. Maybe God isn't some all-commanding Ruler of the Universe—He uses subversion, terrorism, disinformation. Like a cosmic CIA director, sending out spooks to destabilize society."

"George, you're the one who's destabilized. What makes you think you're any less crazy than this motel owner?"

"So who was this woman who tried to kill me?"

"Abramowitz's detective. Or someone else. In case you didn't notice, there are lots of crazy people out there."

"You don't know Richard, Lucy. He's my best friend. He wouldn't lie to me about you. And he would have told me if someone was after me. If I was in danger, he would warn me."

"Richard is not reliable."

"Maybe with other people, but not with me. We're special. No. I think the Rev is behind this. And something else is behind the Rev."

He stared at her. When she didn't answer he sat down on the edge of the bed and began fiddling with the dial of the radio on the table. He got static and eventually a blast of old rock-and-roll. He had found the same station they had been listening to in the car.

"Gilray isn't some alien, George," Lucy said. "He's just the latest example of the kind of crazy preacher that's been around for two thousand years. Except he has a TV satellite." She sat beside him, put her arms around him. Finally he looked at her. "Listen to me."

"I'm listening." He was like a hyperactive child. He nodded at the radio. "I remember some of these from when I was a kid," he said.

He looked so tired. Despite herself, Lucy was moved. "That was before my time. I had to learn them later, like archeology."

"When I was a kid we'd listen on the bus to Kaw Lake," George said. "Seth had a transistor radio. It was small enough to fit into his jeans pocket. He could get two stations. It seemed like a miracle they could make a radio so small."

The radio was playing "Too Much Monkey Business." Too much monkey business for me to be involved in. Lucy agreed. But there didn't seem to be any easy way out.

She watched George in the faint light from outside. "George, why resort to aliens to explain the mess we're in? Look at us. Our problems have nothing to do with aliens."

George kept his eyes on the radio. "I have to find out what's happening, Lucy. I need to know the answer."

"George, there are no answers!"

"There must be."

She racked her brain for a way to pound some sense into him. "Did you ever hear that story about the Voyager spacecraft? You know, the first one to leave the solar system?"

"What about it?"

"The scientists thought it might be picked up by aliens, so they put a recording on board. What a chance to get some big answers, they thought. They packed on as much information as they could, even a couple of hours of music: Bach, a mariachi band, African percussion, Navajo chants, New Guinea tribal dances. And 'Johnny B. Goode.'"

George picked at the strap of the camera bag, his shoulders tensed up around his ears. "So?"

"So the story goes that the scientists wait the rest of their lives for a reply. Nothing. Nations rise and fall. The climate changes. New civilizations come. Ten thousand years of silence. After all this time, a radio message comes from the stars. It's in a code that takes another age to break. Philosophers spend their lives speculating about the significance of this contact. Finally, the descendants of the original scientists manage to decipher the message: 'Send more Chuck Berry.' "

George stared at her. "Don't make fun of me. This isn't some joke. Aliens are invading the earth, and you say 'Send More Chuck Berry?' "

"Little Richard, then. Buddy Holly. Whatever you like."

George tried to get up. Lucy held him tight. She remembered the sight of Luz accepting her "blessing," the narrow face of Kent on the dark road. She laid her head against George's shoulder, made him lie down next to her. He seemed to relax. He sighed. "Maybe you're right," he said. He rested his head on the pillow beside her, his face a few inches away. His cheeks were hollow. If he was the ice man from her dream, he had melted some. "Lucy, I—I know what happened to me," he said. "What I was like before the heart attack. Except it wasn't a heart attack. It—"

A knock at the door undid it all. George leapt for the window. Lucy sat up and yanked the stun gun from her jacket. His edginess was getting to her. It was like living with him, near the end, all over again.

"Supper," came a voice from outside.

George cracked the door. Lucy stepped by him and pulled it open all the way. Barnes's dog stood beside him, tongue lolling. Barnes carried a tray with a couple of ham and egg biscuits, greens, two pieces of pie, and coffee. Lucy took the tray. "Thank you," she said.

Barnes peeked past her. "You folks Christians?"

"We're believers," Lucy said.

"Well, don't forget to say your prayers," Barnes said. "C'mon, Jake." He walked back toward the house.

George watched through the window, a wild silhouette against the exterior light. He let the curtains fall. "I think he's one of them," he said.

"Food, George."

He glared at her, turned his back, paced the length of the small room. "I've got to get to Richard," he muttered.

Watching him, Lucy felt a door close in her heart. She sat down and started on her biscuit. The ham was salty; the biscuit was heavy with grease. It was good. The collards were limp and equally salty. She took a huge gulp of coffee: it was hot but that didn't matter. George threw himself down on the bed, arms behind his head, and stared at the ceiling. "Are you going to eat?" Lucy asked.

"No."

She refused to take her part in the script he was writing for them: Lucy DiPaulo, the self-absorbed, dependent female, and George Eberhart, the self-sacrificing, independent male. He really couldn't see her. She supposed that she might pity him, but too much had happened in the last five months to leave her much sympathy for pathology.

Yet it felt like wrenching her heart from her chest. Their marriage was over. She looked at the profile of his face. The man of ice. Before the tears could come she headed for the door.

"Where are you going?"

"To the bathroom." She left.

The wind had turned cold and damp; she turned her collar up. The bathrooms were in a cinder block building at the vertex of the "V." She sat on a filthy toilet and rubbed tears from her cheeks with the back of her hand. She cursed herself for being so weak: what had they had in the last few years that was worth crying over, in the face of enormities like Kent and the Farm? But she knew she wasn't weak. The weak Lucy would have been turned around and puking into this same toilet. She had changed.

She reached into her pocket for the calculator: she could take the stuff now, follow through with Luz's plan and truly change the world. But it was no longer there. It must have fallen out in the car, or when she pulled out the stun gun in the cabin.

The lights were out in the barn and farmhouse. As Lucy crossed the gravel lot, she saw something move in the shadow of one of the cabins. She did not break step but continued on to the car. While looking for the calculator she watched through the car window. A small figure crept from the shadows.

Lucy forgot about the calculator and went up the cabin

steps as if she had not noticed anything. George was asleep. The radio whispered. The calculator lay on the bedside table. Lucy shoved it into her pocket and shut off the light. She shook his shoulder. "George!" she hissed.

He stirred. "Someone's out there," she said.

He came awake then. "Man or woman?"

"Woman, I think. Somebody small."

George sat up. He crept to the window and peeked out. "Can't see anything," he said. He turned back. "Here's what we'll do. I'll go out the front and try to get to the car. You slip out the widow in back. They're after me, not you, but this way one of us is likely to get free. Head for—"

"No. This is not some alien. She's not going to kill anybody. I'm going to go out and talk to her." Lucy opened the door.

"Lucy, no!"

Before he could stop her she was out. She walked down the row of cabins. Despite herself, she was nervous. "Hello?" she called. I know you're out here. Let's talk."

No answer. The wind, turning colder by the minute, stirred up dust. As Lucy came past the corner of a cabin she was tripped, and someone was on her instantly, driving a knee into the small of her back. Something hard poked into her side. "Quiet," the woman said in her ear.

The woman grabbed Lucy's collar and jerked her back between the cabins. She shoved Lucy against the wall. She was a small woman with short brown hair. She pointed a gun at Lucy's chest. The woman said something, but the words were so slurred they were unintelligible.

"I can't understand you," Lucy said.

A look of intense frustration crossed the woman's face. More slowly she said, "Tuss everhart have a weahpon?"

"A weapon?" Lucy said. "Look, there's no need for this. He's—"

In the lot, the car's engine started. The woman knocked Lucy aside and ran back between the cabins. Tires skidded on gravel; a shot echoed. Lucy got up and ran after her: the woman was trying to cut off the car before it reached the road. Lucy raced across the lot and tackled her from behind. They hit the gravel and rolled. Noah's dog barked. By the time the woman struggled to her knees, George was gone. In a fury, she turned on Lucy and shoved the gun up under her chin, her sweaty face a foot away. The barrel was hot and smelled of powder. The woman's eyes searched Lucy's face, as if Lucy knew the secret that would end a life of trouble.

Lucy realized that she had met another insane person. This one, however, was female.

26: FRIDAY, OCTOBER 15
Fun without Drugs

As he hummed about his apartment at the End of Time Institute contemplating the surprise he would spring at that afternoon's rally, Richard realized that he had now obtained everything he had wanted when he was twenty. At twenty, he had wanted some pastime that would amuse him. Now he was a prophet. At twenty, he had wanted revenge. Now he directed the actions of people he despised. At twenty, he had wanted a friend and a lover. Now he knew that friends and lovers were impossible. They made demands, acted irrationally, needed help. They didn't realize that there was no help to be had.

At twenty he had already known there was no help, that the world was a venue of hopelessness and deceit. He had only wanted to collect the experiences to prove it. In this garden of religious mania he had plucked the crowning proof: human beings were clever idiots. They would accept any attractive lie. Their self-deception amounted to depravity. They were lower than insects. An idealist like George would never accept it; that was what had killed him and would ultimately kill him again. Richard, however, saw. He was charged. He had an image of himself that he knew was true no matter how a photograph might contradict it: eyes that burned with intuition, light shining from his fingertips. He was twisted, buzzed, tripping, yet he had not touched a thing since Sumner's party. He had it in his hands to smash the filthy jewel.

Events had moved fast since Tuesday. At the rally on the Fayetteville Street Mall that night to celebrate their election sweep, the crowd was swollen by pilgrims who had come to the city over the last few months. A hundred thousand people marched past the state capitol, waving torches and signs reading "There are NO Accidents." Waiting for Gilray to address them, the people grew unruly; those police who weren't so much in sympathy as to look the other way were overwhelmed. Hecklers were brutally beaten.

Finally Gilray made his appearance. Richard had never seen him so hot: he had the sex appeal of a major pop star. His sermon was met with an enthusiasm that turned orgiastic by midnight; the torchlight flickered brighter and the flagellants cleared a circle in the middle of the crowd and went to work. Gilray watched with a grim smile. He came down off the platform, took the blood-slick whip in his hand and flogged a young woman into religious ecstasy. You had to respect a talent like that.

The next morning the Governor took a trip to Asheville, where he issued an equivocal statement deploring violence and praising God. In Washington, the state's junior Senator warned the Congress of the increasing fanaticism in the Piedmont and called upon the President to put the army at Ft. Bragg on alert. In Zion the senior Senator, who had taken a few strokes himself the night before, called the Governor an atheist and the junior Senator a secular humanist. No one from the outside was going to put out the fire. As far as most of the state went it was about time the capital city got right with God, and the Army and National Guard were dominated by Rev supporters.

The national media had not given it much attention. Levine, dispatched by Abramowitz to Raleigh, had filed a few reports, but too many weird things were happening across the country for a little religious fanatacism to take much TV time. Richard didn't mind—that would come. The trick now was to make Zion the center of the circus instead of just another animal act. Richard could feel the elements coming together.

On the left half of his HDTV was a text news summary; on the right he ran a collection of Commandante Jesus's video sabotage from the last three years. Research. The disk ran through clips from the Commandante's Greatest Hits:

ECSTASY ROULETTE: This one was a perfect copy of the most popular game show on cable, the one where the unemployed, on the turn of the wheel, could win six-month's supply of nembutal or a month in a sensory deprivation tank. The Commandante had altered the broadcast so that the MC and contestants all were naked. They had grotesque deformities; they suffered from terminal diseases. They conveyed their responses to the questions by articulate farting, accompanied by blue flames shooting out of their asses. The happy winner was euthanized on the set.

THE '98 MIDTERM ELECTION RETURNS: Where the Commandante knotted the California vote totals so inextricably that the results had been thrown out and incumbents had to stay on.

THE FLORIDA EXECUTION RACE: The Commandante had managed to get a camera in on the first U.S. multiple execution and had sent it out to 40 million viewers. He vidsynthed himself into the action to do play by play on which of the three inmates undergoing lethal injection was dying fastest, with mumbled color commentary by his sidekick Otto Da Fey, who wore a black hood and hunchback for the occasion.

THE 1999 STATE OF THE UNION ADDRESS: over which the Commandante had laid subtitles which translated each of the President's hypocrisies into plain English, punctuated by occasional comments on the chief executive's sexual proclivities.

THE 1998 ACADEMY AWARDS: For weeks before the show rumors had flown that the Commandante would intervene. Unprecedented electronic security was arranged: every link in the electronic chain from theater to studio to net to viewer was continuously monitored. The broadcast proceeded with flawless tedium until the Best Picture category, when the aging actress who was to present the award announced the winner as a musical remake of *Triumph of the Will*. Switch to a clip of ecstatic Nazis (resembling the major heads of state of the Western Alliance) dancing around the infield of an olympic stadium singing "Springtime for Hitler." After the clip the dowager actress pulled out a small pistol and shot her co-presenter in the shoulder. Afterward she was unable to explain what had moved her to do this but rumor had it that her hormone injections had been spiked with hallucinogens and her home video center programmed with subliminals.

No one had ever seen the real Commandante: his appearances on rogue broadcasts were all vidsynthed. One time he might appear as a handsome Latino lounge lizard, another as a shaven-headed Orinetal woman in a caftan. Richard couldn't even guess whether the Commandante was male or female—if he was a person at all, and not an organization, or an arm of the government designed to play tricks on itself, or the Alien Richard had portrayed him as to Charlie Sumner. Or an agent of God Almighty Himself.

Until recently Richard would not have given much credence to the last explanation. His fit at the party and his oration outside the polling place had, however, shaken him. Maybe he was being manipulated by the Commandante the way the old actress had been. His outburst at George over the phone—real resentment, real guilt—brought it together for Richard. His rage was breaking loose. Gilray had called him God's hammer. Richard didn't know whose hammer he was, but he liked the idea of smashing things to bits. Why not? He was tired of nudging events from the sidelines.

Wednesday morning, after the rally, Richard cut off George's credit. Without any money even Delano could catch George. Later that same morning he got a message from Delano saying, in her paranoid way, "She would have news for him before the week was out." Wednesday afternoon Gilray set up a meeting for Friday where they would discuss their plans. Thursday night came the biggest surprise of all: Delano called to tell him that she had made a capture. Not George, but Lucy. It was a miracle. Lucy had disappeared from the face of the earth and now, months later, had fallen into his hands. Richard told Delano to bring her to Zion. He could almost believe it was the hand of Providence.

Richard turned off the TV. He saluted his velvet painting of Elvis and went down the hall that linked the apartments to the main building. Gilray, Lucas Boston, Charlie Sumner and Marianne were already in the conference room, along with Helms Griffin, the engineer in charge of the group designing the New Jerusalem Landing Pad. Boston was describing how some doctor on the staff of one of the prisons had been grievously injured by a female inmate. Gilray visibly ignored him and watched Richard enter. Richard had noticed that look from him a lot lately: as if Richard were a prize bull of which Gilray was proud and a little afraid.

Charles began the meeting by reciting the final figures on the election. They had won by the thinnest of margins.

"That's great," Richard said. "But we can't rest on our Bibles now. News travels fast, rots faster. If we don't initiate the next phase by November first we're going to hear some questions. We'll get schisms."

"We're baptizing people twice a day," Marianne said. "Even without our help people have been rallying every night."

"We need to have someone from our ministry at the center of every gathering," Gilray said. "Already there are false prophets. We've got exactly eleven weeks before the End. Thousands more believers will come to Zion. Once the state and national governments really understand what we are doing here we're going to be the focus for the rage of the Antichrist. Conflict is inevitable. Many still here are bitterly opposed to the rule of God."

Gilray turned to Sumner. "What's the latest on the Governor?"

"It looks like he's going to stay in Asheville for a while."

"Is he going to try to organize a government-in-exile?"

"I don't think he's figured out that he needs to do that yet. Does he?"

"It wouldn't make any difference if he did," said Richard. "But we'd better be ready for some opposition. Are you organizing these new recruits into militia?"

Boston spoke up. "Our people are training recruits at the state fairgrounds. We're billeting as many as we can there, mustering and training in the fields. Some of the spillover has moved into the agriculture school."

"All right," said Richard. "We need to keep ahead of this. Infrastructures. Medical care. Dormitories. Free kitchens. And daily public performances to keep the fervor going."

They discussed the progress in acquiring the land across Alexander Drive for the Landing Pad. Before the election they had hit a legal stone wall, but since Tuesday Boston had put the gears in motion to use the public right-of-way statutes to confiscate the land. Environmental groups were screaming and they had some support from the remnants of high-tech industry in Research Triangle Park, but unless the Governor came back the bulldozers would be clearing the mile-square tract of forest by the end of the month.

Helms Griffin got up to show them his model. "It's going to be a job to get ready by Christmas," he said, "but we'll do it." He used a penlight to point out the details of the Landing Pad: the buildings to be demolished, thousands of trees to be ripped up, mountains of earth to be moved, tons of concrete to be poured, the TV camera tower, the sixty-two floodlight poles, the stadium-sized TV monitors on which the hundreds of thousands they expected to gather there would be able to see the platform from which the Reverend would greet the Redeemer.

"Of course we expect some problems with high intensity lumination from the Holy City's descent," Griffin said.

"Our cameras are designed to compensate as much as possible, but we don't know if we're dealing with coherent or incoherent light. We can't know until it happens. We'll have to warn the faithful not to watch the descent by the unaided eye." He hauled out a pair of dark goggles. "All of us will have these, of course."

Richard revelled in the lunacy of it. "Of course," he said.

"Good work," said Gilray. Griffin nodded like a dog fed a milk-bone.

Sumner roused himself. "Let me show you the appeal we're going to broadcast." He touched a switch in front of him and the mural of cloud-borne Jesus opposite the conference table slid aside to reveal a screen. He hit another switch and the disk began: A ragged man and woman trudged down a country highway. The woman's face was etched with fatigue. The man had a burlap sack over his shoulder; the woman carried a Bible.

A bell-like voice, the Rev's: "While smug agnostics debate whether they should sacrifice their condos and health club memberships for Jesus, more and more of the hungry and displaced, escaped government slaves, the sick and the elderly, are flocking into the arms of Christ."

Image of more pilgrims, old, young, some healthy, many weary, joining the original two on the road. "In Zion the Truth is proclaimed hourly: Redemption is at hand. Let all come to the New Jerusalem, Zion, the home of the Saints—" Aerial shot of crowds on the road, the camera flying past them over the rolling, forested hills. In the distance sunlight flares off the white concrete of a mile-square landing pad set in the woods. "—for God is about to punish the world. Let no man fail to join the march, lest he tempt God. Save your soul! Flee from Babylon!" Images of Babylon: ten-year-old, starving prostitutes in Times Square, the New Dust Bowl, scientists shooting bullets into laboratory animals, an old woman committing ritual suicide, the face of a crying child.

"Remember Lot's wife, who turned her face back toward sin even as she fled and was made into a pillar of salt. Don't listen to a wicked husband or wife. Leave them, and children that are unbelieving or disobedient.

"Don't worry about material things. Leave the VCR. Abandon the disk player. Goods there are in plenty for the Saints: bring nothing but money, clothes and enough food for the journey. He who has a knife, a handgun, a hunting rifle or an automatic weapon, let him bring them. If you lack them, buy them." Christian soldiers, men and women and children in white jumpsuits, carrying weapons. "Together, we will break the back of Satan!"

Ascending music, a brilliant glow in the sky, the faint suggestion of the miraculous city beginning to descend. Fade.

Gilray seemed absorbed in thought. Richard wondered what was on his mind. "That's good. But—"

The door opened and Felton entered. "Sorry to interrupt. Mr. Shrike asked that he be informed as soon as these people showed up."

"What people?" Gilray asked.

Felton stepped aside and a police sergeant with an M-16 over his shoulder escorted two women into the room: Delano Amassa and Lucy.

Delano had on a USTS uniform. Lucy wore a man's suit jacket and torn jeans. Her hair was cropped. She looked sullenly around the room. Her gaze settled on Richard. There was a smudge above her eyebrow, and the corner of her mouth was bruised.

Sumner was indignant. "Important things are being discussed here. You shouldn't have brought—"

"That's all right, Charles," Gilray said. "Who are these people, Richard?"

"This is Delano Amassa, a private investigator who was hired by Jason Abramowitz to find George Eberhart. The other is Lucy Di Paulo, Eberhart's wife."

Boston looked uncertain. "Has something been going on behind our backs?"

"Eberhart thinks the Rev is pointing us toward disaster," Richard said. "Jason Abramowitz sent him out thinking he'd come up with something to discredit us, but I convinced Ms. Amassa to work for me. It's only by accident that she picked up Lucy instead of George."

Lucy listened to this with apparent indifference.

Gilray, as absorbed in watching her as he had been in his thoughts a moment before, said, "There are no accidents."

Delano leaned on the table. She acted as if no one but Richard was there. "Nice uniform, Francie," Richard said.

"I've stolen a USTS van," she said. "I'll need some gas."

"Right."

"I'm going to leave this woman here," she said. "Then I'm going to find Eberhart." Voice as flat as a billiard table, not as soft.

There was not much distance between that voice and homicidal rage, and Richard realized that if she caught George, she would probably kill him. He should have anticipated this moment; perhaps he had. George had wanted to die. They would all be dead in a few months anyway. Damn George. He should be here, then he would see the necessity of the end.

Richard's face felt hot, his shoulders cramped. He nodded to Delano. "Okay," he said softly.

27: FRIDAY, OCTOBER 15
....
An Advance Report from Christ the Commander

When the door opened and through it walked the woman from his dream, the Reverend Jimmy-Don Gilray was pierced through by the power of Providence. It was one thing to know intellectually that the Lord managed the fall of the sparrow. It was quite another to feel your loins tremble with the touch of God, to have before you the flesh-and-blood evidence that you are in the grip of a force you have no power to control.

These men, this meeting, the words they spoke, their hopes, fears, the very configuration of molecules in the air—all had been prefigured in the mind of God at the moment of creation. Gilray felt it with a painful sweetness, like the joyful dismay a man must feel when he's hit by lightning and knows that he's dead. The universe had sprung from nothing six thousand years ago, and with it had sprung Jimmy-Don Gilray, this woman in front of him, and his desire. It was his only to play his part.

He had Lucy sit in one of the vacant chairs. He studied her. She looked at him, face empty of emotion. She did not flinch. We are here for a reason, he wanted to tell her. He wished he could convey to her his exhiliration, he wished he could touch her cheek. Her eyes were gray.

Richard sent the detective away. He looked stricken, as if he'd just lost his best friend.

Gilray tried to stay calm. "Is there anything else we need to discuss right now?"

"I would like to talk about Commandante Jesus," Richard said.

"In what connection?"

"I've been studying his work. Either he's a representation of all that we oppose, or he's an expression of the will of God. Yet except for a few passing remarks you've hardly taken a position on the Commandante. After all, the man calls himself Jesus."

"Only to mock us."

"That's not clear to everyone else." Richard's voice gained force as he spoke. "We're in the business of bringing people to Jesus, right? We ought to take better advantage of the opportunity. We should create our own version of the Commandante. We break into our own broadcasts, but we twist the message a little, use it to draw some of his fans into our camp."

"We don't need to trick people," Boston said. "What kind of salvation is that?"

"You can't trick somebody into salvation," Richard said.
"You can't save somebody who won't let himself be saved."
He leaned forward, gripping the arms of his chair. He
wasn't even looking at Boston: he stared at Lucy Di Paulo.
"You're either saved or lost the moment you're born. If a
man wants to die, there's not a damned thing you can do to
save him."

Boston's face reddened. "That goes against—"

Richard turned on him. "This video we've got is loser
material, Lucas! Total white bread. You need some flash,
some edge. These people aren't coming to Zion for their
vacations! It's the fucking end of the world! You've got to
show them the bleeding flesh of the world, the broken
bones of time. Death and resurrection!"

"This isn't some sideshow!" Boston shouted.

Gilray felt himself losing hold of the moment. Acutely
aware of the woman, pulled outside himself, he saw them all
as if through her eyes. It was very disturbing. Through her
eyes they looked small. Boston was the smallest, a fanatic
with no imagination; Sumner equally inconsquential. Richard was larger, but he was insane. He—what was he? He
didn't know. He felt disoriented.

If he was yet to be determined, then he would at least act.
"Richard has a point," he said.

"I think so," added Sumner.

"I'm tired of listening to this blasphemy. This man's totally corrupt. If you can't see that, then—"

"That's enough, Lucas!" Gilray said. "God is more subtle
than you think. He's more clever than any of us in this
room."

"God wouldn't use the kind of travesty he's talking
about."

"God sent his Son to be born in a manger. He selected
his apostles from among publicans and sinners."

He turned to Richard, who had sunk back in his chair,
desolate again. There are forces at work in him that Gilray
was not sure he was prepared to see unleashed. "Richard,
you work together with Lucas on the commercials. We'll
use this one as is."

He rested a hand on Boston's shoulder. "Put your faith to use, Lucas. We're all being tested."

As he spoke, he felt his soul's center return. Another test passed. In the end, he was larger than any of them. And the woman?

Lucy Di Paulo watched. Did she recognize him from some apocalyptic dream of her own? Did she want and fear that fire, too?

Gilray had Lucy installed in a vacant room in the residential wing. Marianne found her some clothes, and later that afternoon Gilray invited her to come along to the rally on the mall. He taped his afternoon broadcast and found her waiting with Felton in the lobby, wearing one of Marianne's ankle-length dresses. Richard sent word he would meet them at the rally.

Felton brought the car around and they left. Lucy had bathed and washed her hair; Gilray could smell the shampoo. When he asked how she had been caught by Delano, she only turned to look out the window. Her clean profile sent a shiver down his spine.

Or perhaps it was simply the weather. In the past twenty-four hours a massive cold front had draped a layer of clouds over the area and the temperature had dropped fifty degrees under gale-force winds. Another portent.

Beyond the gate they passed through a camp of pilgrims. Men and women got to their feet; some of them cheered. "They've come from all over the country," Gilray said to Lucy.

"I bet some of them have been brought." She didn't look at him. "Against their will."

A wild-eyed man, grinning fiercely, boosted his child onto his shoulders to see. "It's hard sometimes to know, when things happen to us, who's will is being done," Gilray said.

"Some dickhead's."

They passed beyond the people. "You have no reason to be so hostile. I didn't know about Richard's detective."

"I was in your prison," she said. "One of your doctors raped me."

"Tell me his name. I'll see that he's punished."

She looked at him. "Will you close it down? You're violating every federal regulation of the last thirty years."

"In the face of what's coming a few regulations are nothing."

Lucy turned back to the window. Her anger intimidated him. The eye of God awaited his reaction, but for the second time that day he felt unsure. He watched out his own window.

Along the road, half of the pine forest was denuded of needles. The forestry school blamed forty years of acid rain, but the real reason was that time was coming to an end. They drove past IBM, where Gilray had worked when he first came to the Triangle thirty years before, a computer engineer designing massively parallel processors for the Pentagon. He had started the first national Christian computer bulletin board. How little he had understood then what was going to happen. But his intention had been clear from the beginning: to do God's will, not his own.

Whose will had sent him this woman?

Along I-40 they passed pilgrims on foot or hanging off the back of pickups. One flock had commandeered a U.S. Transit Service bus and painted a slogan on it: Prepare the Rule of Saints." The call had gone out spontaneously for months, and whether Boston's commercials were effective or not people would continue to come. The converted, the saved, the godly had sent the ecstatic news to their friends outside the Triangle, describing the ideal conditions that prevailed. Maybe they anticipated a little the way things would be when the Holy City descended out of the heavens, but not sinfully, for what the prophets had foretold could be said to be virtually in existence. A matter of weeks would see it come to pass.

As they entered the city a few flakes of snow began to swirl. Trees wove ponderously back and forth like heavy metronomes. Everything spoke of expectation. Lucy quit staring out the window and watched him.

Downtown, the streets were filled with people. Many were living in abandoned stores; others stood around trash barrel fires in vacant lots. Everywhere were signs scrawled on buildings, banners strung across streets and hung from second-story windows: "Free the Undead"; "Remember July 17th"; "The Reverend and All He Stands For!" Behind a street barricade men carrying M-16s chatted with cops. They watched as the limousine passed. Felton stopped at a checkpoint and pulled into the garage below the county courthouse.

A guard opened the door for them, holding his rifle by the pistol grip. He seemed to be in a good mood. "Hoo-ee," he said. "Turning colder than a Zombie's heart out there."

He looked Lucy up and down. She ignored him. Gilray took her up the stairs to the main floor, where they met the deacons who had been running the rally. They mounted the platform in front of the main entrance. Deacon Harrison, red-faced from the cold, was leading a prayer, but the crowd stirred when they saw Gilray come up the stairs behind him. The people filled the mall front to back, and for hundreds of yards in either direction. The deacon's amplified voice echoed off the facing facade, above the heads of the people. Wind whipped down the mall, snapping the flags of the state and Christ on the poles in front of the courthouse, writing cats-paws on the surface of the pool where they had been baptizing. Several of the new Saints huddled in blankets by the water. People hung from roofs and open windows; the only break in the sea of humanity was the open space around the painted figures on the pavement where the July 17 Martyrs had been gunned down.

When the prayer was done Harrison led the people in a hymn:

> Before Jehovah's awful throne
> Ye nations bow with sacred joy.
> Know that the Lord is God alone
> He can create and He destroy.

When the song was done Gilray had the aides keep an eye on Lucy while he stepped to the pulpit. The crowd roared. He let it fold over him for minutes. He bent his head back and gazed into the gray sky. The clouds above them were like the era they lived in: but they were about to lift. As he stared, his body vibrating with the force of thousands of souls focused on his own, a shaft of sunlight lanced down and swept over the mall. Gilray held his hands high and the people roared louder, each man or woman throwing his own tiny mortal force into the common howl, forming a great single voice that rose into the heavens with the message of their frustration and longing. For minutes it went on. Then the sunlight vanished. The cry faded. Gilray braced himself against the pulpit and looked over them, waiting. He spoke.

"These are troubled times. No man or woman whose soul is alive can look around and not see. Evil walks freely among us! It brings us to the edge of despair. It takes our power from us. It makes us sick. We look about us and ask, 'Where are the Strong? Who are the Holy? What is the Truth?'

"There are men today who make a living by fostering doubt. They ask questions. They are so good at asking questions, so serious, so eager to find the 'truth.' But if you ever go up to them and show them the truth on a velvet cushion, watch out! They look it over like a live hand grenade. They back away. They ask another question. 'What *proof* do you have?' they ask. 'Where is your *evidence*?' 'How, after all,' they say, '—how can we accept such *questionable* authority as this, on the basis of such a subjective thing as *Faith*?'

"You've heard them say that word. Faith. They say the word 'Faith' so sadly, but they're a little amused, too. It embarrasses them! They don't want that word 'Faith' in their house. It's like a dog that messes on the carpet. Like a dinner guest wearing last year's clothes. Oh, dear, we can't have that word in here, they say. It's not sophisticated! It's not scientifically justified! It's not a reproducible experiment! As if belief in God is like belief in Santa Claus! As if to utter that transcendent word 'Faith' were an admission of childishness or idiocy or lack of will! They don't know what Christ meant when he said, 'Suffer the little children to come unto me.' No one comes to faith unless he comes openly, innocently, as wiped clean of experience as a child.

"So let's tell them where they can find Truth. Where is Truth? Truth is *here,* in Zion! The Truth of God. Doubt isn't strength, it's a sign that you're sick!"

The snowflakes swirling above them increased. The wind buffeted the microphones. In the crowd he saw faces of every human description, turned up to him with every human expression. A red-haired boy, brow clouded with rage. A slender woman, eyes wide and trusting, clutching a cross. A round-faced man, weeping. A dark man beside him, as grimly intense as if he were memorizing every word. This was the purpose of Gilray's existence. They made him larger than he could ever be by himself, just as God, through him, freed them from their own pettiness, filled them with meaning. He stood at the focus of all their projected emotions, let their force surge through him.

"Here's Truth!" he shouted. "Call it out after me: Christ died and was raised from the dead!"

The crowd shouted back, raggedly: "Christ died and was raised from the dead!"

"Is that all the louder you can shout?" His magnified voice boomed off the buildings. "You expect the atheists of the world to hear you if you can't shout any louder than that? You expect to drown out the voice of the Antichrist with a whisper? Shout it! Christ died and was raised from the dead!"

"CHRIST DIED AND WAS RAISED FROM THE DEAD!"

The roar was an assault, like the wind itself. "No one shall enter the kingdom save through him!"

"NO ONE SHALL ENTER THE KINGDOM SAVE THROUGH HIM!"

"Christ will come again!"

"CHRIST WILL COME AGAIN!" The people leapt up and down, waving their arms.

"He's coming at this moment!"

"HE'S COMING AT THIS MOMENT!" The flagellants hauled out their whips.

"He'll be here in two months!"

"HE'LL BE HERE IN TWO MONTHS!" Pandemonium, ecstacy. A great inarticulate roar.

Gilray held up his arms, and the roar went louder. "Yes!" he shouted. "In two months. In the flesh, standing before you who stand here listening to me, His unworthy servant. Into His lungs He will take the very same air you breathe this moment, to speak words that you will hear with the same ears that hear my words. *In two months!* The joy you will know at that moment will exceed any joy you've ever experienced! It will surpass any any joy that you're capable of feeling now! A joy so overwhelming you'll think that you will die from it!"

The crowd roared and capered. His heart was aflame, in tune with every soul in the city. They were all connected. He knew, if he turned around, he would find awe written on the face of every one of his lieutenants. It was a truth even Lucy Di Paulo could not ignore.

"And you *will* die! You will die forever to sin, and be reborn for a thousand years of peace and freedom here on earth, after which you will experience an eternity in Heaven. And every moment of that limitless time, every millisecond of those thousand years, and eternity beyond, will be filled with this joy that cannot be grasped by our feeble imaginations, a joy greater than the joy you feel in the act of physical love, a joy greater than the joy you feel as the whip comes down on your bleeding back and you see in yourself the image of the Holy Martyrs who have preceeded you!

"Are you ready? Have you made ready for His coming? Will you be surprised to see His New Jerusalem descend from the sky, this great Father Ship, this titanic cube, bejeweled, fashioned of gold and adamantine steel—descend upon the space we are preparing for it not ten miles from where we stand at this moment?"

The people leapt, waving their arms and flags and whips in the air. The snow thickened until a flurry of white swirled above their heads. Gilray raised his fists again, shook them, milked cries and tears and shouts from the crowd. He breathed deeply, totally alive, no speck of weakness in him. He was purified and powerful. He was ready.

He backed slowly away from the microphone. Beneath the cheering he heard the sounds of a scuffle behind him. He turned. Richard Shrike was rising from the floor of the platform; Lucy was being restrained by a couple of deacons. Gilray stepped toward them. "Are you all right?" he said to Lucy.

"Peachy," she said.

Richard stumbled forward. He was wearing a black choir robe, and around his neck a black cord. The cord was connected to a gold-plated hammer. He held the hammer up and shook it, and the crowd responded with another cheer.

"I am Richard the Hammer!" he shouted. The crowd roared. Boston moved forward to stop him, but Gilray laid a hand on his arm.

"The Reverend asks if you are ready." Richard's voice boomed back at them from the buildings opposite. "Are you ready for the Good News?"

The people cheered.

"I am by profession a newsman. So I'm here to tell you the News from Above." Richard pointed his hammer at the clouds and shouted even louder, tearing his voice with the force of his cry. "I have it from an unimpeachable source!"

At that moment, despite the continued swirling snow and howling wind, another break came in the clouds. The sunlight struck burnished highlights from the golden hammer. Richard's body jerked as if he were being electrocuted. His raised arm twitched spasmodically, yet he kept it raised, the poised hammer trembling. After a second's silence, the roar that came back was like the cry of an imprisoned animal. Arm still poised, still trembling, Richard spoke. The character of his voice was changed: lower, steady. Like a rock singer in a stadium, instead of shouting he used the sound system to create volume, "This man speaking to you is now *online*!"

Some of the people shouted, but most were aware that something unusual was happening. Gilray watched, fascinated. There was no moment in all this that was not pre-determined, yet always they stood in the prospect of infinite surprise. This was the way God worked. All prefigured in His mind. Sprung from nothing, playing their parts. Joyful dismay. Desire.

"These words you hear him speak are being transmitted from the bridge of the New Jerusalem, at this moment five hundred parsecs from your world, cruising to you through hyperspace on a mission of mercy. Our advance agents are already among you. Our Commander, the Son of God, salutes Zion, the City of Saints!"

A few people cheered. Richard's raised arm was now weirdly steady. The hammer, clasped tightly in his fist, vibrated like a tuning fork. It had to cost him tremendous effort to keep it there.

"There is no Sin in Zion!"

The crowd responded, more fully now.

"Yet this, our monitor, tells us that something called Private Property still exists in your city of Saints," Richard said. "The sick, the poor, the starving—daily they flock to Zion. They freeze in your public parks. They die for want of a crust of bread. Their children weep from hunger! Our Commander tells us that many of you, by the pain in your own bellies, know that this is true."

A louder roar. Gilray waved an arm to keep the others on the platform from interfering. "Be prepared to act," he told Sumner. "All this is in leading somewhere. It's all true." Out of the corner of his eye he saw Lucy draw back as if to sneak away. He grabbed her wrist. "Listen," he whispered.

"He's crazy," she said.

"He's not the man you know."

"Jesus," Sumner whispered. "Jesus."

Drops of sweat flew from Richard's chin. His hair was wild. "In the face of your pain," Richard said, "the rich sit in their warm homes, eat their meat and potatoes, interact with their obscene cable TV and laugh. Christ the Commander is coming, and they laugh!"

He stopped, and a silence ensued, filled with the hiss of the amplifier, the white storm, the spectral sunlight. From above them came a slow rumble, increasing until it broke deafeningly, a crash of thunder. The echoes rolled over the city: a miracle, a spasm of thunder in a snowstorm. Richard waited, timing himself so that his next rolling words emerged from the tail of the retreating thunder:

"There is no sin in Zion . . . There is no sin in Zion . . . THERE IS NO SIN IN ZION!"

The people took up the chant, louder and louder. Gilray found himself speaking the words aloud. Richard waited; the voices swelled and rumbled like the thunder. His arm stretched upward as if the golden hammer was hooked to the sky and he was hanging from it. After some minutes, as the chanting died, he spoke again.

"If that is to be so—if there is to be no sin in Zion—then you must expunge sin! You must give the sinner a simple choice: leave Zion, convert, or die! The holy City of Saints must be purged of the Sons of Esau! All. ALL MUST GO, OR DIE!

"LET THOSE WHO REFUSE FEEL THE POWER OF THE HAMMER OF GOD!"

And Richard brought the hammer down, explosively, on the microphone nest. A blast of feedback seared over the mall. The roar that ran back was the loudest of the day. Furiously he raised and slammed the hammer down again and again, smashing the mikes to bits. He screamed, seized the podium and wrenched it from its moorings, kicked it over the front of the platform into the crowd.

The people were frenzied. The flagellants lay about with their whips, not caring whether they struck themselves or bystanders. Yes, Gilray thought. The crowd seethed like one huge organism, shot through with the same godly fire that made Richard jerk before them like a marionette. Hopes, fears, molecules in the air. Sprung from nothing. They surged between the buildings and out from the mall, tearing down street signs for weapons, a mob headed for the homes of the nearest nonbelievers.

"We've got to stop them," Boston said. "It's a riot."

Sumner wrested an M-16 from one of the troopers on the platform. "It's only a riot if they aren't led," he shouted. He leapt over the front railing and shoved his way through the dispersing people. They listened to the retreating roar of the mob.

Richard swayed. His eyes rolled up and he slumped to the platform. Boston and the others rushed to his side.

Gilray felt Lucy move forward. No, he thought. As if obeying his silent command, she checked herself. "I've got to get out of here," she muttered.

"All according to plan," he said.

She looked at him sideways, as if not wanting to face him. What size am I now, he wanted to ask. What size am I now, Lucy? The snow had turned into a blizzard. From the distance, blown on the wind from beyond the buildings, came the sound of gunfire. By morning the city would be inhabited only by Saints.

28: SATURDAY, OCTOBER 16
....
George arrives at a Technological Solution

The television in the bar was tuned to the American News Network. "Idaho state police report that they have the Burley area under control following yesterday's gun battle between local Nazis and protestors at the construction site of the city's new swastika-shaped public swimming pool." The anchor wore a red shirt, a white tie, and a blue jacket with stars on it. "Parker Goody, leader of the American Patriot Party, had this to say to ANN's Nola Hawke."

Vid of a man wearing camouflage fatigues with an automatic weapon slung over his shoulder. "The swastika's a historical Indian sign," he said. "The Zionist Occupation Government just wants to stop us from honoring native Americans."

No one at the bar was listening. "Clay, how's your woman?"

"We're not talking. That bitch's so stubborn, if she was to drown herself in the Congaree, they'd have to look for her body upstream."

"—Elsewhere in riot news, the Governor of North Carolina, speaking from Asheville, has declared a state of emergency in the wake of last night's fighting in Raleigh. Since Tuesday's victory of Millennialist candidates in special elections, the Raleigh-Durham area has been in turmoil. Conflicting reports were still filtering in Saturday morning as refugees straggled into Greensboro and Winston-Salem. The Governor ordered those elements of the National Guard still loyal to the state to cordon off the Research Triangle area and give refuge to the victims of the religious persecution that has swept the region . . ."

George sat at a table in the corner of the tavern. The TV stared at him from the opposite corner, above the bar. The room was long and dark with a black-and-white linoleum floor; behind the bar a stuffed marlin leapt across the ranks of bottles, and the rest of the wall was cluttered with softball and bowling trophies, a framed dollar bill, photographs of teams and girls, and a sign announcing "Absolutely No Credit." The clientele consisted of local day workers and the unemployed, nursing draft beers that lasted the better part of an hour each.

Two black men sat at the bar. The one named Clay was either an albino or had contracted some new retrovirus, the reverse of the Black Plague. His skin was pink and his eyes were rose and his curly afro was yellow. A white Negro.

An analyst came onto the screen; he was dressed like one of the Founding Fathers, complete with powdered wig. "Whether the National Guard can manage this crisis without the help of the regular army is an open question. Meanwhile the President waffles. He may be worried about the reaction of his fundamentalist supporters if he should take action against a city of Saints, people who are only acting out the beliefs held by the 80 million Americans who claim to have had personal messages from God in the last year. While he dawdles, religious fervor sweeps across the southeast. Parallel incidents reported in Goldsboro and Wilmington Friday night suggest that by this evening the number of pilgrims going *to* Zion will exceed the number of non-believers fleeing. . . ."

"Turn that thing off, Snyder," one of the men said. "When does the ballgame start?"

The bartender reached for the remote control. Clay took a pull on his beer. "That Reverend's got the setup, let me tell you."

"I hear he's got hot pants, too," said his companion.

"No, Burnette. You just got hot ears."

"I'm thinking of going to Raleigh myself," said Burnette.

"Zion, Burnette."

"Might be the Reverend's right, Clay. Might be we wake up New Year's, hung over, and find out it's the end of the world."

"It only feels that way. It's just Snyder here's cheap bar stock."

The bartender was searching through the TV's menu. "All you can afford," he said, without looking away.

"That's the point," Burnette said. "The Reverend's onto that, too. The working man can't afford to live; it's this here triple economic. The working man's depression. The rich man just gets his shoes polished cheaper."

"Where do you get off talking about the working man?" said Clay.

"Rich man's always had it like that," said Snyder. He found the World Series pregame show, cut the sound to a whisper, and turned to lean on the bar. "There's never been a depression for the rich man."

Clay sat up straighter on his stool. "This ain't a depression. This is the way things *are,* now."

"What do you mean?"

"I mean America's done. It ain't gonna get any better for

guys like us, unless we win the lottery. You feel lucky, Burnette? It's like the damn British after the war, falling apart."

"Which war?"

Clay ignored him. "Only it took them thirty years and we're getting it done in ten. We're part of the Third World, now, or maybe the Fourth."

"Bullshit. When you gonna get off this old line? I—"

Clay rapped a pale knuckle on the bartop. "You want to get out of it, Burnette, ain't gonna do you no good to go to Zion. Go to China, or Brazil."

"When God comes again those Catholics going to get a big surprise."

"Don't hold your breath."

On the table in front of him George had a double shot of whiskey, his calculator and all his money. He separated the revalued currency from the old style, stacked the coins and lined them up: a red five, a three-dollar piece, three new composite quarters, a dime, six pennies. Two old, green ten-dollar bills, worth about a dollar each. $10.91, new style. He wrote that down on a scrap of paper.

He had managed to get another eighty miles out of the Hyundai before he ran out of gas. He'd abandoned it near a state park on Highway 261, searched the back for anything useful and found the calculator on the floor. He shoved the car down an embankment, through the tangle of kudzu into some trees, and started walking. The battered secondary road was empty. A couple of hours later, near dawn, he managed to hitch a ride as far as Columbia. Since then he'd been knocking around the streets trying to keep out of the rain. He avoided thinking about Lucy. He had been scared. A shot from the woman chasing him had shattered the rear window.

"How much money you figure the Reverend's got stored up?" Burnette asked.

"Millions," said Snyder.

"You hear about those two guys they picked up at the Interrail station? They stuck up the concession stand. When the police got them they said they gave the money to an angel, but they needed their guns because of the apocalypse."

George sipped the whiskey. It warmed him. His hand trembled. He looked at the tendons, the knob of his wrist. All his life he had been a big man, twenty or thirty pounds overweight. People deferred to him. His suicide had taken care of that: now he was a powerless scarecrow, on the way out.

Okay, he could accept that. Assuming he could get no more money, how long could he last? Suppose he ate as little as possible: say fifty cents a day. Suppose he slept in bus stations, or local shelters, or outside. Lots of people were on the road with less. He could probably cut the food to twenty-five cents per day if he bought old bread and potatoes. He punched it up on the calculator. $10.91 divided by 0.25 equals 43.64. 43.64 days. It was amazing how little you could make do on if you set your mind to it. He regretted all the money he had wasted. He wished he had the camera he had abandoned at Noah's motel so he could hock it.

"Hey, buddy. You want another drink?" The bartender, Snyder, was looking at him. Burnette looked over his shoulder at George.

George held up his glass, a quarter inch still in it. "Not yet."

"Well, you just let us know," Snyder said.

"I sure will."

George hated thinking about the motel. He tried to tell himself that pursuing the truth was more important than Lucy was. But his mind would not rest easy. He sensed his own evasions, and all he was left with was rage.

He had almost managed to forget how angry a man he had been before he had been revived. That earlier George, living his shadowy pre-hospital life, had been motivated not by hope for the future, but by dread of the present and conviction that the past was meaningless, by alienation that was as much his own creation as it was a reaction to the world. Lucy had been his refuge. But he had not been able to take refuge. The hinges of his soul had rusted shut, and whatever hope had once lived in him had died.

So he had killed himself.

And had awoken in the hospital. But there was no way they could keep him alive if he didn't want it. He saw now that the pursuit of the aliens had been a way to forget the fact that he was still alone, dying by millimeters. He chased his aliens to distract himself from his life. But that didn't mean they didn't exist.

Clay looked up at World Series pre-game. "The Sox were damn lucky to beat the Senators."

"Bullshit. You don't win the playoffs with luck."

"That home run Ellison hit wasn't luck?"

The wind was blowing out for both teams. You don't get to be MVP on luck."

"Did I ever tell you I went to high school with Ellison?"

"Only a thousand times."

"Terry Sanford High School in Fayetteville. He was nothing special back then, either."

"Well who's played better in the second half of the season?"

"Dumb white luck."

"That any different from black luck?"

"African-American luck."

"Black people don't have luck."

"Amen."

"Getting to be more black people every day."

"Getting hard to tell the blacks from the African-Americans."

"No wonder the country's losing big."

They all laughed.

"Pray for the Millennium," Burnette said.

If nobody stopped the Rev, millions were going to be there to welcome the aliens in with open arms. The mammoth, cubical ship settles ponderously onto the concrete of the Reverend's Landing Pad. Ecstatic crowds caper and sing. A Mighty Fortress is Our God. Onward Christian Soldiers. The ramps, made of mysterious metal forged beneath the light of distant suns, extend like greedy tongues. The doors open. From out of the blindingly white interior the aliens descend. Tall, handsome, they resemble your Uncle Charlie, your beautiful sister Sue, Abraham Lincoln, a cross section of the latest pop stars, Jesus Christ Himself. Reassuring, magnetic, brotherly, understanding beyond the wet dreams of sixty generations of homicidal Christian soldiers. The Rev advances to greet them. The fraud is consummated and the possibility of human autonomy ends forever.

It would happen, unless someone stopped Gilray. George could. He could find out if there were, indeed, aliens in the world. Maybe Gilray was one. At the very least he could cram the Rev's sick fantasy of bigotry and salvation down his silver throat, and create a truth that could not be denied. And then he could die for real.

43.64 days. And if he ate half as often—86 days. That would take him to January tenth. More than enough time.

Except George couldn't stop anyone with his bare hands. He subtracted four dollars from his total and recalculated. At 12.5 cents per day he'd have 55.28 days. Maybe enough time. Maybe not.

Unless he ate still less. Why not? Why eat at all?

The street door opened and two men and a woman entered, along with a blast of cold wind. "Hey, Snyder, Burnette," the tallest of them said. He went up to the albino and slapped him on the shoulder. "Clay, my man!"

"What are you so cheerful about?"

The man pulled an envelope from his coat. "Snyder, you want to cash these SRA stamps for me?"

"What? When did you get this?"

"Today. The Post Office released the anodyne markers. Tomanda says some company's standing in as sugar daddy for the government."

Burnette seemed to glow from within. "Set'em up, children! Party time."

Clay was grinning so hard it looked like pain. "Set'em up for sure. Let's dope ourselves to death."

"You're a pitiful man, Clay," Snyder said.

"And you're a businessman, Sny. You don't care. These

stamps're just the rich man's way of getting us to keep our mouths shut."

"Somebody ought to tell them they're wasting their money on you."

"You use those markers, you're admitting you're so worthless the only reason to spend money on you is to get you drugged up. You should use that money against the system."

"Can't use stamps for anything else."

"Can sell them to addicts and use the money."

"I notice you're not out in the streets."

"I'm too mean for the streets. I'm so mean that when I was born, my mamma put me out on the porch to see whether I'd cry or bark."

"You bark, but you don't bite," the tall man said.

"He cries, but he don't bark," the woman said. The others laughed. Clay gripped his glass.

Burnette looked worried. "Calm down, Clay."

"I'll calm down," he said. His shoulders relaxed; he spoke as much to his beer as to the others. "Anodyne stamps. You know what 'anodyne' means?"

Snyder poured drinks all around.

"Hey, turn up the sound," Tomanda said. "They're introducing the teams."

"What does anodyne mean, Mr. Genius?" Burnette said.

Clay lifted his head. "It means it's the end of the line."

Amen, George thought. He put his money and the calculator into his pocket. Snyder watched him as he walked by. Clay raised his head; his pink eyes looked sightless. He looked more alien than any of the phantoms George had chased around the country.

"You come back real soon now, y'hear?" Clay said.

Out in the street it was getting dark. Clouds slid above the buildings, like the future settling down to flatten them. A Mighty Fortress is Our God. Two doors down the street, the plywood that had replaced the plate glass in a storefront displayed the sign, "Felix's Hardware & Guns."

George went inside. Chained to the wall behind the counter was an array of rifles. A display case held rows of pistols.

Onward Christian Soldiers. A man wearing a blue shirt with large orange parrots on it came up from the back of the store. "What can I do for you?"

"I've got four dollars to spend. I need a gun."

29: SUNDAY, OCTOBER 17
On the Theory and Practice of Moral Luck

Without gas Eberhart would have been unable to get far from Noah's Motel. Delano worked the major routes north from Manning and found the Hyundai abandoned beside Highway 261, on the verge of some woods in the Poinsett State Park.

At the bottom of a gently sloping field of rye grass, the car sat among morning glory, honeysuckle and seedling pines. Wysteria hung from the trees. The hood was cool. Delano opened the door and pawed through soycake wrappers and empty gasohol cans. The keys were still in the ignition. She shut the door and leaned against the side of the car, drawing a deep breath that smelled of wet pinestraw. She lit a cigarette and considered what the President would have her do.

Ten minutes later Delano flipped the butt away and got back into the van. A mile down the road, before she had even left the parksite—as if he were meeting her according to some plan—she came upon George Eberhart standing in the road. He was emptyhanded, wearing black. He waved at her as she slowed. She pulled up not ten feet away from him.

He opened the front door and climbed in. "Thanks for stopping," he said.

He did not seem to recognize her. Delano became alert for a trick. She accelerated back up to speed.

"You're lucky I came along," she said. "You could have stood out there for a week without getting a ride. USTS service on this road has been curtailed."

"I knew I'd get a ride."

"Why?"

"Because you've been chasing me down the East Coast for the last month. Well, you caught me."

So it was going to be mind games. Delano felt as if she were peering out at the road from behind a mask. A squad of workies clearing brush looked up from the roadside at the speeding red-white-and-blue van. A scrawny old man, leaning on a rake, flipped them the bird, but they were already past.

She had stopped taking the Truth, but she didn't need any drug to see through Eberhart. "I didn't catch you. You waved me down. If you think you can turn this situation to your advantage, you're wrong. Make a false move and I'll blow your fucking head off."

"Whoa! Don't get hostile. Here I am, in your van, you're driving—what, seventy miles an hour?—and you've got the gun. Not much I could do that wouldn't get us both killed."

He sat back, hands folded in his lap, calm as a Christian martyr. He did not look half as haggard as he had in Tallahassee; in fact, he looked as if he'd been eating three squares a day and getting ten hours of sleep each night. "From what I've seen of you," Delano said, "you don't care much about whether you live or die."

"Do you?"

"Yes."

"That's good. That's very healthy. But still, accidents happen."

"I don't believe in accidents."

Eberhart snorted. "You're not serious."

"I am."

"So it wasn't just an accident, then, that you missed getting me in Tallahassee?"

"You got away."

"And at Noah's Motel? You missed me there, too. Whose fault was that?"

Delano didn't say anything.

"Must be a cruel world for you, having to fail so many times."

"You had some help the second time. But yes, I should have had you. I take responsibility for my mistakes."

"No sin to make a mistake." Eberhart leaned back still farther, pulled his feet up and braced them against the dashboard. "You ever hear about Moral Luck?"

"Get your feet down. Slowly."

Eberhart did, leaving two muddy smears on the plastic. "The Theory of Moral Luck applies the discoveries of quantum physics to morality. It proves that the morality of a person's actions is a matter of chance."

Delano wondered what he was after. "That's bullshit. People know when they're doing right or wrong."

"No, no. People can't control everything."

"So? They can control their intentions."

"It's not just a matter of intentions," Eberhart said. "Take an example: two neighbors, Mr. Smith and Mr. Jones. Mr. Smith doesn't check the brakes on his car. He knows they're in bad shape, but he hasn't got around to fixing them. Then one morning he's driving to work, well below the speed limit, when a kid dashes out in front of him from between parked cars. Smith hits the brakes, but doesn't stop fast enough to keep from killing the child. Is he guilty of manslaughter?"

"Of course. He should have fixed his brakes."

"Okay. Now assume Mr. Jones's brakes are just as bad, but a child never jumps in front of his car. Is he as guilty as Mr. Smith?"

Delano hesitated. "Yes, he is."

"So we should check his brakes, and if they're not up to snuff we charge him with manslaughter."

"No. That's crazy."

"But you just said he's as guilty as the guy who hit the child. The only difference is he was luckier."

Delano thought hard. "Maybe Jones isn't as guilty as Smith, but he's still guilty. Kids run in front of cars all the time. He could guess something like this might happen, whether or not it ever does."

"Ah. So sin isn't simply a matter of right or wrong the way you said earlier? Jones is ten percent as guilty as Smith? Thirty percent? Fifty percent?"

She didn't like the way this was going. "Something like that."

"Exactly. The Theory of Moral Luck says morality is a matter of probabilities, not certainties, fixed by events, not intentions. There is no difference between the moral states of Mr. Smith and Mr. Jones until the kid runs out in front of Mr. Smith's car. And that's purely a matter of chance. Smith's sin is in a mixed state until circumstances fix it so we can see it, just as in quantum mechanics we don't know the position or momentum of a particle until we measure it. We could say the particle has no position or momentum until it interacts with our detector. Same for morality. The kid jumping into the street is the morality detector."

"Wait a minute. That doesn't make sense."

"Where's the flaw? Humans aren't responsible for accidents."

"I already told you I don't believe in accidents."

"And I already laughed at you for saying such a stupid thing."

It started to rain. Delano turned on the wipers, feeling a vivid contempt for the man. "This isn't some game we're playing, Eberhart. There are things going on around us that look like accidents but that are really part of a plan. Who's to say that kid jumping into the street isn't a message, designed especially for Jones?"

"Smith."

"What?"

"Smith. It was Smith who hit the kid."

Delano ignored him. "So? Who's to say it wasn't a warning for Jones to fix his brakes?"

"Yes. That's the other point of view. Einstein said it best: God does not play with dice. There are no accidents. The kid runs out there for a reason—either to define Smith's guilt, or warn Jones, or punish the kid."

"Or for some other reason. Who knows?"

"Certainly not I, Ms. Amassa. If you can't face the twentieth century, I can't make you. Einstein had the same problem."

His sarcasm reminded her of her father, who had never let any weakness pass—until he wanted something from her. Her father would have been a big fan of Moral Luck. "You're sick, you know that? I'm not listening any more."

"That's the mature response. If it helps you to think your life's being regulated, go right ahead. Everything that happens to you is being watched by the Man in Charge. You're at the focus of the big Morality Detector. You didn't pick me up by accident; it's all part of the Plan. It's a test. Don't ask me to tell you how you're doing, though."

"Will you shut up!" she said. "Don't you understand that you're dead meat? I've *got* you. Don't try to twist my mind."

"Sure," he said. "You should lighten up." He stared out the window. They were passing a dying strip of businesses along the bypass around Camden, South Carolina. The road was slick with rain, and drops streamed diagonally across the side windows. Eberhart followed one of them along the inside of the glass with the tip of his finger.

She had had enough. "For forty years, because of attitudes like yours, America's been turning into a fucking *sump*! Moral Luck! Just another way to avoid responsibility. You don't care if America dies like a dog in the road."

"America will be fine if it doesn't dash out between parked cars."

"America's rotting. And you're the poison, not the cure."

"Me? I'm a newshound. I'm out to help people."

Delano laughed bitterly. "Help people! You ever read Thoreau? Thoreau said if he knew for sure a man was coming to his house to help him, he'd run for his life. Everybody looks out for himself. Especially the ones who tell you they want to help you."

"The lion doesn't lie down with the lamb, huh?"

"If he does the lamb doesn't get up afterwards," Delano said. "Anyone who doesn't know that is a halfwit. You're no halfwit."

"No, I'm not."

Delano leaned on the accelerator. Tires hissed on wet pavement like frying bacon. The wipers slapped out a nervous rhythm. "I'll tell you what morality is," she said. "Morality is something you feel deep inside yourself. It's an instinct. You know what's right and wrong, and you don't need any laws or commandments or Theories of Moral Luck to explain it. It's purity. It's radical innocence."

"Sounds very American."

She was surprised that he saw it. "It is American—or it used to be. America's lost her innocence. When it started out it wasn't buried under laws and so-called civilized behavior. Civilized behavior!" she laughed. "Who makes up those rules of civilized behavior?"

"The Rosicrucians?"

"—the people in power, in order to keep their power! I learned that the hard way. The only reason to appeal to civilization is to disguise your own attack. The only legitimate purpose of polite discourse is to create a climate where the enemies of America can be exterminated."

Eberhart smiled. "Now *that* sounds modern."

"Shut up. America used to be the only moral state in the world. But we listened to too much static about 'international law' and 'diplomatic propriety.' As if those weren't the things we fought a revolution to get away from! We lost touch with our instinctive rightness. And TV hypocrites like you pushed it along."

"Ms. Amassa, I couldn't agree more. But I think you're being too pessimistic. Mr. America still owns all those instinctive virtues: arrogance, sloth, self-delusion. And innocent—you bet! His innocence swells like a goiter. It doesn't matter who jumps out in front of his car: his intentions were good."

"You're so fucking funny."

"So is America. God bless America! Not just holier-than-thou but holier-than-the-universe, perpetually innocent, perpetually surprised, perpetually ignorant, protected from reality by a fortress of myth, keeper of the sacred lies, cloaked in an impenetrable fog of masturbatory obsession with self. Bring me that mirror. No, that's not a running sore. It's a beauty mark."

"Don't attack my country."

"You're the one who called it a sump, Ms. Amassa. How do you think it got that way? Quantum mechanics?"

Delano had a realization. "How do you know my name?"

"Take your choice: accident or plan."

The van sped along. The rain came down in sheets. She took her eyes from the road long enough to look at him, and he turned toward her. The ease and deliberation of the movement terrified her.

"You're not Eberhart," she said.

"Finally figured it out, Francie?"

She glanced at the road, then back at him. "Who are you!"

"Part of the plan. We've been around for generations, working it out bit by bit. We hate America. We're destroying it. Everything bad that has happened in the Twentieth Century has been our doing. We're everywhere. We sell drugs to eight-year-olds. We design the curriculum of public schools. We control the Supreme Court. We spray paint subway trains in New York. We manipulate commodity prices in Chicago. We beam microwaves into people's homes to cause cancer. We program network television. We engineer diseases. We plant subliminals in popular songs to encourage miscegenation. We run abortion clinics. We fluoridate milk."

"That's insane."

"You think so? Good. That's our best defense."

"You couldn't keep a thing like that secret."

"It's no secret. You've known about us; you just haven't

gone far enough. Everyone you know is one of us. Richard Shrike. The Reverend Jimmy-Don Gilray. Your mother." They passed a field where a man in a plaid jacket plodded through mud with a shotgun broken open over his elbow. Eberhart pointed. "That man. His name is Vernon McCollum and he just murdered his family and buried them in the woods. Unbelievable, isn't it?"

Delano struggled. She pushed her foot to the floor. The van raced on as if it could carry her away from her fear. Eberhart regarded her with an air of amusement. "Scared, Francie?"

"It's not possible," she said.

"You've seen the signs. You've received messages from the President of the United States. But even the President is one of us. He sends me secret orders. He told me to jump in front of your van. Fortunately, your brakes were in order."

There were tears in her eyes. "No."

"You're drifting off the road, Francie. Watch out! You might have an accident."

Delano yanked the .38 from her waistband and shot him. The report was deafening. The van swerved; she jerked the wheel and kept firing. Eberhart's body flew back against the passenger's door; his eyes were opened wide. There was no blood. He took the slugs like a bale of hay in a shooting range. His hands spasmed, turning open toward her, as if in appeal. She drew away, pulling the trigger on the empty clip.

The van's tires slipped off the road onto the shoulder. The steering wheel spun out of her grip. There was a sickening lurch, a feeling that they were taking flight, as the van flipped. Through the windshield, just before it exploded into shards, Delano saw the trunk of a tree, tossed upside down as if gravity were meaningless. She heard a scream of tearing metal, saw the still-smiling face of Eberhart, recognized a whispered voice in her ears, and felt a tremendous blow to the top of her head.

December

··

And I looked, and, behold, a whirlwind came out of the north, a great cloud, and a fire infolding itself, and a brightness was about it, and out of the midst thereof as the colour of amber, out of the midst of the fire . . . . came the likeness of four living creatures. And this was their appearance; they had the likeness of a man.

—*Ezekiel 1:4-5*

30: WEDNESDAY, DECEMBER 29

Sneak Previews

There was fighting in the east and in the west. Open race war raged in Robeson County. In Chapel Hill secularists seized the public television station and declared the city a socialist republic. Charles Duke Sumner, elected mayor of Zion, declared himself Holy Governor of North Carolina and moved into the Governor's Mansion.

On December 14 an earthquake measuring 7.2 on the Richter scale, centered off the North Carolina coast, sent a tsunami sweeping over the outer banks. A second earthquake on Christmas morning toppled the tottering Cape Hatteras lighthouse and ruptured water and gas mains as far east as Zion. The effectiveness of the seige on the Reverend's Millennialist state was hampered by the earthquakes, the abnormally cold weather, and the number of National Guardsmen who had defected to his cause. In Zion, all healthy males above the age of fifteen were pressed into the militia. Despite the lack of weapons and ammunition they managed to hold most of Wake and Durham and part of Orange County. Nevertheless, by mid-December the blockade had taken hold.

Within the City of God there was less and less food. Medical supplies were scarce. The winter was turning into the hardest in the last fifty years: temperatures had not risen above freezing since Thanksgiving and eighteen inches of snow had fallen since the first of December. The pace of UFO sightings had increased daily. Various believers were contacted by Moses, the Apostles, Abraham, King David, Mary and Joseph, Martin Luther, and the Radar Men of Venus. On Christmas, several spoke with Santa Claus. As quickly as heretics could be condemned and punished new prophets arose from the streets to replace them. The nightly rallies and daily pageants fused together until, by the last week of the year, the region had been driven by hope and desperation into a state of continuous hysteria. Through it all work on the Landing Pad proceeded, and according to Lucas Boston would be completed by Thursday night, a full twenty-four hours before the expected arrival of the New Jerusalem.

There was no sin in Zion. The Reverend Gilray and Richard Shrike had resorted to measures ranging from rewarding informants with food to starting a holy basketball league in order to keep the city under control. The Reverend recognized the importance of wholesome recreation to even the most devout believers, even at the End of Time itself, but it was Richard's idea to show continuous free films. And it was his idea that, only two nights before the Second Coming of Christ, Lucy and he should attend the evening showing of the full-color, stereophonic, wide-screen synthesized revision of *It's a Wonderful Life* at the Christian Valley Theater.

The crowd parted for the limousine as Felton pulled up in front of the entrance; they pressed closer as Lucy and Richard got out. Lucy felt as if she had stepped into a Bosch painting: the people gathered in the freezing parking lot had the same sudden, tortured reality, intensely human at the same time they were grotesque. Richard wore his Hammer costume: a severe black suit, pointed black boots, black turtleneck, and the gold plated hammer that hung around his neck. Long hair slicked back, he looked like a match for the devil himself. Felton stood by nervously while Richard embraced an old woman, bent with age, who bled from the palms of her hands. Behind her a weeping boy spoke in tongues, and a man with the sober face of an insurance executive wrestled an invisible demon.

Lucy reached into her coat pocket and found the calculator that she carried with her all the time now, fondling it like a return train ticket in its folder, seeking the reassurance that it was still there, ready to take her away at any moment.

Living under house arrest at the Rev's complex for the last two months reminded her of her life with George back in New York. She was physically comfortable. Once she persuaded the Rev to let her work on public health for the refugees, she had a job just as demanding and ultimately futile as her work with the corrections department. Dr. Vance, who ran the program, was just as arrogant a boss as the attorney general, a secular humanist among the believers, taking notes for a paper on glossolalia, spontaneous bleeding, miraculous cures and other physical manifestations of hysteria. The Reverend Gilray stood in for George. Except for the Rev's increasingly high-pressure sexual advances, he ignored her just as much. Richard was Richard.

But of course it was totally different. The world around her had gone from the merely troubling to the insane. Back in Manhattan she had at least had the hope of a refuge in her marriage. Here she had none. She could not ignore the fact that the world was sliding down the slope to apocalypse. Her desire to throw gasoline onto the fire was hard to resist. She hung on.

She was keeping a diary, witnessing. Gilray fascinated and repulsed her. He clearly saw his desire for her as more than simple lust. She had seen enough strange and violent things in the last month in Zion to make the outcome of his preachments an open question. If it was possible for so many thousands to believe, if the fabric of reality could become so warped that even the whippings and witch hunts seemed ordinary, then who knew what was real?

But still she kept her ticket out. Whenever the millennial world threatened to overwhelm her, she pulled out the calculator and totaled up the numbers of her rage.

Felton opened a path for them into the theater. Christian Valley had been constructed in the eighties during the last flush of prosperity before the collapse, and although the building itself was made of cinderblock that had not taken the years well, a lot of money had been spent on the lobby. The ticket booth was fronted with bulletproof glass, as if the architects had been afraid that the place might be taken by force. Emblazoned on the lobby carpet were matched Greek masks of comedy and tragedy, representing the twin poles of teen sex movies and slasher flicks that had dominated the screens of the era. The "Coming Soon" poster case held a large picture of Jesus. Chains of tinsel swooped from the walls, and red and white paper bells hung from the stained acoustic tile. The building was heated to barely above freezing. Stereo speakers played a medley of Christmas favorites, at present "Silver Bells." Lucy wondered that nobody objected to the secular lyrics.

The concession stand had until recently been reduced to displays of Bible quotations. Richard, however, on the theory that they wouldn't need it past Friday, had persuaded the Rev to free up some food, and behind the counter workers were handing out free biscuits and honey. A woman, whose bald head was covered with scabs, trembled as she bit into her biscuit. She wore a fur coat that must have cost twenty thousand dollars: another convert, Lucy thought, with a husband back in Chicago or Dallas wondering what had happened as he drugged himself into insensibility. Or maybe her husband was dead. Or maybe he was there in the theater.

Felton led them to seats that had been roped off for them. "I love this movie," said Richard. "It's a perfect expression of God's love for us."

"You're out of your mind," Lucy said.

He leaned close and whispered. "That's the problem with

you, Lucy. You're never out of your mind. You're stuck in there. I keep calling you to come out and play. But no."

"It might be dangerous if I came out, Richard. You don't have any idea what I'm thinking."

"It's possible for someone to know you better than you know yourself. The Rev, for instance, spotted some things in me I never saw."

"Did he make you Richard the Hammer?"

"Who knows? Maybe I was Richard the Hammer all along. Maybe there is no Richard the Hammer, except what people think."

"Maybe Jimmy Stewart got saved by an angel."

"Stranger things have happened."

Lucy gave up. It was clear that Richard had turned some corner in his mental life and was bound for apotheosis or self-immolation. The seizures were only the most obvious sign. Lucy had taken to calling him "The Hammer," to his face. He liked it. He reacted with the same irony that he'd used in their other life; it was as if this Richard were the earlier Richard wearing a plastic disguise. He invited you into a conspiracy not to ask what lay beneath it, not to wonder whether there was anything to Richard other than a series of disguises, one nesting inside the other, like Russian dolls. Lucy was convinced that Richard was not aware of this conspiracy himself. It had gone beyond the point where a final reality was ascertainable. When she could divorce herself from her anger, Lucy supposed what she was observing was in some way tragic: the dissolution of a character that had once had some nobility. But that nobility had been so far submerged by masks that she could not tell whether it in fact had ever existed, and in the end she could not bring herself to care. She wasn't up to saving the unsavable. Anyone that serious about killing himself ought to pick a less clever method.

The lights faded. The screen lit with the image of a lush green landscape. Gentle music swelled from the speakers as the camera swept past dark woods, fields full of daisies, sparkling streams, over a lake that reflected back crystalline skies. The music encircled them like the arms of a loving mother. On the horizon appeared a brilliant light in which shone some complex structure. Lucy heard the audience draw in its collective breath. A chorus of voices burst forth as the camera swept closer to the celestial city, and a bell-like masculine voice spoke: "And I John saw the holy city, the New Jerusalem . . ."

The audience sighed. Towers of glass and steel, broad streets paved with gold, parks full of children and old people, bejeweled plazas where azure-robed choruses of fair-skinned men and women—sprinkled here and there by the occasional black or Asian face—lifted their voices in a single hymn of praise to the Lord. Then a flash of beach and spindrift as the camera soared out above the ocean, banking to look back on the glory of God's paradise, skirting the beach and blue water to cross back over the breakers at the site of a cluster of condominiums. A man and woman rode horses in the edge of the surf. "Canaan by the Sea," the angelic voice said. "A satellite community of the New Jerusalem. Yours—on the first of the New Millennium."

The chorus spun to inspiring heights. The camera swooped down to the courtyard of the development, where a long-haired man stood, arms outstretched, smile dazzling as the sun. The camera zoomed in until his bearded, loving face filled the screen. The image froze. The final, triumphant chord echoed in the theater, and the image faded to pearly white.

"Jesus saves," Richard whispered to her.

It's a Wonderful Life started. Lucy had seen the original version on TV many years ago, but not this latest avatar. The video-synthesization was at first distracting: James Stewart and Donna Reed and Lionel Barrymore had all been dead for years. The producers had decided not to update the film, so that it was still set in the forties and the story was still the same. You could almost believe that a contemporary company had gone back to 1945 to reshoot the film with modern equipment.

As the story of George Bailey unfolded from disaster to frustrating disaster, Lucy found herself wondering at its continued popularity. She had not remembered the first part of it, which told about a man as whipsawed by fate as the hero in a Greek tragedy. As a boy George saves his brother from drowning and as a reward loses the hearing in his left ear. He prevents the druggist from accidentally poisoning a customer and is slapped around for his effort. He longs to escape his provincial home town but is trapped by circumstances. His father's sudden death forces George to forego a college education. His every attempt to seize happiness only adds to his burdens. His wife is a homebody. His children demand his sacrifice. He manages a one-horse savings and loan through the Great Depression, never making a dime, lives a life of service to his friends, family and community, and at every step of the way sees his simple desires thwarted.

Beneath its sentimentality the film grappled with a serious question, and Lucy realized that it was the same one that her George had pestered her with: What is the source of evil? In the world of the film evil seemed to be a result of the actions of bad men like the crippled banker, of insensitive people like George's brother Harry, of human fallibility like his Uncle Billy's forgetfulness, and finally of chance, or perhaps some supernatural agent—God? Satan?—such as that responsible for the stroke that killed George's father. Evil was ameliorated only by the efforts of good hearted people like Bert the cop and Ernie the cab driver, and by the love of a good spouse.

Whatever their source, however, the disasters came one upon another until George was driven to the brink of suicide. The Christian Valley audience was sucked in. What would happen? Given the chain of events, there was no way the George in the movie could be saved.

At this point the film made its abrupt turn into pure fantasy. God sends an angel. The angel's name is Clarence. Clarence convinces George that all of the disasters which occurred are not really disasters—not even the loss of the money that drove him to the bridge in the snowy night. The bank examiner who was prepared to have George indicted ends up singing Christmas carols with his family, and the

missing ten thousand dollars is made up from the cookie
jars of every citizen in Bedford Falls.

The reaction of the audience was orgasmic. In that moment Lucy understood the movie's appeal. The audience
lived in a world where human effort was useless. They were
ready to be seduced by any view of reality that promised
relief from the forces that had destroyed George Bailey and
were destroying them. That was how people like the Reverend got hold of them.

Lucy realized that this quest for an explanation was *her*
George's quest, as well as the Rev's. She understood something about George she had never grasped before. She felt a
real sympathy. But George and the Rev, unlike her, were
egomaniacs. They thought, because they saw the problem,
that gave them humanity, and because they had a theory of
evil—aliens or Satan—that gave them the solution. In the
service of that solution they would do anything. Abandon a
wife, institute a reign of terror. They would create chaos in
their efforts to make order. And they couldn't see real people because they were blinded by theories.

Lucy looked around the theater into the sullen faces of
the audience, lit now, in the rising lights, by fatuous hope.
The followers. God was coming for them at the end of the
week. They would get Jesus, the Prince of Peace himself,
instead of some cherubic character actor. They would pursue this chimera to their own destruction. There would be
no January 1, not because Christ was coming, but because
crazy men, expecting a miracle, would destroy the world.

Well, she had a miracle in her pocket.

She looked at Richard. He was as intent on the credits as
any of them, as open in that moment, unaware that he was
no longer protected by the dark, as a young boy.

"They don't make them like that any more," he said.

"They made this movie last year," said Lucy.

In the lobby people blessed Richard, called him "Reverend"; one woman tried to clean his shoes with her hair.
Outside, thick snowflakes drifted from the skies, haloing
each of the lights in the parking lot. The people climbed
onto the yellow school buses that had brought them from

the pilgrim relief centers. Richard chattered on about the movie's "radical semiotics" as Felton drove them back to the Institute. Lucy wanted to take Richard's hammer and beat him to death.

Across the road from the Institute the floodlights showed bulldozers still going strong, clearing the forest around the fresh concrete of the landing pad. The diesels roared. Geysers of exhaust from their stacks were fingers pointed at heaven saying, "We're getting ready. Are you?" Thousands of pilgrims had already gathered and the militia had thrown a barricade across the road. The guard waved the limousine past the checkpoint and they turned up the drive, past the newly constructed bunkers, around the statue of Christ, to the Institute.

When they entered the residential wing, Lucy said, "Richard, could we go to your room and talk?"

Richard was surprised. "Certainly."

The only sign of Richard's former life in his room was the elaborate video/satellite center that filled one wall. He had enough gear to produce his own newsbroadcasts, and could siphon information from anywhere on the globe by satellite and cable.

"I need to tell you something," he said, closing the door. He turned on the video, turned up the volume. It was HCR: some report about a bride and groom dousing themselves with gasoline and setting themselves afire. Richard look nervous. "George killed Delano."

"You've seen George?"

"No. Not since October. But Delano's dead. I've know that since October, too. She was killed in a wreck in South Carolina. I'm assuming George killed her."

"How do you know?"

"I don't. But George may be dead, too."

"Well that's interesting, but I don't care."

The phone beeped. Richard jumped, looked at the flashing red light and walked over. He put on the headphones and tabbed the speaker switch. It was time. Lucy went into the bathroom and locked the door. She poured a glass of bottled water, sat on the toilet seat and set the calculator on the edge of the sink. She wedged her fingernail file into the seam along the edge and popped it open.

There was no packet inside the calculator. She cursed. She kicked the corner of the vanity so hard she hurt her foot. Once again she had been screwed by fate.

She resealed the calculator and went back into Richard's room. He wasn't there. From across the room she could see that the record light on his phone was on. Then she found him, lying on the floor at the foot of the chair. His breathing was shallow. A bruise on his forehead was just starting to seep blood; he had hit the table going down. Another seizure.

The phone was still taking an incoming message. She punched the monitor key and the screen lit to show a ragged man: "—see him before the end of the week. The Aliens—" The man broke into a fit of coughing.

It was George. His face was deeply lined. He was bearded and gray.

"—something I want to give him. You owe me this, Richard."

Richard's breathing slowed into regularity. Lucy wondered if, after a seizure, he dreamed. George rattled on.

"He has to be stopped. But they're very clever. Ask yourself who stands to benefit when this father ship lands—"

"George, shut up," Lucy said.

He stopped.

"This is Lucy, George. Your wife, Lucy."

"Lucy! But I was calling Richard."

"Right. You were calling Richard but you got me instead. Richard isn't available right now. Maybe *I* can help you. You want to see the Rev, right?"

"You know why I've got to see him. I've got to know what—"

"I understand you have many vivid and poignant desires, George. I'm prepared to help you. But first you have to give me a sign of your good faith."

"Good faith?" George sounded hurt. "I've always been true to you, Lucy."

"Well, George, there are schools of thought on that."

"I'm sorry about what happened at the motel, believe me. But I'm glad you got away."

"Fine. Here's what I want you to do, George. Did you by any chance find a pocket calculator in your car?"

George looked bemused. "Yes."

"Good. Are you in Zion?"

"Yes. I'm—"

"I want you to leave the calculator in a place where I can get it. I want you to do this without questioning why."

"What do you—"

"Shut up, George! For once just listen! You deliver that calculator and I'll see that you get your crack at the Rev within twenty-four hours."

"I don't understand."

"Of course you don't. That's why it's a test. If you do what I tell you then I'll know you love me."

"Love doesn't ask for tests, Lucy."

"Stencil that on a T-shirt, George. Meanwhile, do what I say." Lucy knew she could get Felton to do the pickup for her. "By noon tomorrow," she said. "It can be your little New Year's present to me."

Richard stirred, mumbling something. Lucy told George where to drop the calculator and hung up. She sat back in the chair. Maybe her luck was turning. George's calling at just that moment, and Richard's having a seizure—she couldn't have asked for a better break if she had prayed for it.

She was glad the virus was not in her calculator. That would have been the wrong way to do it. Inelegant. No, she would give the virus to the Rev. He wanted her. She would let him have her, and a little something extra. And through him, his followers, and through them, the whole human race. It would be a pure act of will, gratuitous, for herself alone. And for Luz.

Lucy sat. Richard's face was calm. She stretched him out more naturally, propped the chair cushion under his feet, and got a wet washcloth from the bathroom. She dabbed at his bruised forehead. The gold hammer rose and fell on his chest. Lucy imagined him in the depths of his sleep, dancing slow motion aquatic tarantellas with those unknown dreams. She envied him. She had not slept well for a long time, but now she felt drowsy. She ran George's telephone message back to the beginning, erased it, then stretched out on Richard's sofa and fell asleep.

31: THURSDAY, DECEMBER 30

....

George delivers the Goods

George awoke stiff, cold and hungry on the floor of the university lounge, to discover that overnight the courtyard outside the windows had been blanketed by another layer of snow. He stared dumbly, blinking. A sparrow landed on the branch of an oak, shaking off a flurry of powder that drifted to the unmarred ground. In a trance, he picked his way through the forty or fifty others sleeping on the floor to the doors at the end of the lounge. He stepped outside. Although the sun had not yet risen, there was enough light, gray and indirect, to see everything clearly. It was as beautiful a morning as he had ever seen. The air was still: no traffic, no sirens, no planes or people. His breath came out in billows. The cold woke his senses. He felt strong.

After a few minutes he went back inside. Others were stirring, checking their shopping bags full of clothes and their purses full of useless money. He had been wrong to worry about running out of cash. In Zion there was nothing to buy, and the few things worth buying could not be bought.

George hobbled back to his corner. The calculator, pistol and extra ammunition clip were still there. Despite Zion's calls for pilgrims to arrive bearing weapons, George had not been fool enough to think the border guards would let him keep the gun. It had taken him a week of planning to find the right spot, well away from the roads, where he could avoid both the National Guard laying siege to the Reverend's utopia and Zion's own border militia. He did not suppose himself to be the only pilgrim in Zion in possession of a weapon unknown to the city's rulers; he probably wasn't even the only one there with the intention of killing the Reverend, but he was going to be the one who succeeded.

People were up now, heading for the bathrooms near the dead elevator, rolling up their blankets and sleeping bags. The director of the lounge-turned-barracks, a flustered woman with the sad eyes of a basset hound, got up on a chair and tried to get their attention. "Praise God!" she called.

"Amen," responded a few of the people.

"Let us pray." She led them in a fervent, somewhat erratic prayer thanking God for their lives, the snow, and the television, and asking Him to keep them one more day until His arrival. George stared at the tattered cuffs of the man in front of him.

After it was over the woman surprised them. From the cupboard in the abandoned snack bar she produced a coffee urn and a box filled with vending machine pastry. The sugar coatings of the sweetrolls were crystallized from age. The woman assigned two of the female pilgrims to cut the pastries into pieces small enough so that everyone would get one. She loaded the urn with water from the tap, poured a single pack of ground coffee into the brewing basket, and plugged it in.

The pilgrims' good cheer was undeniable. George was moved. He knew that some of these people had hounded nonbelievers out of the city. Others had done worse. Yet their fellow-feeling was genuine. It was a mystery, perhaps *the* mystery.

While George sat, staring out the window at the snow and sipping his ounce of coffee, a man next to him spoke. "Where you from?"

The man was in his mid-fifties. He wore a plaid jacket over at least a couple of shirts; an orange hunter's cap pulled low over his forehead, green rubber workboots with yellow soles. He was freshly shaved. A bit of bloody brown paper towel was stuck to a cut in the dimple on his chin.

"New York," said George.

"I'm from Texas," the man said. He stuck out his hand. "John Field."

"George . . . Lowell."

"George, when did you get onto God's team?"

"In April."

"A latecomer. But praise God, not too late!"

"How about you?"

John Field leaned forward, forearms on his knees. "I can tell you the exact minute: December 11, 1997, 11:45 pm. Waco, Texas. I was watching the TV, feeling as bad as I ever felt in my natural life. My wife had just left me, I was out of a job for seven months, drunker than a skunk, and I hadn't had but one bath in maybe three weeks. I was flipping through the cable channels, climbing up through the stations into the high numbers that didn't have nothing on them, just snow and hissing. You can tell just what a sorry piece of work I was at that time, George, when I tell you that suited me just fine. I liked going up through the numbers, higher and higher, getting back nothing but noise. It was like I was climbing up through the layers of my brain, and there was nothing there but noise, too. I was pisseyed drunk, and pisseyed mean. If you'd come in that room just then I would of spit in your eye."

"What happened?"

"As I was watching I came across a station that had a picture on it, and the picture was the face of Our Lord Jesus Christ Himself. I can even remember the channel—channel 777. Jesus said to me, 'John, I want you to stop acting like a rodeo clown. Clean up your act. Pick up this room. Take a bath. Find yourself some honest work. When Tolene comes back, you get down on your knees and beg that good woman to forgive you. The End Time is coming. You hear me?'

"I thought it was some kind of movie. I didn't say nothing. But Jesus keeps looking at me and then he says, 'Wake up, John!' and he points his finger at me. A pink laser beam shoots out from his finger and hits me right between the eyes. A blast of cold fills my skull. All that noise up there goes away as if he pulled a plug. It about melted me right there in my chair. I was dazzled. I knew that I was all right, and when the last day came, I was going to sit by His side. I must of passed out, because when I woke up the TV was full of snow again. But I wasn't. I remembered it all just like it happened, and there was a fire burning in my heart."

John Field looked across the snowy courtyard. "It burns there still, George. I got the greatest gift you can get, the gift of grace. Tolene did come back. She told me she was halfway to her momma's house in San Antonio when she decided she would give me one last chance. I asked her what time that would of happened, and she told me about a quarter to twelve. I got down on my knees and kissed her feet. I promised her I would never give her a day's worry again."

A woman came over and put her hand on Field's shoulder. "John. We have to get ready." She smiled at George. "Hello," she said.

"Hello," said George. To John Field he said, "Thanks for the testimony."

"We had better get ready," said Tolene.

"See you later." Field took his wife's hand and they went over to a group of people who were getting into costumes. John Field sat on one of the low tables, stiff as a bride being dressed for her wedding, while Tolene Field took off his hat and pressed down upon his head a crown of thorns. She helped him off with his jacket and, one by one, the layers of shirts, to reveal his back, criss-crossed with suppurating wounds. He did not flinch. Around the room others were donning burlap robes. Two men struggled to get into a large paper-mache costume that had once been a pantomime horse but which now represented the ten-horned Beast of the Apocalypse.

George felt very alone. A Mighty Fortress is Our God.

The people took up their whips, their signs, their crosses, and set out for the penultimate rally.

After they had gone George got to work on his own costume. He fashioned a burlap robe from some bedding. Out in the courtyard he scraped the snow from the remains of a bonfire and blackened his face with ashes. He teased his straggly hair into further wildness. Using the knife they had cut the pastry with, he began cutting a six-foot staff from a dead dogwood. His breath steamed in the cold air and despite his exertion he was freezing. He told himself he was a crazy religious fanatic. He tried mumbling to himself. It was easy. As he worked he heard cheers from the street. A couple of young men ran across the quadrangle, kicking up clouds of powder. They saw him hacking at the tree, laughed and ran on.

He got the staff into shape, adjusted the pistol in his belt beneath the robe, made sure the calculator was still in his pocket, and examined his reflection in the lounge windows. Quite respectable. He set off for the Capital Square.

The streets were filled with people. Most headed downtown, but a significant number were going the other way, starting the long trek to the Landing Pad. George fell in step with a man who was talking to himself and a woman carrying a sign that had a taped-on photo of a silvery UFO and the slogan "Fish Cannot Carry Guns." George clutched her coat and peered into her face. "Have you seen Him?" he demanded. The man came close—it was the Lord's Prayer he was chanting—but made no move to stop George.

"No," the woman said. She pulled free. George let them go. No one cared about George's performance: in the City of Saints, he did not even rate a second glance.

In front of the Brownestone Inn a group of pilgrims was building a cross of snow. Children broke from the effort to throw snowballs at each other, their laughter edged with hysteria. A boy dashed by, wearing a woman's sweater and a winter cap with the ear flaps pulled down. There was some tumult up the street. A block away, in front of what had once been a pricey hotel, a crowd spilled across the trampled snow. From the hotel balcony a man harangued them through a bullhorn. Scuffles broke out between listeners supporting and attacking the speaker.

Something about the man with the bullhorn was familiar. George pressed closer through the mob until he could get a good look. Men in fatigues stood by the rail on either side of the man, automatic rifles held at the ready, and scanned the mass of people filling the street between the hotel and the burned-out shell of the Green Party headquarters. The speaker wore a blue swallowtail coat and American-flag pants. His white hair hung over his collar and the point of his Van Dyck beard stuck out beneath the bell of the bullhorn. It was Uncle Sam.

"Millions now living are already Dead!" Uncle Sam shouted. "From the neck up, anyway." His cackle was turned mechanical by the horn. "Following around these *preachers*. You're Americans! The Constitution guarantees you freedom from religion. But you've pissed it all away!"

That drew angry shouts, but among the crowd were some who yelled support. "It's time for us to act like free people and throw off the shackles of medieval superstition! This Reverend Gill-face interprets the Bible for you and you suck it up like pigs at the trough. Well, I'm here to tell you to grow up! The man who does the interpreting is the man who has the power! You give up your power to him just because he tells you he can read better than you can? I don't know whether to laugh or spit!

"You know St. Paul? Well, St. Paul says, 'Though I speak with the tongues of men and of angels, and have not love, I am become as sounding brass, or a tinkling cymbal.' You've been deafened by the biggest sounding brass in America! I wonder if you can hear anymore! Can you hear me? Are you listening? Are your brains working?"

Curses and cheers. George got shoved and almost lost his balance. He was directly in front of the balcony.

"Your Reverend Jimmy-Don's voice booms like a church

bell: loud because it's hollow. He has force but no authority. Noise but no signal. Power but no—"

Someone threw a brick, which narrowly missed Uncle Sam and whanged off the wall behind him. The guards raised their rifles and searched through the crowd. Someone screamed and the mob surged forward. Uncle Sam pointed into the seething mass. "Deconstruct that fella!"

A couple of supporters attacked the brick thrower. Others came to his defense, and a melee broke out. The gunmen on the balcony could not get a clear shot. Uncle Sam started to clamber over the balcony to drop into the parking lot, but before George could see what happened next he was knocked down by someone hurtling into him from behind. He took a knee in his temple, grabbed hold of someone's coat to keep from getting trampled. His vision swam. He staggered to his feet. The rally had become a riot. George struggled forward, was shoved through a row of junipers against the wall of the building. He sidled away from the thick of the fighting.

From downtown came a siren. A police truck, beacons flashing, pressed into the crowd. Garbled commands roared from its roof loudspeaker and a bunch of men jumped out of the back wielding baseball bats. The crack of a rifle from the balcony above George was answered by fire from the militia, and the body of one of Uncle Sam's riflemen flopped over the rail to land a yard in front of George among the bushes. George didn't wait to see what happened next: he slid around the corner of the building and, still clutching his staff, hurried to the alley between the houses on the sidestreet. Behind him he heard a cheer.

Several others, like George, were high-tailing it through the backyards. A middle-aged man shouted out a back door, "What's happening?"

"That Uncle Sam! He started a riot!"

"He's crazy," another man said. "The Antichrist." The man looked George up and down.

"I'm the Wandering Jew," George said. He threw his staff over a chain link fence and clambered over into a snow-covered garden. His hands were numb. Panting, he hurried up the next street away from the fighting. Numbers of people spilled into the side streets, but the sounds of gunfire had been replaced by more cheering. George had no interest in finding out who had won, but he would not have put much of a bet on Uncle Sam's chances.

As George crossed a bridge over some railroad tracks a pickup full of militia shot by him up the snow-rutted street, horn blaring. A couple of refugees from the fight skidded into the gutter to keep from getting run down. George bent to help a woman in an expensive coat. Her companion, a red-faced man in a threadbare blazer, brushed snow from the knees of his pants. The pickup spun out as it took the turn at the end of the street and disappeared on the way out of town.

"Attack on highway 54," the man said.

"The heathen armies," the woman said. "The President's made a deal with the Japs. They're going to attack!"

"You're crazy," an angry man said. "It's a holy revolution in Greensboro! Christians have risen up and are marching to break the blockade."

"They're trying to get the power plant from us," a man on the other side of the bridge shouted. "The nucular plant—cut off the power and freeze us out."

"It's the Advance Landing Modules." Another man had crept up beside them and whispered in George's ear. "The ALM's are distributing manna. We should get to the Landing Pad."

George stared at the people. "It's the Second Coming," he said. "And I've got to meet Him this time." He hobbled to the end of the bridge and slid down the embankment, through snow-covered kudzu vines to the railroad tracks. As the people above watched, he started down the roadbed toward the center of the city.

By the time he reached Capitol Square he was exhausted. The militia ringing the old capitol building looked tense. For three days George had been hearing rumors of a massacre of the Saints' militia in the west. One of the commanders had had a vision of invincibility. He would march his men outside the lines; the guns of the National Guardsmen would throw flowers. He and his men were slaughtered before they'd gone a hundred yards. Their bodies still lay there. Some believed that when the Savior came on Friday night they'd rise up, truly invulnerable, and complete their sortie, devastating the army of the Antichrist.

The militia at the Capitol, however, didn't look reassured by that expectation. Behind the barbed wire and metal-stake barricade encircling the statehouse, young men in fatigues clutched rifles and mugs of steaming coffee. They stood stiffly around trash-barrel fires, expecting to be shot by some sniper or raptured out of their bodies at any second. Only the statehouse and its surrounding park of memorials stood indifferent, as if waiting for this, too, to pass. Across the snowcovered lawn, a man with a chainsaw cut a dead oak into firewood. The snarl of the saw bit sharply through the cold air.

Uncomfortably aware of the snouts of the machine guns, George approached the south entrance of the square. The young man posted there trained his rifle on him. He would not make eye contact. The name strip across his breast pocket was blank.

"They haven't told you your new name yet?" George asked.

The boy looked confused. "Who are you supposed to be?"

"I'm the Wandering Jew."

"Well, wander away from here."

"I can't do that."

The young man poked the M-16 at George's belly. "Go away."

A couple of other men came toward them from behind the barricade. "He can't come until I find Him," said George. "It's prophesied. I'm the Jew who denied Him."

One of the advancing men heard George. "Do tell," he said. "We've been expecting you."

George forced himself to be bold. "You could give me a better reception, then. It's hard traveling for a two-thousand-year-old man."

"It's hard even on the younger ones, pilgrim."

"It's no thanks to your sort that I got here in time. Two millennia of suffering for me and my people! Every corrupt politician, whenever he got himself into trouble, just had to point at a Jew to get the heat off his back."

"It's the truth," the third militiaman said.

"Let me tell you, pal," George said. "I'm not going to make the same mistake twice. Have you seen Him around?"

The oldest man smiled. "Not yet. Come back tomorrow night."

"How about you let me in now?"

"Why?"

"I want to pray at the foot of the statue."

"What statue?"

"General Washington."

"What's that got to do with Jesus?"

"I believe in all martyrs."

The man looked skeptical. "Okay," he said. He gestured with the barrel of his rifle. "But you try anything funny and you won't last till tomorrow."

They pulled back and let George past the barbed wire. The statue, surrounded by a short iron picket fence and bracketed by two cannon, stood on a little rise before the south portico. Washington, in a bronze greatcoat, leaned on a walking stick like a country gentleman. George knelt down beside the righthand cannon. He folded his hands up under his robe and bowed his head. He pulled the calculator from his pocket. He had forced himself not to speculate why Lucy wanted it. Maybe she had arbitrarily picked an absurd task. Maybe she needed to balance her checkbook.

George wondered how she had gotten from South Carolina to Richard's phone. For the hundredth time he pushed back the thought of her pursued in the dark by who knew what while he ran away. He looked at the statue. To the militia who idly watched him he must look like some devout religionist, some worshipper of the American republic. George supposed that in some ways that was accurate. He believed in America as much as Uncle Sam. He couldn't define exactly what he meant by America, but he knew that he genuinely cared for it. Even though Americans were crazy.

Lucy thought *he* was crazy, but he'd cared for her, too.

His knees were freezing. When he stood, he reached out to the cannon as if to steady himself—it was hardly feigned—and slipped the calculator into its muzzle. The iron felt no colder than his hands. Leaning on his staff, he made his way toward a group of soldiers warming themselves around a fire. A few flakes of snow swirled from the sky to melt in the heat rising from the trash barrel. "Bless, you, my Christian brothers," he said. "Can you spare some food for the Wandering Jew?"

"Ain't got no food," one of them said.

"You aren't really a Jew, are you?" another said.

"Two thousand years of waiting!" George poked the man in the chest. "All because I didn't know the Savior when I saw Him. Don't you make the same mistake! If you see this Reverend of yours, tell him I said so."

A tall man dumped an armload of firewood by the barrel. "You'd best try the courthouse, old man," he said. His voice was not unfriendly. "They've got some food for the pilgrims, I think. We'll keep our eyes peeled."

"See that you do," said George.

An explosion echoed out of the west. The men's heads jerked up; one climbed up on a sandbag to see better until a corporal pulled him down. A smudge of black smoke rose against the sky. They pushed George out of the enclosure. He shuffled across the street toward the pedestrian mall.

In front of the courthouse a group of penitents scourged each other with barbed wire between rows of heads on stakes. They chanted and cried. Nearby a man hooked jumper cables to a storage battery, then pressed the claws of the cables to the genitals of a naked child lying on a blanket. "Depart from this accursed boy, Satan!" he shouted, while beside him another man stood with his hands at his sides and wept.

There was no food.

32: THURSDAY, DECEMBER 30

Attacks, Alarms, Warnings, and a Promise

He stood on the roof of the apartment where they had lived when he was a boy. The lights of Memphis spread out below him, brighter than he ever remembered them, and he looked across city blocks in the fervid night, past the bars and warehouses, down to the dark edge of the Mississippi. Above him in the sky shone different lights, lights of religious significance. They carried an apocalyptic message, but try as he might he could not read it. Time was short. A hot wind blew.

Then the glare from the lights below began to flicker. Looking down from the parapet he saw that the streets were on fire, that they were not the streets of Memphis but of Hell. He was trapped. He scanned the rooftop, and among the plumbing vents and TV antennas and brick chimneys with tin hats, he found the figure that saved him from being alone: Lucy Di Paulo.

She wore a thin chemise, blown against her body by the wind. Her hair was long. It streamed behind her like a flag. She reached out to him; he smelled her perfume. He pulled back, but her arms were around him and she drew him toward her. She kissed him; her body pressed against his and the flush of pure lust swept over him. The first notes of the last trump began to split the skies, but he ignored them, wrapping her in his own arms, pushing her down. They struggled as if in mortal combat, awkward, comic, terrifying.

At the edge of the building they stumbled. They fell. They fell for miles and miles, and he could see the hungry flames waiting below, hear their red voice, feel their hot breath, but he had her now and it did not matter how much he lost in the end. They hit the flaming pavements of Hell together and her jaw was driven through his face like a cold steel chisel through a pine board and he was dead.

Gilray woke, gasping, in the middle of his orgasm. He lay there halfway between dream and reality while his heart slowed and the semen went cold on his belly and his thoughts turned from confusion to trouble. He looked at the clock: it was already late morning. He slid from his bed and stumbled into the shower. The hot water steamed away his distress, leaving only the mystery.

He spent the next hour working with the camera crews that would broadcast from the Landing Pad. He took a light lunch, a salad, including what was probably the last avocado left in three counties. In the afternoon he stopped by the studio and joined the countdown broadcast with a last-minute appeal for the faithful across the nation to rise up against Satan's government and come to the aid of Zion. Richard waited for him off camera at the end of the broadcast.

He wore a black jumpsuit, black Italian calf-length boots, black gloves of the thinnest leather, and the gold hammer. His hair was slicked back so that his head seemed weirdly large. There was a bruise on his temple.

"Crisis time, Rev."

"What's the matter?"

"There's been an attack on the front gate. Some people were killed."

They left the studio. "An old man came up leading a group of about thirty men and women," Richard said. "He claimed he was the Sword of America, and it was his duty to strike out against God's Hammer. He was dressed up in a costume like Uncle Sam. Felton sent for me. I thought I could talk to them, calm them down."

Richard looked sheepish. "They got pretty excited. They

started shouting, throwing stones. When I tried to talk to them, they charged the gate. The guards opened fire."

"Is anyone hurt?"

"Yes. Some pretty bad. Vance is taking care of them."

They went to Vance's clinic, down the hall from the residential wing. Blood smeared the tile floor. Marianne and Felton directed traffic; a militiaman sat on the floor outside the clinic door holding a bloody towel to his shoulder. Inside, Vance and a nurse worked on an unconscious woman who had been shot in the face. Two or three other people were laid out on tables; at least one of these was dead.

"What's going on at the gate?" Gilray asked Felton.

"The area is secure. Most of the intruders got away, including the Uncle Sam character. They may try to disrupt the Landing Pad. I've put the men over there on alert, though there's not much chance we can find the attackers in the crowd."

Gilray took Richard to his office and they discussed strategy. Richard reported a rumor that Charles Sumner had had a vision naming him ruler of all Zion. Richard thought it was probably true. A half hour later the door opened and Vance entered, angry. "This idiocy is getting out of hand," he said. "This isn't the worst of it. I haven't heard anything from the community hospital in two days."

"Sumner has charge of that," Gilray said. "There are lots of other problems to worry about. This is the end time."

Vance looked grim. "I don't suppose you'd let me try to revive any of these people. I think I can."

"It's out of the question."

"They were due to check out by Saturday morning anyway," Richard said.

"It's all part of the plan," Gilray said. "We're caught up in the gears, little cells in the body. It's going to work out."

"I don't know how I got myself into this mess." Vance brushed unconsciously at a droplet of blood on his forearm and stared out the window at the snow-covered lawn.

"You've got no choice at this point," Richard said. "You might as well hang on and do as much good as you can. If we're crazy it will be evident to everybody by noon Saturday. I'll personally turn over my hammer to you and you can bash my brains out."

"That will be a treat," Vance muttered. He jerked the door open and stalked out.

Gilray turned on Richard. "I don't know why you wanted him here. There are hundreds of Christian doctors who could do his work just as well."

"I wouldn't trust my tender body to one of them. Vance is tough-minded. What you don't understand about him is that he's just as hung up on saving the world as you are. But he doesn't think he can do it."

"I don't believe this Uncle Sam attack is any accident. I think Charles is behind it."

Richard played with his hammer. "That's quite possible."

"He's very jealous of you, Richard. Before you came along he was a more important person."

"He calls himself the Governor now. That should satisfy him."

"It doesn't. I don't think he's going to surrender the spotlight to us tomorrow night."

"It will be hard for him to compete with Jesus Christ himself."

Gilray smiled. It amused him that whenever Richard thought he was being cynical he said things that were simply true. "That won't stop him from trying to disrupt things. I'm going to declare him a heretic."

"You won't be able to enforce any punishment," Richard said. "His people are too loyal."

"When I expose his heresy a lot of pilgrims will desert him. He'll be busy anyway. If the National Guard attacks before tomorrow midnight, they're more likely to hit the State Capitol than us out here."

They talked about the preparations. Richard estimated the number of faithful camped around the Landing Pad at more than one hundred thousand; it would be twice that by midnight Friday. He was going to inspect the platform and TV tower that evening. Gilray listened with only half attention. His mind was on his dream. Were all prophets tortured? He had to pay so much, and nobody knew it. Not even Richard, who in his own way was paying as much. He broke into Richard's monologue. "Are you still afraid to admit you believe?"

"I believe in you, Rev. You may be crazy, but you have Sumner figured out pretty well."

"I only tell the truth."

"Right." Richard breathed on the golden hammer, then polished it against his sleeve. He studied his reflection in it. After a moment he looked up. "Meanwhile, we'd better firm up security. Everybody and his brother's getting messages right now, and all of them will show up here. I'm not even too sure about Felton."

"Who's to say some of these visions aren't real?"

"I'll let you figure out which ones. I've got to go."

Gilray had to admit that, from a certain perspective, and for the wrong reasons, Vance had been doing heroic work in the last month. Richard had convinced Gilray to let Vance come to Zion. Richard stressed their need for a level-headed professional; Gilray wanted someone to keep an eye on Richard. He expected that Richard had described to Vance the opportunity he would find in the City of the Saints to observe the effects of religious hysteria on a population of average Americans. Oh, he could imagine the entire conversation. Richard was quite capable of assessing Vance's prejudices and using them to manipulate him.

Once Vance arrived, however, he concentrated on useful work. He organized the remaining hospital personnel. He trained a paramedical staff. He stockpiled medical supplies. He worked eighteen-hour days and kept his cynicism in check. Gilray could not deny that he was effective. He knew Vance had brought equipment for doing revivals, but until the incident at the gate he had not come right out and said so.

In the early evening Vance came by to report that two more people had died. "Also, do you know that your guards are letting unauthorized people into the grounds?"

"What sort of people?"

"Sick people, most of them. I've got a pregnant woman down the hall right now who claims her unborn child's the second coming of Christ, and that she's going to deliver at midnight Friday. She says the baby tells her what to do by sending vibrations up her spinal cord."

"That's not the way Christ's going to come."

"Well maybe you can read the Bible to her. The point is that she just showed up in the building yesterday. No one admits to letting her in."

"These people are called by God. I don't expect you to understand it, but I expect you to respect us."

"You realize that Shrike is deteriorating? I can't speak for his actions anymore. He needs treatment, not stress."

Vance twisted like a man on the rack. Maybe that was the real reason he was here. They'd come full circle from that afternoon in the doctor's office last summer; then Gilray's faith had been tested by science. Now Vance confronted the world of faith. "You're the one who looks to be under stress," Gilray said. "Could you be a little worried we might be right?"

"Shrike is a psychotic! He's completely snowed you."

"We'll see."

Vance's jaw muscles worked. "Jesus. I just hope there are some people left alive once this whole thing blows up in your face." He got up to go. "Ms. Di Paulo asked me to give this to you." He reached into an inside pocket and gave Gilray an envelope.

After Vance left Gilray opened it:

Reverend,

I have seen the way you look at me. You think perhaps that this is wrong. You think I don't feel the same. I don't know about wrong or right, but I would like for you to explain it to me before the end arrives. No one needs to know. Let's meet in your room on the evening of the last day.

Lucy

Gilray trembled. Now, the culmination. He had been fashioned by God and given power, had kept himself pure through the barren years, for this: to create, for the Lord, the first Millennial child.

He folded the letter, put it back in the envelope, and put the envelope into the pocket of his jacket closest to his heart.

33: THURSDAY, DECEMBER 30

Richard hosts a Party

Richard broke his drug fast with a tab of LSD, preparing for his last-night tour of the Landing Pad. There wasn't much time: the Big War might start at any minute. Nuke city, with Zion at one of 10,000 ground zeros. The Japanese were in league with the Brazilians who were clients of the Soviets and everybody knew the Soviets were the nation of Gog that would start the apocalyptic war predicted in Revelations. Wouldn't Vance feel like a fool then, wasting the last weeks of his life sticking bandaids on people busy rearranging their faces with claw hammers—except there wouldn't be time to feel bad when the flash hit. There wouldn't even be enough time for you to realize you were crisped, and all Vance's revival equipment would be bloody useless. Then it wouldn't matter how you'd spent your time, and it wouldn't matter what had happened to George or whether, before George died, he realized that Richard had betrayed him.

Felton waited for him out front. Felton was a psychopath. The Pad, just down the road, was full of psychopaths, which was why Richard had to drive instead of walk. They had been gathering in the thousands since Christmas morning. Already hundreds had died from malnutrition, exposure and overindulgence in penance. The faithful shouted their prayers at the leaden sky, which responded with bullets of frozen rain and wind like the scythe of the reaper himself.

Tonight, however, the clouds had blown away and the sky was clear as vacuum. Richard headed for the lobby. As he walked down the dimly lit hall past rows of windows, the acid started kicking in. Stars leapt out of the darkness like beacons. Richard stopped to stare out the window through the fog his own breath printed there, like the breath of a comatose man on a mirror proving he was still alive. And he was alive, wasn't he? Nothing that the world had managed to do to him in thirty-six years had managed to snuff him yet. He was too rude for it, a collection of atoms conjured into a temporary pattern, and he could as easily dissolve in the next instant as hang together. There was no special dispensation. Dispensations were the Rev's business.

Something ached in the area of his heart. He was about to go back to his room and take cap to get rid of it when Felton found him standing in the hall. They went out to the limo. Richard watched the lights from the buildings flick off and on as the car passed by the boles of pines, and as he did he had a vision of the random pattern as an infinitely complex code that only he could decipher. It was a beautifully hot idea. But what did it say? How to read the grammar of random occlusion?

They reached the gate and were let through. Felton nosed the limo through straggling masses of pilgrims, who gave way readily once they recognized the Rev's car. A few touched the windows; most simply stopped and stared. The militia had given up trying to keep the road clear and retreated to the Glaxo building, on the edge of the Landing Pad. When the limousine pulled up to the parking lot checkpoint, Felton rolled down the window and one of the guards leaned in.

"There's been some fighting inside," he said. "Some of Sumner's schismatics. But we got it under control."

Something seethed in the woods at the edge of the lot.

Richard realized it was people. There were like big, clumsy black ants, scrabbling among the trees. He got out of the car and started toward them. A hand touched his shoulder.

Felton. His face was a beautiful mask. Richard had never realized how handsome Felton was. "Not such a good idea, Mr. Shrike."

"You take care of me."

Smoke from bonfires streaked the sky ahead, underlit by spotlights from the last-minute construction. As they drew closer Richard saw that the woods had been stripped of brush and many trees hacked down for firewood. The cold wind blew the stink of porta-toilets past them. He heard singing and the gabble of voices. They passed a child, no more than five years old, crouched in the frozen mud by the edge of the lot. Face smeared with grease, he bashed a labelless tin can with a rock. He held the can to his mouth and sucked at the juice that dribbled out. When he saw Richard and Felton he ran off into the woods.

At the edges of the campground they went unnoticed, but by the time Richard could feel the heat of the outermost bonfire on his face people were turning to stare. A few entrepreneurs had made a killing selling dark goggles to the faithful; others carried around everything from sunglasses to greased cardboard. A big woman in a long coat and stocking cap struggled to her feet. Richard couldn't hear her voice, but he saw her lips form the words, "The Hammer." She reached out toward him. Others turned and soon he was surrounded. Their hands were clawlike. Their expectations hovered in the air like ozone from the high tension of their belief. Felton shifted nervously, as if he wanted to be somewhere else.

"Any news from the Capitol?" one of the men asked.

"No news," Felton said.

Richard looked around him and imagined one hundred thousand insane people, huddled in layers of clothes around myriad bonfires, flowing like a carpet of beetles around the cleared square mile that would be the landing site for the New Jerusalem. Starting with this haggard woman, these desperate men, they spread out from him in twos, threes, tens, hundreds, thousands, fifty thousand or more in this corner alone, pressing in on him, and out all along the side of the pad parallel to the East-West Expressway. Others were gathering on all four sides of the dark field, ready to greet the great City when it descended in its blaze of glorious light, opened its twelve gates and welcomed the faithful onto its streets of gold. Through the people Richard caught a glimpse of the pad itself, surrounded only by a wire fence. Such was the power of faith that so far they had refrained from crossing inside. Across the dark plain of hastily poured, frost-rotted concrete, on the distant north side, Richard saw more bonfires dance, intermittently obscured by crowds.

He pressed through the campgrounds toward the southeast corner, where trailers for the construction bosses crouched at the foot of the observation tower from which they would broadcast the descent of Christ in his Father Ship. The floodlights, heavily filtered cameras, optical fiber cables and satellite uplink were already in place. Beside the tower a platform faced halfway between the dark, empty square and the crowded pilgrim camp. Technicians were testing the network of stadium-sized HDTV monitors they had set up at intervals about the perimeter so that people on all four sides of the Landing Pad could watch the Rev and Richard pray to bring in the New Age. They had wired in a generator at Glaxo to ensure electricity should the Antichrist's rumored attack on the Shearon Harris nuclear plant manage to cut off power. The flickering of the monitors joined the bonfires, reflecting off tents, clumps of bedding, heaps of cleared snow, tree stumps, ridges of frozen mud and the chapped faces of the multitude.

As Richard pushed ahead, the faces of the hopeless were imprinted on his brain. They were diseased. Richard recoiled. He tried to keep them from infecting him. If he touched them as he passed, it was only to push them aside. But recognizing him, the people got excited, so that each new person he encountered as he made his slow progress was more aware than the last that he was coming. They would suck him dry. Yet there was an energy to them that surged into him at the same time they sought meaning from him. They believed in the power of prayer. In a little more than twenty-four hours their prayers would be answered in a more direct way than any prayers in Christian history: by the arrival, in flesh and blood, of the Savior himself. As Richard flashed on this—the entire Christian network of belief stretching back in time to Golgotha and outward in space to cover the entire planet like an information virus—his fear evaporated. Contact with the insane was a source of infinite strength. It was the best excuse for a party he had ever heard.

And what a party! Already the flagellants had spiked themselves into dazed ecstasy. From Data General, the Microelectronics Center of North Carolina, the Dupont Electronics Development Center, the University of North Carolina RTP office, and countless other abandoned high-tech research centers, Luddites had dragged machines ranging from personal computers to antique clocks, which they had then smashed to flinders. Thousands of people wore hammers around their necks. Volunteer preachers spouted their own variations on Revelations; in the background rose the voices of people speaking in tongues, the singing of spirituals, the blaring of holy music from boom boxes. A man wearing a videocam, his face painted into a Indian mask, stopped to focus his eyepiece on Richard, while he whispered commentary into a throat mike. Richard looked straight into the face of the camera and imagined someone three hundred years later watching him. Hello! he thought. Greetings from the late Twentieth Century!

By now his progress toward the tower was completely halted. Filthy people mumbled and fell on their knees. Women locked eyes with him in open invitation. Others averted their gaze as if he were too bright for them to see— as indeed, perhaps, he was. It was possible. How could Richard know what they saw when they looked at him? Perhaps they saw an angel of the Lord dressed in fiery robes. Perhaps they saw the image of Christ Himself. God was great; he could do stranger things than that.

And as he watched these people, as he inhaled the stink

of their latrines and the smoke of their fires, as he listened
to their voices edged with hysterical faith, Richard began to
hear the buzzing in his ears and taste the metal at the back
of his throat, and was swept under a memory of the days
when he was Gene Lethal. Despite the cold, he was sweating. Felton tried to guide him toward one of the trailers, but
Richard shrugged him away. The darkness, the glare of the
spotlights, and the excited crowds were a lot like an outdoor
concert, except this was a lot larger than any concert Six
Million Jews had ever played. He was shot through with
galvanic forces, as if indeed his mind were a receiver and
Aliens were lancing messages into his neurosystem, charging
his limbs with cosmic energies. The crowd was an extension
of his firing neurons. The fires glowed brighter. The flickering of the nearest video screen, around which a swarm of
crazy saints gathered like a group of addicts around their
connection, seemed pregnant with meaning. *He,* Richard
Shrike, was their connection. Richard felt his eyes glow and
flicker like the screens. The people around him saw it too;
he could see his light reflected in their wasted, expectant
faces, their trembling limbs, the hammer that weighed between the breasts of the still beautiful girl who pressed closest to him in the crowd.

"One day more," Richard said.

The people near him responded eagerly, nodding, repeating: "One day. Only one day more!" The girl in the front,
reaching out to touch him said it too, "One day!"

"One day!" Richard shouted. He laughed, and more of
the people crowded around. Felton tried to pull him away;
Richard pushed him aside.

A man stumbled forward out of the press of people,
reaching out his hand as if to take Richard's own. In the
man's hand was a gun. Richard could not back away. The
moment stretched in comic slow motion: the bearded man,
his blond hair and hollow cheeks, his scrawny arm, his
gnarled hand, the remarkably clean, matte-black gun, the
people struggling to fall back, the light and noise and the
man beginning to speak.

"Secularist pornographer—" he began, and the hand

tightened for the shot that would kill Richard, but as he did the girl knocked the man's arm down. There was a small report, tiny amid the large sound of the crowd, and the shot spanked the frozen ground. Screams and cries, bodies surging away and back. The people fell on the man, riding him down. They beat him with their fists. Some used their hammers. Felton tore a person or two from the top of the heaving mass, but he could not get near the man.

"Come away now!" Felton shouted in Richard's ear, but still Richard ignored him. This was much better than any rally so far: this was much closer to the quick heart of sickness inside him. He wished George were there to see it.

In a minute the people had beaten the man to death. Eventually they fell back from his battered corpse. Richard thought he ought to be revolted, but he was not. "One day more," he whispered again.

The people swayed, breathing heavily. Blood dripped from the young girl's hammer. Someone vomited, someone laughed. They waited. Richard told them to carry the body to the landing site and throw it there, beyond the wire.

They did. They would do whatever he told them. What a miracle belief was! For the first time in his life Richard knew what it meant to say that faith could move mountains. Mountains? Planets! Faith could move solar systems, it could draw alien races across light years, from galaxy to galaxy on the pure beams of hot, passionate belief. They were up there waiting for him. He was charged up, electrified, online. Inside, he knew that there was nothing up there waiting. At midnight Friday night no one would descend; there would be no salvation. He didn't care. He had it, he was *on*. There was nothing more.

Richard pushed through the crowd and boosted himself up on the lowest girder of the TV tower. He stood on the corner of one of the camera platforms and raised his fists into the air.

"One more day!" he screamed. The people screamed back, "One more day!" It spread like a TV broadcast through the thousands, fast, a real information wave just like the textbooks said.

"One more day!" They all got the signal, it turned them on and turned on them, and the shout became a roar from a thousand and then ten thousand and then countless more angry, believing throats, a great inarticulate beast given one voice by their faith and by Richard's penetrating transmission: "ONE MORE DAY!!!"

Laughing, he pulled the gold-plated hammer from around his neck and windmilled it around his head like a cheerleader at a football rally. Darkness, smoke, fires, television. "ONE DAY! ONE DAY!"

The full hundred thousand screamed it, echoing between the woods and the trailers, rebounding back, out of phase because of the time lag, from a mile away on the other side of the dark graveyard that was the Landing Pad. The crowd surged around the base of the tower. He spotted Felton down there struggling to maintain his place: Felton believed. He spotted the girl in the robe. She believed. She probably thought she had saved his life. He had no life. He leapt down, pushed forward and embraced her. The chant of the crowd battered them from all sides. She pulled herself to him, weeping. Richard could feel the cold steel of her hammer against his chest.

The believers crushed them. They might be suffocated, and if they fell it would certainly be death. Richard didn't care. He could feel the girl's scrawny ribs, smell her unwashed flesh, rub his cheek in her dirty hair. This was what he had come to the Reverend for. He was in total control of a people out of control. He was making it up moment to moment. It was an apotheosis of Creative Nihilism. He was a rotting piece of meat, he was in love, and Lucy was his at last. He was a fucking lunatic. Stinging tears welled up in his eyes, and he knew that he was alive.

. . . .

Surf's Up

George waited around the university lounge for twenty-four hours without hearing anything from Lucy. Either she had not gotten the calculator and had written him off, or she had been prevented from contacting him.

Three people died in their sleep Thursday night. One of them was John Field. While Tolene Field wept and the flustered group leader attempted to console her, George helped two other men dig shallow graves in the quadrangle. A lay preacher from Pennsylvania led a prayer. George stood there in the cold, hardly able to draw enough breath to fill his lungs, and strained so that he might hear, beneath the words of the Twenty-third Psalm, the ringing of the phone in the stairwell by the lounge. His teeth were loose in his bleeding gums, his shoulders were permanently stooped and he could not feel his toes. Outwardly calm, he was filled with rage. A Mighty Fortress is Our God. The aliens look down on them and laugh. Uncle Charlie, beautiful sister Sue. The human race was comprised of idiots, and all it took was a pleasing homunculus, a likely pattern of phosphor dots, a charismatic psychopath like the Reverend Jimmy-Don Gilray to lead them down the rathole.

By afternoon the remaining pilgrims had all packed up and left for the Landing Pad. Still no call. George tried Richard's telelink code but got nothing. He could not wait any longer: he would have to find a way to get at the Reverend himself. He looked up the address of the local HCR bureau, tore the city map from the phone book, and set off.

George tried to stay off the streets. Followers of Charles Duke Sumner and remnants of Uncle Sam's Deconstructionist Army had fought all night. Sinners were dying so fast that, upon His arrival, Jesus was going to have to resurrect a few just so he would have someone to conquer. George cut across yards behind houses. The sun was a bright brass spot in the clouds. Blue shadows lengthened beneath the oaks and in the lee of buildings. Away from the main streets the city seemed deserted. In the wake of the fighting it was almost silent, a collection of dumb buildings spread over hills within a forest, the trees more real than the houses.

He emerged onto a commercial street: Peace Street, the sign said. An old stone high school dominated one corner; the shattered plate glass windows of a florist's shop gaped across at it. On the roof of the shop stood a white billboard: above the slogan "The Reverend and All he Stands For!" someone had spray-painted "Fuck" in big red letters.

Down the street, in the parking lot of a gutted convenience store, a crowd of people was scourging prisoners. George felt a throbbing in the air. The people looked up. The roar swelled and three military helicopters shot over them from the northwest, flying low. The gunships rocketed toward the capitol, and after a moment George heard an explosion and machine gun fire. The people in the lot ran for cover; George was almost bowled over by a woman who rushed past him clutching a fistful of UFO photographs.

He ducked down an alley beside a paint store and crouched behind a dumpster. Two more helicopters skimmed over the rooftops; these bore insignia he didn't recognize. He heard automatic weapons fire and saw figures flash by on the street. The rear of the alley butted up against a building and there was no way out except the way he had come. Night was falling fast.

While George hesitated, a figure carrying something long and unwieldy jogged down the alley. It was a young man with a surfboard. He leaned the board against the wall and joined George behind the dumpster. He looked George up and down. "Let me guess: The Wandering Jew, right?"

"Psychic," said George.

"Gonna get hot in old Zion tonight," the young man said. He wore a down jacket; on his forehead was a diving mask. He saw George looking at the mask. "Keeps the tear gas out of your eyes."

"And I suppose the board is just camouflage," George said.

"I'm on my way to the coast, but I lost my damn ride. Since the earthquake it's the best surfing on the east coast in a century."

"Did they surf a century ago?"

"Probably not."

"It's a little cold for water sports."

The young man jerked his chin toward the knapsack on his back. "Wetsuit. It's no sport for pussies."

Another flight of helicopters roared overhead. Cries and riflefire from the street. Onward Christian Soldiers. "What about all this?" George said. "It's supposed to be the end of the world."

"If I'm going out, I'd rather go out riding a big one. Catch a tube, smash to splinters in the sea foam. I'm telling you, the waves at Nag's Head right now are prehistoric!"

George looked over at the man's board. It was yellow, with an orange stripe down the center. A sticker on top said, "Zeus, Moses, Jesus and Elvis." With his long ponytail and scruffy beard, the surfer looked a bit like Jesus himself.

"Pretty irreverent sticker," George said.

"Hey, I figure if Jesus was alive now, he'd be riding the waves. It's a form of worship."

An explosion echoed from the street and a cloud of smoke whipped down the alley. George's eyes began to water. The young man pulled his mask down over his eyes and nose.

George coughed. The surfer found a rag, wet it with snowmelt and made George hold it over his mouth and nose. It helped. That made George mad: he didn't want to be helped by the likes of this kid. His mind felt hot, swollen. There were too many maniacs running around. A Mighty Surfer is Our God. It was too easy. Who would take responsibility for all this?

The fighting surged and eventually passed by. They waited in deep twilight.

"Wish I could get a ride on one of them choppers," the surfer said. "I'd be there in an hour."

"Not much chance of that," George muttered.

"Special Forces is full of surfers. They'll probably head for the beach right after the battle."

If George had not needed the bullets he might have shot the kid there on the spot. But that would be killing the wrong maniac. He pulled himself painfully to his feet. "Follow the railroad tracks east," George said.

"See you later." The surfer grabbed his board and jogged down the street. George wondered if he'd get out of Zion alive.

It was dark by the time he reached the HCR bureau. The front doors of the building were chained shut. George cupped his hands around his eyes and pressed his face up against the glass but couldn't see anything. He circled around to the back. The ground fell away. A dumpster was shoved up against the basement fire door, but someone had pried it away from the building enough so that George could squeeze inside.

He fumbled his way up the unlit stairwell, leaning on his staff to catch his breath on each landing. The muscles in his legs quivered. The second floor corridor was dimly lit. He passed a large glass panel, an interior window on the wire room, found the door and entered. The system was up and running. That put him on his guard: the Reverend must have had the place closed down months ago. The VDTs sat with blank screens, green cursors winking in the upper left corner of each. George went to the copy desk. He sat down at the slot editor's machine, pulled open the desk drawer and began searching for a manager's output report. He came up with one that was three months old.

An output report, used to monitor efficiency, listed the number of items filed, the time and length, according to employee computer prompt. From the list George stole a prompt and typed it in on the VDT:

LOGON DOC,EDR

The screen went momentarily blank, then the computer responded:

DOC,EDR LOGGED ON
1647 est 12/31/99
DOC:

George called up the 4 p.m. national news writethru from AP. He read the headline page.

1600 edt NATNEWS WRITETHRU—HEAD-LINES
   WASHINGTON—Secession "Not a federal concern," President Says.
   WASHINGTON—Second Lady feeds multitude on Mall.
   NEW YORK—Asian Economic Coalition threatens intervention to stabilize U.S.
   DETROIT—Detroit secedes from union.
   CHICAGO—Computer radicals push One-World Information state.
   GLENS FALLS, NEW YORK—Angel delivers ultimatum at New Year's Eve service.
   DAVIS, CALIFORNIA—Ozone Layer 40% gone, scientist says.
   KEY WEST, FLORIDA—UFO aliens take over offshore island.
   GREENSBORO, NORTH CAROLINA—Pilgrims clash with National Guardsmen.

That one was worth checking out. He called up the story:

   GREENSBORO—Dec 31—At least one hundred pilgrims attempting to break the seige surrounding the Rev. Jimmy-Don Gilray's Zion state were killed in a clash with North Carolina National Guardsmen Friday.

Christian guerillas armed with makeshift bombs and hunting rifles clashed with guardsmen near the town of Apex, at a checkpoint on a highway entering the rebel counties. The fighting raged for two hours, sources reported, killing nine guardsmen and wounding twelve. Pilgrims attempting to join the Space Savior movement have attempted to penetrate the blockade several times in recent weeks.

An aide to Gov. Melville Smith told the press, "The Guard will maintain this blockade as long as it is necessary to restore order to central North Carolina."

Meanwhile, refugees from inside the beseiged city report fighting between rival religious factions. The religious government has reportedly resorted to public torture and executions in order to maintain control.

The pilgrims, whose arrival in increasing numbers has threatened the stability of neighboring cities, discount such reports. "They're just trying to slander God's Saints," said Peter Castillo, a machinist from Louisiana who has been attempting to enter Zion for two months.

The fighting came amid rumors that military commanders at Ft. Bragg were considering an Asian Economic Coalition offer of assistance in the wake of the President's refusal to declare a state of emergency in the riot-torn southeast. On Thursday, Lt. Col. Dan Calloway, spokesman for the Commander, 18th Airborne Corps, Ft. Bragg, denied the army had any plans to attack the Rev. Jimmy-Don Gilray's 'Christian Utopia.'

Rumors of Asian intervention have prompted further dissension in Gov. Smith's already shaky government-in-exile. A spokesman for Smith said he had not been notified of any AEC offer and insisted that such action would be a matter for civilian authorities to decide.

In Atlanta, Goro Yamada, Press Secretary for the AEC regional office, said only that, "We are naturally concerned about our loan exposure in the State of North Carolina, and will take whatever steps are necessary, in keeping with international and civil law, to protect our sphere of influence."

Something moved. George looked up from the screen. A man hustled down the aisle of desks at the side of the wire room. George was about to slide beneath the desk when the man, seeing that George had seen him, ducked behind a bank of display screens.

George felt for his gun. "Come out of there," he called. "If you don't squeal on me I won't squeal on you."

The man peeked above the top of a monitor on which a young woman wearing a black mask delivered the silent news. He looked familiar. George recognized him as Stanley Levine. "Jesus. Stanley."

"Look, pal, I don't know what you're doing here, but whatever the locals say this is still private property. I'll give you five—"

"Stan, it's George. George Eberhart."

Levine stared. He came around the desk toward the slot. He had a grease-stained paper bag in his hand. "George. Son of a bitch. What are you doing here?"

"I might ask you the same."

"I'm in exile. After you left Abramowitz decided he didn't like my style. He sent me down here to check up on Richard. Then all this happened and I got caught in the gears."

"You've been in touch with Richard?"

"Sure. From 100 yards away, minimum."

"I need to reach the Reverend. I was going to message New York and see if anyone at HCR had access to Richard."

Levine slumped into one of the copy editors' chairs. "Old

Richard the Hammer? Forget it. He's *non compos*. Or else he's running the best scam of his life. Either way he's not going to want to hear from us." He pulled a stale croissant out of the bag and bit off a corner. George's stomach growled.

"We're lucky we even got in here," Levine said. "They used to have a couple of Saints guarding this place, but now that the crunch is coming they're all off killing each other."

"Happy New Year."

Levine grinned. "Come the New Year, you and I will be the only folks in town, looks like. The rest will either be playing Space Alert with Jesus or riding the mother ship to Heaven."

George wanted to laugh; it hurt his chest. "How have you been spending your time?"

"Starving my ass off." Levine gnawed away at the croissant. He didn't offer any to George. "Hiding out here. This is the last food in the building." He crumpled the bag and threw it into a wastebasket full of month-old hard copies. "Oh, I've taken some vids, too. I could do a great book on these loonies, if there was anybody left who could read."

"Could be a nice piece." George tried to keep a lid on his anger.

"You bet. If I could get out of here alive. I've had to hide out from the Rev's men. I'm not a popular guy with him."

Beneath his robe, George hefted the gun. "How sad for you."

"You bet."

"Stan, I've got to see the Reverend, alone, in person. Tonight. You're going to help me."

"Tonight?" Levine laughed. "Sorry, George. Mrs. Levine didn't raise any idiot children."

"You won't run any risk."

"Neither did General Custer. Have you been downtown lately? They stick heads up on street lamps for swearing. How do you think they'll feel about a Jew blasphemer?"

"Isn't that the point? Somebody's got to stop this insanity before it comes to its climax."

"Sounds pretty sexy, George. I'm getting hot."

George couldn't stand it any longer. He lunged for Levine and knocked him over backwards. Levine's head banged against the floor. His eyes clouded. George shoved the fallen chair away and climbed atop him, his knee in the pit of Levine's stomach. He was shaking with weakness, but inside he was completely calm. He searched himself for the place where his humanity had dried up and could not find it; his mind ticked cool and steady as a Newtonian clock, with just about as much sympathy in it. He took the pistol out, made sure the safety was on, pressed the muzzle up under Levine's chin and waited for him to come around, thinking what a mess it would make if he shot him.

Levine groaned, moved his hand to touch his head. "Listen to me," George said. "First we're going to message New York and see if they know any way to contact Richard. You're going to make an appointment to see him. You've had a vision. You've got to see him tonight. The fate of the human race hangs on it. I'll tell you what to say."

Levine looked up at him. "Okay, George," he gasped.

"If that doesn't work we're going to try something else. You're going to create a diversion and we're going to get onto the grounds of the Reverend's institute."

"We won't even get there."

"We'll get there."

"But they've got that place sewed up tighter than a surgical virgin—"

George leaned on his knee. Levine stiffened. "You've been there, Stanley? You know the layout?"

"Not really. I was only there once."

"That doesn't matter. You're perfect for the job."

"How about moving the knee."

George leaned harder. Levine twisted in pain, but George felt no satisfaction in it whatever. His grip on the gun tightened. Sweat glowed on Levine's forehead. Eyes like white slugs, veins standing out red and barren as winter tree limbs, skin like a damp cellar wall, beard like fungus on a corpse. George had never looked at a man's face in quite this way—not as the expression of a soul, or as the flesh of an animal, or even as an inanimate object: it was a phenomenon, a sequence of events as unconnected to personality as the weather. As the cold wind in the alley. As the white snow, which would eventually turn into dirty slush, which would turn to water, which would flow to the sea, which would evaporate and form clouds, which would produce snow, which would turn to slush and filth and around and around again until the sun flared up and ashed the entire planet, Levine and George with it. Until midnight, when Christ came again. Until the saucers landed and the aliens revealed themselves. Until the devil tore away the curtains of illusion that he'd raised to confuse them and revealed the quotidian hell that George inhabited. Until—sweet merciful God, yes—until he awoke and found this was all a dream.

35: FRIDAY, DECEMBER 31
....
Lucy gets Engaged

And now, this very evening, Lucy was invited to watch these men usher in the Millennium that other men had predicted every fifty years for the last two thousand years of man-ruled history. A Millennium ruled by the male God, who had created the universe for the benefit of man. This male God would send his son, the Prince of Peace, to slaughter his male enemies and run the world for a thousand years. Those who did not accept the truth of revelation would depart, cursed, to an everlasting fire ruled by a male Satan, who in these last terrible days before the Second Coming was attempting to pervert as many believers as possible by means of the male Antichrist.

Where did women fit in? Where else: they took their accustomed roles as worthy followers, innocent victims, or damned unbelievers. And oh, yes—as temptresses. Satan's agents were often female. Indeed, one of the signs that the Millennium was imminent was that women had not been keeping their place. And all this massive machinery of history had been set in motion because the first woman, created by the male God to serve man in the Garden of Eden, was too stupid or too contrary—male theologians had debated this point down through the ages—to follow instructions. And her husband, who ought to have known better than to listen to her, had followed his dick into perdition.

The Reverend Jimmy-Don Gilray and Richard "the Hammer" were going to lead them out again. But even under the shadow of the end the Reverend wanted something from Lucy.

She could hardly wait. They had arranged that she would go to his rooms while he visited the Landing Pad at dusk. He would slip away and meet her at ten.

Lucy set the bottle of pinot noir, glasses and towel on a silver tray. The calculator was beneath the towel. She had already checked this one: the packet of virus was inside.

It was 8:30, time to become invisible. She showered and washed her hair, blew it dry. In honor of her prison days she had kept it short: not very feminine, but it would have to do. She plucked her eyebrows, applied the eyeshadow, liner, mascara and lip gloss. She put on the dress the Reverend had given her, dark blue velvet with a tight bodice. The high-heeled boots laced to mid-calf. Balancing on the heels, she tottered over to the mirror. She looked like a religious fanatic's vision of heaven: demure, ready to submit, with a hint of wildness to come that would keep him preoccupied while she slipped him the bug. He would never even realize who had done it. Lucy Di Paulo was hidden away inside the perfect woman. A traditional role. The purloined person.

Lucy avoided looking into her own eyes. When she and George had been going well, they had spent a lot of time in bed. She had assumed many roles for him, and he for her. There was a playfulness to it that pulled them together instead of apart, an understanding that this was not all they were, a mood of giving instead of extortion, an underlying gentleness. Had she had been used even then? It hadn't felt that way.

Sudden remorse overcame her: those days were so far behind her now it was as if they had never happened.

She laid out the jeans and sweatshirt she would change into for her escape, then took the tray down the corridor to Gilray's rooms. Everyone had left the building for the Landing Pad. She punched his door code and went directly to the bedroom. It was even more spartan than Richard's: a simple dresser, an altarlike computer table with a Bible set below the monitor on a shelf, a double bed with a single pillow and no headboard. Above the bed hung a print of Da Vinci's *Madonna of the Rocks,* and above the computer a framed Master's degree in computer engineering from Memphis State University. From the wall near the dresser hung a reading lamp, and beneath the lamp sat an armchair. Off the bedroom were a small bathroom and a dressing room with a louvered door.

Lucy set the tray on the dresser. Using her nail scissors, she clipped off a corner of the virus packet, then dusted the smidge of pink powder into his glass. She uncorked the wine and filled the glasses. Here's to the rearrangement of the world: universal death or the transformation of the left brain.

At a few minutes to ten someone knocked on the door. How polite. She opened it to find a gaunt man in a burlap robe pointing a gun at her. "Lucy!" he said.

The man's hair stood out like an uneven growth of lawn. It was George. She grabbed the hand with the gun and pulled him into the room. "How did you get in here?"

"I had some help. Are you all right?"

George looked much worse than he had at the motel. He slumped in the chair before the Reverend's computer, the gun in his lap. "Why didn't you get in touch with me?"

Lucy swirled past him to the sideboard. "I never got the calculator. I decided you were standing me up."

"I passed it on just like you said!"

She slipped the calculator into a drawer, then turned to him. "Well, I never got it."

He rubbed his brow as if to massage his brain into life. "I'm sorry. I guess a lot of things haven't worked out."

"That's too bad. Now get out of here."

"I need to see the Reverend."

"*I* need you to leave."

"I've worked too hard for this. There's too much at stake."

"I don't care, George. I can't help you."

George hefted the gun. "I can stop him, Lucy. Maybe the whole world—"

"Fuck the whole world, George."

George looked sullen. It was all she could do to keep from laughing. "Do you know how absurd you are?" she asked. "It would be funny if people like me hadn't spent so much time worrying about you."

"Don't worry about me, I—"

"I'm not. Now get out."

There was another knock at the door. Lucy grabbed George's arm—through the robe it felt painfully thin—and yanked him out of the chair. She shoved him into Gilray's dressing room. "Keep quiet!" she hissed, "—or you're a dead man." She closed the louvered door, then hurried to the door to the apartment. It was Gilray.

"Hello," she said. "I've been waiting."

Instead of a suit Gilray wore a black turtleneck and black denim trousers. "Look at you!" he said. "The Eternal Woman."

He looked so ordinary, not like any kind of threat. Lucy reminded herself of the people in the Christian Valley Theater ready to follow this man to annihilation. She led him to the bedroom and fetched his doctored wine. "How are the preparations going?"

"Everything's going according to plan. The sun will rise on a new world."

"Well, let's drink to it."

He took the glass. He brought it to his lips. Lucy felt a

joy so savage she trembled. Drink it, you bastard, and let it rot you alive. Infect the rest of them. You deserve worse.

He looked her in the eyes, and without drinking set the glass on the computer table. "You shouldn't patronize me."

"What do you mean?"

"I know you don't believe in the Millennium."

"I believe it's time for a change. I'll drink to a new world. It might not be the one you expect, though."

He sat down on the bed. "Let's talk about that," he said.

She had been prepared for destruction, perhaps lust—not conversation. She leaned over and kissed him. He sat there, arms at his sides.

He was going to make her seduce him. She went back to her glass and had some more wine. It was really quite bad. First George, now this. "I guess you need a little warming up," she said, her back to him. She bent down and started undoing the laces of her boot.

She heard him move, felt his hand on her back. "Why are you so hostile?" he asked.

"I've got good reason to be hostile." The balls of her feet already ached from the high heels. "I've been hurt. Women all over the world are being hurt, and you tell us it's God's will."

Leaning against him, she slid off the boots. She picked up his glass and handed it to him. She took a sip from her own. "It's not a complaint, it's a simple fact."

He put the glass down without tasting it. "You want to know who's been hurt?"

"Yes."

"Men. Women have caused men pain since the Garden of Eden."

"Men treat women like objects."

"Your body is an object. You're not—you're a soul inhabiting it."

She wasn't going to be able to do this if he started talking about souls. She made herself stay calm. "Let's not talk anymore," she said. She pulled him over toward the bed.

They lay down together. He ran his finger along the neckline of the dress, his leg folded over hers. His face was inches away. His skin was smooth and there was no smell to him at all. He kissed her, and she kissed him back. His tongue slid into her mouth and he rolled half onto her. He found the zipper of her dress and drew it down to the small of her back. Expertly, with one hand, he unclasped the hooks of her bra. There was something clinical about the way he did this, as if he had read all about it in a book, had practiced it repeatedly and was checking off stages from some mental list. She felt sick. She held him close to try to smother it, but he drew back and slid the dress from her shoulders. He breathed evenly. He cupped her breast in his hand. "Souls can be saved many ways," he whispered.

Lucy couldn't do it. She pushed him away and sat up. "You're not going to save my soul by fucking me, if that's what you think."

He didn't react. "Why did you agree to see me, Lucy?"

"Don't ask questions you might not like the answers to."

"I know the answer," he said. "But you don't."

Lucy had her back to him, facing the closet. She wondered what George thought of all this. She had come into the room resolved to lie as much as was necessary to get him to drink the wine, but the rage that she had repressed for so long was overwhelming any planning. She was damned if she would hide her emotions for him. She would tell him off and take the virus herself. "You know my motives?" she said. "You don't even know your own! You've been after me ever since I came here. Jesus is landing in an hour and here you are with your hand on my ass."

"My motives are entirely pure. This meeting is part of God's plan."

"How nice for you."

"I'm only doing my duty."

Lucy wished Luz and Concepcion were here. It was the same colossal arrogance she had gotten from her drunken father, from Detweiler at the A.G.'s office, from George's UFO mania, from Dr. Kent.

It was more than she could stand. "What a coward! You can't take responsibility for your own lust. You invent God to justify it."

"It's not just God, it's biological fact."

"So is shit."

He put his hand on her shoulder, tried to make her look at him. She refused. "Why do women have more endurance than men?" Gilray asked. "Because you have to suffer childbirth, and are constructed so that you can bear the pain. Men are physically stronger so we can fulfill our role, protecting wife and child."

"And beating up wife and child if they get out of line."

"Someone must lead, and someone follow."

She pulled the dress up to cover herself. "I suppose God gave you testosterone so you can come up with theories like this."

"You think you're enlightened, Lucy, but you're only lost. Women rise to greater heights of self-sacrifice than men, but when they fall, they fall to lower depths. They can be better, and lead men upward, or worse, and lead men down."

He still had his hand on her shoulder. She shrugged it off. "Let me guess which one I am."

"You're more noble! Nobility is the mother who runs back into the burning building to save her child. The man who saves his family is a pale imitation. 'Women and children first,' isn't sexism, it's necessity. Call it evolution, if you can't believe in God. When men are willing to die to save women, when women are ready to bear and nurture children, then God's in His Heaven and all's right with the world. But that's not the way we've been living, and you see what it's come to. Tonight the order will be restored."

"By screwing me."

"Right here, on this bed. I will engender the New Man, and you will bear him. That's my motive. And no matter what you might think your motive was, that's the real reason you agreed to meet me tonight."

"I'm here for my own reasons!"

"I'm sure you feel that way, Lucy. If you didn't, your eventual submission wouldn't be so gratifying."

Her hands trembled. She surged off the bed, almost tripping on the hem of her dress, and turned on him. "Gratifying!" she said. "That's what it's all about, isn't it. Well, forget it. Not tonight. I have a headache."

"You can't fight God, Lucy."

She reached behind her back and tugged up on the zipper. "Don't you understand that every time you say 'God' it's just an excuse for you to do what you want? You're not some holy TV receiver! You're just a fucking man!"

Gilray came off the bed and grabbed her, swung her around. Lucy struggled to get free. His eyes were emotionless as a shark's, and the size of the risk she had been running hit her. Gilray was monstrous. He was capable of anything. She would be doing the world a favor if she killed him; it would be no sin, only justice.

Something strange happened then. "I would be doing the world a favor if I killed you," he said. "It would be no sin, only justice." He shoved her away. As Lucy watched, Gilray shrank. He looked small. Far from the fear and hatred she had felt an instant before, all she could see now was his weakness. Dangerous, unjustified, he was also pitiful.

"Why do you think I'm here?" he said. He pointed a trembling finger at Lucy. His hand was frail. It was a woman's hand. It was like her own. "You think it's just sex I'm offering? *I'm* opening the door to the new world, but you're too afraid to walk through it. Christ is the answer! He rules over men because men cannot rule themselves. Men rule over women for the same reason."

Lucy's rage drained away. Gilray's ideas were transparent. In the mind of the crowd they might kill, but from his lips they seemed only an inadequate reaction to his pain. All he knew was killing, all he knew was force.

She thought of George crouched in the closet behind him. They really were birds of a feather, dazzled by theories of salvation while the blood that pulsed through their arteries rushed along unheard. Thinkers. The philosophers praised it as humanity's greatest achievement, but right now, to Lucy, it looked a little desperate. George had wasted away to nothing pursuing his theories. Neither of them was any stronger than Lucy. Christ, she was stronger than both of them put together!

She saw the drawer of the dresser where she'd put the calculator, slightly ajar.

"You really need help," she said.

Gilray glared at her. He picked up his glass from the computer table. He raised it to drink.

"No," she said.

He stopped, the glass at his lips. "No what?"

She came over, took the glass from his hand and set it down on the table. "I don't want it that way," she said.

It was as if that was what Gilray had been waiting for. "Good," he said. His face went blank, like a TV monitor at the end of a disk. He put his arms around her waist and pulled her close.

George burst out of the closet. "Let go of her!" he shouted. The gun was in his hand.

"No, George—" Lucy began. She pushed away from Gilray.

"Someone has to stop him," said George. He fumbled with the gun.

"George," Lucy said, "this is stupid. Just because he's crazy doesn't mean you have to be." She moved between them.

George didn't listen. He pointed the gun past her shoulder and squeezed the trigger. Nothing happened.

"Damn!" He fiddled with the pistol. Gilray made no attempt to escape.

She would end this farce, then knock some sense into George's hormone-sodden brain. He pointed the gun again. Lucy reached toward him. As she did she tripped on the hem of her dress. She fell. Her cheek slapped the side of the gun's barrel, and the gun went off.

She felt a blow at her temple. The floor rose up to strike her; the room grew dark. How typical! she thought. The invisible woman. Shot by her husband while trying to keep him from killing a man who had wanted to rape her. Her only regret was that if this was death, no one would ever know that she had done it, not to save either of them, but for herself.

36: FRIDAY, DECEMBER 31
....
Richard Escapes

Richard had gone far over the top the previous night. Lost in the crowd, he'd gotten separated from Felton, swept up and clinging to the blond girl like a man clinging to a life raft in some voodoo hurricane he had conjured up himself.

After whippings and chantings and ravings the tide had deposited him and the girl on the west side of the Pad, in a tract house that had been taken over by a horde of pilgrims. There Richard organized certain rituals of his spontaneous invention. He ended up alone in the house's bedroom with the girl, whose name was Dawn. The bedroom, furnished in bogus French Provincial, had been untouched by the disruptions of the last months, and in this room, with preterhuman disinterest, Richard abused the fervent young woman through the night. She in turn abused him. By candlelight he saw reflected in her eyes the vision of a God of glorious extermination, a God that he did not relish the prospect of ever having to face.

When daylight came up he saw no reason not to continue. Richard explained to Dawn that they had been kidnapped by aliens, who had filled their heads with false memories to cover up their abduction. The bedroom was a cage in some extraterrestrial zoo, and the sounds outside were their captors studying them to determine normal human behavior. The girl believed him. They barricaded the door and put on an exhibition. At some point during his tenth or twelfth hour with Dawn, Richard passed out. When he awoke it was dusk and the house was deserted. His head throbbed and his stomach felt as if it were filled with cinders. Dried blood and bits of hair were stuck to his hammer. From beneath a mattress on the floor stuck a young woman's bare legs.

It was dark before he could find his way back to the Institute. He had some trouble persuading the guards at the gate who he was, but with the End so near their vigilance was relaxed. He slipped and skidded on the icy drive, past the snow-cloaked statue of Christ and into the lobby. The place seemed empty, but on the way to his room he met Felton in the hall.

"The Reverend had been worried about you. We thought you were dead."

"Not yet," Richard said, rubbing his temples. "What time is it?"

"After nine." Felton looked nervous. "Everyone's at the Landing Pad. The Reverend will be back here at ten, though, briefly."

Richard was too fuzzy to wonder why. "Tell him to come get me before he goes back. I'll be ready."

He showered and shaved and found clean clothes. Images of the sick, pretty girl flashed before him. He could not shake them. He remembered the first time George had introduced him to Lucy. Lucy was so sincere, so serious. She expected a lot from George. Richard was astounded that George would let himself get hooked up with someone so straight; he couldn't believe that George would seriously try to make a commitment that they both knew would never work.

Well, it hadn't. Richard remembered the last time he had seen George, over the phone from Tallahassee, how thin he had looked, how troubled.

Enough. He forced the memory away. He cleaned and polished his hammer and draped it around his neck. The hammer's weight pressed reassuringly against his heart; the cord tugged at his collar. He checked himself in the mirror. The skin below his eyes sagged a little, but a simple foundation took care of that. By all outward appearances, he was ready for the end of the world.

Richard went out to the next room, slid open the drawer and selected another tab of acid. He poured an inch of Glenmorangie to wash it down. He fell back in an armchair and waited for the Rev. While he sat there he had a wonderful idea: when Christ came again maybe Dawn would be resurrected. Except Richard didn't believe in Christ. He tried to figure out whether that made any difference. The LSD began to take hold. The intensity of the room's light increased, his black robe became blacker, the texture of the wallpaper stood out. The rush of the heating system drifted up into audibility. After awhile the light began to hurt his eyes. Richard found an old pair of mirrored sunglasses and put them on.

Still Gilray did not show. It seemed to Richard that the room vibrated with the steady thrum of distant engines, as if he were indeed on a space vehicle. With some relief he realized it was only the sixty-cycle hum of the lamp on the end table. He turned it off. He lit the candles. The flames threw faint shadows of the furniture against the walls and ceiling, and the room became a monastic cell. Richard sat in his chair and imagined he was living in 999 A.D., waiting for the end in a world of faith instead of one of video executions and phosphor-dot politicians.

He heard the footsteps approaching his door long before the knock came. Richard pulled the cloak tight around his shoulders. "Come in," he said. "It's open."

For a moment whoever it was outside the door hesitated, and then it opened. At first Richard did not recognize the man: big, rumpled, with a heavy beard and thick, unruly hair. He wore black jeans, a black turtleneck and a black jacket. In the shadowed room he looked like a bear in man's clothing. George.

"Fancy meeting you here!" said Richard. He got out of the chair and went to George, extending his hand. "A pleasure, a real pleasure! Where you been keeping yourself, pal?"

George stared at Richard's extended hand as if it were a dead fish. He kept his hands in the jacket's pockets. "You look ridiculous, Richard."

"I do, don't I. It's this robe. All the prophets have them. I don't want to wear it, but it's in the contract."

"I want to talk to you."

Richard turned his back, paced the room. On each swing by he peeked past George at the door. George stood still, blocking the way out. "Nothing I'd like better than to have a little chat with you, George. Only, you see, I've got an important meeting tonight. Big rally. You might have heard, it's the end of the world."

"I've heard."

"You didn't see the Rev out there, did you? Any murders? Fighting? Angels?"

"Lots of murders. No angels. I don't think angels are very likely. What do *you* think, Richard?"

"I think it's time I got going. I'm already late. Who can say where that wacky Reverend is, huh, George?"

"He's been unavoidably delayed. Tell me about the end of the world."

"Catastrophes. Lights in the sky. Messages. Sudden and miraculous change."

"You really think that's going to happen?"

Richard looked at his watch. Its ticking was like a hammer striking an anvil. "In . . . one hour and thirteen minutes."

"Eastern Standard Time."

Richard smiled. "Still got the old sense of humor, George. Of course Eastern Standard Time. That's where *we* are. God sets his clock to go along with ours." Richard wondered, if he simply went up to George and pushed him aside, whether George would let him go. George looked fit and well fed and not easily moved. He was a different man from the one who'd called Richard from the road.

"Are you looking to leave, Richard?"

"Not a bit. What gives you that impression?"

"I just thought something about talking to me was bothering you. Why don't you tell me what's on your mind."

"George, I didn't mean that you should get hurt. That Delano's a crazy woman. I told her to go easy, but she was out of control."

"Do I look hurt to you?"

"Actually, you look pretty good, George. You surprise me. I thought you would be in much worse shape after being on the road for so long, especially the way things have gotten in the last few months."

"Delano gave me a shot in the arm."

"Delano did? Imagine that."

"You lied to me, Richard. You could have told me Lucy had disappeared."

"Sure. I could have done a lot of things, but would it have made any difference? I didn't know where she was. She was furious at you. At least this way you could go on believing she cared."

"You let me make a fool of myself."

"Face it, George. You've never needed much help. After all, you're the one who killed himself."

"And I remember how you tried to stop me. All those talks we had about lethal genes and absurdity had nothing to do with me offing myself. I don't hold you responsible in any way."

The room seemed very hot and bright. Richard could see George's eyes even in the candlelight. He turned away and stared at a candle flame on the dresser. It undulated like an erotic dancer in the faint breeze as either of them moved.

"I'm glad you feel that way, George. That's the way I feel, too. Well, what say we get on and find the Rev? Time's wasting. There's work to be done."

"What's going to happen, Richard, after midnight?"

"The world's over then, George. Catastrophe."

"What if there is no catastrophe?"

"That would be catastrophic."

"You don't believe that."

Richard couldn't take much more of this. He had a wonderful idea. Oh, was he on tonight! He grabbed himself by the throat. He jerked his head back as if he were being pulled from behind, held his finger to his temple like a gun.

"Don't make any false moves, pal," he threatened, "—or the hammer-man gets it!"

"Richard, are you out of your mind?"

"Please!" Richard said in his own voice, "Do what he says! I don't think he's kidding."

He shoved his head back further, almost falling over backward. "You bet I'm not, Chucko," he growled.

"This is a pretty desperate move," said George.

"You bet I'm desperate."

"You can't escape that easily."

"We'll see about that, copper."

"You'll never get out of this building alive."

Richard grabbed for the imaginary arm around his neck and jerked it forward and down, pulling his nonexistent captor over his head. He kicked the invisible man in the groin. "Thank God you showed up, George!" he gasped. "I've got loose of him! Now's our chance to escape. Help me."

"I'm trying to."

Richard felt his anger build. "Let's go! It's rally time, bozo! I've knocked this madman out for now, but who knows how long before he comes to? You don't realize how dangerous he is. He's had me trapped in here for months. I've tried everything. Notes on toilet paper. Morse code on the pipes."

"But you were unable to escape."

"How could I? Lives hung in the balance! And he knows all about you, George. He made me tell him. You sicken him, George, you know that? He hates your guts, and it would please him greatly to see you dead. He was the one who made you kill yourself. He says you come on like a cynic, but you're full of pollyanna crap. You never could grow up so you just opted out. He says the only reason Lucy stuck with you is that she was a professional martyr."

"There's a lot of truth in that. He must know me pretty well."

Richard felt the sweat gather on his brow. The room seemed full of noise. "I don't know. But this kidnapper's a desperate man. He'll stop at nothing."

"Does the Reverend know about him?"

"The Rev's been taken in by him. He thinks this guy is some sort of prophet."

George indicated the crucifix on one wall and the velvet Elvis painting on the other. "He's got terrible taste."

"Run for help, George. Hurry. I'll keep an eye on him."

George stared at Richard. His eyes were pure and direct as the candle flames. It made Richard realize that people were sort of like biological candle flames, slowly combusting, burning up. That was how they kept alive. Everything they did was the product of this combustion. It was a wonderful idea.

"Richard," George said, "there is no kidnapper."

"He's invisible! Just because you can't see him doesn't mean he can't have a gun pointed at my head."

"There's no one here but you and me."

"George, why would I make up such a stupid story? You're my best friend. We haven't seen each other in months. I thought you were dead. You show up and what do you get—some warmth, some surprise, some joy? No. Instead I treat you like the straight man in a farce. You ask me tough personal questions. I evade them. If it weren't for this kidnapper, why would I put you through such a pointless conversation?"

"I don't know."

"You've got to believe me!"

"Why? Do you really care what I think about you?"

Damn him! They were both burning up, he and George, as they stood there. Yet George wanted Richard to abandon the Game before it was over. Why should Richard commit himself first?

He couldn't. He pointed at the imaginary kidnapper. "He's coming to. Let's go!"

George looked only at Richard. "Goodbye, Richard."

"Goodbye? You're not leaving?"

"Yes. I think you've got the situation under control." George turned toward the door. "That's a nice hammer you've got there."

It was like the touch of a knife against Richard's throat. It took all of his skill to keep the Game together. "It is, isn't it. And it comes in handy, too, sometimes. You should get one for yourself."

"I don't need one. I'm not saying you don't, though." George walked out, closing the door softly behind him.

Richard had never felt so strange. Success. Total success! He had broken through into a new reality. He was absolutely alone. His stomach lurched as if a trap door had opened beneath him. He looked around a room gone suddenly alien, his senses pitched to a raging storm. The clock display on the phone vidunit read 11:03. The numbers glowed with fiery intensity. As Richard watched, the readout changed to 11:04. He could hear everything in the building. The murmur of voices. The faint squeal of the disk brakes on the Reverend's Lincoln as Felton drove up out front. The prayers and screams of pain from the crowd at the Landing Pad. The sound of cancer cells dividing in his brain. The hum of spinning atoms, the rumble of entropy increasing as time slipped irrevocably by. It was late.

He knew what came next. The candle flames swayed, bright as souls burning in Purgatory, amber with hearts of faltering gray. He listened to the hiss of their burning. He sat down on the edge of the chair and leaned forward, elbows on his knees. He took the hammer in both hands, gripping it in his fists like a baseball bat, claws toward his face. Their gold tips pointed at his eyes. The handle was slick with his sweat. His forearms trembled. He closed his eyes, imagined the force it would take, the awful scene it would create. The muscles in his arms ached. His heart raced and he could hardly catch his breath. Convulsively he jerked the hammer upward. But his head pulled back from the blow, and he struck himself glancingly, the claws biting into his forehead and sliding off. The shock was brutal. He flopped to the floor. He lay there for a moment. The blood streamed over his brow and into his left eye. He'd done no more than gash his forehead. Coward.

He forced himself to his knees. He blinked, saw the candles on the table, heard voices in the living room. Quickly, now. He squeezed his eyes tight, on his knees in front of the velvet of Elvis. That was a good one. His laugh was a muffled bark. Blood from his forehead slid down his cheeks like tears, dripped off his chin onto his hands. No more time. The candleflames roared like a furnace. His pulse thrummed in his ears, a racing engine. He felt stronger than he had ever felt in his life. He pushed the hammer down and away, steady as a machine, then yanked his fists toward his face with all the force of his will. There was no resistance. The hammer flew up as if falling from a height. He felt a stinging at the bridge of his nose, saw a flash of light.

37: FRIDAY, DECEMBER 31
....
The Reverend Wrestles with an Angel

Time was running out, things were going wrong. Richard had been missing all day. Felton searched for him, but the crowds at the Landing Pad were in such disarray that it was hopeless. Men and women fleeing from Zion reported the army had retaken the capitol in heavy fighting. Charles Duke Sumner had gone down with his state. Hysterical rumors said they would attack the Landing Pad next, and in truth the Reverend Jimmy-Don Gilray could see little reason why they wouldn't.

Still other rumors said that Richard had been taken up into Heaven, been killed by jealous rivals, was passing in disguise among the people. The staff panicked. Gilray pressed forward with the broadcasts. He spent most of the afternoon on the platform, hoping that Richard might show up, but as the early twilight was succeeded by darkness his thoughts turned to his upcoming meeting with Lucy. He grew anxious. It was no time for second thoughts, but maybe it was inevitable that a man should have second thoughts on the eve of the Second Coming.

It was well past ten before he was able to slip back to the Institute. He was greeted by another problem. An hour before, Felton had been attacked by two strangers at the front entrance, and had felled one of them with a cross-kick. The man, slender, bearded and vaguely familiar, might have a broken neck, according to Dr. Vance, and Felton was thrown into despair at the thought that this act of violence, coming on the verge of the End, might condemn him to perdition. Felton was the last person Gilray expected to have doubts. He assured Felton that the Lord would recognize the goodness in his heart, but Felton confessed he'd enjoyed hurting the man. Impatiently, Gilray made him get down on his knees. Together they prayed for forgiveness.

There was no time. Instead of love, Gilray was filled with anger. After this fuss Felton told him that Richard had returned and was in his room. Gilray realized that Lucy would have to wait while he sent Richard over to the Landing Pad. He told Felton to get the car and hurried to Richard's apartment.

The door was unlocked, the living room dark. He heard a rustling like the crumple of stiff fabric, but with an organic swish to it that raised the hairs on the back of his neck. Across the room an object jerked in the shadows. Some animal—a person crouched over upon himself. Gilray fumbled for the light switch, turned. The figure untwisted, straightened up and stood facing him. It was Lucy Di Paulo.

He felt no relief. "What are you doing here?"

"Waiting for you."

The woman wore a black turtleneck, black pants. She looked deadly as a pistol. "You're not Lucy," he said.

"Don't I look like Lucy?"

"I saw you change."

"Don't believe everything you think you see. I'm here in the flesh. You can touch me." The woman held her hand out toward him.

He backed away. "Who are you?"

"I should think you'd be eager to talk with me."

"I haven't got the time." If only he could will the clock to slow! Two thousand years of history were being wedged to their end through these minutes, in this place. Seconds crammed together so tight he could feel their heat, every event full of implication that flitted by too fast for him to read. Richard, Felton, the crippled man. Prefigured in the mind of God. He edged toward the door.

The woman smiled. "I've been sent by God to talk."

He stopped.

"I'm here to answer your questions," she said. "Your faith has earned you a direct revelation. Go ahead. Ask me anything."

"You're not from God. You're one of—those creatures."

"I'm an angel."

"You're no angel."

The woman moved gracefully toward him. "I don't fit the cliche. I'll admit that. I'm also capable of doing a few things that angels are not generally known to do. Still, I am an angel."

"You're made of flesh."

"As far as that goes, yes. The word 'angel' means simply, 'Like a man.' In this case, 'Like a woman.'" She reached out and touched his cheek. "Exactly like a woman."

He inhaled her perfume, then, convulsively, stepped back. No time. "You're one of those that impersonated Vance, back in Lexington."

"An instructive experience."

He grabbed hold of himself. It was just another test. Was he large enough for this moment, able not to be tricked again? "If you're from God, answer me some questions."

"Sure will."

"Will the world end tonight?"

"Can there be any doubt?"

"Answer me."

"Yes. The world you know will end tonight."

"Will it happen as the prophets predicted?"

"Yes, it will."

"Exactly as they said?"

"More or less. All prophets are subject to interpretation. You've made a career interpreting them."

Gilray wondered whether this might be Lucy after all. "If you're an angel, then you know what God wants."

"He sort of wants you to be good to one another, but to tell the truth He hasn't been too consistent on that. Sometimes we wonder if He's sincere."

"You mock Him. That's blasphemy."

"Right. That's what he's really worried about. The Golden Rule is salad. The main course is that you should believe in Him. If you don't He'll damn you to eternal perdition."

"Don't turn this into a joke."

"Who's joking? He means it. Believe or get microwaved. That's why He loves your little Protestant bottom so much, my beloved. You're one of His true disciples. You brought the Good News. If anyone has seen so much as ten minutes of one of your broadcasts and still refuses to believe, he's toast. No second chances with The Big Juan."

"An angel wouldn't use sarcasm, either."

"It must be your ears. I'm just telling the truth—as much as I, a mere angel, am able to understand His divinity."

Gilray kept his distance. Where was Richard? The door to the bedroom was closed; he glanced at his watch. 11:18. He needed to get back to greet the Savior—but the Savior could come in a manner they did not expect. "Will I be saved, then?"

"Sure. Everybody who believes will be, regardless of his actions. Don't worry about how people take what you've preached. All those suicides, those murders. Your motives were pure. You never told anyone to do anything wrong. If you did you didn't mean it, and if you meant it that was only because it was necessary to save the world."

"What about those who fought me?"

"Straight to Hell. Doesn't matter what they think they're doing. Their souls are twisted, they'll pay for it forever. They've got only—" the woman closed her eyes, "—thirty-nine minutes to find Jesus."

"Then God approves of my ministry?"

"God *loves* you. Remember where he said, 'I will show thee thy bride.'" She spread her arms wide. She was beautiful. "Well, *I* am your bride. You've been preaching salvation through love. Here I am, the lamb's wife, sent to fulfill you."

He looked at the closed bedroom door, and was afraid. "You aren't any angel. You're an alien."

"How do you know that?"

"You're a physical being. I saw you change."

"Only thirty-eight minutes left. A bad time to start doubting."

"I won't be cheated."

"You can't cheat an honest man. If you're going to doubt, then why not just call me a demon from hell, a Satanic ruse?"

"You are a Satanic ruse."

"Test me. Recite the Lord's Prayer and see if I vanish." She held out her hand again. "That cross on your lapel—press it against me and see if it scorches my skin."

Gilray slid away from her. She had circled around until she was between him and the door.

"God knew you would doubt, Jimmy," she said. "He gave me a parable to tell you. The parable of the Woman who Believed in Aliens."

"I don't have time."

She came toward him. He stepped back and stumbled into a chair. "You have time for this story."

He gripped the chair's arms. "I—"

"Once there was a woman who believed in Aliens from Outer Space—"

He tried to get up; she pushed him back down.

"Her childhood was hard," she continued. "Her mother was an invalid, and her father molested her. When the girl went to her, her mother called her a wicked child. She turned inward. Because her cold mother was a churchgoer, the girl rejected religion. She turned to science. She came to believe that a greater than human intelligence existed in the universe.

"At first this belief was based on nothing more than need. But as time went on she accumulated evidence. First were statistics: there are more than a hundred billion stars in the Milky Way galaxy, and as many galaxies in the universe as stars in the Milky Way. Out of this huge number it stood to reason intelligent life would arise on more than one world. To think otherwise would be to give humans too privileged a place in the universe.

"She took consolation in this. When her mother died she moved in with an aunt. She was an untidy girl, tongue-tied and awkward. She did well in school but got no reward. Instead of a prominent college, she managed only to get into the state university. There she fell in love with a brilliant young pre-med. They slept together. She got pregnant. She and the boy married, and she dropped out in order to raise the child and support him."

"What has this got to do—"

"—with you? Just listen!

"The only way to imagine the human race alone, the woman thought, would be to suppose that it had been created uniquely by a God that wanted only one race in the cosmos and had fashioned the rest of it just for show. But the woman who believed in Aliens didn't believe in that stingy God, so she peopled the universe with the many races her common sense told her must exist out there. She wondered whether these Aliens might ever contact human beings. Perhaps they had contacted us in the past. Perhaps they were in contact with us even now. Perhaps they even were available for contact with her personally!

"Eventually she got a job as a teacher's aide. She took care of her husband and their children without calling too much attention to her beliefs. But then, in the last year of his residency, her husband fell in love with a nurse. He filed for divorce. The woman who believed in Aliens did not contest it, so long as she received custody of the children. She enrolled in school and worked toward her teaching certificate.

"Meanwhile her mind worked furiously over the possibility of Aliens. She decided that, having evolved on distant planets under vastly different conditions, Aliens must be vastly different from human beings. Their thought processes would be strange. To come in contact with such beings might be horrifyingly disorienting. They might seem superficially to be reasonable beings, or even to resemble humans, but then, when one might least expect it, they would reveal their true colors. To trust them would be madness."

It was madness for him to risk himself here. But he couldn't be sure that the woman wasn't sent to him. She sat on the arm of the chair, looking directly at him as she spoke. Warm voice. Smooth skin. Her body close to his. The seconds raced by.

"The woman began to write a book. Though she received her degree with honors she could not find a teaching job—she gave very bad interviews. She ended up working as a waitress. In her book she expounded her theories, but she received little sympathy. This only reconfirmed her conviction that she was right.

"The Alien mind, she deduced, must be antithetical to all that was humane, while carefully maintaining a mask of humanity. Perhaps this mask of humanity even went so far as to convince the Aliens themselves, so that they could act abominably toward humans while still, sincerely, insisting on their good will. If you challenged an Alien's behavior it would react with stunned innocence. It would suggest that any protest was only paranoid delusion. This is how devious and subtle, how truly unlike human beings, they were."

He felt desire. He felt afraid. He tried again to get up, but the woman put her hand on his chest and pushed him back into the chair.

"Listen," she said. "Here comes the interesting part. About this time her ex-husband sued for custody of the children on the grounds that he could better provide for them. The woman who believed in aliens could not afford a good lawyer. Her husband used her manuscript as evidence that she was mentally unbalanced. He received custody. The woman did her best to accept this decision. Perhaps she was not a fit mother. She poured her energies into her theories.

She explained them to her friends at the restaurant. When they stopped listening she turned to the customers. She was fired, and soon after was committed to an institution.

"There she completed her book on the science of Alien Hating. For she had discovered the true nature of aliens: they are alien. Men are good. Men are reasonable. Aliens are evil. As a result of their millions of years of evolution in different corners of the universe, as a result of their bizarre genetic makeup, as a result of travel over killing distances through unknown radiations, Aliens had become devious, subtle, bent, many-faced, hypocritical, superior, uncouth, self-righteous, programmatic, inconsistent, sexually imperialistic drones, incapable of existing in harmony with human beings. Such vile creatures were beneath contempt. The only sane response to them was fear and hatred. It was not necessary to understand—understanding them was an impossibility—one's duty was only to identify and exterminate them.

"Unfortunately, by this time she also realized that the hospital was being run by Aliens. That her husband was an Alien. That her father and mother had been Aliens, that in fact Aliens had conquered the world. She was helplessly in their power. The woman who believed in Aliens did not respond to therapy and remained in confinement for the rest of her life. And that was that."

Smiling faintly, she caressed the hair at his temple. He flinched. It was near twelve. Out in the fields the thousands were gathered, waiting. For him. For Jesus. He didn't know whether this woman was here to save him or damn him to hell. Her eyes were clear and direct. She was so close. He had dreamed about her. He cast about for a sign, seeking certitude in the place in himself where he had always found it, but all he got was a great silence. My God, my God, why hast thou forsaken me?

"That's it?" he said. "Some murky story? After all I've suffered? After all this pain? God wouldn't tease me like this!"

"This is no tease. It's a warning against doubt! Forget these Alien delusions, these satanic theories. Trust only in the Lord. The fearful, and unbelieving, and the abominable, and murderers and whoremongers, and sorcerers and idolators, and all liars, shall have their part in the lake which burneth with fire and brimstone.''

"Don't taunt me."

"Taunt you?" She leaned closer. Her face was inches away, her breath fragrant. "An angel would never taunt you," she said. She kissed him. Her lips were warm. Molecules in the air. History ending. Prefigured in the mind of God.

She slid onto his lap, arms around his neck. "Let me save you now," she whispered. "It's not only what you want; it's what God wants for you. It's why he sent me here—only for you, Jimmy."

Her flesh was so warm. Seconds crammed with heat, the last moments of the world. He could not think. His body responded to her. Inside him was no certainty, only panic and desire. He wanted her. She beckoned him into the world of doubt. She would make him give up everything for her, and he would never know if it was right or wrong.

He jerked out of the chair, dumping her on the floor. "No."

She calmly picked herself up. "It's only what you want."

"No." He pushed away. "It isn't."

"You're missing a great opportunity."

"Then I'll miss it."

"One time only."

"Go away!"

"Sale ends at midnight."

"Get thee behind me!"

She sighed. "Whatever you say, Jimmy." She walked to the door, opened it and left.

Gilray breathed hard. He had done it. He was strong. But after some moments came a feeling of unutterable loss. There was a void where his heart should be. He was sweating; he could not catch his breath. He fell back in the chair, realizing he was having an asthma attack. He stuck his head between his knees and tried to calm his spasming lungs. His vision blurred.

After awhile it stopped. Gilray looked up. The building was silent. His watch read 12:10. It was as if the woman had never been there. He got up and opened the door to Richard's bedroom. It was lit only by the guttering stubs of a couple of candles. Richard lay on the floor with the claws of his hammer stuck into his crushed forehead. The carpet was black with his blood. Gilray reeled. He fell back into the living room. After some minutes he forced himself to search through Richard's pockets until he found the room key. He locked the outer door and left.

Felton was still waiting in the foyer. "It's after midnight!" he said. "Where's Mr. Shrike?"

"He's gone on ahead," said Gilray. He avoided Felton's stare and led him out to the car. They drove to the Landing Pad. From the road Gilray could see the searchlights scanning the empty sky, hear shrieking and tumult. He rolled down the window. Bodies pressed close. From somewhere near the highway came the sounds of automatic gunfire. People in the Glaxo lot cheered as the limousine slid to a stop. They reached out to touch the car; they left handprints on the windows. Felton and two militiamen cleared a path for him. Gilray tried to identify the stirring in his chest as something other than the return of the illness that had tormented him through his childhood. Near the platform, behind the barricade, Boston rushed up to him.

"It's past Midnight! He didn't come!" Boston grabbed him by the arm. "Harrison has a plane ready. We need to get away!"

Gilray wanted to slap him. The anchor of Boston's universe had broken loose and all he could do was cluck like a chicken and run.

Gilray mounted the steps, strode to the pulpit. From this vantage he could see that thousands had broken through the fence into the Landing Pad. They waved torches. They leapt toward the sky and begged for the New Jerusalem to descend and, if not save them, then crush them beneath it. Gilray raised his hands and out of the havoc of the crowd came something like an articulate cheer. It howled about him like the wind, heavy with the same hysteria that whipsawed Boston. The Reverend lowered his arms, but it was minutes before they subsided. The people were on the verge of insanity. They were not prepared to face another morning. Had he shown up an hour later they would have been gibbering like lunatics, dancing on the corpses of the ones who had killed themselves, an inch away from slaughter and cannibalism and worse. The void in his chest had grown, was growing still.

"Brothers and Sisters!" he shouted. "I come to you with Good News!" Feedback squealed and echoed across the pad. The people cheered. The twisted bodies on the concrete paused. He could imagine them lifting their bloody heads to listen.

He felt the eyes of the cameras focus on him. On the stadium screens, and on a million other screens around the world, they watched him. "We have had a close encounter! Not half an hour ago God sent to me one of His angels. The Time has come!"

A great roar.

"But the End is not yet!" he shouted. He grabbed the microphone and left the pulpit. The cameras followed. "God has made a New Covenant with me, His unworthy servant. A covenant of cosmic significance that we must guard as jealousy as did the Israelites the first Ark of the Covenant! The unbelievers will mock us, but we must persevere. God assures us our salvation, in a little while longer, if we will do His work."

Gilray felt the void in him, cold as outer space, sucking his life away. He strode across the stage in fury.

"And He has given us a sign! He has given us a sign, good people! He has gathered into His bosom His servant Richard the Hammer!" The wind and the people howled. "This very night I saw the angel of the Lord touch him on the forehead. I saw him ascend into the heavens; the blinding light of salvation streamed from his extended fingertips as he was carried into the Ship of our Lord and Savior Jesus Christ. Tears of joy, of totally fulfilled hope, were flowing down his face and mine, when Richard said to me these last words:"

Gilray stood at the edge of the platform. Beyond were darkness, bonfires, madness. He let the void propel his voice outward. " 'Tell them, Jimmy!' " he shouted, weeping. " 'Tell all God's people to hold fast to their faith. They've got to have faith. In this time of trouble, faith is all that stands between them and the pit of despair. It's up to you, Jimmy, to keep on. Their faith in you is going to save them.' "

38: FRIDAY, DECEMBER 31
....
The Secret Reagent

George hid in the dressing room listening to Lucy try to seduce Gilray. Through the louvered door he watched their silhouettes against the light, and once he was even tempted to shoot Gilray in the back. But he did not. Listening to Lucy's angry voice, he heard things he had not heard before.

He had seen her angry many times, but now he heard the undertone of fear. Hers was the voice of a reasonable person stressed beyond endurance, about to do something drastic. In Lucy's dance between accusation and seduction, George heard echoes of a hundred resentful bedroom debates from his life with her. The gun hung in his hand, heavy as a cinder block. He had never listened before. She had been crying for him to listen, and he had not.

Now she was trying to make herself sleep with Gilray, as if through that she could get revenge. Couldn't Gilray hear that? It was clear from every word Lucy spoke, from every silence. She didn't care that George was there; he was less than nothing to her. He felt impotent and ashamed.

Gilray was ranting; he sounded as if at any moment he might attack her. Lucy, incredibly, grew calmer as Gilray became enraged.

"You really need help," she said. It was not sarcasm, but realization. There followed a silence.

"No," Lucy said.

"No what?" said Gilray.

George glimpsed the hem of Lucy's dress as she rose from the bed and went over to Gilray. "I don't want it that way," she said. The faint clink of a glass being set down.

George slammed open the dressing room door. They stood together in the middle of the room. "Let go of her!"

Lucy pushed away from Gilray. "No, George—" she began.

"Someone has to stop him," George said. He fumbled with the gun. Gilray watched.

Lucy stepped between them. "George, this is stupid," she said. "Just because he's crazy doesn't mean you have to be."

George raised the gun and pointed past her. Gilray's face was placid. George yanked on the trigger, but it would not budge.

The safety was on.

"Damn!" he said. He pried at the lever. It was stuck. Gilray made no attempt to move. Lucy stepped forward just as George got the thing unlocked. He jerked back from her grasp; she tripped, fell against his arm, and the gun went off beside her ear. The recoil flipped the pistol out of his hand. Lucy slid to the floor.

"No!" George shouted. He knelt beside her. He had not hit her, but the blast had bloodied her ear. Her temple was blackened with powder. "Lucy."

"She'll be all right," Gilray said.

"You hope!" George said. "I was trying to kill you."

"I noticed."

"I could still do it."

"No doubt."

Lucy breathed shallowly. George helped her to lie more comfortably. He ought to get a wet cloth and see if he could bring her around.

"Don't worry about her," Gilray said. "It's time to get to the Landing Pad. Jesus will arrive soon."

George looked up. "You know better than that. These aren't some agents of God you're meeting. They're aliens."

"They're God's aliens. We call them angels."

George scrambled across the carpet for the gun. Gilray waited, calm as Christ before Pilate. When George jumped up his vision swam. He leaned against the chair in front of Gilray's computer. "You're doing their work," he said. "I've been keeping track of them, and I know the havoc they've caused. They've destroyed people's lives all over the country."

"Unless you lose your life you cannot save it."

"I'm talking about real, technological beings!"

"The Bible tells us to expect the return of Christ."

George began to see that he could bash his brains out against Gilray's God and not make a dent. "They're just using those prophecies to get their foot in the door!" he insisted. "Who's to say that these beings haven't been setting up events for forty years so that they would fit in with your interpretation of the Bible?"

"Who's to say they didn't inspire the prophecies in the first place, two thousand years ago?"

"Okay. But now they're ready to step in and pick up the pieces. And you've prepared millions to welcome them with open arms."

"Don't give me all the credit. Your friend Richard was a big help."

"What matters is that you've convinced people what's coming is salvation! It will be slavery."

"Lots of people call salvation slavery. They don't want to accept limits. That was predicted, too." Gilray looked at the pistol, then turned and picked up one of the glasses of wine. "Even if you kill me you can't stop what's been set in motion, George. You're exhausted. You're sick. Put down the gun and have a drink. Here, take mine. I'll pour myself another."

George *was* exhausted. He could use a drink. He looked at Lucy, still unconscious on the floor, and his anger grew. Alien ships were even then screaming through the ionosphere. Their hulls heated. Inside, the invaders assumed new disguises. Uncle Charlie, beautiful sister Sue. It was no time for drinking. "Forget it," he told Gilray. He gestured with the gun. "Put the glass down—slowly."

Gilray set the wine on the arm of the chair. "Suppose what you say is true," he said. "Suppose these angels that come tonight—"

"They're not angels," George said. "They're aliens. And they're not arriving tonight, they've been here for months, infiltrating and disrupting. I can give you a stack of stories this high of people hurt by them. They've lost their jobs, abandoned their marriages, killed themselves, all because of what the Alien did. He played a number on their heads."

"So did Jesus."

"Don't try to trick me. I'm talking about broken lives here."

"How can they do all this?"

"I don't know. They're unimaginably powerful. They must have group minds, infinite mutability, telepathy."

Gilray smiled. "Sounds pretty unlikely. But suppose I grant you that such superbeings exist. I'll even grant that they've been intruding in human affairs. Why assume they want to take over? Why can't they be angels of the Lord, sent to save souls?"

"They're terrorists."

"Maybe they're God's terrorists."

"They're physical beings—aliens."

"Aliens, angels—let's not argue terminology. Let's call them Prigoginic Agents."

George became wary. "What?"

"Don't be so dense. Suppose you've got an unstable society. Think of it as a thermodynamic system. Maybe at a lower input it was capable of dissipating incoming energy. But the stresses have increased, the energy input has doubled, tripled. Subsystems have broken down or new ones have been created that don't fit in. Positive feedback loops that blow up like a bad program. The whole system teeters on the brink of collapse. Yet we know that new energy input is going to come; we can't eliminate that."

In his black clothes, Gilray looked more like a spy than a preacher. George kept the gun on him. The UFO fleet banks over the Eastern seaboard, heading for Zion. Their advance agents are everywhere. "In such a situation there are two possibilities," Gilray said. "One: maximum entropy. The system collapses, disastrously. But there's another possibility: reorganization. A sudden change. The old patterns are swept away in an instantaneous state change, and a new structure emerges."

"I've heard this before," George said.

"Good news gets around," said Gilray. "The big question is, which result is more probable, collapse or reorganization? That depends."

"On what?" George's head was spinning.

"Suppose you introduce a reagent," said Gilray. "This reagent can push the system toward chaos, or toward the new structure."

"A reagent?" Infinite mutability. Unimaginable power.

"A reagent. It causes a reaction. The reaction converts one pattern of organization into another. Like a virus. It infects the old system, attacks the individual cells, imposes a new template on them . . ."

George realized what he had been trying to ignore: where had his shot struck? He pushed past Gilray and searched the wall behind him. There was no mark on it.

George had shot him, and it hadn't made any difference.

"You *are* one of them," George said.

The man looked completely like the Reverend. "Yes, I am," he said.

George felt as if a door he'd been pushing against had suddenly been jerked open. "You—you've been running this crusade just to destroy us."

"No. The real Rev did that. I'm just filling in for him with you and Lucy. The real Rev has been unavoidably detained."

"How? Why?"

"Imagine a creature with a group mind, infinite mutability, telepathy."

George gripped the useless gun. "What, is this a game to you? If you're that powerful there's no way humans can compete. Why not just take over?"

"Do a teacher and student compete? A parent and child? More to the point, do a bird and gravity?"

"Gravity isn't personal. It doesn't come to individuals and disrupt their lives."

"Ask the man falling off the cliff. Ask the hawk in flight."

George struggled to keep up. "Are you saying you're some force of nature?"

The Alien pointed at the wine glass. "Drink up, George. This getting at the truth is thirsty work. You've been at it for months. You deserve a little drink."

George laid the gun on the bed. "Please. I'm at your mercy. Just answer my questions."

"I'm prepared to answer them all," the Alien said. His smile was smooth as a well-told lie. "To invoke a change of state. Take Lucy here, for example," he said, gesturing toward her. "Her body is a system. It's been under stress. Being alive is stress enough, but there are other stresses. Rape. Imprisonment. Fear. Rage. A gun going off next to her head. Who's to say how her system will react to all that? It can collapse—we call it death. Or, under the influence of the Han virus, it can reorganize. But afterwards, it's never the same."

George had forgotten about Lucy. He looked down at her—and saw she was not breathing.

After all that had happened, he had not thought his body was capable of feeling such a jolt. It was as if someone had jerked his spine, snapping a long-dislocated vertebra into place. He dropped beside her. He felt her throat and found no pulse. How long?

He propped himself up on his knees, crossed his hands over one another and began CPR. He felt so weak. He looked up. The Alien stood there, watching. "Help me!" George said.

"The Lord helps those who help themselves."

George lifted Lucy's head, bent it back and opened her mouth. He covered it with his own and breathed into her. Her chest rose. Her lips tasted of wine. He blew again, then shifted back to chest compressions. He counted fifteen for every two breaths.

"I have to go now," the Alien said. "It's been nice talking with you."

"Wait!" George gasped. Eleven, twelve. "I need to know—" Thirteen, fourteen. "—what you've been doing here!" Fifteen. He shifted back to her mouth, blew hard once, twice.

"I can't talk with you while you waste time with her," the Alien said. "Come with me."

George felt Lucy's throat. No pulse. "I can't," he said.

"We've got all the big answers, George. We'll give you the universe."

George started the compressions again. "Fuck you."

Without a word, the Alien turned and left.

George kept at the CPR for some minutes with no success. Despair swept over him. He had been too slow. One last, fatal time he had failed to pay attention to her. He staggered to his feet and rushed out of the room. Levine had said there was some sort of clinic. He yanked a fire alarm and rushed down the corridor. "Help! Help!" he shouted. The building echoed with the buzzing alarm. It was deserted. The clock in the lobby read 12:15. The Millennium had arrived.

Around a corner he found a door open to a white room that smelled of disinfectant. Inside, Levine lay on a bed with his neck in a brace. George found a first aid kit and dashed back down the hall. Back in the Reverend's room he ripped open the case, found a prepared hypo of SOD, searched for Lucy's carotid and inserted the needle. He resumed CPR, hoping to infuse some of the chemical into her brain.

It seemed like hours later when a blond, bearded man in a flannel shirt came into the room. He got down on the floor. "Let's get her to the clinic," he said. "Grab her arms." Together they lugged Lucy down the hall. While George struggled to get her out of the dress, the man wheeled over a defibrillator. He moved with silent efficiency, directing George with simple commands. On the third try Lucy's heart started. "Lucky," the man muttered. He gave her a series of injections, hooked tubes to blood vessels in her arm and ran them through another machine. He examined the bruise on her temple, then got out a very long needle. "We'll need a nerve tissue sample," he said. "Who are you, anyway?"

"I'm her husband," said George.

"I hope you're not one of these religious nuts."

"I'm not."

"Thank God."

George focused on doing what the man told him. The rest of reality sloughed away until only Lucy occupied his attention. She seemed so fragile, the chance for her survival so slim. Her face was quiet. He had left her dying on the floor, an arm's length away.

The doctor, whose name was Vance, put Lucy on a respirator. He noted that she responded to a pin prick and that her irises contracted when struck by light. He could not say whether she would ever regain consciousness, and if she did whether she would have suffered serious brain damage.

George sat on a chair by her bed and watched. Vance went to work with the tissue sample.

After awhile George's remorse drove him from the clinic to the lobby. It had begun to snow. He stepped outside. In the distance he heard sounds of riot from the Landing Pad. No Father Ship yet. No saucers skipping across the sky in meaningful patterns, no archangels in glittering space suits. Everything was the same.

Big snowflakes swirled out of invisibility into the glare of the floodlights illuminating the statue of Christ, which wore a halo of accumulation. George stared at the back of the statue. It was not often that you got that vantage point on Christ. When Christ had hung there, nailed up on the wooden cross of Golgotha, there had been people in back of the hill as well as in front. Bystanders instead of participants. Maybe they had passed by in the night, saw the torchlight and the long, flickering shadows. Did they know that, up there, an age was ending and a new one beginning? Did they know that history was turning on the pivot point of that cross, that millions would live and die differently because of the man hanging on it? Trudging by in the Palestinian night, had the camel trader felt the change?

Probably not. Probably he'd had other things to worry about. People had gone on living, and nothing had seemed changed, or if there was a change, the reasons for and effects of it had not come clear to them. For the first time in his life George understood that, from a certain point of view, there were things more important than the end of the world.

It was cold. He went back to the clinic and watched Lucy. The respirator whirred. No change. Restless, he returned to the Reverend's apartment. All his anger was gone. He felt tired. The room was as they'd left it: the gun lay on the bed, Lucy's boots lay on the edge of Gilray's worktable, a bottle of wine stood on a tray beside the computer. Pinot noir—an inferior vintage. The corners of the room vibrated: each object looked infinitely strange, as if it had been constituted just before he walked in and would disappear the instant he left. Wearily, George sat down. The glass the Alien had given him still rested on the arm of the chair; throughout their conflict it had stood there without spilling. A miracle. He picked it up, leaned back, and drained the wine in one long pull.

It tasted like ambrosia. It was just what he needed.

April

················

Something further may follow of this Masquerade.
　　　　—*Herman Melville,* The Confidence Man

39: SATURDAY, APRIL 15

A Rupture of the Hypothesis

Some things did not change. April was still April. In the morning the trees still stood silent as columns in empty cathedrals, and mist still cloaked the ground below. Shoots of grass still thrust themselves blindly from the earth, unaware that they had done this innumerable times before, and the mockingbirds still called early outside the window, waking her with exhausting, beautiful song. On Saturday mornings it was just as hard for Lucy to pull herself from bed. Just as before, when she did, she found George already up and about.

Food was still a problem and work still a necessity. But the nature of the problem, and the work, had changed. Lucy was no longer a lawyer, exactly. There were no more lawyers—at least not in the way there had been lawyers before. Luz had been right about that. The law books didn't make any sense. Lucy could read the words all right, but some time soon after beginning a passage she would lose track of their meaning as they climbed pyramids of abstraction into atmosphere she could no longer breathe. Even the parts she could understand seemed needlessly complicated.

So instead of being a lawyer Lucy worked with some other people in a large building downtown, the former revenue building, trying to figure out how to keep things running well enough so that people got food and a place to sleep. Lucy had no official title, but if she had been required to come up with one it would be something like "mediator" or "diplomat." The military had made a deal with the Asian Economic Coalition to insure the area's economic independence. Traditional powers in the state reasserted themselves elsewhere, but within the Triangle things were a fertile mess. Lucy spent most of her time negotiating between the various interest groups that had fought with each other in the wake of the collapse: the religious factions left after the Reverend Gilray's departure, the neighborhoods, the returning secularists, the Green Party, various claimants of civil authority, Uncle Sam and his followers, the multinationals, the universities, the farmers, the elderly, the international relief agencies, Dr. Vance and his hospital cooperative.

In truth the people were not interested in fighting, or maybe they were just tired. Things had gotten pretty bad in January, after the end refused to come. The Reverend, undeterred by the failure of his prophecies but unable to wield power in the Triangle, had escaped to Haiti. You could watch him on TV, talking about the Millennium that was yet to come and warning about Women from Hell. Many people were disillusioned, many were angry. Even the ones who weren't had some thinking to do.

Saturday was the co-op's day to work on the garden. Lucy pulled herself out of bed. The bathroom shelves were littered with old Mr. Howard's collection of broken clocks, not one of them still working. But she knew it was late. Lucy drew a few ounces of water to wash her face, then saved the waste water in the tub out back. Her hair was coming back much more evenly than George's had. She kept it short. She put on an old sweatshirt and blue jeans and ate some of the ubiquitous brown rice the U.N. was distributing for the multinationals. George and the others were already gone. She walked to the garden they had planted down the block, in the vacant lot where two houses had been burned out. George, Mr. Howard and Pam Scully were planting the last of the tomatoes and beans. Rudy Karamajian was not there. Lucy took a shovel from the carport they used for storage and started turning over the earth in what was to be the potato patch. After awhile George joined her.

"Good morning," he said.

"I overslept," she said. "Why didn't you wake me?"

"I said you were exhausted. We took a vote. Sleep won, 3-1." George set the blade of his shovel into the ground and leaned on it with his broken work shoes. The cuffs of his khakis gathered around his ankles. He followed along behind Lucy, cutting the second half of the row she was forming and turning over the earth. They worked methodically. George's face became flushed and he drew deep breaths. Lucy tried not to get too far ahead of him. She could smell her own sweat and feel the knots in her shoulders and arms loosen. Without realizing she was doing it, she started humming a song in rhythm with her spadework.

After a minute George started to sing the words:

> I know an old woman
> Who swallowed a fly
> I don't know why
> She swallowed a fly
> Perhaps she'll die.

> I know an old woman
> Who swallowed a spider
> That wriggled and jiggled and tickled inside her

> She swallowed the spider
> to catch the fly
> I don't know why
> She swallowed the fly
> Perhaps she'll die . . .

And so on. Lucy remembered the song from grade school; Mrs. Hadge's class, the second grade. She had beaten the rhythm sticks. "That must be an old song," she said. "Since we both know it."

"I think it is," he said.

His singing refreshed her memory and soon they were chanting the words together, shoving their blades into the ground on one line, turning the earth on every other one. The work became a kind of dance. Lucy let the song pull her along, and the future and past slipped beneath the expanding present. They worked. The sun got higher. Lucy giggled. She lost her breath. George lost his own. Soon they had worked over half of the potato plot. They leaned on the shovels, taking a break. Lucy's hands were sore, but the blisters of a month earlier had hardened into calluses. Pam came over with a jug of sun tea; they sat in the shade of an oak and drank.

Rudy showed up with a sack of seed potatoes and while Pam cut the potatoes into eyes the others started planting the pieces. Lucy and Mr. Howard worked on the second half of the plot. He had been a programmer before the change, had taken them all in, and he still talked about organizing the house like a parallel processor. Lucy was unsure exactly what a parallel processor was. After awhile Rudy reminded George that he had work to do at home. George kissed Lucy goodbye and left. His lips tasted salty.

Before she knew it, it was afternoon. They put the tools away and walked home. Lucy enjoyed feeling the sweat dry on her skin. The spring breeze was cool. She was pleasantly hungry. After they got back and washed up she found George in the workroom. Tables cluttered with dead radios, televisions, phone machines. Stacks of *National Geographics.* A lawn sprinkler. Thirty feet of hose. A rebuilt mimeograph machine. Beneath the window a shelf of seedlings. Posters of Krishnamurti and Da Vinci. Bottles of homebrewed beer. George sat in front of the computer, editing an advocacy piece for the Commandante's newswire. As he searched for an open phone line he listened to a baseball game on one of the few working radios. Some things had not changed. The

Red Sox had vowed not to let last September's collapse affect the new season and then promptly went out and lost their first seven games. George still expected such disasters.

"How's it going?" she asked him.

He looked up at her. "Inflammatory," he said. "We're talking about starting a new series. Every week we'll give away software that can penetrate a different government's intelligence system."

"Can you do that?"

"I don't know. The Commandante says governments are too messed up to act unilaterally and too suspicious of each other to unite. The multinationals will see it as good for business."

George filed his copy. In January, Commandante Jesus had revealed himself to be a syndicate of media hackers led by a guy in Toledo named Sid Wasserman. The announcement came from Reykjavik, where Wasserman had found backing to transform the underground network into a new multimedia information line, Absolute Truth. The Icelandic socialists had offered him asylum despite threats from the U.S., Japan, the Soviet Union and France. George thought it was a great idea. As soon as he was on his feet again he had signed on as a correspondent.

"How about something to eat?" Lucy asked.

"Lunchtime?" George said it like an incantation that would conjure up the hunger in him. "I guess so."

They joined Pam, Rudy and Mr. Howard in the kitchen and ate some peanut butter and corn bread. For dessert they shared the orange the others had given Lucy and George as an anniversary present. Over lunch they talked about the Commandante.

"You know," George said, "At one time I would have sworn there would be more to the Commandante than just some hacker."

"Maybe there is," said Pam. "It could be your aliens." From the time she had first heard about George's theories, Pam had enjoyed teasing him.

"No," George said. "He's just a man. You can't blame aliens for everything."

"Give us hackers some credit, Pam," Mr. Howard said.

"I thought there was going to be an invasion," said George. "The Rev thought Christ was coming. We were both wrong."

"When I was sick," Lucy said, "I remember you telling me some story about the Rev being an alien, George."

"The Rev is just a man, too. I talked to someone who looked like him, but that was different. Maybe I could believe that one was an alien, but in the end what he was doesn't matter. All that matters is what he did."

"What did he do?" Rudy asked.

"He made me take care of Lucy."

Lucy watched George's face. He had gained back some of the weight he had lost, but he was far from being the bear he was in her memory. George had cared for Lucy during her revival, despite the fact that he'd gotten so sick after the first of the year that it looked for awhile as if he would die again. Then Lucy got it. They called it a flu epidemic. Lucy suspected otherwise. She had died trying to stop Luz's virus from getting out, but somehow it had happened anyway.

She remembered coming awake in Dr. Vance's clinic. She had stared at the ceiling, convinced that this was the beginning of the afterlife. That George was there seemed strange. He waited patiently, sitting by the window. His eyes were sunken and his brow damp—he must already have been feeling the first symptoms. He came to her, leaned over the bed to kiss her on the forehead. "I'm sorry I left you," he said. "I won't ever again."

It did not seem to her then that she was alive and in the world so much as that George had somehow managed to come with her to this new, illusory world. She awaited the final judgment. The reward, the punishment. Certainly she had done enough things that warranted punishment, and some few that deserved reward.

Instead she was in the world again, living with George and the others in Mr. Howard's junk-filled house. George understood what she was going through. He persuaded her that to deny reality was only an escape. He told her to trust her senses. She tried it. What a discovery! There was physical work, air to breathe, food to find, music and stories. Everything seemed more solid. She wondered how she had been able to ignore the reality of things so easily—of work, sex, weather, animals, food. Now they filled her days. Even when she could not think things through consecutively, the way she had before, often the resolution to problems would come to her, neat and clear, dazzling as a jazz solo, a quilt pattern, the veins of a leaf.

After lunch Pam and Rudy went to the park. Mr. Howard went to spend the night with his friend Dillard Stamp. George took a nap. For the first time in a month Lucy had an afternoon alone, with no work to do. It made her nervous. She tried reading a book, but she could not concentrate. As the day wore on the sky clouded, threatening rain. She turned on the TV and flipped through the channels. The epidemic was raging worldwide. Many had died. In North America the worst seemed to have passed, but elsewhere public health systems were overstrained. Wirsen, a Swedish brain specialist, had reported that the virus, though resembling influenza, caused subtle neurological alterations. Unfortunately, the Swede had contracted the disease himself and others had been unable to substantiate his results. Lucy hoped Luz was still alive to appreciate her success, and to take some responsibility.

Around five o'clock the front bell rang. George was still asleep and no one else was back. When Lucy opened the door she was stunned to find Richard standing there.

But immediately she saw it was not Richard: it was someone who had undergone manipulation to make himself look like Richard. The process was not perfect. The man's hair and skin were Richard's, and his eyes were right, but the jaw was too square and he carried himself all wrong. Lucy supposed it would take a long time to get down Richard's solipsistic grace. She hoped it never would be possible.

The man held up a home-printed pamphlet. "My name is Richard Shrike," he began.

"No it isn't."

The man tried again. "I carry the reborn spirit of our recently departed prophet Richard Shrike—"

"No you don't," said Lucy, but the man's eyes and voice, close enough to Richard's to raise an echo, upset her.

"I have been restructured with a fragment of the True DNA of Richard Shrike—"

"Richard is dead," she insisted.

"Can't let that ruin the weekend, can we?" the man said. "Death's just a genetic accident."

Richard might have said that. Lucy clutched the doorknob.

"I represent the Church of the New Age. You've heard of us?"

"No."

"We believe," he said, "that the Millennium has indeed come, but it has come to each person individually. That God's agents, extraterrestrials, have met us all individually in the last years, and that we have been measured and judged. That all that has happened is part of His plan—"

The man's switch from cynicism to earnestness effectively destroyed the illusion, and Lucy was free. "I'm not interested," she said.

"This is an important message."

"I'm sure it is."

"The Aliens are still among us. They are running the world."

"I don't believe that."

"We have proof."

"We'll have to negotiate about that," Lucy said. "But not today."

The man stared at her, and the rage fueling his belief was visible for a moment. If she would not listen, then she was not worth talking to. He thanked her, then walked away toward the next house on the street.

"You don't look a bit like him," she called out.

The man stopped. In his black suit, with the gold hammer hung round his neck, he looked like a hole punched through the late afternoon into the past.

"You never knew him," she said.

"I saw him. I've ingested him. I *am* him."

"Not even close," Lucy insisted, and closed the door.

George came down the stairs, rubbing his eyes. "Who was that?" he asked.

"Nobody important," she said.

That night, as had become their habit in their new life, before they went to sleep George gave Lucy a back rub. He poured lotion on his fingers, warmed it with his hands. The scent of trees came through the open window. George worked the stiff muscles of her shoulders. Lucy closed her eyes. The threatened storm began: thunder rumbled, rain drummed on the roof. Downstairs, Pam and Rudy played "The Four Seasons" on a salvaged CD player. Lucy listened to the faint sound of George's hands on her back. He sighed. She remembered how George had looked lying in the hospital bed a year ago. How resentfully he'd watched her, out of the corner of his eye, as if he knew she was keeping some secret from him but didn't want to let her know that he knew. She had felt both his desire and his fear. When she'd touched him, how he had flinched!

Now he was touching her. Nothing was held back.

She rolled over and embraced him, and they made love silently in the dark. Afterward George fell asleep, his arm curled around her waist and his belly warm against her back. Lucy lay awake and listened to the sound of the rain falling on the roof, and on the new leaves of the trees outside their window, and on last year's leaves below. As she lay there she had a vision of the house made of glass, seen from high above, as if from a ship hovering in space. Everything in it made a pattern: each person alive and in place, rooms full of machines broken and repaired, of plants, furniture, books. She saw electricity in the walls, light and heat and sound. Numbers read off a disk, turned into music. Letters on a TV screen. Blood pulsing through their bodies. As she watched the pattern extended forward in time. She saw years of work ahead. Trouble and success. Questions with no answers. Irreversible change.

Cool air brushed her cheek. She huddled further beneath the blanket. She could feel George's regular breathing against the nape of her neck. He mumbled something: he was lost in some dream.

Here, too, was change. She used to lie next to George and worry. No matter how warm the moment or how firm his heartbeat, she could not escape the knowledge that hearts always stop and moments never last, because no one lives forever. Now she knew that this moment was the only immortality that she and George would ever share, and she was glad to have it, and it was enough.

AUTHOR'S NOTE

In writing *Good News From Outer Space,* I found invaluable information and inspiration in A. Alvarez's *The Savage God: A Study of Suicide,* James Burke's *The Day the Future Changed,* Norman Cohn's *The Pursuit of the Millennium,* Douglas Curran's remarkable *In Advance of the Landing: Folk Concepts of Outer Space,* Gwynne Dyer's *War,* T.F. Glasson's edition of *The Revelation of John,* Carl Jung's provocative *Flying Saucers,* Hal Lindsey's *The Rapture,* Ted Peters's *Futures—Human and Divine,* Oliver Sacks's *The Man Who Mistook His Wife for a Hat,* Alvin Toffler's *The Third Wave,* Clifford Wilson & John Weldon's bizarre *Close Encounters: A Better Explanation,* and *The Complete Books of Charles Fort.*

In particular I must single out E.R. Chamberlin's engrossing and amusing survey of millennialist movements, *Antichrist and the Millennium.* Readers of Chamberlin's book will readily recognize my debt to him, and to his description of the events occurring in Munster, Germany in 1534–35.

I also recommend a remarkable newspaper, the *Weekly World News,* available in most supermarkets.